# NATIONWIDE ACCLAIM

Blend FBI-CIA antagonism, high-tech surveillance and terrorism. Stir with reality. It doesn't get better than that. Couldn't put it down!

*Fielding L. Pope, California*
*Former Member - White House Communications Agency*

Echelon takes you on a post 9/11 roller coaster ride through the inner workings of the intelligence community still tortured by self-doubt as it suddenly confronts a new and unexpected threat. It's a white-knuckle ride. Hold on tight.

*Edmond J. Boran, New York*
*Retired FBI Special Agent*

Echelon: a rich mix of derring-do, engaging characters, kaleidoscopic plot twists, assassins, government rivalries, incisive detective work, eavesdropping by the good guys, rough justice, and snappy dialogue.

You won't want to put it down. Don't. Pick it up. But be sure your calendar is clear...

*Bruce Powers, California*
*Former Pentagon Director of Naval Aviation Plans*

Echelon propels the reader at flank speed into the post-9/11 world of contemporary intelligence gathering capabilities within the competing jurisdictions of the FBI, NSA and CIA. Lifelike characters leverage these networks to their own advantage... a "must read" for those who enjoy an action-packed thriller with intrigue and a surprise ending!

*Rear Admiral Wallace N. Guthrie, Jr., Florida*
*U.S. Navy (Retired)*

ECHELON grabs your mind and won't let go. Filled with intrigue; it keeps you thinking, page after page. It's cunning. So visual and real; crafted with the insider knowledge that speaks with authenticity. My favorite novelists have been Dan Brown and David Baldacci; now, I have to include Jack O'Neill. I am waiting for his next one.

*William Utz, Virginia*
*Attorney*

Jack O'Neill weaves an exciting tale that vividly contrasts the diverse worlds of high-tech intelligence gathering and high-finance venture capital. Well researched and cleverly conceived, Echelon is a good, easy reading book.

*Ben Bentzin, Texas*
*Private Equity Investor*

Money and mystery in today's digital world of intelligence gathering exhibits Jack O'Neill's superlative skills in mixing fiction and reality. Echelon begs the question: Is somebody listening to you?

*Laura J. Kilcrease, Texas*
*Venture Capitalist*

As fresh as today's headlines, Echelon weaves a thrilling tale of FBI-CIA conflict. Fast-paced action, crackling dialogue, and vibrant characters drive the story toward a dazzling conclusion.

*Constance Sorrentino, Virginia*
*Economist*

Intoxicating from start to finish. Intriguing characters and intense staging launch you into a world of mystery and suspense. The FBI-CIA battle for post 9/11 supremacy is alarming. The ending... startling.

*Angela Wacker, Maryland*
*Professional Golfer*

I don't usually read thrillers, so you can imagine my shock at being totally hooked by Echelon. It kept me on edge from start to finish with its vivid cast of characters and a fast moving plot that opened my eyes to festering CIA/FBI skirmishes and the huge amount of eavesdropping and international money laundering going on in today's world. For a short period of time I was part of that exciting world and was sorry when it ended.

As for the ending, don't bother trying to guess; you can't.

*Jessie East, Maryland*
*Educator*

# ECHELON, *Somebody's Listening*

Six weeks after 9/11, CIA agent Michael Stone is assigned to the FBI's Strategic Information Operations Center, the heart of the war on terror. On his first day, a top-secret Echelon message mysteriously appears on his terminal. Denied access, Michael manipulates the system, gaining access to the message and a puzzling web of illicit activity. The FBI's SIOC director is enraged.

From his terminal in FBI headquarters, Michael assembles the world's most powerful eavesdropping system. His eavesdropping begins to reveal a global conspiracy of deception and greed.

As the CIA flexes its intelligence-gathering muscle and the FBI struggles with the restraints of its law enforcement mandate, the conspiracy spreads from Miami to Key Largo, the Florida Everglades, Key West, California and Acapulco.

The frantic chase culminates in a stunning conclusion in Washington, D.C.

ECHELON, *Somebody's Listening* is an explosive page-turning thriller with an extraordinary cast of characters caught up in a CIA and FBI battle for expanded roles in a changing world.

# ECHELON

*Somebody's Listening*

# ECHELON

*Somebody's Listening*

**Jack O'Neill** *First Edition*

*Jean,*

*Enjoy!*

*Jack O'Neill*
*1-18-06*

Word Association Publishers
205 Fifth Avenue
Tarentum, Pennsylvania

# Echelon: Somebody's Listening
by Jack O'Neill

Published by:
**Word Association Publishers**
205 5th Avenue
Tarentum, PA 15084
*www.wordassociation.com*

This book is a work of fiction. Names, characters, places and incidences are either the product of the author's imagination or used fictitiously. Any resemblance to actual events or locales or persons, living or dead, is entirely coincidental.

Printed in the United States of America.

## Library of Congress Cataloging-in-Publication Data

O'Neill, Jack
Echelon: Somebody's Listening / Jack O'Neill.
     p. cm.
ISBN 1-59571-071-X (pbk.) – ISBN 1-59571-089-2
1. Intelligence officers–Fiction.   2. Terrorism–Prevention–Fiction.
3. National Security–Fiction.   4. Eavesdropping–Fiction. I. Title.
PS3615.N444E27 2005
813'.6–dc22

                         2005021763

# Acknowledgments

ECHELON, Somebody's Listening would still be in my computer if it weren't for the courage of my publisher, Tom Costello. I'll never be able to thank him adequately for taking a chance on me.

I wouldn't have dared venture this far without the persistent encouragement of my daughters Carolyn Thomas and Janet Jacobe.

Theresa Doerfler, Kay Garrett, and Robert Middlemiss have sculpted my writing forever.

Beverly Dale, the smartest woman I've ever known, ruthlessly annihilated flawed grammar. Bebby, you are truly missed.

Janet Jacobe's polishing cloth bestowed an outstanding sheen.

Lisa Pickard, an around-the-world sailboat racer and Lisa's husband Wade, a sailor extraordinaire, sprinkled generous quantities of needed reality.

There are so many others: Shannon Hiskey, Jenette Nowakowski, Steve Dennis, Jackie Schwimmer, Elsa Gomez, Claire Drew, Mary Leddy, Tracy Mercier, James Jacobe, Greg Fair, Kevin O'Neill, Chris Boyd, Sara Jane Maloney, Ward O'Neill, Sally Dail, Patsy Collins, Miho Hiroshe, Nancy O'Shea, Julie Rogers, Kathy O'Neill, Jane Caudill, Bette Hogge, Pat Drake, Ron Phillips, Janice Marcom and Iris McMahon.

To all I have failed to mention, I am sorry. You know who you are. Your fingerprints are all over this novel.

Thank you all.

For

Michael Sanford O'Neill
and
Linda Ann O'Neill

**Facts:**

Eavesdropping is the business of governments worldwide.

The United States government has two identical Strategic Information Operating Centers, one at FBI headquarters in Washington, D.C., and the other at CIA headquarters in Langley, Virginia. These centers respond to information collected by the world's most advanced global-eavesdropping networks.

Echelon, Carnivore, Magic Lantern and Rapid Start are code names of systems supporting U.S. eavesdropping.

The USA Patriot Act enhances these U.S. eavesdropping systems.

The CIA controls a company called In-Q-Tel located in Rosslyn, Virginia. In-Q-Tel is run as a venture capital firm.

Money laundering is a serious international threat.

A scapular is a pair of small cloth squares joined by shoulder ribbons. Catholics wear scapulars under their clothing as an expression of religious devotion: one square on the chest, the other on the back.

# Prologue

CIA agent Michael Stone never liked sneaking out of the house in the dark. The world was too quiet. Even the birds hadn't started their predawn chatter. He walked to his car parked at the curb—the garage door opener was too damned noisy. It would wake Sarah. He smiled. A twenty-one-gun salute couldn't wake Linda Ann or her baby sister Kathleen. Which reminded him. He had to be sure to be home Saturday afternoon—nine children, all under three, their mothers, and an unknown number of siblings would be arriving for Kathleen's first birthday party. He'd have to charge the camcorder battery and buy a high-quality tape.

At the airport Michael scanned the newspaper while he and the clerk behind the counter waited for the day's first pot of coffee to brew. It would be the only time he had to catch up with the rest of the world. He wanted to review his presentations one last time during the flight. At Gate 22 he tossed the newspaper and coffee container before boarding the shuttle.

The world was still sleepy when Michael landed. That suited him just fine. He wouldn't remember making his way through the airport to the cabstand or the long bumpy ride into the city. He was going over his presentations, slide-by-slide, without opening his attaché case. The cab pulled to the curb. He paid the driver, entered the lobby, and joined a small crowd waiting for the elevator.

Michael was the last one to get off the elevator. Standing alone in the vacant corridor, his suit jacket tossed over his shoulder, he read the suite-location sign on the wall. He had turned two corners making his way to Suite 4573 when the doors on both sides of the corridor began flying open. Moments later he stood motionless, wedged in a crowd.

Michael unclipped the cell phone from his belt, slid it up along his body, and dialed.

"Sarah, it's me."

"Hi, me."

"Just wanted to tell you I caught the first shuttle from Reagan National okay."

"You haven't missed a flight since I've known you. Why ya calling?"

"Something's happened, Sarah. Just wanted to tell you I'm okay."

"So, what happened?"

Michael and Sarah had sworn never to lie to each other. In his heart he knew she never had. He had. Often. His security clearances required him to lie. His chin dropped, his eyes and lips squeezed closed. "Sarah, I don't know. I'm closeted. You know how it is."

"I know I never know," said Sarah. "That's what I know."

Michael's eyes wouldn't open. He whispered, "Sarah... I love you."

"I know Michael. I love you too, even if you are one spooky spook. Hurry home." She hung up, knowing not to question further.

Michael opened his eyes. The woman standing next to him pleaded with hers. Michael handed her his cell. She gave him a nervous smile before dialing.

He heard so many names—Sidney, Connie, Fran, Shuji, Ernesto... He tried not to listen.

A grousing male voice, "Damned answering machine."

A tearful female voice, "Mark, I'm okay. Honest I am."

A loud male voice, "*Get my wife!*" Michael looked in the man's direction. The voice muttered back at him, "It's the maid."

The tearful female voice again, "I love you." Silence, and then, "I've always known you loved me Emilio."

A calm male voice, "We're blessed. God has blessed us over and over again."

An impatient voice, "Where are the children?" Silence. "*Harriet,* get the children home." Silence and then, "I'm sorry. I didn't mean to yell."

Forty minutes later, everyone on the forty-fifth floor had shuffled in place. Forty-four floors below had to evacuate first.

The elevator banks came into view. Michael passed along the information he received from a voice in front of him: "The stairwell is around the corner after the elevators."

When they had passed the elevators and the woman in front of Michael reached the corner, Michael leaned forward, peering over the woman's shoulder. He looked around the corner. His heart sank. Another mass of somber-faced individuals was coming towards them from the other direction. The two masses joined at the stairwell door still twenty feet ahead.

When he turned the corner, Michael scanned the faces of the

oncoming crowd. It was like being at a stadium during a baseball or football game. He never saw anyone he knew in those crowds either.

Everyone froze. Something had changed. Soon the word spread. The air conditioning had stopped. The lights began flickering, came back on, and then suddenly it was pitch black.

An eon later Michael stood at the entrance to the stairwell. Emergency lights cast crisscrossing beams of light. Minutes later, he and three others stood side by side encased in the body heat rising from below. They were poised to take their first step down. As soon as the four in front of them abandoned the step, Michael and his three partners took their place. Three steps later the four were in unison, leading with their left foot as they descended to each lower step. It seemed natural—left foot first.

Step-by-step, landing-by-landing they descended. The stairwell began filling with smoke.

A deep baritone voice from somewhere below: "Thirty-ninth floor."

An exhausted female voice much closer and above: "Is it getting hotter in here or is it just me?"

The emergency lights continued to dim. Between the fortieth and thirty-ninth floors, as the four step-partners left one step for the next, the stairwell went dark. Michael's foot landed squarely on the step below. He sank to a squatting position to keep his hundred and eighty pound frame from tumbling down the stairs. The woman on his right tried to balance herself by grabbing his arm. She couldn't find it. She let out an "Ohhhhh…" as she fell over Michael. Michael grabbed the woman and pulled her back down beside him.

"Don't move! Don't move," echoed everywhere as the woman regained her balance. Penlight beams appeared. They became beacons.

Sitting on that step in the darkened stairwell, the woman next to him apologizing needlessly, Michael felt a festering anger emerge. He burrowed into its heat as he remembered CIA employees that had lost their lives. The seven agency officers who died in the suicide car bombing of the United States Embassy in Beirut. The station chief in Lebanon, William Buckley, who was kidnapped by terrorists and died in captivity. Richard Welch, the agency's Athens station chief, shot to death by Greek terrorists.

A sudden chill caused Michael to shudder as he remembered the cold and sunny January morning in 1993. Frank Darling and his wife of three months were sitting in their car on Dolley Madison Boulevard just outside CIA headquarters in Langley, Virginia. They were locked in a left turn lane waiting for the light to change.

Mir Aimal Kasi pulled up behind the last car, got out of his car with an AK-47 assault rifle and began his well-planned murder rampage. He shot Frank and walked the line of cars, firing point blank at their occupants. When he returned, Frank was lying on his wife, trying to protect her. Kasi shot Frank again before fleeing the scene. That day Frank Darling and Lansing Bennett, a medical doctor, joined William Buckley, Richard Welch, and seventy-five others on the CIA's wall of honor in Langley, Virginia.

Mir Aimal Kasi had obtained a job as a courier to the agency, and had been living in a low-income federally subsidized apartment in northern Virginia. Immediately after Kasi's rampage, vows that this murderer would be caught were reinforced with signs that went up throughout the Agency.

"NO MATTER HOW LONG"

CIA operatives located Kasi three times but his well-connected family spirited him away each time. Four and one half years later CIA agents located Kasi in a $3 a day Pakistan hotel room. The FBI arrested him while he was visiting from his hometown of Kandahar in southern Afghanistan. Two days after Kasi's conviction in 1997, terrorists shot and killed four American oil company employees in Pakistan.

Michael fumed that Kasi still received three squares under the full protection of the U.S. government, nine years after having committed cold-blooded murder.

Michael forced himself to return to the present. He looked around and saw almost nothing. It was pitch black. He stood up. He felt the woman on his right and the man on his left do the same. He called out. "Okay?"

A voice a few steps below said, "Wait, my penlight... Got it."

"Everybody ready?" Michael asked. He paused. "Get ready." His step partners moved closer together. "Now together... *slowly.* One step down."

The CIA station Michael was visiting this morning was headed by the CIA's first female station chief. It had been working espionage operations under cover, primarily involving Russian intelligence officers at the United Nations. It worked with the FBI conducting counterintelligence while spying on and recruiting foreign diplomats from the United Nations.

The counter terrorism investigations of the 1998 bombings of two United States Embassies in East Africa and the 2000 bombing of the U.S.S. Cole in Yemen had been the responsibility of this CIA station. These investigations resulted in Osama bin Laden and his Al Qaeda network being accused of both attacks.

This CIA station was an ideal test bed for Michael's In-Q-Tel projects. He was within minutes of describing them when the corridors of the forty-fifth floor flooded with people and overwhelmed him.

All chatter had ceased by the time they reached the thirtieth floor. Concern shifted to legs that began failing. Everyone suffered when someone could no longer stand. It was like shutting down one lane on a four-lane highway during the rush hour. Michael knew of three relay teams of men that were already carrying two women and a man from landing to landing. Two more flights and a young woman clinging to her forearm crutches would be passed to Michael and the man on his left. She had exhausted herself using her crutches to go down the stairs, but her spirit hadn't waned. She gave the brass engraved signs Michael had read so often as he waited for elevators, "In case of an emergency do not use the elevators. Use the stairs," an entirely new meaning.

On the eighth floor landing a vague sense of excitement seeped into the stairwell. Was the descent moving faster? Was the air cooler? No one dared ask. On the seventh landing eyes strained. Were flickers of light imagined or caused by trying to see in the dark too long? Suddenly a clear beam of light shot up the middle of the stairway. The bottom of the staircase had to be close. Michael began hearing voices, strong encouraging voices, but couldn't make out what they were saying.

Three landings later a brilliant light beam raced back and

forth across their faces, blinding them. "Come on. Move it."
They froze, not wanting to fall this late in their descent. The
fireman insisted. "Move it. Let's go."

The four grasped hands. They began using alternate feet on
each step as they descended. It felt strange. Their grasps
loosened as they descended floor after floor. Hope was rising.
They were going to make it. On the ground floor they went
through the staircase doorway. Fireman and policemen
positioned in the lobby directed them toward the rear of the
building, through a door, a corridor, and then through a darkened
aisle that passed dozens of office cubicles. They ran through a
final door trying to keep up with the four in front of them. They
cried when they realized they were out of the building and on the
street. Michael swore he'd never lie to Sarah again.

"Go! Go!" shouted another line of firemen. The street and
the firemen were covered in the ghoulish gray-white ash that was
floating in the air. They choked as they ran in the direction they
were told to run. They had no idea where they were or where
they were going. They were out of the building. They were
alive. Nothing else mattered.

Michael ran for two blocks before stopping and looking
back. It was 10:20 a.m. The needle-nose antenna atop the north
tower was descending straight down into a cloud of debris. He
watched as it disappeared behind the building they had just
escaped—the forty-seven-story structure at 7 World Trade
Center.

# Week One

# Chapter 1

### Key West, Florida
### October 23, 2001
### Tuesday 1350 ET

Gonzalo Santes took off his favorite floppy hat, wiped the sweat from his brow and looked around. The bar had filled as suddenly as the light afternoon shower had turned into a downpour. Outside, a crowd mingled under the huge canopy spanning the three-door entrance. Inside, most of the new arrivals shook their heads no as waiters approached. A few gave a why-not shrug followed by a nod.

Gonzalo flinched when the waitress suddenly appeared at his table. She was carrying a tray of beers high on her upturned palm. She put a frosted mug on his table, snapped up his empty, and continued twisting and turning her way through the crowd without losing a step. Minutes later, the afternoon's gutter-gusher abruptly let up. A few under Sloppy Joe's canopy began dashing through a light mist, attempting to make up for lost time.

Gonzalo stood. He had no trouble seeing over the crowd but couldn't spot his waitress. Then he heard her. She was bending over a table on the far side of the room, laughing hysterically with five twenty-somethings. He tossed a few bills in the direction of his drained mug and made his way out of the bar, his t-shirt clinging to the folds of his massive belly. Small beads of sweat dotted his forehead. Across the street The Lazy Gecko beckoned. He hadn't been there. Another beer seemed to be just about right. Maybe two. He began grinning. He found it hard to believe that he would soon be a free man.

A few hours later, Gonzalo found his way to the Hilton Key West Resort and Marina. From his second floor window he looked down on the yachts docked side-by-side from one end of the pier to the other. *Descifrar* was the sixth one from the right end of the pier and directly below his window. Two massive cruise ships were docked outside the small, cement-enclosed harbor. The top decks of both were higher than everything else on the Florida Keys. They made the yachts moored below his window look like toys.

He showered, tossed his belongings into two suitcases, and brought them aboard *Descifrar*. A final meal in Bistro 245 would be a perfect send-off. He found a table by the rail, overlooking the harbor. He would watch the sun set over the Gulf while enjoying the African breeze trying to sneak through the palms unnoticed. He glanced at the tiny red welts on his arms and legs. They were old bites inflicted by gnats he had never seen or felt. He smiled. The no-see-um repellent he had applied was keeping their cousins at bay.

Gonzalo's mother and father were born on the outskirts of one of the worst Bogotá slums. His mother blossomed into a beautiful little girl. On the eve of her fourteenth birthday, bursting with hope and confidence, she made her way to the heart of Bogotá. She knew something better had to be her lot. Two months later she was back with her mother in the shanty where she was born, pregnant with an American conventioneer's child. Before her pregnancy showed, she married the most promising young man she and her mother knew. Three months before Gonzalo was born he abandoned the woman he believed would give birth to his child.

His mother's beauty continued to attract young men. She swore never to have another child. She would dedicate her life to Gonzalo. When six-year-old Gonzalo started school, he was a head taller than his classmates. His mother continuously nurtured and encouraged his curiosity every way she could. She believed if he was to go on to high school and then college it would be an unquestioned act of intervention performed by the hand of God himself, a true miracle.

In the third grade Gonzalo still towered over his classmates. He was an awkward child. Each limb had a mind of its own. His passion was soccer. One day as Gonzalo loped across the field, a classmate shouted, "Gringo." The game stopped. Everyone began laughing and then intoned—Gringo. Gringo. Gringo. From that day on Gonzalo was known by his new name—Gringo.

Gonzalo's mother believed in miracles, but with no one able to tell her when or why a miracle might occur, she couldn't trust her son's future to their hit-or-miss nature. She used the only means available to her. As a courtesan, she worked her way up the social ladder, each time moving her mother and son closer to Bogotá. One beautiful day during her son's seventeenth year, his mother, on the arm of a wealthy lover, accompanied Gonzalo on his first day at the University of Colombia, School of Finance and International Relations. That day his mother confirmed the true nature of miracles.

Gonzalo had grown to a lanky six-foot four. Just as they had in elementary and high school, his university classmates made fun of him, no longer because of his ineptitude at sports, but because he was acknowledged to be the smartest student in the university. He retreated to his passions: finance and mathematics. Forced to choose, he majored in international finance.

Jose Valderrama, Colombia's shrewdest and most insightful financier, hired Gonzalo on graduation. Jose had established a worldwide network of wealthy clientele from the Middle East, Central Asia, and the Balkans. All operated beyond the fringes of their countries' laws and regulations. Each had rivers of cash they were eager to have Jose launder and then invest. In Colombia, Jose's greatest fear was drug lords. If they infiltrated his network they would swamp him with cash, demand every detail of his operation, and put him under a perpetual threat of death.

Over the years Jose and his young protégé Gonzalo developed absolute trust in each other. Jose moved his family to Acapulco, away from Colombia's violence, government corruption, and malignant labor unions. Because Gonzalo's mother and grandmother had no interest in leaving their home, Gonzalo stayed on in Bogotá.

Gonzalo quickly became the brains of Jose's operation, investing funds and keeping track of each client's account. To obliterate the sources of money, he followed the rule of five, transferring all money through five countries before investing it. Secure voice and video communications kept his business transactions running smoothly.

Jose never fully understood how Gonzalo shifted and invested funds around the world so easily. He dubbed it all, "Gonzalo's miracles." Jose concentrated on nurturing his clients while enjoying the good life from his plush Acapulco compound.

Eagerly embracing every technological advance available, Gonzalo had no trouble protecting Jose's empire. He created and changed encryption codes frequently. Jose eventually abandoned keeping his copy of the encryption keys—the only copy other than Gonzalo's—current.

As the American economy of the nineties flourished beyond financial experts' wildest forecasts, Gonzalo's conventional investment strategies were stretched to their limits. The rate of return stagnated. In search of the higher yields Jose's clients were demanding, Gonzalo decided to join the cadre of venture capitalists. He began bankrolling emerging companies with nothing but promising concepts needing cash to be brought to market. One successful company in twenty could turn into a fortune within months.

Jose insisted Gonzalo contact Royce Palmer, a lawyer in San Diego. Royce set up corporations. Gonzalo used them to funnel laundered money to unsuspecting venture capital firms. The names of Royce's firms changed almost as frequently as Gonzalo's encryption keys.

Gonzalo spoiled his mother and grandmother. During the first several years with Jose, he sent them on month-long holidays to Cartagena, where his grandmother loved to gamble in the casinos while his mother lounged on the Caribbean beaches. Another favorite was Lanceros, the Colombian countryside resort in Paipa, where they both enjoyed the hot-spring pool and long drives into the magnificent Colombian countryside.

During the next decade his mother and grandmother spent eight weeks or more abroad each year. They explored Madrid, Paris, Miami, Washington, and New York. During the final years of the twentieth century, his mother and grandmother lingered in Boston, Rome, Athens, and Dublin. In the first year of the new millennium, they added Bangkok and Sydney.

Gonzalo's most-prized gift to his mother and grandmother was a four-bedroom luxury apartment in an upscale Bogotá gated community. It boasted three teams of armed guards that patrolled the perimeter carrying both shotguns and pistols, day and night.

Gonzalo found working for Jose a blessing and a curse. Although Gonzalo could indulge his every whim, he had no time to do so. Fourteen-hour days were the norm. The wealthier Gonzalo got, the more isolated he became. His one passion was his yacht. He named it *Descifrar*, "decipher" in Spanish—a challenge of sorts to anyone who might try to decipher the encryption codes he used to shield the empire of Jose Valderrama.

It had taken a concerted effort on Gonzalo's part to convince

Jose that his lifelong dream—the solitude of a long cruise aboard his prized *Descifrar*—would not endanger the empire they had so carefully crafted. Jose demanded that he mix business and pleasure. Gonzalo agreed. He would cruise from Barranquilla, Colombia to Key Largo, Florida.

Jose's son lived in Key Largo under the alias Doug Crosby. Jose hoped Gonzalo would be able to motivate Doug—something Jose had never been able to do. Gonzalo was to spend time in Key Largo encouraging Doug to create an East Coast office similar to the one Royce Palmer ran in San Diego.

The moment the sun set on the Gulf of Mexico, Gonzalo flipped a coin to decide whether he'd start the last leg of his journey from Key West to Key Largo by cruising north on the Gulf or the Atlantic side of the Florida Keys. Tails. He'd follow the Intracoastal Waterway on the Atlantic side and then cross to the Gulf at Seven Mile Bridge on his way to Blackwater Bay in Key Largo. Minutes later he left the Bistro 245 restaurant and boarded *Descifrar*. He freed the dock lines and began making his way to the busy traffic area of the Key West bight. It wasn't long before he cleared Ft. Taylor on the western end of Key West and headed east. Shallow waters combined with the traffic of freighters, tankers and recreational boats forced him to stay at the helm. An hour from Seven Mile Bridge he decided, against his better judgment, to set the autopilot and settle in a deck chair.

The swells that had rocked Gonzalo to sleep now threatened to wake him. Fighting drowsiness, his finger began tracing the outline of the scapular against his chest. A wave rolled Gonzalo's head onto his shoulder. The deck chair went out from under him. Adrenaline surged. Strange objects flashed in front of his eyes with shutter-lens speed. His shoulder took the brunt of the fall. He rolled and thrashed on the deck, trying to locate the vertical— any vertical—for what seemed like an eternity. His hands and knees reverted to long-forgotten instincts. Together they raised his bulk, but threatened to lay it prone again at any moment. He opened his eyes. The deck was just inches from his nose. He rolled onto his side and sat with his back against the bulkhead. His adrenaline slowed. His heartbeat retreated from its break-neck pace. He reached up, grasped the gunwale with both hands, and labored to get his 290 pounds upright.

Gonzalo held fast with one hand and massaged his aching shoulder with the other as he regained his bearings and the feel of the deck. The droning inboards told him *Descifrar* was still following the course he had set. He looked off the port stern and searched for the glow of Key West. It wasn't there. He looked skyward. A strong breeze crossed his face. Fast-moving clouds were threatening to hide the full moon rising in the east.

Gonzalo crossed the deck, trudged up the ladder, and steadied himself with a hand against the bulkhead while he inspected the image on the radar screen. The nearest blip was forty degrees off the starboard bow, a nautical mile away. Heading east it posed no danger. He stepped behind the wheel and released the autopilot. The solitude of exploring the dark waters ahead took on the task of returning his calm and clearing his head.

As he crossed under the three spans of the Seven Mile Bridge and entered Gulf waters, his finger began tracing the outline of the PoKéRoM disk secreted in the pocket of the scapular dangling on his chest. The disk contained the encryption codes used to shield Jose Valderrama's empire. They were the only copy of his encryption codes. They were the key to his freedom.

The yacht's heading continued to waver about its setting. Gonzalo turned to the Global Positioning Satellite display. It would be a few more hours before *Descifrar* would make its final run to Blackwater Sound and then into Doug Crosby's private inlet at Key Largo.

Visibility neared zero as *Descifrar* approached Blackwater Sound. Ten-foot swells driven by gusting forty-knot winds glued Gonzalo's hands to the wheel. His feet were spread wide, one slightly in front of the other, to counter the swaying deck. His eyes darted among the radar, compass, GPS, and shoreline while his ears listened intently to every ping of the depthfinder.

In Florida's shallow waters *Descifrar's* six-foot draft meant he had to augment the 10-foot accuracy of his differential GPS with sightings of buoys and channel markers. Some were lit. Most weren't.

His eyes ached trying to see unlit buoys, the shoreline, and then each of the electronic displays in front of him. His injured shoulder throbbed a steady drumbeat. His legs pleaded for rest. He checked the fuel gauge. The needle sat on the lower half of the empty mark. *"Good God, how long has it been there?"* he heard himself say.

Gonzalo piloted *Descifrar* toward the narrow entrance of Doug's cove. If his rudder and throttle commands weren't perfect as he passed through the narrow entrance, sharp boulders would pierce *Descifrar's* hull. *Descifrar* would be lost.

It was time. Gonzalo drove the throttles to full power, turned the wheel ten degrees starboard, and then held it firm. *Descifrar* responded, picking up speed, her props deep in the water, her rudder locked to its task. She outraced the crest of a swell and began sprinting down its face, gaining speed with every turn of her screws. *Descifrar* raced toward the entrance of the cove now forty meters to starboard, her twin screws whining in perfect unison. The inlet neared. Thirty meters. Twenty meters. Gonzalo eased the throttles back, his eyes riveted on the inlet opening. Ten meters. Five meters. He tweaked the rudder, then the throttle, and then the rudder again, *Descfrar* responding to each command. Finally, there was nothing more Gonzalo could do. He stood at the helm as *Descifrar* slipped through the narrow opening unscathed. Gonzalo reversed the thrust of the engines until *Descifrar* bobbed on the quayside of Doug's sheltered cove.

Gonzalo swept the shore with his floodlight. Its beam found the guesthouse Doug had told him to use. It was at the end of the dock. He then scanned the berths. There were three. Two were vacant. He chose the end berth. There would be less chance that *Descifrar* might be damaged. He positioned *Descifrar* into the berth and then opened the cabin door. Wind lashed at his clothes while rain flushed the sweat from his face. He held tight to both rails of the ladder getting down to the deck. He threw a bowline and then a stern line far across the dock. A swell lifted *Descifrar* just as he jumped off his yacht. His chest hit the edge of the dock, knocking the wind out of him. He had no idea how he had been able to scramble onto the dock before the yacht pinned him. It didn't matter now. *Descifrar* had to be secured.

He secured the bow and stern lines with quick triple clove hitches. He timed his movements carefully before jumping back onboard. He launched three bumpers and threw six more lines across the dock, then another bowline and stern line, and finally double forward and aft springs. An hour later he finished adjusting the lines and bumpers. His most treasured possession was secure. As he stood on the deck, checking again just to be sure, he looked at the date on the face of his watch. In twenty-one days the "time lock," his final defense against fatal exposure that had embedded in the PoKéRoM disk, would have to be reset, or the encryption keys would be erased and impossible to recover. His fingers began tracing the comfort hidden within the scapular. There was plenty of time.

Gonzalo threw his two suitcases onto the dock. The second one slid across the weathered boards, landing in the water on the other side. He didn't care. All he wanted was to get into the guesthouse at the end of the pier.

With each wind gust, the remaining suitcase pulled on his arm, threatening to send him flying into the water. Lurching from post to post, he reached the guesthouse door and turned the doorknob. The door flew out of his hand. Inside, he used his weight against the back of the door to close it. In the bedroom he stripped, showered, and changed clothes.

On the empty refrigerator Gonzalo found a note. Doug had left a car in the garage. The key was in the ignition. There was a good place to eat a few kilometers north on Route 1. Doug would be back sometime after midnight.

The thought of a grilled steak and a cold one to calm his raw nerves revitalized Gonzalo. He found a slicker on the back of the bedroom door. He wrapped it around him as far as it would go. He held the slicker against his chest, hunched his shoulders against the wind, and made his way across the lawn to the main house.

He found his way to the garage door and flung it open. Inside was a 1988 red Mercedes convertible, an SL560 roadster. He opened the driver's door. The car was designed for a driver considerably shorter than six-foot four.

With his feet still on the garage floor, he sat sideways in the driver's seat. Slowly he wedged each leg in turn under the steering wheel while twisting and turning his torso to get it facing forward. By sucking in his gut more than he ever thought he could, he wedged himself behind the wheel, his feet pressing hard on the cowl, his thighs pressing against the underside of the steering wheel column. The bottom arch of the steering wheel disappeared into a fold on his belly. He turned the ignition key. The roar of the engine echoed in the garage. He started out of the garage, a broad smile of relief across his face.

As the car left the protection of the garage, rain pounded on the hood and windshield. He couldn't see a thing. His right knee was jammed on the side of its enclosure, not allowing him to raise his foot onto the brake pedal. His left knee had more room. He braked using his left foot. The car jolted to a stop. He sat, his breath coming in short bursts as he searched for the windshield wiper controls. A twist of the turn signal arm sent the blades whipping back and forth across the windshield. He kept the sole of his left foot over the brake. He started forward again. Struggling with every turn of the wheel, he drove up the driveway and turned onto the road.

Gonzalo began offering extravagant thanks to the Lord for his survival at sea as his fingers searched his chest for the comfort of the scapular and its hidden treasure. He couldn't feel it. He pressed harder, searching every inch of his chest. The scapular wasn't there. His heart raced. He had left the scapular on the guesthouse bathroom floor, on top of the pile of his wet clothes.

He tried to brake using his right foot. Confused, he pressed hard on the gas pedal while his left foot stayed hovered over the brake pedal. The kick-down engaged. The tires found traction. The car flew down the road. His head snapped against the headrest. In the split second it took him to realize what he had done, he pressed hard with his left foot on the brake pedal.

All four wheels froze. The car hydroplaned and began spinning. The road appeared and disappeared as he twice saw where he had been and then where he was going. A yellow sign warning of a sharp curve came and went from view. The road turned. The car didn't. It flew off the pavement and landed upright in the inlet.

The Mercedes bobbed helplessly on the white-capped waters. Gonzalo searched frantically for the door handle. His large hand couldn't find the small finger well where the door handle was hidden. Seawater filled his shoes and began climbing his legs. He squirmed in every direction, struggling to get free. He pushed with his feet against the cowl, trying to move away from the steering wheel. The seat kept him firmly wedged behind the wheel.

He couldn't budge. The front of the car began sinking faster than the rear. Gonzalo stared at the waterline marching up the windshield, slowly at first. Then, with a gurgling sound, the windshield went under.

As he floundered, he tore the turn-signal arm from the steering column in a desperate attempt to stop the windshield wipers from pretending that nothing had happened. His will to live revitalized with the muffled thump of the front of the convertible hitting bottom followed by the sensation of the car dancing on the bottom. With the few moments of breath remaining, he found the finger well hiding the door handle, encircled the handle with his forefinger, and pulled. The handle moved but the large heavy door didn't budge. With a final desperate effort, he threw his weight against the car door. The door slipped free of its latch. He slithered out of the shallow-water tomb.

Gonzalo surfaced bobbing like debris in white foam while he gasped for air. Minutes passed before his feet struck bottom. He tried steadying himself but couldn't. The wind was relentless. Swell after swell washed over him as he fought for every breath. One swell lifted him higher than the others, sending him tumbling toward shore. Over and over he rolled. He crawled through the froth, making his way ashore as shells and sharp coral cut, gashed and bruised every extremity. His body refused to complain. It was fighting for its very existence. Finally, he was prone on the rocky shore, sobbing with relief as unrelenting sheets of wind, rain, and salt-water spray stung his bleeding wounds.

He struggled to his feet, lurching toward a house less than thirty meters away. Totally exhausted, he crawled under the shrubbery against the foundation of the house on its leeward side. Gonzalo fell asleep.

# Chapter 2

## Arlington, Virginia
## Tuesday 1725 ET

Carolyn Hughes stepped into the elevator of Crystal City's Water Park Towers North Apartments, pushed the ninth floor button, and slumped against the rear wall. She hoped no one would get on before she got off. She unclipped the keys dangling from her purse, grasped the small plastic tiger, and jiggled the keys until they hung freely. As she walked the hallway to her apartment, her fingers robotically chose the key on the right side of the tiger. She had it ready the moment she reached her door. Inside she tossed the tiger on the small foyer table, took a few steps, and then flopped onto the couch. With the sound of the spring-loaded door hitting the jam every muscle in her body went limp.

At the office lately, her days had been dreadful, sitting there at her desk, avoiding all eye contact, sneaking out to lunch alone and going across the Mall hoping against hope that no one from the office would see her slumped on a park bench somewhere. Damn him. Why had he done it?

The living/dining room in her one-bedroom apartment had its full complement of starter furniture: two small cloth-covered living room chairs, a glass-topped coffee table, and a floor lamp. A teardrop chandelier hung over the cherry-veneer dining room table-and-chair set. Two pictures hung on the long wall—abstracts she loved. She had been thrilled when the beige berber wall-to-wall had accented them nicely.

A 13-inch color TV—the only TV she owned—sat on the small kitchen counter. In the bedroom, a computer and an all-in-one printer, copier, fax and scanner fit nicely in the corner next to the dresser. On the opposite side of the bedroom she had ample room in front of the accordion closet doors.

Carolyn never closed the vertical blinds on the sliding doors leading from the living room to the balcony. She never lowered the honeycomb shade on the window next to it either. More than once she had sat alone in the dark with a glass of white zinfandel, enjoying the view on the far side of the Potomac. After dark, the buildings of Washington, D.C. sparkled like gems in a jewel box.

Now, all she wanted was to be alone—no music, no TV—just to be alone with her thoughts. She slid out of her shoes and slouched until her head rested on the back of the couch. She hated avoiding her co-workers. Most were friends. It just wasn't time yet to let anyone into the emotional turmoil roiling inside her. She needed more time by herself—much more time. A few of her friends knew about him, others probably guessed. Such things just can't be kept secret in an office environment. She prayed to God no one would ever find out why she had ended her affair with Greg McNulty.

Carolyn glanced at her watch. *Oh God, in ten minutes I have to leave*, she realized. She wasn't hungry but knew she had to eat. She struggled to get up, went into the kitchen, and scanned the refrigerator shelves. She didn't find a thing she felt like eating. Her old standbys would have to calm her stomach. She unwrapped a slice of American cheese, folded it, and took a bite before pouring a glass of milk.

Weeks had gone by since she watched the Attorney General hand Greg-the-Bastard *her* plaque. So when would this fatigue and anxiety go away? Wasn't time supposed to be the cure all? She went into the bedroom and stood in front of the dresser mirror. Her hazel eyes replied: *Get over it. Move on.*

Carolyn had used up her leave trying to stay away from the Department of Justice. No matter how hard she tried, reminders of her gullibility and naiveté continued to materialize—in the middle of the night, at work, almost everywhere she went or whatever she did. They surfaced without the haziest hint of a warning, out of nothing at all.

At the office she had stayed behind her desk, her head down. Most people sensed she didn't want to be bothered. At lunchtime she had strolled the Mall all the way to the Lincoln Memorial—it was farther than walking to the Capitol. Exercise was supposed to help, wasn't it? Thank goodness for the bag of gummi bears in her desk. The afternoon had dragged. She just wanted to get out of there, to go home. It was strange. She couldn't remember a thing about the trip home. Now, she had to leave the sanctuary she had yearned for all day.

Sending a resume to Taylor Associates was an "oh-why-not" thing. Besides, it took little effort. Her computer and printer were on autopilot. It was the twentieth, thirtieth resume. Oh who cares. Beside, sending resumes helped. Each one mailed might be *the one* that would get her out of Justice.

When Taylor Associates had called and asked for an after-hours interview, she told them no problem. She jotted the caller's instructions on the edges of the editorial page of *The Washington Post*. Stepping into another world, if only for an hour or two during the interview, might prove to be the catalyst she needed to get her through the night without seeing the image she fought so hard to vanquish—Greg-the-Bastard receiving *her* plaque from the Attorney General of the United States.

Carolyn tore off the edge of the editorial page and jammed it into the zippered pocket on the outside of her purse. She turned to the swivel-mounted full-length mirror in the corner on the other side of the dresser. Not being gorgeous had never bothered her. Twinkling eyes and a vivacious and energetic nature had always canceled that out, no problem. She stood erect, threw her shoulders back, and sucked her belly button toward her spine. She adjusted the drape of her form-fitting black business suit. She turned left and then right. Few could match her stunningly svelte five-foot nine-inch figure.

Carolyn stopped at the foyer mirror on her way to the door. She fingered her bangs, studied her largest freckles, and then scowled at the hazel orbs staring back at her. Discouraged, she compressed her lips, tested the body of the red hair resting on her shoulders, and decided there was nothing more to do. She opened the door and stepped into the hallway. After a few steps she stopped. Her shoes were still on the floor by the couch where she had kicked them off.

She had no idea how long she had stood in front of the elevators before noticing both up and down buttons were dark. *Thank goodness I'm alone. Nonsense, if anybody came they would have smiled, hit a button, and thought nothing of it.* She shook her head wondering, have I always talked to myself like this?

Carolyn stared vacantly at the changing floor numbers as the elevator descended to the lobby. She tried distracting herself with positive thoughts: I'll be meeting new people. It may be a wonderful opportunity. Maybe I'll meet someone else. Nothing worked. *That son-of-a-bitch used me. Looked me right in the eye and lied. And I believed everything he said. How could I have*

*been so dumb? Shit! Shit! Shit!*
The elevator came to a slow stop. The doors to the lobby opened. Carolyn sprinted across the lobby, opened the heavy front glass doors, and went out onto the sidewalk. She hurried south on Crystal Drive, her red hair bouncing on her shoulders with each stride. At the corner, she stood at the front of the evening crowd waiting for the commuter traffic to pass.
Six years ago she had graduated from New York University. Three years ago she had obtained an MBA from George Washington University in Washington, D.C. and had taken a job in the Antitrust Division at the Department of Justice. Two years ago she had rented her one-bedroom apartment in Arlington, Virginia. Its living room and bedroom shared a balcony overlooking the George Washington Parkway, the Potomac River and the District of Columbia beyond. The kitchen was small and efficient. She never used the balcony and had often wondered if anyone did. Maybe when entertaining.
A year ago Carolyn told her boyfriend that he could move in with her. Overnight the apartment shrank. Four months later she told him to move out, happy to get her apartment back. Six months ago Greg-the-Bastard walked into her office with the Cayrod file.
The bulk of the traffic had passed through the intersection. The crowd pressed forward, eager to defy the no-walk sign. Someone brushed her arm. Annoyed, she decided the last two approaching cars were damned laggards. She darted in front of them. Horns blared. Without giving them a glance or losing a step, she threw a stiff bird their way.
On the far curb Greg's image returned. Damn him! He preached to me. Consumers are being hurt. Don't offer Cayrod any way out. Pen the bastards in. They don't deserve a break. They're stealing.
She quickened her step. Her neck and shoulder muscles coiled. Her stomach churned a flood of acid. She walked faster hoping somehow to leave Greg behind. He didn't stop. Cayrod is lying. *No Greg, you're a fucking liar!*
Shit, he looked so good. Damn, he was good. No, he was great. And after... lying on his back beside me, stretched full length, exhausted, our sweaty bodies touching. *Oh God, it hurts.* She forced herself not to run. It would attract attention. She

didn't want attention. Her stomach blazed. Carolyn stopped. She hunched over, her face twisted in torment, fighting tears.

The woman walking behind Carolyn didn't expect her sudden stop. She bumped into Carolyn. "You all right?" the woman asked as she grabbed Carolyn's arm to prevent them both from falling.

Carolyn struggled to regain her composure. "Yes," she muttered, willing herself to regain normalcy. "I'm fine." She took a slow deep breath. "Everything's okay. Just a little out of breath, that's all." She stood erect, smiled, and began walking. She had to compose herself. If she couldn't keep the torment hidden on the street, how could she do it during an interview? Maybe it would be better not to show up.

Bosses get credit for the work of their staff. No problem. But telling me to litigate with Cayrod while Greg negotiated, in secret. That's so unprofessional. Why didn't he just tell me?

Her face tightened as she broke into a power walk. That damned press release. The bastard didn't say a word about that either. It just appeared in the press. Out of the blue, a settlement—a consent decree. He had told me not to mention those words—consent decree. It's not the right time for that sort of thing. What the hell's wrong with that man? She brushed her cheeks to ward off tears.

*Going to that damned auditorium. Stupid, stupid, stupid. How could I have been so stupid? Do I have some deep need to beat myself to death or something?* Then it began. The scene began to unfold. She knew it would. She knew every detail. She had seen it dozens of times. At home. At work. And worst of all, in the middle of the night. Oh God, now on the street? She grimaced hoping to stop it, knowing she couldn't. *Please no.*

The spotlight flared. Carolyn's eyes followed its beam as it swept across the seats of the auditorium and stopped center stage, its circular beam now badly distorted, half spread out on the stage floor, half climbing the heavy curtains hung high from something well out of sight. The curtains began to move. Then they parted. The deep voice of a commentator filled the auditorium and began describing what was happening. A voice she knew but couldn't place. She listened. She had no choice.

Justice department officials are now coming through the parted curtains. They're crossing the stage and clustering around

the podium. They're squinting trying to see through the glare of
the spotlight while feigning smiles. They're noting who from
their staff had accepted their recommendation to join them in this
tribute to their management skills.

All the officials are now leaning forward. They're focusing
on the rear of the auditorium, trying to identify the woman sitting
in the shadows of the last row. The woman is slouching lower.
Her eyes are now barely clearing the seat in front of her. It looks
like, it's...

Wait, the curtains are moving again. The Attorney General
of the United States is coming on stage. He's walking tall in his
blue pinstriped suit. There's a broad smile on his face. He's
making his way to the podium...

Everyone on stage is turning. They're looking back toward
the curtains. Greg McNulty has stepped on stage. He's standing
there, tall, proud, shoulders back. He's... he's inviting the
audience to feast their eyes on him. The Attorney General has
begun encouraging him to come to the podium. Now everyone
on stage is waving at Greg to come join them. He's sauntering
toward the podium.

What...? A woman in a bright blue dress has just freed
herself from the weight of the curtains and appeared on stage.
The spotlight is blinding her. She's standing there alone,
confused, her hand shielding her eyes from the glare of the
spotlight.

The Attorney General is signaling the woman to come to the
podium. The woman's turning away. No... she's parting the
curtains again. She's looking backstage. The woman in blue is
holding the curtains back for someone. Muffled gasps are
coming from the audience. It's a girl. A ten-year-old girl. And
now a boy. He's younger. I can't quite see what the boy's
carrying. Now I can. It's an infant wrapped in a blue blanket.
The girl is taking the arm of the boy. The lady in the blue dress,
the little girl, and the boy carrying the infant wrapped in a blue
blanket are heading for the podium. They are at the podium,
standing next to Greg McNulty, smiling up at him adoringly.

The Attorney General is reaching under the podium. He's
taking out a plaque. There's a proud grin on the face of the
Attorney General as he looks at Greg McNulty.

Carolyn shuddered. She knew the final scene of her

nightmare. Knew every detail.

The spotlight froze the events on stage. Greg McNulty's outstretched arms are accepting a plaque. Standing by his side are the woman in blue, the ten-year-old girl, and her younger brother cradling an infant wrapped in a blue blanket. They're mesmerized by the sight of Greg receiving *her* plaque from the Attorney General of the United States.

Carolyn tried purging the scene. She began counting windows on the top floor of the building on the far side of Crystal Drive. She avoided the cracks in the pavement. She counted the cars stopped at the light. Nothing worked. She knew it wouldn't. Nothing ever worked. Exhausted, she surrendered.

I knew he was married. I did. But I didn't know about the children. Oh God, his wife was pregnant while he panted on his back beside me. "The bastard," she muttered. *Oh God, I'm making a fool of myself.*

Ahead, the pedestrian crossing signal began flashing its warning hand. Carolyn slowed, almost stopped, her lungs now taking in smaller and smaller gulps of air. Carolyn waited at the rear of the crowd gathering on the corner. She pleaded to whomever was in charge of such things: Please let me forget.

A few minutes later Carolyn looked up. She stood in front of a tall office building. Above the entrance, carved in gray marble, was the name: Taylor Associates.

# Chapter 3

### Vienna, Virginia
### Tuesday 2315 ET

Michael Stone stood at the curb on White Cedar Court, sweat dripping from his nose, his chest rising and falling rapidly beneath his stained t-shirt. He felt great. Mowing the yard was a good workout if you hustled. He looked toward Lemontree Lane, the only cross street in the Tall Oaks development. He was the only one outside. He turned the other way, looking into the cul-de-sac. Four large, two-story colonials shielded White Cedar from a two-lane road and Nottoway Park's basketball courts on the far side. A small gravel parking lot confined by an aging split rail fence invited pickup games until a timer extinguished the court lights at midnight. His neighbors on the cul-de-sac, like those living along railroad tracks or on arterial highways, had long ago accepted the realities of their surroundings.

His eyes focused on the glow of basketball court lights coming from behind two of the homes. The sounds of the players took him back to high school. Michael liked high school, particularly sports, math, science and girls. He never told anyone about the math and science. He played varsity basketball for three years. His Irish ancestors had given him a lanky six-foot one frame that had speed and great balance. He often marveled at how everyone seemed to know him as he walked the halls after a game. Girls grinned or nodded as they passed him in the halls. He'd respond by accenting his sparkling blue eyes with a slight but genuine thank-you smile that he had practiced in front of a mirror the summer before his sophomore year.

In his senior year the team had made it to the regional finals and Manhattan's Madison Square Garden where the final game had been televised nationally. The game had been hard fought. Tied as the final buzzer sounded, Michael launched a two-handed high floating shot from beyond mid-court. Madison Square Garden went silent. Finally the net snapped over the rim. He had won the game. The crowd went wild. His teammates raced to his side and then carried him on their shoulders through the crowd anxious just to be near him.

In college Michael found sports too time consuming and

serious. He concentrated on math, science and girls. One day everything changed. Michael met Sarah. She was it for him. He'd never forget the moment he told her. It was six months after they met. They were standing on the balcony outside the great hall of the Kennedy Center for the Performing Arts. It was after a performance of Shear Madness. He had never been so nervous in his life. It was a warm, still September evening. There wasn't a cloud in the sky. A crescent moon hung high over the Potomac River, its beams dancing in her auburn hair. The world stopped, waiting to hear his words. "Sarah, I love you."

Sarah told him she too had felt the same way from the moment they met. They were married the following summer. Sarah took a job with the U.S. Bureau of Labor Statistics. He started working for a computer service firm. Four years later the CIA lured Michael away from his secure but mundane career.

Now the big 4-O was two short years away. He wasn't looking forward to it. His younger neighbors sensed his concern. They reminded him of it when given the slightest chance. He sucked in his gut, pulled up his t-shirt, tightened his stomach, and gave it a hard slap. He smiled, not too shabby for an old man. No question, he could still play full court. He knew all the moves, had been there, done that. The old eye-hand coordination wouldn't let him down, that's for sure. He squared his shoulders, planted his feet, and let a one-handed jump shot go over the head of his defender. Swish.

"Michael."

Michael turned, looking toward the front door. Sarah was heading back into the house. From the way she called his name he knew it was getting late. He held his watch toward the security lights high on the house. It was ten thirty. His work shift started at midnight. He finished emptying the mower's clippings into the plastic garbage bag at the curb and then began running behind the mower and its protruding grass bag.

Tyson's Corner, two miles from White Cedar Court, boasted two sprawling shopping malls and a business park with a surging government contractor population. The Vienna Metro station just a mile from Michael's home provided thirty minute rides into the heart of Washington D.C. Together, Tyson's Corner and the Metro had transformed Vienna into a coveted close-in bedroom community.

Michael and Sarah moved onto White Cedar Court soon after the CIA had assigned him to Langley, just eight miles away. They became the third family to occupy the house since it was built. The previous families also had been CIA families.

A car turned onto White Cedar Court from Lemontree Lane as Michael emptied the grass-catcher bag for the last time. His neighbors waved as they turned into their driveway across the street and pulled into their garage. They had asked Michael and Sarah to go to a movie with them, even offered their 13-year old to babysit Linda Ann and Kathleen. Sarah had turned them down. Michael would be working. In truth, most of their neighbors had stopped asking. Michael vowed to change. Starting with this new assignment he would work reasonable hours and shed his well-earned workaholic reputation.

A few years ago Michael had begun working for In-Q-Tel, a company owned by the CIA and located in rented quarters in Rosslyn on the Virginia side of the Potomac. It was a straight twenty-minute Metro commute. An added perk was the panoramic view of Washington D.C.'s signature landmarks from his twenty-ninth floor window. He beamed with pride every morning when he looked out his window before beginning his workday. After dark the view was more spectacular.

Like all CIA employees at In-Q-Tel, Michael had been tasked with sharpening the technological edge the agency had demonstrated in decades past. It was an edge that had produced spectacular results, including the U-2 reconnaissance aircraft that helped end fears of a "bomber gap," its follow-on, the A-12, and then the A-12's retirement in favor of the Air Force's SR-71 Blackbird. When the KH-11 imaging satellite had taken those dramatic images of Jimmy and Rosalyn Carter during their inaugural walk along Pennsylvania Avenue from the Capitol to the White House, the world had gasped.

The rapidly-changing technologies of computers and telecommunications created both opportunities and challenges for the CIA. In response, the agency had conceived In-Q-Tel in order to get outside of governmental bureaucracy and tap new and unrestrained talent. In-Q-Tel provides venture capital to private hi-tech firms with promising solutions to the Agency's twenty-first century concerns.

Michael's five contractors focused on developing Trojan horses capable of galloping into unsuspecting databases, scooping up intelligence, and departing without leaving telltale residue. Their long-term goal was to support the creation of automatic intelligence alerts by gathering and processing intelligence from as wide a range of databases as possible.

Michael had sought and obtained more than just talent from his contractors. They were aggressive and demonstrated out-of-the-box thinking. However, their aggressive behavior had caused problems. Three times Michael had been called on the carpet. Three of the five contractors had gone off on their own, confident their ideas would be better accepted if they proved them by first implementing them. The three government agencies that had their databases probed caught the probes and complained to Michael.

Michael fought to keep his contractors unrestrained and untainted by failure. He took the time to calm the violated agencies and convince them not to formalize their complaints. He never told his three contractors they had been caught. He simply explained to them the different defenses each of the three government agencies might use to halt and then identify the source of probes.

Six weeks ago, Michael's superior had told him to pack it all in. He was to hand over his In-Q-Tel projects to a junior project officer in Rosslyn.

Michael and Sarah had assumed the training for his new assignment would be less pressing than his In-Q-Tel assignment. It wasn't. His training at Langley had been intense, finishing just six hours before he had begun mowing the lawn. Tonight would be his first twelve-hour shift at FBI headquarters in Washington, D.C. With a car in the repair shop for a few days for a new transmission, Sarah had to find a babysitter for the ten minutes it would take her to drop Michael off at the Metro and return. She'd have to cash in favors to get a neighbor to commit so late at night.

Michael rolled the mower into the garage and went inside. He took the stairs two at a time and jumped in the shower. Twenty minutes later he was dressed, standing in the foyer. Small beads of sweat were forming on his forehead. He picked up the newspaper on the foyer table, found the sports section and checked the statistics of the Chrysler Championship golf tournament. David Duval led Tiger Woods by three shots on the first day.

Something was wrong. It was too quiet. Michael called out to Sarah. There was no answer. He looked out the front window. Sarah was sitting in the car. Linda Ann and Kathleen were strapped in the rear seat. His heart pounded as he threw the paper back on the foyer table. She hadn't been able to get a babysitter. The kids had to go with them to the Metro stop.

Sarah backed out onto White Cedar Court before Michael had time to secure his safety belt. "Tomorrow's a school day."

"I know," Michael mumbled.

"Marie and Christine both called while you were mowing. They said it was too late to be making so much noise."

Michael nodded. "Won't happen again."

Sarah turned into the Vienna Metro parking lot and followed the Kiss-And-Ride signs. At the curb, Michael leaned across the bench seat to kiss her goodbye.

"Let's talk," said Sarah. She followed him from the car so the children wouldn't hear.

"For two years I've worked my butt off," Michael began. "Twelve hour days."

"I know. It's been more than three months since we…"

"Oh God."

"You're never home, Michael."

"Because I'm working, Sarah."

"Twelve hours every day?"

"I'm not having an affair."

"Right."

"I'm being transferred to the goddamned FBI, Sarah. Don't you understand?" Michael looked at his watch. Sarah turned and headed back to the car.

Before Michael entered the overpass leading into the station, he turned. Sarah was turning onto Nutley Street. She was heading back to their Tall Oaks home.

The Metro train entered Federal Triangle station. The three blocks to the FBI building would be his last chance to raise his pulse rate for the next twelve hours. On Twelfth Street he power-walked to Pennsylvania Avenue and then turned east. The sudden sight of the Capitol, its white marble glistening in the glare of floodlights sent a shiver down his spine. Up close like this it was even more beautiful than from his In-Q-Tel office window.

Michael stopped on the corner of Tenth and Pennsylvania. The streets were deserted. In thirteen hours, about twelve thirty tomorrow afternoon, Sarah would be at the Vienna Metro waiting for him. The kids would be in school. That would be when he would apologize.

Michael heard the low rumbling sound of a high flying jet. He scanned the sky hoping for a glimpse of it. Suddenly he saw it, the silhouette of an F-14 crossing the face of the full moon now hovering directly over the Capitol dome.

Michael Stone stepped through the doors of FBI headquarters, unclipped the badge from his inside jacket pocket, and re-clipped it to the outside of his jacket. He put his keys and change in the small plastic container the guard slid to him. On the other side of the arch he reclaimed his belongings and headed for the elevators. On the fifth floor he stood in front of glass doors engraved with the words George H. W. Bush Strategic Information Operations Center. It was referred to as SIOC. He knew exactly what was on the other side of these doors even though he had never gone through them. He had been trained in the CIA's SIOC located in Langley, an exact duplicate of the one at FBI headquarters.

Each SIOC covers forty thousand square feet. Five hundred elite agents and prosecutors operating on twelve-hour shifts, processing, coordinating and dispersing evidence and intelligence are assigned to each SIOC. These agents and prosecutors are obtained from over thirty different federal agencies.

Michael cleared the SIOC lobby. He went to the leads center at the far end where he joined forty-one other analysts. His computer terminal was at the end of the first row. To its right was the leads center briefing room. To its left was the analysts/investigators area.

Michael listened to the debriefing from the FBI agent who had manned his terminal the previous twelve hours. Satisfied he understood what the agent had told him, Michael sat. The seat was warm. He signed on, taking responsibility for the terminal. He immediately began organizing his first report. In seven hours the FBI deputy director, Vinny Campbell, the person responsible for the operation of this SIOC, would convene the first of two daily briefings in the amphitheater-sized executive briefing room located back at the lobby end of the SIOC.

The disposition of each of Michael's leads, whether discarded or not, had to be documented. His summary report, most of which would never make it to the deputy director's briefings, had to be passed forward in two hours.

# Chapter 4

### Florida Keys, Florida
### Wednesday 0055 ET

It had been two hours since Doug Crosby left Key West on his way to Key Largo. Two hours of staring at the rear of that damned oversized SUV that had cut in front of him on Duvall Street. He had stayed tight on its bumper for almost an hour but in this stop-and-go traffic, tailgating had proved to be a waste of time. He backed off the SUV, shifted his weight to get comfortable, and began searching for a new radio station. It was no use. All he could get were updates on when and where Hurricane Fabian might hit the Keys, followed by on-the-scene announcer after announcer describing how the Overseas Highway was crowded with campers, trailers and cars fleeing the Keys.

"And oversized fucking SUVs," Doug screamed at the radio.

It was four in the morning when Doug Crosby turned into his driveway. The garage door was open. His Mercedes convertible was gone. *Gonzalo has arrived, probably found my message on the refrigerator and is eating at the restaurant a few kilometers up the road. Maybe not. Who gives a shit where he is?*

His father's words echoed in his head. *Gonzalo is coming to teach you many things. Listen to Gonzalo. Learn from him. Gonzalo is family. Like a son.*

Doug turned off the car motor, slumped in his seat, and muttered to his father. *"I'm your son."*

As far as Doug knew, no one outside of the Bauer family knew that Bauer Industries was going public. Bauer was his find. His father would be proud of him. Hadn't *Forbes* attested to the quality of his choice?

In the kitchen Doug snapped open a can of beer and then sprawled on the living room couch. He clicked on the television. He would wait for Gonzalo. In minutes he was absorbed in Real Sex 28, an HBO original presentation.

Doug awoke at five-thirty in the morning. His neck and back ached. A car chase blared on the television. Four empty beer cans sat on the coffee table. A fifth lay overturned on the rug. The last he had heard, the Keys were on a hurricane watch. Residents were to evacuate the Keys if the storm veered westward from its northerly course in the Atlantic. *Yeah right. Everybody's already gone.*

Doug found the Weather Channel. A graphic displayed a yellow wedge showing the range of possible routes the eye of the storm might take during the next six to twelve hours. Fabian was now eighty miles southeast of Key Largo still maintaining a due north course. The most westerly edge of the yellow wedge touched Key Largo. The commentator said, "If the eye of the storm continues on its northerly path as we think it will, the Overseas Highway should be reopened sometime in the next few hours."

Doug staggered to his feet, went through the kitchen, and opened the door to the garage. The Mercedes wasn't there. Shit. Jose had to be told.

Doug called his father. It took whoever answered the phone a few minutes to locate him. When Doug heard his father's voice he anxiously told him that Gonzalo hadn't come home all night. Jose hung up on him.

Doug's face turned blood red, every muscle in his body tensed. He was furious he had made such a dumb mistake. He picked up a beer can and hurled it. Beer splattered his face and traced a trail as it flew into the kitchen. *That fucking Gonzalo.*

# Chapter 5

## Washington, D.C.
## Wednesday 0547 ET

At five forty-seven in the morning an icon appeared and began blinking on Michael's terminal. Michael double-clicked on the icon. Echelon, an international eavesdropping system, had intercepted a message. He attempted to open the message. A boxed message appeared on his screen.

> Access Denied
> SIOC's Multi-Agency
> Operations/Intelligence Room may override
> this restriction if deemed urgent.

The Echelon system, capable of intercepting virtually all global telecommunications, provoked worldwide scrutiny. Foreign governments expressed the strongest reservations about the system. Their chief concern was fear one of the five countries under treaty to operate the system—the United States, Great Britain, Canada, Australia, and New Zealand—might employ Echelon to obtain confidential and proprietary information that would provide unfair advantage during international competitions. The world community considered the United States to be the chief suspect.

Michael knew Echelon eavesdropping required approvals at the highest level of the requesting federal department or agency. It often included the Departments of State and Justice, and the National Security Council. It wasn't uncommon for final approvals to be requested from the executive office of the president of the United States.

Echelon taps were rare. Michael had never seen one. He initiated a search to identify who had requested this Echelon tap. In 0.7 seconds he knew—a joint FBI, Department of Justice, Drug Enforcement Agency, Customs Service, and Security and Exchange Commission task force. All confirmed intercepts resulting from this request were to be reported to the task force leader, Greg McNulty, at Justice.

Rapid Start, a computer program, had sent Michael an Echelon intercept and then denied him access to its content. Why?

# Chapter 6

### Miami, Florida
### Wednesday 0615 ET

Alan Dickie couldn't remember a day that he hadn't wanted to be an FBI special agent. For four years he rode the Metro to Foggy Bottom in the District of Columbia to attend George Washington University. For three more years he rode the Metro to the Clarendon station to attend the George Mason University, School of Law in Arlington, Virginia. Three months before graduation he applied for a job with the FBI. After graduation he bided his time as a law clerk in a District firm that was struggling to gain a foothold within the sphere of the Federal Communications Commission. A year later, with the FBI interviews and background checks complete, he was offered a job and began his FBI career.

Alan expected the thirteen-week long training program at the FBI Academy on the Marine Base at Quantico, Virginia to be demanding and nerve-wracking. At five-foot six and one hundred and thirty-five pounds, Alan was the smallest male recruit in his class. Three women were taller. One was heavier.

Alan had an insatiable desire to analyze. No detail was so small that it didn't deserve further examination. Building the foundation of his career on solid grunt work, he greased through his early years as a bona fide FBI agent. His criminal complaint analyses were textbook accurate. He listened to wiretaps and uncovered leads that seemed to others to have materialized from the dead time between words. He used his long overnight surveillances to identify informants who would later testify and convict their schoolyard playmates. When his interrogations didn't supply a confession, they almost always provided new information that often led to a later conviction.

Defense attorneys soon started to seek delays with the hope that Alan would be reassigned or come down with a terminal illness. The promotions rolled, faster than most, until now at thirty-one, he had his dream assignment. Alan became the youngest special agent ever appointed to the head of the FBI's Miami Field Office, known as MFO. He was determined to mark his territory from day one.

He sat bolt upright in the black high-backed chair behind his desk to survey his new office. His rearrangement of the government-issued furniture pleased him. He walked to the opposite side of the room to see what it would look like to those entering his chamber. An American flag hung from a pole to the left of his desk. A Department of Justice flag hung on the other side. Alan's heavy combination-lock safe on the Justice flag side of his desk didn't quite match the color or height of the desk. He made a mental note to have it replaced. Along the left wall, end tables with tall brass lamps crowned with yellowing shades sat on either end of a brown cracked-leather couch.

Alan's gaze found the lithograph he brought with him to every assignment. It hung on the wall over the couch. It was the picture of FBI academy recruits threading their way through a mock town infested with pop-up citizens that might kill, surrender, or be going about their everyday chores. His hand caressed the .40 Glock semiautomatic in his belt holster.

Opposite the couch were two matching brown cracked-leather armchairs. He had bought a mock Oriental rug the day before at Wal-Mart. Now it lay between the couch and chairs on top of the worn beige wall-to-wall carpet.

Alan sat on the couch, sinking deep into the tired cushion. He looked toward his desk and smiled. The inches he had added to the height of his desk chair would leave no doubt who was in charge here. It wasn't an accident that in courtrooms everyone had to look up to judges.

There was a light tap on the door. A tall heavyset woman peered in. "It's 6:30, Mr. Dickie," Sally said. "Holt is here."

Alan waved Sally to come in and close the door. "Tell me again, what's Holt's last name?"

"Brown. Holt Brown."

Alan nodded and headed for his chair behind the desk. "Right. Give me five seconds before you send him in."

Alan banged his thigh on a corner of the desk as he hustled getting to his high-backed chair. He sat upright, adjusting his tie. Then he rose, pulled the back of his suit jacket down, and sat on it. First impressions are so important. Both of Alan's hands worked the knot in his tie.

A gangly six-foot man with a close-cut Afro came into the office. The collar of his short-sleeved shirt was open. He wasn't wearing a tie.

"Mornin'," said Holt.

Alan waved him to the couch.

Holt sat on the arm of the chair closest to Alan's desk. He leaned forward, putting his hands on his knees. "We've got kind of a surprise," Holt said, dribbling it out for effect. "It's an intercept. *Jose Valderrama.* Within the hour. From our 305 area code."

Alan remained stone-faced.

"An *Echelon* intercept. *Jose Valderrama.* One of our ten-most-wanted."

Alan nodded.

"We've been tracking Jose for three years. We think he heads one of the largest, most sophisticated money-laundering operations in the world."

"It's Holt, right?" said Alan.

Holt's brow wrinkled. He sat up.

"You're my chief of staff."

Holt nodded.

"You'll be my eyes and ears to the staff."

"Okay," said Holt.

"As my chief of staff, you should know that it's my policy to begin our daily briefings with a review of your daily report. You will submit these reports every evening before you leave for the day."

# Chapter 7

## Arlington, Virginia
## Wednesday 0730 ET

Carolyn Hughes left South Waterpark Towers for her 7:40 a.m. appointment with Simon Tully, the CFO of Taylor Associates. There was a refreshing nip in the air. She looked up, savoring the deep blue sky and filling her lungs with the cool morning air. Sated, she headed off at an invigorating pace along Crystal Drive. It had been weeks since she had felt this good.

Everything had gone well—surprisingly well—during her interviews the evening before. Not one negative vibe. A large part of the give and take had been about the specifics of her assignments at Justice. Then they switched to hypothetical case histories. Her MBA gave her a technical edge—the ability to sprinkle academic principles into every theoretical world they created. Final questions were light—her hobbies, sports, that sort of thing—just the right amount of filler laced with smiles.

Carolyn entered the Taylor Associates building lobby. She told the receptionist she had a meeting with Simon Tully. The receptionist slid a sign-in sheet to Carolyn, handed her a visitor's badge and then nodded to a gray-haired man sitting at the far end of the lobby.

Although Simon Tully had been a slight five-foot eight in high school, he had played varsity football ferociously. One day a vicious blind tackle drove a helmet into the side of his right knee, tearing ligaments and shattering cartilage. In the emergency room doctors stabilized his knee with an air cast. They told him he would need surgery.

Simon didn't trust doctors, refusing all suggestions involving corrective surgery, and now, decades later, walked on the ball of his right foot. Over time he had convinced himself that his limp wasn't bad, that few people even noticed.

The man that had been sitting on the couch on the far side of the lobby had crossed the lobby and was standing at Carolyn's side when she finished signing in. When she looked up, he introduced himself. "Good morning, Carolyn. I'm Simon Tully."

Carolyn followed Simon across the lobby and up the staircase to the third floor. She couldn't help noticing the heel of his right shoe was new, the left worn. She followed Simon into his office several feet from the stairwell door. She pegged him to be in his late forties or early fifties. His loosened tie, opened collar, and turned up sleeves this time in the morning put her at ease, at least for now.

"Emily, this is Carolyn Hughes," Simon said to the middle-aged woman sitting behind the desk in his outer office. The two women nodded. In his office Simon waved Carolyn to a chair facing the window.

As he walked around his desk Carolyn looked out the window. His view of the Potomac and Washington, D.C. is almost the same as mine, she thought, as she settled into the chair.

After a few get-comfortable exchanges, Simon began, "So, tell me about yourself, Carolyn."

Carolyn repeated what she had told her Taylor Associates interviewers the night before. She had a business administration degree from New York University. Her major was finance. A George Washington University MBA followed; her thesis: Alternative Corporate Financial Strategies and Their Impacts on Mergers. She went on to cite two antitrust cases her financial analysis had supported at Justice. She concluded by saying three years at Justice were enough. She wanted to become a part of creating wealth, not impeding it. Her entire discourse flowed with remarkable ease. Everything was going well.

Simon explained that his staff had been impressed with her interviews, the company was investigating possible merger candidates, and that the preliminary results of the merger survey would be presented to Jack Taylor, the CEO, in the next few days.

"I'm not free to provide detailed information," said Simon. Carolyn nodded understanding. "Three days ago, Jack came into my office. He handed me a tear sheet from *Forbes* magazine. It announced this year's fastest-growing company in Florida." Simon stood, walked to the window and gazed across the Potomac. "I asked Jack if he was thinking of adding this firm to our merger candidate list."

Carolyn didn't feel the least bit uncomfortable looking at Simon's back. This man put her at ease.

"Jack just looked at me. Didn't say a word. That's his way. I read the tear sheet and then reminded him that the firm mentioned in the tear sheet was privately held." Simon returned to his desk and sat facing Carolyn. "I told Jack that getting information on a private firm in the next few days would be impossible. Then he surprised me. He said, 'Why not give Carolyn Hughes a shot at it?'"

Simon smiled at Carolyn's quizzical expression. "How did Jack find out about you? I had no idea at the time. Later when I thought about it, it was obvious. A key member of my staff is leaving, starting her own firm. In fact, we're providing her with venture capital. Anyway, I'd just prioritized five resumes as possible replacements for her. I gave them to Human Resources to arrange interviews. Jack must have spotted your resume there." Simon leaned back. "I wish I could tell you our hectic pace is unusual. It's not. Everybody travels at a hundred and ten miles per hour around here. Every day. Tomorrow's always too late. Interested?"

"In what?" Carolyn probed.

"A permanent position with Taylor Associates. Our recent growth has been through acquisition. I need someone with your experience."

"My responsibilities?"

"Initially, follow up on Jack Taylor's interest in the *Forbes* article."

"And?"

"And find out as much as you can. Something like what you did with that Cayrod case."

Carolyn froze. *Oh God, is this all going to crash?* Her heart began pounding against her ribs. *Will I ever be free of Cayrod? Of Greg?* She felt her face flush. She stared at Simon, every nerve in her body keyed to pick up any inflection in Simon's voice, the slightest body language, anything. She fought to keep her voice from betraying her. "I never mentioned Cayrod, last night or this morning. It's not on my resume."

Simon didn't respond right away. Then, in a matter-of-fact tone, he said, "One of your interviewers last night has a friend who has a friend. The word came back you did a great job at Justice. I followed up some… another friend." Simon sat back smiling. "Cayrod *should* be on your resume Carolyn. Seems it paid off big."

Carolyn shifted in her chair. She needed time to let her emotions do whatever they were going to do. Her mind raced, digging to unearth hidden agendas. Was this his way of testing her? It all sounded innocent. But was it? Suddenly she knew. She realized that for the first time since sitting in that last row of the Justice department auditorium the word Cayrod was just another word. Calm swept over her.

"In a strange way, I suppose it did pay off," she said.

"Human Resources has the full offer package," Simon continued. "A twenty percent salary increase, full benefits, 401K, incentive and bonus awards, of course."

"I'd be working for...?"

"You'd be my special assistant," said Simon.

Carolyn smiled. "Your special assistant?"

"Um-hum, I need someone able to take in-depth looks... on a variety of financial issues... flexible. Able to work well with people." Simon hesitated. "I have to be honest though. There's no one to help you. You'll have just a few days. The firm's in Florida. I'll schedule your presentation last. That would give you until 11:30 a.m., three days from now." Simon studied Carolyn and then smiled again.

"I know. The schedule is asinine. But, these merger briefings will be going on for weeks to come. Your first presentation will be little more than a placeholder. Jack will understand."

Carolyn didn't know if she had heard Simon correctly. She asked, "Before even talking with you about what I might find, I'll be briefing the CEO, Mr. Jack Taylor?"

"There just isn't enough time. If you uncover something critical, something you think I should know before you brief, call me." He took his business card from his wallet and slid it across the table. "We turn out the lights about eleven. You decide on a pre-brief or not. If you do, we can get together the morning of the briefing, five-ish. That wouldn't be unusual."

"I'll start tomorrow," Carolyn told her new boss.

# Chapter 8

## San Diego International Airport, California
## Wednesday 0535 PT

Janet Griffin nodded idly when the flight attendant asked if he could put her carry-on in the overhead rack. She slid her purse under the seat in front of her and sank into the plush leather seat, eager to nap until changing planes in Dallas. The flight attendant asked if she would like something to drink before they took off. Janet shook her head without looking up, signaling she didn't want to be disturbed.

San Diego was Janet's retreat from the demands of her hectic life, if only for a few days. It was where she recharged, usually by doing a little shopping, maybe seeing a show downtown, and eating in first class restaurants. Most of all she loved sitting poolside while soaking up the surroundings and devouring paperbacks.

Just before she had left for this trip she had gotten back into her high school dress size and had her long hair highlighted and styled. She had hoped this trip would turn out to be special. Everything had started so well, right here in the San Diego airport.

Four months ago, she had arrived from Miami and was making her way to the rental car counter. Sporting a new summer dress, she was feeling so frisky she had to force herself not to prance across the concourse.

Suddenly a man grabbed her arm from behind. She tried but couldn't break free. She faced him with her fiercest how-dare-you look.

The stranger released her and stepped back, contrition spread across his face. "I'm sorry," he stammered. "So sorry. I thought you were Phyllis. Phyllis, my cousin."

"I'm not Phyllis," Janet said slowly, giving herself time to take him in. She shifted her luggage from the arm he had grasped. It was hurting, so she knew it was going to bruise.

"I know. But from the back..."

"From any direction I'm not your cousin." *This guy is hot!*

"Of course I understand," Royce said. "It's my fault. I'm late. My cousin's plane arrived on time, nearly twenty-five

minutes ago.   At least that's what they told me at the gate.
Apparently, I've missed her.  I'm sorry."
  "I've got it," Janet said.  "You're sorry.  Right?  Do you get
it?  I'm not Priscilla."  Janet knew the man had said Phyllis but
wasn't exactly sure why she responded with the name Priscilla.
*Thick dark hair, wide shoulders, piercing eyes.  Jesus.*
  "It's Phyllis," Royce said.  "My cousin's name is Phyllis."
  "Okay, Phyllis.  I'm not her either."
  "I'm Royce, Royce Palmer."   He scanned the terminal,
looking for his cousin.  "Look, I'm really sorry.  I didn't mean to
grab you that way.  I know there's no excuse for what I did.  But,
would you consider…  Would you allow me to make amends?
Maybe buy you a drink?"   Royce began to search the terminal
again.  Janet didn't respond.  Royce turned.  His eyes nailed her.
"In the restaurant over there?  Please?"
  She stepped back, trying to concentrate.  *Irresistible.*
  "Please.  One drink?" Royce pleaded.
  "Just one," Janet said.  *Gorgeous.*
  "I'll call Phyllis on her cell."   Royce dialed his cell.  Janet
listened as Royce apologized to a recording of the weather
forecast.  Royce snapped his cell closed.  "She is so demanding."

  The waitress centered their drinks on small cocktail napkins.
  "Is she wrong about you usually being late?" Janet said.
  "Obviously, she didn't wait one damned minute today."
Royce paused before adding, "Others know us so much better
than we know ourselves, don't you think?"
  They went through the usual preliminaries.  He was a lawyer,
had his own firm, albeit a small one—just him and Ginny, a part-
time secretary, receptionist, and all-around office administrator.
His clients were mostly from California—San Diego and San
Francisco.  Two were Washington State—all nascent
companies needing capital.   That was his specialty, providing
venture capital for emerging companies with promising ideas but
no money to get their ideas to market.
  In response Janet disclosed she was a realtor and often came
to San Diego to relax.  She didn't mention her daughter Nicole.
  After drinks, Royce's interest in her was palpable to Janet.
"I'd *really* like to see you again."
  Janet looked away, not knowing what to think.  She

reengaged. "We've just met."

"Tell me your last name."

"Griffin. Janet Griffin." She pushed her chair back, stood, and looked toward the exit.

"May I call you?"

Janet looked back at Royce. He was standing.

"Jet lag won't be a problem?" he asked.

"Going east to west?" Janet replied mockingly.

"At least tell me where you are staying," said Royce.

Janet picked up her luggage from beside her chair and positioned the strap of her purse on her shoulder. "Thanks for the drink."

This morning Janet had walked hand-in-hand with Royce through the nearly empty airline terminal for her flight back to Miami. They had arrived early. The concourse was almost empty. Her flight would be the first to leave the San Diego terminal.

She squeezed Royce's hand, smiled up at him and then skipped a few yards ahead. With the sound of her final steps ricocheting from the walls of the concourse, she turned, raising both arms offering to embrace him. *Please Royce. This once. Be what I want you to be. Please.*

Royce walked into her embrace and lifted her off her feet. He hugged her slight five-foot four frame so tightly that Janet couldn't breathe. Laughing, Royce began swinging her feet from side to side in front of him. As he loosened his bear hug, she slid down his chest. Her skirt rolled up, exposing her panties.

Janet protested. "Royce, I told you I can't breathe when you do that."

Royce grinned, grabbed her buttocks and slammed them against his groin.

Janet wanted to sleep, to be fresh when she arrived home in Miami. *He shouldn't have exposed me that way. And then pressing me against him...* Janet closed her eyes. *I'm sick of his third degrees when we get together, wanting to know everything I do, everyone I talk to, where I've been... He's way too possessive.*

Janet positioned the small white pillow against the window and rested her head on it. *Royce will never change. So disappointing. Why couldn't he have behaved this morning instead of acting the way he did? I gave him a chance.*

"We're passing through twelve thousand feet to our cruising altitude of thirty-two thousand. We anticipate an on-time arrival in Dallas. If you're continuing on to Miami with us, our on-time arrival there will be 5:30 this evening."

Janet made her decision. It was firm. There would be no backing down. The next time they talked, she would tell him. *You're history, Royce.* She looked out the window. *Break-ups suck.*

At that moment Royce Palmer's plane was taking off for Acapulco, Mexico.

# Chapter 9

### Washington, D.C.
### Wednesday 1230 ET

Michael Stone checked his watch. It was twelve-thirty. It had taken him several minutes of banal conversation on the telephone to convince Greg McNulty to meet him for lunch. Now he was beginning to think it had been a waste of his time.

Michael wandered among the tables in the Department of Justice cafeteria, trying not to appear like a lost soul. On the other hand no one seemed to pay any attention whether he stood in one place or wandered around. He knew he should have called Sarah earlier. She would be waiting at the Vienna Metro station. He had thought the meeting with Greg would be quick but it wasn't turning out that way.

Michael saw a stocky dark-haired man walk briskly into the cafeteria, stop and look across the tables toward the cashier's area. Michael raised his hand. The man nodded and headed toward him. McNulty's rumpled shirt hung loose at the waist yet the knot in his tie was precise and snug to the buttoned-down collar. Michael extended his hand as Greg reached his side. Greg peered through rimmed glasses that matched the tint of his hair. He shook Michael's hand indifferently.

"I thought you might be a no-show," said Michael.

"Sorry I'm late," McNulty said. "My meeting went on and on. Find a table. I'll be right with you." Greg turned and joined the line of those waiting to buy their meals. Michael sat at the nearest empty table. If he called Sarah now, she would be annoyed. She hated changing plans at the last minute.

A few minutes later Greg sat opposite Michael, flipping a dangling strand of cheese over a wedge of warmed-over pizza. "You say you're part of the SIOC team?" He bit into the pizza.

Michael sat a little straighter. "Right."

Greg spoke through a mouth full of pizza. "It's the place to be these days, what with the budget and all."

"There's a lot of drudge work." Michael watched Greg bite into the pizza again. This time he guided a strand of stretching cheese to his mouth.

"Tell me about it," Greg mumbled. "Okay, so what can I do

for you?"

"Work with us," said Michael.

Greg stared in mid bite.

Michael waved Greg to continue eating. He wanted to go so he wouldn't have to tell Sarah not to meet him at the Metro station. "You'll be getting a request. From our SIOC's Office of Multi-Agency Operations and Intelligence. Just wanted to give you a heads up."

Greg swallowed hard. "What?"

"SIOC is the command center for federal investigations. We're across the street in FBI headquarters. Fifth floor."

Greg folded the crust, stuffed it into his mouth signaling with his hand he would speak as soon as he swallowed. He did. "Work with you?"

"We'll be monitoring your task force. Just a formality."

Greg glared in disbelief. "No way. Classified." He leaned closer. "Compartmented."

"We know."

Greg picked up the final wedge of pizza. "Yeah, I guess you guys would know."

Michael leaned back in his chair. "Having us onboard will give your task force high-level exposure."

Greg shook his head. "I don't know. Look, Justice's been after this money-laundering cartel for years."

Bingo, thought Michael. Money-laundering is a legitimate link to the missions of Operation Enduring Freedom. "Of course, you'll stay in charge," Michael added quickly. "All we'll do is monitor."

Greg chewed deliberately, his eyes searching Michael's face through the black rims of his glasses. "Tell me, how'd you find out about us?"

"You know I can't disclose intelligence sources," said Michael.

Greg opened a napkin. He wiped his lips and hands slowly. "There are procedures, forms, channels of approvals. Need-to-knows. It all takes time."

"As I said, I'm just here to grease the skids, give you a heads-up. The request will be on your desk when you get back to your office. It's your decision, of course; your responsibility, not ours." Michael put both hands on the edge of the table in preparation for leaving. "If you want to go through all the hoops, by all means do. If you want to approve it this afternoon, we know you can."

"I'll think about it," said Greg.

Michael pushed his chair back. "As head of your task force, you'll get the highest level of national attention. Your name might be used during our daily briefing to the president." Michael looked at his watch. "You may be asked to brief at some point." He stood. "Got to go. Been out of the office too long."

"Sorry I was late. Couldn't be helped."

"Take care." Michael's face broke out into a broad smile as soon as his back was turned to Greg.

# Chapter 10

### Washington, D.C.
### Wednesday 1250 ET

Michael left Justice and walked along Pennsylvania Avenue toward the Metro. Sarah had certainly gone back home by now. After all, this wasn't the first time he hadn't been able to arrive at the Metro stop on time. They had developed an understanding. Sarah would wait for the train after the one he normally arrived home on. If he weren't on that one, she would return home without him.

Michael stopped at the corner of 12th and Pennsylvania, his mind racing. He had no doubt that he had convinced Greg to authorize him access to the content of the Echelon message. Greg had inadvertently told him that his task force was investigating a money-laundering scheme. Had been for years. Why hadn't they moved on it? Who was laundering what money? Drug dealers? Terrorists?

Money-laundering schemes were a SIOC priority. Echelon intercepts were of critical national importance. They demanded immediate action. Someone had directed that Echelon intercept to his terminal. He had to go back to work. He would call Sarah as soon as he arrived at his SIOC terminal.

Michael returned to the leads center and found a terminal with no one sitting at it. As soon as he signed on, he smiled. The Echelon icon was blinking. He double-clicked on it. An array of information filled the screen. Greg had approved his access to the Echelon intercept.

The Echelon telephone intercept originated from area code 305: Miami, Florida. It had been placed to an Acapulco, Mexico telephone number. Michael called up the reverse telephone directories. The call had originated from Key Largo, from a phone owned by someone named Doug Crosby. The Acapulco telephone number didn't list a name. Michael launched a Spanish-English translator program. After a long silent delay he heard a grunt and then a voice.

"Good news. Gonzalo arrived.
Bad news. Gonzalo and Mercedes missing."

The connection broke. Michael attached his unique Operation Enduring Freedom tag to the Echelon intercept. With his OEF tag attached, the Rapid Start software program would ensure that he received all international calls from the Acapulco telephone number as well as future information that correlated with this Echelon intercept.

Money laundering was what Greg McNulty had said. His Justice task force had been investigating a money-laundering scheme. Money laundering. A top priority at SIOC. Michael opened the technical analysis portion of the intercept. This Echelon intercept was based solely on the Acapulco telephone number.

Michael searched the screen for follow-up action being taken. He found none. He opted for human intervention. He queried Langley. Two hours later Langley relayed the response from the CIA's Acapulco office.

Confirm. Subject number within Jose
Valderrama compound. What's up?

Michael created a summary of what he had found. He sent it to Greg, Langley, and the CIA's Acapulco office.

A new icon began flashing on his screen. Additional correspondence related to the Echelon intercept was available.

Greg McNulty, the Justice task force leader, had forwarded the Echelon intercept and Michael's summary to Alan Dickie, at MFO. Greg's message assigned Alan Dickie follow-up responsibility. Michael found and then added Alan Dickie's telephone and fax numbers to his OEF Rapid Start file.

An administrative message appeared on Michael's screen.

The FBI is a member of Greg McNulty's multi-
agency task force.
The FBI MFO is assigned follow-up.
The cryptonym for FBI support to SIOC is
PENTTBOM.

An FBI PENTTBOM tag should be used, not
an OEF tag.
V. Campbell
FBI Deputy Director

Michael sat back.  He reread the message, then read it again.
Vinny Campbell.  He's the guy in charge of this SIOC.  Michael
looked around the room, wanting time for his mind to clear, to
understand the intent of the message.  He reread the message a
fourth time.  He wanted to be sure he hadn't missed a word or
misunderstood a phrase.  He sat back.  He understood.  *This is
fucking bullshit.  Unadulterated bullshit!*

# Chapter 11

## Acapulco, Mexico
## Wednesday 1230 CT

Jose Valderrama hurled his half-empty glass at his study wall. The heavy Waterford crystal chipped the edge of a mahogany picture frame and fell to the floor. He whirled around. "Damn it Royce, how many times have I told Doug never to call me? What the fuck does he do? He calls me. I'll have his fucking phone torn out." Jose paced the study, his hands trembling with rage.

Jose was in his mid-fifties, dressed in jeans and a denim shirt. His jet-black hair was plastered to his head. Brown eyes smoldering beneath thick black eyebrows, a lean six-foot frame and an effortless step conveyed a deadly shrewdness.

Jose stopped at the French doors, grasped the handles and flung the doors open. On the patio he placed both hands on the waist-high marble wall, breathing hard. It was a minute before he returned to the study and settled quietly into the Elizabethan chair.

"He's concerned," said Royce, watching him. The guy could move like a snake.

"Who the fuck isn't?"

"He's just getting started. He wants to be sure you know everything that's happening, when it happens." Jose looked at Royce. "He loves you, Jose. He wants to please you."

"Maybe the feds didn't get a chance to record it."

Royce went to the bar. "Right. You said you hung up without saying a word." Royce held up a Tequila bottle. "Want one?"

Jose wasn't listening. "Fuck."

Royce poured his drink and then stood by the window. "We have to know if Gonzalo is okay."

"Jesus, Royce, don't treat me like an idiot. I know that."

"Doug doesn't know the Keys well yet," said Royce. "After all, he's been there less than a year. He needs time to blend in, to get to know everyone."

Jose waved impatiently for Royce to go on.

"This guy you said helps Doug sometimes, what's his name? Pepe…"

"Pepe Gomez," said Jose.

"Yeah, Pepe Gomez," said Royce. "Why don't you ask Doug to have Pepe help look for Gonzalo?"

Jose's eyebrows rose. "Good idea, Royce. Doug told me Pepe's lived in the area for years and knows the Keys well."

"We have to assume your telephones lines are bugged. We'll use one of those Internet stores in town to send Doug an e-mail."

# Chapter 12

## Washington, D.C.
## Wednesday 2400 ET

Michael Stone was exhausted as he walked into the FBI headquarters building. Sarah had been furious when he had arrived home yesterday afternoon, more than three hours late. He hadn't remembered to call. The more he denied having an affair the more upset Sarah had become.

He couldn't tell her about the Echelon intercept that had appeared on his terminal. How Echelon intercepts demand immediate follow-up, much like CIA night letters. How he had gone to the Justice department cafeteria to hoodwink Greg McNulty into disclosing his task force mission—money-laundering. How he had decided to intervene by calling Langley. How, once he had called Langley, he was obligated to stay at the SIOC until the reply arrived. How it was a good thing he had waited because Langley had confirmed the call was to the Valderrama compound in Acapulco.

And what did he get for all these efforts? Sarah was as convinced as ever that he was having an affair and, after only one day on his new job at the FBI's SIOC, he had managed to get on the FBI deputy director's shit list.

Michael passed through the security checkpoints, entered the SIOC, and headed to the leads center at the rear of SIOC. On his way, he detoured to the washroom on the floor below. Water flew as he defogged his mind by splashing water on his face.

Back at his terminal he heard the word of the day at his debriefing before taking responsibility for the terminal: Deputy Director Vinny Campbell had stressed the need to identify and follow-up every suspected money trail no matter how faint it might appear, where it might lead, or how improbable the suspected money-launderer might appear to be. Never underestimate the sophistication or resourcefulness of the enemy, Vinny had told the attendees at his 4 p.m. executive briefing.

Michael's OEF icon was blinking. He double-clicked on it. Rapid Start was forwarding an intercept. The intercept content was preceded by a message.

The Acapulco Internet service provider has allowed the installation of Carnivore software. The message went on to explain that Rapid Start software had identified this intercept to be of interest to Michael by linking this international Carnivore intercept to the Echelon intercept that he had put his OEF tag on yesterday. The common telephone number linking them was that of Doug Crosby. The message concluded by saying the Florida attorney general and the judiciary had previously approved monitoring Doug Crosby's telephone number.

Michael smiled. *Zeros and ones. Zeros and ones. Love 'em.*

Michael called up the Spanish-to-English translator. He read the Carnivore intercept. It was e-mail from an Acapulco library terminal to Doug Crosby in Key Largo.

> How many times have I told you never to call
> me? Don't call again. Ever. Give Gonzalo
> more time. He's never been near a hurricane.
> Maybe he's holed up somewhere. If he doesn't
> show in the next few hours, have Pepe Gomez
> find him. Pepe knows the area better than you.
> Pepe has more contacts than you. Pepe's
> contacts will be more useful than yours.

Michael looked for confirmation that Greg McNulty had received this Carnivore intercept. He hadn't. Michael summarized the linkage between the Carnivore and Echelon intercepts. He sent it along with the English translation of the Carnivore message to Greg McNulty, Alan Dickie at the FBI's MFO, and the CIA's Acapulco home office.

Michael suggested that the CIA Acapulco home office put the Acapulco library under surveillance.

# Chapter 13

**Arlington, Virginia**
**Thursday 0730 ET**

Carolyn felt a huge weight come off her shoulders when she resigned from Justice. For the first time in weeks she felt free. Now she walked briskly with her head high as she made her way from her apartment to Taylor Associates. She was eager to immerse herself in her new world. She picked up the temporary badge waiting for her at the front desk. Instead of going to Human Resources as the receptionist had instructed, she crossed the lobby, walked up two flights and went directly to Simon's third floor office.

Emily smiled. She waved Carolyn in. "He's expecting you."

Simon was engrossed in something on his desk. He looked up and waved her to the chair in front of his desk. He took the *Forbes* tear sheet from his desk drawer. He held it up so Carolyn could see it.

Carolyn didn't tell Simon she had bought a copy of the magazine on her way home after accepting the job.

"That's Charles Bauer," said Simon pointing to the picture. "It's his firm Jack is interested in—Bauer Industries. They're located in Bayside, Florida." He passed the tear sheet to Carolyn. "Find whatever you can about their financial situation, their profit to loss ratio, revenue flow, debt to equity ratio, lines of credit, stockholders, if any, that sort of thing. What's their product line, who are the movers and shakers, customers, competitors? Anything and everything." Simon leaned back in his chair. "As I said yesterday, you have a place-setter report due in two days, at 11:30 a.m. I'll support you one hundred percent. Count on it."

As Simon summoned Emily, Carolyn folded the blurb and put it in the flap of her day planner.

Emily guided Carolyn to her assigned cubicle on the floor below Simon's. She introduced Carolyn to others in neighboring cubicles, explained some of the office procedures, and showed her where the supplies and ladies room were. Carolyn was surprised to see every cubicle occupied. She thought she had arrived earlier than most.

Returning to the entrance of Carolyn's cubicale, Emily said, "The first few days can be confusing, I know. Feel free to call me anytime. Extension 334."

"Thanks," Carolyn said. Emily headed back up to her office. Carolyn sat in her low swivel chair. She extracted the blurb from her day planner, hunched over the gray desktop, and began reading it... again.

> Although detailed information is not readily available, sources indicate Charles Bauer, founder and CEO of Bauer Associates, now heads the largest firm in Bayside, a small town on Florida's Intracoastal Waterway. Located several miles north of Miami, Bauer Associates has become the fastest-growing firm in Florida. It is believed to be on the verge of becoming a serious Internet player. Their principal efforts are in software development and network systems. Asked if any of the firm's work was applicable to the Internet, Mr. Charles Bauer replied, 'No comment.'

Carolyn sat up, pressed her spine against the chair back, and crossed her forearms on her chest. Ten minutes later she picked up the telephone. It took three calls to learn that the author of the *Forbes* blurb had just left on a European assignment.

From her experiences at Justice, Carolyn knew general information could be obtained on privately-held corporations with diligent digging, but financial and technical information was notoriously tough to uncover—legitimately at least. There wasn't enough time to conduct the type of investigation she had done in the Cayrod probe. It had taken significant clout and many weeks to identify sketchy sources. Mining them was tedious. It had been almost a year before a documentable pattern of abuse began replacing hunches and guesses.

Bauer Industries had no known tipster or disgruntled employee willing to provide an entry point. Not yet anyway. All she knew was the name of the CEO, Charles Bauer, and the location of the firm's headquarters: Bayside, Florida.

Now that's luck, thought Carolyn. Janet lives in Bayside. I haven't seen her for a couple of years—since Nicole was about two.

Carolyn decided the direct approach would be best. However, she would have to offer Mr. Bauer something to entice him to talk to her. She called Simon. He authorized the release of the identical packet of material being used by the other merger teams. Within minutes, Emily brought the packet to her cubicle. It was impressive, but much too long and detailed for a first meeting. She spread it out along her L-shaped desk and on the floor. She reassembled it into five-minute and fifteen-minute versions and then asked Emily to make her copies of the two smaller versions.

Satisfied her plan had been set into action, Carolyn picked up the telephone to make final arrangements. She dialed Janet.

"It's me."

"Carolyn?"

"I know we just talked last week," said Carolyn.

"What's up?"

"I'll be in Bayside." Carolyn hesitated for effect. "About five today."

"Are you kidding me?"

"Nope. What do you say? Five in the Carp's Landing bar?"

"Yeah, okay. Good timing. The hurricane has passed. Why're ya coming?"

"I have to run," Carolyn said.

"You're not in trouble or anything?"

"Got to catch the plane."

"Me too."

"What are you talking about?"

"I'm in Dallas. We're about to take off."

"I thought I called Bayside," Carolyn said.

"My cell and I are roaming."

They exchanged flight arrival times. They were landing at the Miami International Airport at virtually the same time. They agreed to meet in T.G.I. Friday's for a drink before heading for Bayside.

At one-thirty, Emily told Carolyn that Simon was out of his office. She put Carolyn through to his voice mail. "Mr. Tully, this is Carolyn. I have an appointment with Charles Bauer at eight in the morning. My flight to Miami leaves Reagan National within the hour." Carolyn paused. "I doubt I'll have detailed information for Saturday morning's briefing. Either way, no earlier than eleven-thirty. *Please.*" Carolyn paused again. "I'll be with Janet Griffin, my former college roommate. Emily has her number."

On her way to the cab that was waiting on Crystal Drive, Carolyn stopped by Emily's desk. She picked up her travel advance, plane tickets, neatly bound copies of the two briefings she had created, and a third bound set—the originals.

# Chapter 14

## Miami International Airport
## Thursday 1740 ET

Carolyn walked the length of the plane's exit ramp into the Miami Airport. She found her way along the crowded concourse to T.G.I. Friday's. The only booth available was in the back on the far side of the bar. She started to slide in when she saw Janet coming around the bar. "Done roaming?" Carolyn asked when Janet reached the booth.

"For today," said Janet. They hugged and slid into opposite sides of the booth.

"Who's taking care of Nicole? What were you doing in Dallas?"

"Nicole's in daycare as we speak. She's been sleeping over at her best friend's house the last two nights, having a ball. Dallas? Just a stopover. I was coming home from San Diego. Visiting a friend there."

Carolyn's eyebrows rose. "A friend?"

"Yeah, I met this guy in San Diego, a few months ago. Real good looker, tall, handsome. I never mentioned him because I didn't know where it would go what with him in San Diego and me in Bayside."

"Is it serious?" Carolyn said.

"I thought it might be, but no. He's way too possessive, wants to know everything I'm doing, where I go, who I meet, that sort of thing." Janet looked down. "To tell the truth, he's too rough."

"Gotta watch that. So why are you still going all that way to see him?"

"This was my last trip."

"Just like that? This is it?"

"I really decided while the plane was taking off from San Diego. I didn't like the way he said goodbye. He embarrassed me."

"Have you told him you're breaking up with him?"

"I will," said Janet. "Let's not talk about him anymore. He's history."

Carolyn changed subjects. "That's a preppy outfit you're

wearing. You know what it reminds me of?" Janet waited for Carolyn to tell her. "Remember when we decided to change our goody-goody image back in Greenwich Village?"

"What are you talking about?"

Carolyn's eyes sparkled. She was nineteen years old again, crossing Washington Square Park on her way to class. "Remember? Only the nice guys asked us for dates?"

"Oh God." Janet laughed, realizing exactly what Carolyn was talking about.

"It didn't take much did it?" Carolyn teased. "The guys had only one thought on their minds."

"We set the stage and then performed flawlessly on it," said Janet. "We're a great team. I remember being scared to sit down in that mini-mini skirt you made me wear. I had to press my thighs together or cross my legs real quick when I sat or the guys would look at nothing but my crotch. And I couldn't pick anything up without squatting like I was about to pee."

"What about my skintight leather pants?" Carolyn said, laughing. "I had to lie on my back on the bed, flail my legs in the air, and wriggle and squirm my little butt something awful just to get them on."

"And that cropped blouse you insisted I wear without a bra," Janet continued. "It barely covered the bottom of my boobs. I couldn't raise my elbows above my shoulders. Remember?"

Carolyn's eyes assessed Janet. "They're still looking good. Wish I had 'em."

"Hey girl, you've got more than I'll ever have upstairs," said Janet. "I wish I had as much in my noggin as you do."

"What are you talking about?" said Carolyn. "You're no slouch."

"Remember our real problem?"

"There weren't any problems," said Carolyn. "Once we stepped on that stage, everybody believed our act. I thought it was an incredible way to live. We started dating two, three guys at a time."

"Yeah, but then..."

"So we got felt up a lot," Carolyn conceded and then realized what Janet was really referring to. "Oh. ...You mean...?"

"Right. Put up or shut up," said Janet. "And we shut up."

Carolyn remained expressionless. "Right?"

Suddenly, Janet got out of the booth and hunched over squealing. "Oh my God, you did." She spun around, her hands over her mouth. "With Bruce. Right?" She froze, her eyes daring Carolyn to deny everything. "After that away basketball game. Right? Oh my God."

Carolyn smiled.

"Carolyn, Bruce was a rascal. A certified scoundrel. Everybody knew that. Oh, you didn't?"

"Wish you had?"

"A blackguard. A rogue for gosh sake," said Janet. "You didn't?"

"Yeah, I did," Carolyn said as she slid out of the booth. They gathered their luggage and headed out of T.G.I. Friday's without ordering.

"Carp's Landing," Janet said, her eyes still tearing with laughter.

"We were great on that stage, weren't we partner?" said Carolyn.

Janet headed for the parking lot, Carolyn for Alamo.

Thirty minutes later Carolyn pulled into the Carp's Landing Hotel garage. She found her way to the entrance of the bar, an opened archway visible from the Carp's Landing lobby. The mirror over the bar framed an elaborately-designed oasis on the far side of the room where water tumbled over black lava rocks into a pool accented with broad-leafed tropical foliage. A live parrot sat on a T-perch on the side of the waterfall.

"There's usually a school of carp at the base of that waterfall you're looking at," the barmaid said. She put a cocktail napkin in front of Carolyn. "At least during the heat of the day. They left just a few minutes ago."

Before Carolyn could respond, she heard Janet's voice behind her, "Still drinking vodka tonics?" Without turning, Carolyn ordered. "Two vodka tonics, one with lemon, one with lime."

"On my tab, Natalie," said Janet as she hopped up on the stool next to Carolyn.

"How's your father?" Carolyn asked.

"Bert and I are doing just fine. Since I've been back in real estate, that is. So, why are you here? It's great and all, but…"

"I'm as surprised as you are." They grasped hands and squeezed, enjoying the sight of each other in a place they both enjoyed.

"Come on, why are you here?" Janet insisted. "Give me a clue."

Natalie put the vodka tonic with lime in front of Carolyn.

"I took a new job," said Carolyn. "What day is today?"

"Oh lord, we're starting from there are we?"

Carolyn laughed. "Well, after talking with you last week, I went on another interview, a firm called Taylor Associates. They're located just a short walk from my apartment. Actually, I started working for them this morning."

"You're no longer with Justice, protecting the public from big bad business?"

"Okay, you get one, but that's it. And yes, I've left Justice."

"So, what are you doing here? On your first day no less."

"We're interested in a firm called Bauer Industries," Carolyn said.

"They're big here," Janet said.

"I know nothing about them. Except that I have an appointment with Charles Bauer in the morning."

"Old Charlie?" said Janet. "He started the firm. Years and years ago. He and Bert are great friends. But it's Gil you want to talk to. He's Charlie's son. Gil runs the company on a day-to-day basis."

"Bauer's well-known then?" said Carolyn.

"Uh-huh. They're pillars of the community. You'll meet some of 'em tonight."

"Tonight?" Carolyn asked.

"I'm changing a previously-planned dinner party to a welcome-to-Bayside-Carolyn party."

"Oh Janet, don't go to such a fuss. It's just me."

"You were in such a rush when you called I didn't get a chance to tell you. Bert will be there, of course."

Carolyn smiled. "Of course."

"Janet, I'm surprised to see you here," a male voice said from behind them. "Aren't you supposed to be picking up Nicole about now?" The two women looked into the mirror over the bar. A slight young man in jeans and an open-collared sport shirt stood behind them.

"Oh my God," Janet exclaimed as she swiveled on her stool. "We were just talking about you." Janet turned toward Carolyn. "Carolyn Hughes, this is Gil Bauer. Gil, this is Carolyn. She's my very best friend. She's in town for a few days. From Virginia."

Gil feigned a slight bow toward Carolyn as he extended his hand. "Nice to meet the best friend of Ms. Janet Griffin."

Carolyn took his hand, smiling. "Mr. Bauer."

Janet gulped her drink. "Gil, you're right. I have to pick up Nicole. Daycare schedules aren't negotiable. Come on, Carolyn." Janet stood. Carolyn followed. "By the way Gil, Carolyn's meeting with your father tomorrow. Right, Carolyn?"

"Eight in the morning," Carolyn confirmed over her shoulder as Janet nudged her toward the lobby.

Gil called after them. "Don't keep him too long, Carolyn. He's got a nine o'clock tee time."

"I know," Carolyn said without turning around. She touched Janet's arm, slowing their pace. "*He* runs Bauer Industries?"

"Don't let that skinny boyish look fool you," said Janet. "And he has a love."

"Oh?"

"You know her. Her name's Bauer Industries. The Carp's Landing bar is the Bauer whiz kids' hangout after work. He's just one of the guys in there."

"He looks like a kid. Eighteen or nineteen?"

"Twenty-seven," said Janet. "We have to go."

Carolyn stopped walking. "I can't. You go. I'll meet you at home."

Janet looked up, questioning what she had just heard. "What?"

"I'm here on business. Sevenish okay?"

Janet looked resigned. She had to go. "You remember how to get there?"

"I'm sure I can find it."

"I really have to run," Janet said. "Heard from Greg?"

Carolyn winced. "Please, don't mention his name. Okay?"

Janet raised a hand. "No problem."

Carolyn turned and started back into the bar. Janet called after her, "Hey, I've got news about my mom."

"Welcome back," said Gil. "Want a fresh one?"

"Sure, why not?" Carolyn sat on the stool. She swiveled toward Gil. "Is it true, what Janet just told me?"

Gil signaled to Natalie to freshen Carolyn's drink. "I've never known her to shade the truth."

"It's true then. You have a mistress."

"Whoa. What are we talking about?" said Gil.

"Your mistress. Is it a problem?"

"I'm lost," said Gil.

Carolyn smiled. "I work for Taylor Associates. We're interested in your mistress—Bauer Associates, of course."

"Oh," said Gil, displaying a broad grin.

"Taylor Associates is expanding, talking with potential merger candidates." Carolyn picked up the drink Natalie had put on the bar. "Our CEO, Jack Taylor, has sent me to tell you about our company and, if it sparks an interest, we hope to learn a little bit about Bauer. I have a few charts in the car that I'll be showing your dad in the morning. Want to see them?"

"Now?" said Gil.

"It would only take a minute to get them."

Gil looked up and called to Natalie, standing behind the bar several feet away, "We'll be in the dining room."

When Carolyn returned from the parking garage with her charts, Gil waved for her to join him at the corner table in the back of the dining room.

Carolyn slid in beside him and opened a small A-frame stand between them. She would use it to display the 15-minute summary presentation she had prepared for Gil's father in order to entice him to tell her something about Bauer Industries. Being able to show her presentation to both Gil and Charles Bauer could only enhance her chances of obtaining information on Bauer Industries in return. "Shall we start?"

"Why not."

Carolyn slipped from the fifteen-minute version to the thirty-minute version as Gil became more and more interested, wanting to know additional details. Ninety minutes later they had gone over the full set of charts that the other Taylor Associates merger teams were using.

"That's it," said Carolyn.

"Very interesting," said Gil emphatically. He looked up as he slid out of the booth. Catching Natalie's eye, he pretended to write on the palm of his hand. "There's not enough time for me to tell you about Bauer right now. But I will. I promise. Right now, I have to meet with my guys at the bar."

Carolyn drove across the Intracoastal Waterway Bridge to the mainland. She turned onto Bell Boulevard, Bayside's main drag. A few minutes later she found her way through a community of upscale single-family homes. She parked in Janet's driveway.

Janet's mother, Fannie, had married Bert Griffin, a bank clerk, when she was seventeen and Bert was twenty. Two years later she showed him a plane ticket—a one-way ticket from Bayside, Florida to San Diego, California. Fannie told Bert she would divorce him in California. Bert pleaded. Fannie told him she was too young to settle down. Bayside stifled her. She wanted to see the world before she got old. The harder Bert pleaded the more abusive Fannie became. She had never loved him, never wanted to be a mother, and hated changing those damned diapers. When she blurted out that she was having an affair with his boss at the bank, Bert picked up the telephone. He called for a cab. He sent her to the airport with the clothes on her back and all the cash in the house—eighteen dollars and seventy cents. He would ship her remaining belongings to any address he received on a postcard. The postcard had never arrived.

Janet had wondered about her mother over the years but had never brooded about her absence. After all, she had reasoned, three of her closest playmates lived with their mothers in single-parent households, so it wasn't that unusual. Besides, everyone in Bayside loved Bert.

At first, school hadn't been easy for Janet but by her third year she was at grade level. By the sixth she had made the principal's honor roll for the first time, the same year Bert received his charter for the Bayside Savings and Loan. The following year her class witnessed American industry in action by going to her father's bank on a field trip.

One day eighth-grade Janet played hooky from school. She stayed home. Bored, she explored the drawers in her father's dresser and discovered an envelope under his socks. Its postmark was San Diego, California. The envelope didn't have a return address. In the envelope was a snapshot of Bert and Fannie on their wedding day. With the snapshot was a clipping torn from the *CURRENTS* section of a Sunday edition of the *San Diego Union-Tribune*. The clipping included a picture of a dozen celebrities posing with the governor on the steps leading up to the California governor's mansion, an ornate three-story Victorian home crowned with square turrets. The caption explained that the governor was being honored for his support of the arts.

A circle had been drawn around the head of Janet's mother, Fannie. She was standing next to the governor on the bottom step. Janet showed Bert the clipping with the picture of her mother when he came home. Bert took the envelope from Janet. He refused to talk about it, scolding that she should never go through other people's personal belongings.

In high school Janet had been a member of the National Honor Society, a cheerleader, captain of the tennis team, and class president her junior and senior year. She didn't want to leave Bayside. Her best friends all lived in Bayside. Her quasi Peter Pan complex of not wanting to grow up reinforced Bert's fear that the small town of Bayside might someday stifle Janet just as it had her mother, Fannie. He wanted Janet to be whatever she dreamed, to meet the right people, to experience the world well beyond southern Florida. Bert insisted his daughter apply to out-of-state colleges.

Accepted by New York University, Janet left Bayside, Florida for Manhattan. Janet Griffin and Carolyn Hughes roomed together their first year. Their Goddard Hall unit overlooked Washington Square Park in lower Manhattan. The following three years they lived in an apartment on Perry Street in Greenwich Village.

Carolyn rang Janet's front door bell. Moments later there was a thud on the other side of the door.

Janet opened the door and helped Nicole up from the floor. "Nicole wants to be the first one to answer the door bell. Sometimes she doesn't stop in time when she gets there. You didn't get lost did you?"

"No," said Carolyn. "Gil and I got involved."

"You're faster than I remember," Janet teased. Turning to Nicole, she said, *"Tu recuerdas a la tía Carolyn?"* Nicole smiled and then ran the length of the hall, disappearing down the stairs.

"She's so adorable," Carolyn said.

Carolyn and Janet retreated to the kitchen just off the foyer.

"Did you get to day care on time?" Carolyn asked.

Janet looked puzzled.

"When you left Carp's Landing you were running to get Nicole from daycare. Remember?"

"Oh, so much has happened since then. Being a mom…"

"Makes you forget?" Janet interjected.

"No, smart-ass," Janet said, smiling. "They've trained me."

"Who trained you?"

"Day care. They charge a buck a minute after closing time. Sixty dollars an hour."

"Whew! Expensive," said Carolyn. "Where'd Nicole go?"

"Downstairs." Janet opened the refrigerator and took out a tray of hors d'oeuvres. She put it on the kitchen island.

"Why are you guys speaking Spanish?" asked Carolyn.

"Spanish is all Nicole speaks. Her day care's a Spanish-speaking day care." Janet took a bottle of stuffed olives from the refrigerator. She emptied it into the cup in the center of the hors d'oeuvre tray.

"Won't Nicole just pick up English from those around her everyday?" asked Carolyn.

"Hope not," said Janet. "I want her to be bilingual. I've asked everyone to speak Spanish when she's around or refrain from speaking at all. That includes you *tía* Carolyn." Janet pointed to the kitchen island. "Pass the tray, will you?"

Carolyn swiped an olive before she did. "Does Bert speak Spanish?"

"You forget that I was brought up in the Miami area. Bert's the one who taught me."

"So Nicole'll learn English when she goes to kindergarten."

"You got it," said Janet. "The kids she's playing with downstairs speak only Spanish. Their parents in the living room speak Spanish. They're from Bogotá. I'm told that's where 'high Spanish' is spoken." Janet popped an olive into her mouth. "Want another?" Carolyn waved her off. "Bert will be here soon."

A short gangling man with a thinning crown of gray hair entered the kitchen. His white Rockports and color-coordinated shirt and slacks accented aging yet still sparkling sky-blue eyes. "What d'ya mean, soon?" Bert said.

"We didn't hear the doorbell," said Carolyn.

"Let myself in. Knew you'd be busy. Besides, can't ring the bell if I want to surprise my granddaughter." Bert embraced Carolyn. "It's good to see you."

"I just told Carolyn about Nicole learning Spanish," said Janet as she started for the dining room with the hors d'oeuvres. "I've been neglecting my guests. Let's get inside." She nodded for her father to take a second tray from the oven.

"How's the banking business?" Carolyn asked Bert as he took the tray from the oven.

"Had some close calls, but that's history," said Bert. He called after his daughter, "Leave some of those olives for your guests."

Carolyn and Janet wandered out onto the patio. Ground lights lit the flowerbeds edging the patio. A slate walk led to the swimming pool in a far corner of the yard. Janet said, "Guess what? I've met my mom, Fannie."

Carolyn gasped. They had never talked about Janet's mother. Carolyn had assumed the topic to be off-limits. As far as she knew, Janet had never even seen her mother, other than the pictures in the sock drawer that Janet had told her about one night in Greenwich Village while they were both smashed. "You met your mom?"

"And Bert's pissed."

"I'm all ears," said Carolyn.

"It's a long story." The two women headed along the slate walk for the pool. "Mom grew up on a San Diego dairy farm— dirt poor. She had a terrible time in school, barely staying on grade. I remember Bert telling me she had dyslexia. Her mother claimed she was just dumb and lazy." They stood by an orange tree. "Her mother hounded her: Buckle down. Try harder. Her classmates ridiculed her, called her slow, retarded. You know how brutal kids can be. By her teen years Mom had low self-esteem, big time." They meandered toward the pool again. "She drank, had romances, got caught shoplifting, the works."

"Your mother really opened up didn't she?"

Janet's grandmother had harangued Fannie incessantly, so

much so that Fannie ran away during her junior year in high school. Three months later Fannie ended up in Bayside, Florida. Within months, she and Bert were married. Janet arrived ten months later. Before Janet's first birthday, Fannie told Bert she was too young to be a mother. She returned to San Diego. Bert and Fannie divorced before Janet was three.

A few years later Fannie married a forty-year-old celebrity, James Jacobe. He ran for the California legislature that year but lost. Two years later he won. Twelve years later he was elected to the U.S. Senate, only to lose his reelection bid. Because of his wealth and party loyalty, the president appointed him ambassador to Yugoslavia. Last year terrorists had kidnapped Ambassador Jacobe. They demanded a million dollars ransom. Fannie paid. Two weeks later the ambassador was found on a dirt road, decapitated. Days later Fannie wrote to Janet, asking to come back into her life.

"I have dyslexia too," said Janet.

"No you don't," said Carolyn.

"Yes, I do. I remember hiding it, not wanting anyone to know. Being ashamed, I couldn't read or write as well as the other kids. Keeping it to myself was awful. Probably why I never told you." Janet sat quietly before continuing. "Bert told me he saw it early. That's when he told me Fannie had it too. Bert told the school about me. I got special help starting in preschool." Carolyn frowned. "So I begin thinking, maybe Nicole… I listen and watch carefully. Damn, she has it too."

"She'll be okay, right?" Carolyn said.

"It'll take work. I wish I hadn't started this bilingual thing, though."

"Stop blaming yourself. Look, you got help. It worked. It'll work for Nicole too."

Bert called from the patio doors. "Hey Carolyn, you're going to Crosby's party tomorrow, right?"

"Of course she'll go," Janet yelled back. Turning to Carolyn, Janet said, "You'll have a great time."

"Who's Crosby?" Carolyn asked.

"Doug Crosby's a client of mine. Has a fabulous home in Key Largo. He parties like only the super-rich party."

"I'm here on business," Carolyn said. "Remember?"

"You don't want to miss a Crosby party—Key Largo."

"I don't know. I'm meeting with Gil's father, Charles, first thing in the morning, a get-acquainted meeting." Carolyn started to smile. Her hazel eyes rose, lingered just below her eyelids, and then snapped back. "He has a 9:00 o'clock tee-time. Soooooo, I'll be free about then." Carolyn mulled the timing over again. "I'll do it. I won't be able to stay long, but I'd love to see Key Largo."

"You're on," said Janet. "Let's get back inside. Gotta mingle."

Carolyn and Janet found Nicole in the living room, sitting on the Oriental rug. She was holding a stuffed koala bear at arm's length. She waved a menacing finger at it with her other hand. A slight woman sat cross-legged on the rug next to Nicole. A large window looking over the backyard silhouetted a heavyset woman sitting in a chair near both of them. Neither woman was paying any attention to Nicole's jabbering. Two men on the couch were in a heated debate. They were oblivious to everyone in the room. Carolyn couldn't understand anything anyone was saying. They were all speaking Spanish.

Janet turned to Carolyn. "There are three boys about Nicole's age downstairs. They won't play any of the games Nicole wants to play. For some reason, it's Freddie's fault and Nicole is scolding him." Janet smiled. "Oh, you haven't met Freddie. See that koala bear? That's Freddie. Nicole has adopted Freddie. Or vice versa, I don't know. Freddie has become her security blanket."

"Nicole's all alone," Carolyn lamented.

Janet laughed. "No. No. You don't understand. The boys won't play her computer games because she always beats them."

Nicole headed for her mother, Freddie dangling from her hand.

Janet picked her daughter up. "Freddie no parece felíz."

The doorbell rang twice in rapid succession. Nicole wiggled free. She started running the moment her feet hit the floor.

"That's got to be Pepe," said Janet. "Trying to impress. As usual."

They watched as Nicole slid on the hardwood floor into the door, beating Bert. Bert helped her up and then opened the door. It was Pepe.

"Well, you finally made it," Bert said.

A short man with disheveled gray hair and a luxuriant salt-and-pepper mustache stood in front of Bert and Nicole. Nicole headed back to the living room.

"Urgent business demanding my attention," said Pepe. "You know how it is." He unbuttoned the final button on his white ruffled sports shirt, exposing a thick gold chain nestled in gray chest hair. He brushed past Bert. "Last minute as usual, it never ends."

"Oh, before I forget," said Bert. Pepe turned, looking toward Bert. "Janet told me to tell you that Doug called."

"Everybody wants a piece of me." Pepe headed down the hall to the living room.

Bert reemphasized, "Doug wants you to call."

"Got it," Pepe yelled without looking back.

Nicole reached into Freddie's pouch, pulled out a piece of brightly-colored metal and handed it to Carolyn. Carolyn read the word PoKéRoM on its face. She had no idea what it meant. Nicole got down, and tugged on Carolyn's hand, guiding her into the hallway. Carolyn followed her to the staircase leading upstairs. Using pantomime, Carolyn told Nicole they would go into the kitchen first.

Not wanting Nicole to hear English, Carolyn whispered in Janet's ear, "Nicole wants me to go upstairs." She then showed Janet the piece of metal Nicole had given her. "What is this thing?"

Janet smiled. "You haven't been around kids lately, have you? It's PoKéRoM."

"I read *that*," Carolyn said.

"PoKéRoM is a kid's educational computer game. You'll soon be immersed in Yu-Gi-Oh."

"What?" said Janet. "This thing's no bigger than a business card."

"That little thing fits in the CD tray."

"If you say so."

"You've hit it big with Nicole," said Janet. "Freddie the koala bear is the protector of her latest and greatest PoKéRoM disk. I've never seen her show her hiding place to anyone." Janet turned to her daughter. Speaking Spanish she said, *"Aunt*

*Carolyn asked if it was okay to go upstairs, honey. I told her fine. Go ahead."* Janet rubbed noses with her daughter. *"Watch out Nicole, Aunt Carolyn's really smart. She's good at games."*

Nicole told Carolyn what her mother had said by tugging on her hand. When they reached the staircase, Pepe called from the living room, "Te quiero, princesa."

Nicole pulled harder on Carolyn's hand.

# Chapter 15

## Vienna, Virginia
## Thursday 2315 ET

Michael tried not to make a sound as he came into the kitchen. Sarah heard his every step as she gave the oatmeal on the stove a few needless stirs. She listened as he sat, pulling his chair to the table. She turned slightly, her head still bent over the stove. After a few more stirs she brought the pot of oatmeal to the table and ladled it into Michael's bowl. "So there we are. Rested now, are we?" Sarah brushed strands of her auburn hair off her face with her forearm as she returned to the stove.

Michael smiled meekly at Linda Ann and Kathleen. Having them up at this hour was unusual. It probably meant she wasn't able to get a babysitter while she drove him to the Metro station. He was already in the doghouse. Not being able to get a babysitter wouldn't help.

Linda Ann looked at her baby sister Kathleen sitting in a high chair on the other side of the table. Neither of them made a sound. They knew their mother hadn't just asked a question. But unlike Michael, they didn't understand why. Michael had run five miles along the paths of Nottoway Park soon after coming home late from work, well after 2 p.m. When Linda Ann came home from school at four o'clock, Michael was asleep. Michael had insisted to Sarah that running released the tensions of the job. Sarah had let him know in no uncertain terms that he had been on his new job just one day. No job could possibly involve him so quickly. His tension couldn't possibly need releasing.

Sarah sat at the table, scoffing at Michael. "We'll be okay for our twelve-hour shift today, will we?"

Sarah's tone triggered Kathleen. She began banging her spoon on the tray of her high chair. Getting no response, she threw the spoon on the floor. She then began an elaborate display of licking the spray butter off her raisin toast. Linda Ann began laughing at her sister's antics. Sarah cut her down with a single glance.

Sarah wouldn't let Michael help feed the baby, clear the table, put the dishes in the sink, or help with the kids. Several times she mumbled something about not wanting to exhaust him.

Michael stood outside the driver's side window at the Vienna Metro station to say goodbye as he usually did. When their eyes met he mouthed, "I'm sorry." Sarah didn't flinch. When Michael glanced toward the Metro, Sarah drove off for White Cedar Court.

Michael sat at his terminal in the leads center staring at a blinking administrative icon, a message from the office of the FBI's deputy director Vinny Campbell. Michael had ignored his last message requesting him to change his OEF tags to PENTTBOM tags. He put off opening this message. Instead, he opened the confirmation of his e-mail delivery to Greg McNulty, Alan Dickie and the CIA Acapulco home office. It was the e-mail he had used to relay Jose Valderrama's Carnivore intercept to them. He looked at the time notation. It had taken almost twenty hours to be sent.

Michael had been called into the Multi-Agency Operations room when he initially tried to relay the contents of the Carnivore intercept. Multi-Agency Operations had balked. Their concern centered on the privacy rights of Doug Crosby. Then they shifted to wanting to know exactly how the Carnivore message had anything to do with Operation Enduring Freedom as suggested by his OEF tag. Back and forth they went—privacy/relevancy, relevancy/privacy—until the Multi-Agency Operations room concern waned but still smoldered. An hour later the concern shifted to whether SIOC would be infringing on the task force's turf. They were on the brink of being satisfied when they got busy. Rather than make a decision, they deferred to the Intelligence side of the room. Michael had to start all over again. The Intelligence side eventually decided to query Greg McNulty. Greg was out of the office when the query arrived. He concurred six hours later. By then Intelligence had had a crew shift. The new Intelligence crew insisted on re-reviewing the relevancy of Michael's request.

Suddenly, Michael stiffened. He had committed the cardinal sin of intelligence gathering. He hadn't prioritized his request properly. Worse yet, he hadn't followed up quickly enough. Over and over during his Langley training he had been told time was of the essence in the war on terrorism. Delays gave advantages to the enemy. More than three thousand people had died on 9/11. The least the nation could expect from their government was fast action with aggressive follow up. Intelligence information in the war on terror had to be treated like a CIA NIACT or night action cable. When a NIACT arrived you dropped everything, no matter what. You responded. The twenty-four hour delay was a day the enemy gained and the U.S. lost.

Now he knew why he had received a second administrative message from the office of Vinny Campbell.

Michael opened the administrative icon.

> The Carnivore intercept relayed to Justice,
> MFO and the CIA Acapulco home office used
> an OEF tag.
> The cryptonym for FBI support to SIOC is
> PENTTBOM.
> V. Campbell
> FBI Deputy Director

Michael stood, walked out of the leads center and went down the stairs to the restroom. By the time he returned to his computer station, his decision was firm. Administrative reviews would have to take a back seat. There might be other leads in his queue of leads more relevant than the administrative concerns of Vinny Campbell. If there were, he had better identify them before he responded to Vinny Campbell and his administrative trivia. He wouldn't fail the more than three thousand souls lost on 9/11.

For now he would ignore the second message from Vinny Campbell.

Many of his leads turned out to be well-meaning citizens trying to help. Each could take a minute, an hour, or days to close. Michael scanned ahead to see if any looked more promising than the rest. None did. He settled in with hours of work in front of him.

Within a few minutes a new intelligence icon began blinking. He double-clicked it. The Rapid Start software program had automatically scanned its databases. It had correlated Doug Crosby's Key Largo telephone number with a telephone intercept that had been authorized by a Florida judge. Michael called up the intercept. Doug Crosby had called a Bayside, Florida telephone number. Michael reviewed the intercept record. Doug had asked to speak to someone named Janet. Doug had left a message with a male voice. The male voice had explained that Janet wasn't available. Doug had asked the male voice to have someone named Pepe call him as soon as he arrived.

Pepe's name had appeared twice now, first in Jose Valderrama's e-mail that Carnivore had intercepted, and now in Doug Crosby's telephone call to someone named Janet. Michael used his reverse telephone directory. The telephone number Doug had called was in the name of a Janet Griffin.

Michael checked to see who had received copies of this intelligence. Greg McNulty and Alan Dickie hadn't. Michael forwarded it to them both. He then attached his OEF tag to Janet's name and telephone number before sending them to the Rapid Start program.

Rapid Start immediately rejected Michael's attempt to record Janet's name and telephone number. A computer-generated message explained that Rapid Start could not accept telephone numbers or names without the prior authorization of an attorney general and approval by the judiciary. Zeros and Ones were on the job.

Michael summarized his intelligence-gathering efforts to date and assigned his next message a high priority action item. Vinny Campbell was to seek the United States Attorney General's approval to have Janet Griffin's telephone number monitored.

# Chapter 16

### Bayside, Florida
### Friday 0745 ET

At seven forty-five in the morning, Carolyn was standing on Bell Boulevard in front of the Charles Bauer Building. Already she was feeling the heat of day. She entered the lobby and looked at the directory. She rode the elevator to the twelfth floor and entered doors marked Bauer Industries. The receptionist told Carolyn to go right in, Mr. Bauer was expecting her.

Charles Bauer rose. "Good morning, Ms. Hughes. Come in. Come in." He waved her to a chair against the wall before coming out from behind his desk. He sat in a matching chair. The buttons on his sport shirt strained to contain his stomach while his hips challenged the arms of the chair. "You arrived in Bayside last evening, is that right?" he drawled.

Carolyn smiled. "I did."

"And you are a college friend of Janet Griffin."

"New York University."

Charles raised his bushy white eyebrows. "And you've met my son."

"I have. He told me you have a 9:00 o'clock tee time and that I mustn't keep you. Right?" Carolyn smiled at the eyes peering over horn-rimmed glasses.

"Yes. I have to be on the tee, ready to play at nine o'clock."

"Which means you must be on your way very soon. I'll be brief."

"Twenty minutes." Charles slouched in his chair signaling Carolyn to begin. "I'm not as agile now."

"As I told you on the telephone yesterday afternoon, Mr. Bauer, I'm here representing Taylor Associates. We are in the process of analyzing merger candidates."

"Acquisition or merger?"

"Merger, Mr. Bauer. The article on Bauer Industries in the current issue of *Forbes* magazine caught Mr. Taylor's attention."

Charles's hands gripped the chair arm, knuckles whitening. "That article caused me nothing but grief."

"I have a packet containing what I am going to tell you about

Taylor Associates." Carolyn reached into her attaché case. She withdrew the fifteen-minute version without changing her cadence. "It starts with a description of our line of work, profiles of our customer base, revenue, and net income growth during each of the last four years." She opened the packet of material. "It's designed to show you what we believe are the benefits to Bauer Industries of a merger. I'll leave this packet with you."

Charles made a motion to reach for the packet. Carolyn put it on the floor, leaning it against the side of her chair, well out of his reach. She didn't want him to be browsing through it while she spoke. "Of course, if things work out, a memorandum-of-understanding will be drawn." Fifteen minutes later Carolyn finished.

Charles rose. "Thank you. Most interesting." He retreated behind his desk where he added a note to the bottom of a pre-typed letter lying there. "Please see that Mr. Taylor gets this personally—after you present your report, of course." He put the letter addressed to Mr. Jack Taylor in an envelope and sealed it.

As the two walked out of the suite, the receptionist called to Carolyn. She had something for Carolyn and asked if she could give her a moment to retrieve it. Standing in the elevator Mr. Bauer said, "I really have to run. Thank you for coming, Ms. Hughes." The elevator doors closed. Carolyn headed back to the receptionist.

"I assume I'm supposed to give this to you, Ms. Hughes," the receptionist said. "I'm a temp, so I'm not absolutely sure. I found it after you went into Mr. Bauer's office. It's addressed to you."

Carolyn took the envelope, thanked her, and pushed the down button. As she waited, she opened the envelope. She pulled out a bound document. Printed in large bold type on the hard front cover were two lines.

**Q2 Report**
**Bauer Industries**

# Chapter 17

**Bayside, Florida**
**Friday 0845 ET**

Pepe Gomez stepped into the center of the shower enclosure, closed his eyes and put his face toward the ceiling. Streaming water massaged his face while wall nozzles sent pulsing jets onto his torso. Today Pepe would cap off a fantastic string of good luck. He stretched his arms out and spun like a pinwheel. The tips of his fingers never touched the walls of the enclosure.

Pepe had had a hundred and thirty grand put in his hand by Janet's former husband, Scott Graves. It seemed so easy, Scott getting Janet's father, the banker, to give him the money he had lost to Pepe, and Scott, in turn, handing the money to him. Pepe decided to have a go at repeating the gig.

After Janet and Scott split, Pepe had seeded an inveterate gambler, a handsome glib Italian, with Janet. They had dated for a short time. Suddenly, for no apparent reason, Janet would have nothing to do with him.

It was just about then that Pepe's best-heeled gambler began doubling down on the outcomes of baseball games. Still flush with most of the hundred and thirty grand, Pepe let him. Astonishingly, Pepe came out on the winning side of seven consecutive double-down bets. When the man then put up his home on the eighth bet and he lost, Pepe cut him off. Gaining possession of his house as payment for the debt had been a bad scene—one of the worst Pepe had experienced.

Pepe shook his head side-to-side sending water from his hair to the walls his fingers couldn't reach. He turned the shower knob to cold. He wanted to erase the image of the former owner crying and pleading not to have to sign over the deed. He had lost his job. His wife was divorcing him. If he lost the house, he would have to move into an inner-city Miami apartment. His two boys would be forced to change schools in the middle of a school year.

Pepe had experienced sobbing and pleading losers often. It was one of the realities of loaning money to people willing to pay exorbitant rates to get their hands on it. To collect your money you had to be firm, threaten, hire muscle, and even injure clients if that's what it took. Everybody knew that. If they didn't, well, they learned. A broken leg. A broken arm. For this man it had taken two broken legs. He spent three days in intensive care followed by three weeks in the hospital recuperating from a collapsed lung and a variety of other internal injuries.

The payoff for Pepe had been the man's house, a mansion— a mansion Pepe had never dared dream of possessing. Owning the house would create a new image for him. It would raise his prestige. A million-dollar mortgage-free home and nearly a hundred and thirty grand in cash was his ticket to a level of society that didn't know he existed.

Most importantly, Janet would fall in love with him and the house.

Pepe's black BMW purred north on Route 1, its top down, the early morning air invigorating his spirits. The speedometer needle rose: 75, 85, 95 miles per hour. He tossed his head back and threw both hands in the air. He let out a scream of delight. He was invincible, ten feet tall.

Pepe slowed, turned east, and made his way to Dania Beach. In the parking lot he ripped off his shirt, took off his shoes and socks, and rolled up both pantlegs. After a fast drumroll on the dash, he ran to the shore. His thoughts riveted on Janet—her face, the fullness of her breasts, those legs, those beautiful, perfectly formed legs. He could feel her love, her desire to be with him. He just knew it. And if she had his baby…

He ran a few strides, kicking at the cool sand. Settling into a stroll, he closed his eyes. The world around him faded. She'll look great on my arm. After all she's only two—no more than three inches taller without heels. She'll be so proud in my new home. He envisioned himself with her at cocktail parties, strolling the malls, frolicking on the beach. Every man who saw her with him would be envious.

Pepe ran along the water's edge. His spirits soared with the sounds of the waves breaking on the shore, the feel of the water on his feet. He ran faster and faster, toying with every crest.

Pepe settled on his stomach in the sand, put his forehead on his crossed hands, and closed his eyes. Soon he felt Janet laying next to him. She was naked, her head and a shoulder resting on his back. His heart hammered as she slid her hands up along his shoulders to his neck. She gently massaged his temples while her lips smothered his neck with slow damp kisses. Janet slid full length on Pepe's back. She raised herself and slowly brushed his back with her erect nipples.

Suddenly Janet's hips drove Pepe's hips hard against the warm sand.

"I love you Janet," Pepe shrieked,

Drained, Pepe struggled to his feet, retraced his steps along the shore, and then across the beach to his BMW. He ordered breakfast at a McDonald's drive-through window, went home and changed.

Pepe parked in front of Janet's house, bounded up the walk, and rang the bell. He heard a thud. Janet opened the door. Nicole got up from the floor.

"Hey Pepe," Janet said cooly. "We're famished. Let's go."

Pepe bent over and asked Nicole if she was ready to go. "Estamos todos listos, mi pequeña?" Nicole retreated into the kitchen. Pepe called after her, trying to charm her with thoughts of brunch and an afternoon on the Keys. "Estamos listos para el desayuno-almuerzo, y para pasar la tarde en los Cayos?"

Janet called Nicole, took her hand, and followed Pepe to his car. Janet wore white shorts. The shirttails of her sleeveless blouse were knotted above her bare midriff. At the beamer, Pepe picked Nicole up and swung her into the miniscule rear seat.

"Wait!" Janet said. "I'll be right back." Pepe's eyes followed the white shorts as they made their way to Janet's front door.

Back in the car Janet knelt on the front seat and put a scarf on Nicole. "What time are we due at Crosby's?" she asked. She glanced at Pepe. He was ogling. She did a quick one-eighty, flopping into her seat.

"Four or five. Plenty of time for brunch and the Parrot Jungle." Turning to Nicole, Pepe gushed, "Una gran gira por la Jungla de los Loros, mi princesa?"

Nicole turned her head away.

Janet glared at Pepe. "Look, I don't know why you offered to drive us to Key Largo. But we accepted the ride. That's all."

Janet couldn't hear the phone ringing in her home.

# Chapter 18

## Miami International Airport, Florida
## Friday 1100 ET

Across the waiting area from where Carolyn stood, the last passenger in line handed the agent her boarding pass and hurried down the ramp for the flight to Reagan National. Carolyn waited impatiently for Janet's answering machine to finish telling her Janet would return her call as soon as possible. The repetitive beeps that followed her message seemed to go on forever.

"Hey Janet. Sorry I didn't catch you at home. Look, I have to return to Virginia right away. Turns out I have a lot of work to do preparing for tomorrow's presentation. Sorry I'll miss the Key Largo party. Maybe next time. Oh shit, they're closing the boarding ramp. Gotta go."

# Chapter 19

### San Diego, California
### Friday 1120 PT

Ginny repositioned the colorful flower arrangements until she had a firm grip on all of them. She crossed Market Street and headed toward the parking garage a few blocks away where she arranged the flowers carefully in the trunk of her car. Finding the flowers on sale had saved the Mission Hills Women's Club at least sixty dollars.

Ginny never knew when Royce Palmer might come into the office. She felt guilty for having snuck out. He had told her more than once not to leave the office unattended. She drove along Market to Pacific Highway. In less than ten minutes she was driving up Washington Street's steep grade to Falcon Street. She was pleased that no one had taken her reserved parking space behind the building.

She walked up the narrow staircase, unlocked the door with "Palmer Investments" painted in bold black letters on frosted glass, and settled herself behind her desk. There were two e-mails: one was advertising from a cruise line, the other from Jose Valderrama. She opened Jose's message.

No word from the east. Find out what's going
on firsthand.

Ginny knew "east" meant Key Largo. "Firsthand" meant Royce had to catch the next flight to Miami. Twenty minutes later a travel agent e-mailed Ginny Royce's e-ticket from San Diego to Miami.

# Chapter 20

### Key Largo, Florida
### Friday 1430 ET

Doug Crosby lived in a home his father, Jose Valderrama, had bought in Key Largo just after the turn of the millennium. Jose had given it to Doug on his twenty-fourth birthday. Jose hoped that being on his own in a new environment would trigger some responsibility, even a little enthusiasm, in Doug's lackadaisical approach to everything.

The home was large for the Keys, built in the 1920s by a railroad tycoon. Successive owners had refurbished it, first after the Second World War, and again in the late 1980s, maintaining its original elegance. Jose had the kitchen and bathrooms redone with marble counter tops and rosewood cabinets, installed all new jet-black kitchen appliances, put a Jacuzzi in the master bedroom suite and a hot tub on the rear deck of the guesthouse, repainted the main house and guesthouse inside and out, and put new roofs on both structures. The furnishing he left to the discretion of a noted Miami interior decorator.

Beyond the lanai-pool and small manicured lawn was a cove dredged by the railroad tycoon. It was lined with giant granite boulders. The granite jetty and dredging were done well before regulatory restrictions prohibited such environmental damage. A yacht and a fifty-foot sailboat floated calmly in berths protected by the rugged jetty. A third slip was empty. The guesthouse sat a few feet off the dock.

A uniformed maid greeted Pepe, Janet and Nicole at the front door. She escorted them to the kitchen where an impeccably-dressed Doug Crosby stood with a Bloody Mary in his hand. Pepe extended his hand. "Doug, great to see you. This is Janet and her daughter Nicole."

"I'm told this is your first visit to the Largo Key," Doug said to Janet.

"Nicole and I are happy to be here." She stepped forward and offered Doug her hand. "Thank you for inviting us."

Doug's limp hand barely grasped Janet's. He walked to the window, turning his back. He looked out. "I have to talk to Pepe." Pepe turned to Janet and shrugged, not knowing what to

say.  Janet took Nicole's hand and went into the living room.
When they had left Doug said, "Gonzalo's here. That's his yacht
out there."

"Gonzalo?"

Doug snapped. "*Gonzalo*, Dad's right-hand man."

Pepe tried to calm Doug. "Right. Gonzalo's here."

"I don't know where he is," Doug said.

"You can't find him?"

"Jesus Christ, Pepe, are you stupid or something?" Doug
choked down his drink and slammed the glass onto the marble
counter. "I didn't want him here. I can handle everything myself
without his fucking help." Doug picked up his glass, tossed its
remnants into the sink, and headed for the ice bucket, vodka and
Bloody Mary mix sitting on the counter. "Why didn't you call
me back?"

"Janet's father told me…" Pepe began.

"So why didn't you call me?" Doug pressed.

"It was late."

"Goddamn it.  When I call, you call me back the minute you
get the message. Understand?"

"Okay. Okay."

"I want you to find Gonzalo."

"Why me?" asked Pepe.

"Dad said, 'Get Pepe on it.'"

"You called Jose?  I thought you weren't supposed to..."

"I don't need you to tell me what I'm supposed to do." He
turned his back to Pepe and finished making his fourth Bloody
Mary. "You told me Bauer would be a done deal by now."

Nicole held tightly to her mother's hand as they went into the
living room.  A bay window framed the lanai swimming pool, the
guesthouse, dock area, and the protected cove beyond.  The tall
mast of a sailboat swayed on muted swells from a motorboat now
out of sight.  The guesthouse, painted a brilliant white with a rich
blue trim, gleamed in the afternoon sun.

Janet and Nicole headed toward the two women that had
been at her house the night before.  Other than the location,
nothing seemed to have changed.  The slight woman sitting
crossed-legged on the carpet was talking with the heavyset
woman sitting in the chair beside her.  Their husbands sat outside

by the pool, having what appeared to be a friendly and spirited argument. Three boys played Marco Polo in the pool.

The larger woman saw Janet and Nicole coming into the living room first. *"Oh, look who's here. Wonderful,"* she said in Spanish.

The woman sitting on the floor welcomed Nicole and Freddie with open arms. "Mi querida Nicole, tu trajiste a Freddie."

Nicole headed for the woman on the floor. The woman spoke to Freddie in Spanish. *"You didn't want to stay home alone on such a nice day, did you?"*

The heavyset woman in the chair pointed out the bay window. "La casa de huéspedes no les parece una casa de muñecas?"

Hearing the guesthouse described as looking like a dollhouse, Nicole begged to go see it. "Puedo ir a la casa de muñecas? Puedo? Puedo?"

The younger woman sprang up and whispered to Janet, "I'll take her, if that's okay. I need a little exercise."

Janet kissed Nicole, sending her on her way.

When Nicole and the woman reached the guesthouse front door, Nicole opened it. "Espera," said the woman, restraining Nicole. The woman leaned inside. "Hello." No one replied. The woman knew everyone she had seen in the main house. None were occupying the guesthouse. Nevertheless she called louder. Still no reply. They stepped inside the guesthouse.

To their right was a kitchen, on the left a living room/dining room combination. Twin bedrooms occupied the rear of the house. Sliding glass doors opened from each bedroom onto a deck. The deck sported a built-in hot tub.

Nicole put Freddie on a high-backed wrought iron chair at the kitchen table. "Freddie está sediento."

Responding, the woman opened a kitchen cabinet, took out a glass, and poured water into it. She put the glass of water on the wrought iron table in front of Freddie.

"Freddie tiene hambre."

The woman took a set of dishes from the cabinet and put them in front of Freddie. Satisfied Nicole was occupied, the woman walked through the house, going into the bedroom on the left and then out onto the rear deck.

After serving Freddie dinner, Nicole held her koala up to the window. "Ves, ahí está mami." Satisfied Freddie had seen her mother, Nicole wandered into the right bedroom, opened the closet doors, and glanced up at Gonzalo's clothes. She went to the other side of the bed. Gonzalo's pile of wet clothes was on the floor. On top of the clothes was a scapular. Nicole's eyes riveted on the edge of a PoKéRoM disk protruding from the scapular's cloth pocket. Nicole picked up the scapular, slid out the PoKéRoM disk, and quickly secreted her new treasure in Freddie's pouch.

The woman re-entered the other bedroom from the deck. She called, "Nicole, dónde estás?"

Nicole ran from the bedroom, through the living room and out the front door. She made a beeline for the safety of her mother now lounging by the pool.

Pepe finished strapping Nicole in the back seat. He pulled out of Doug's driveway, heading north on Route 1. Janet slumped low, putting both feet on the dash. She shut her eyes. Pepe began stroking her thigh. Without opening her eyes, Janet brushed his hand away.

When they arrived at Janet's, Pepe carried Nicole upstairs and tucked her into bed. He went quietly from Nicole's bedroom into the bathroom where he opened the medicine cabinet carefully so Janet wouldn't hear. He found Janet's birth-control pillbox and counted the pills. He then removed pills from an identical pillbox he had taken from his pocket until they both had exactly the same number of pills. He exchanged the two boxes.

For the next nineteen days, Janet would be taking sugar pills instead of birth-control pills.

When Pepe came back downstairs Janet was fading fast on the couch. A drink cupped in her hand, rested on her bare stomach. Her eyes closed, she felt Pepe sit.

"Pepe, it's late. Time to say goodnight."

Pepe stayed seated.

"I'm tired. It was sweet of you to drive us to Key Largo. I never expected it."

Pepe feasted on the sight of her so close to him. The pain in his groin became unbearable. He bent over and embraced her.

Janet squirmed free, splashing margarita on her stomach.

"*Stop!* Don't ruin a wonderful day."

Pepe sat back, his face grim. "I take you places, show you a good time. I do whatever you want. I get nothing?" Janet sat up. "Scott had nothing. For Christ sake, he owed me $130,000."

Janet bolted from the couch. "Pepe…"

"I have money. We can do things. We can go places."

"*Stop,*" Janet shouted in a shrill voice. "You've never mentioned the money to anyone. Right?" Pepe sat quietly. "Have you?" Pepe glared at Janet. "Damn it," she shouted. "Tell me you haven't."

"Our babies will be so beautiful," pleaded Pepe.

"*Our babies?*" Janet screamed. "*Our babies?* What the hell are you talking about?"

# Chapter 21

## Acapulco, Mexico
## Friday 1000 CT

Jose Valderrama gazed from his hillside vantage point toward the arc of Acapulco's tall buildings, his eyes following a brightly-colored parasail as it deposited its passenger onto Icacos Beach. When the parasail collapsed on the sand, Jose turned, strolled to the almond tree, and sat in its shade with his back against its trunk. The grass field to his right was filling with cars. The one to his left filled with pick-up trucks with attached horse trailers. All were covered with a brown dust raised when they drove into the riding center on their way to the grassy knolls where they parked.

Young girls dressed in jodhpurs, riding boots, and white blouses with ready-made black bow ties groomed their tethered mounts. Jose watched one girl strain, trying to tighten the girth of her English saddle. He had no idea that the quarter horse had bloated its stomach in protest. An Arabian strained its tether trying to reach the taller grass just out of its reach. As each new car or pick-up truck arrived at the riding center, a new brown dust cloud rose. They seemed to linger forever in the still, early morning air.

Riders in the far ring practiced jumping over split rail fences and mock hedges. Their coaches barked demands every few minutes. In the smaller ring, the one nearest Jose, six younger riders sat side by side on their ponies waiting for a judge to decide who would receive the blue ribbon. Jose saw only his granddaughter Lucita. She sat rigidly straight and proud on her pony. Jose's cell phone rang. The riders and the judge looked his way. He turned away. "Yo."

"Dad?" said Doug.

"I'm on the cell phone, son. Everything okay?"

"Still no sign of Gonzalo. He arrived. That's for sure. I left a note saying he could take my car. I told him where there was a good place to eat."

"Gonzalo's still missing then?"

"And my car."

"What'd Pepe say?"

"He didn't find shit. Said Gonzalo and my car vanished into thin air."

"Talk to me, Doug."

"Pepe looked along the Overseas Highway up to the mainland. Said the highway had been closed. Hurricane Fabian. I don't trust that weasel."

"Get off Pepe's back, Doug. You told me he knows the Keys and a lot of people. You don't."

"He didn't even want to look, Dad. Can you believe that?"

"You keep shitting on Pepe and, I'm telling you, he's gonna go over the edge. We need him, Doug." There was a pause. "Tell me what you know. Nothing more, for Christ sake."

"Gonzalo's here. I found his suitcase on the shore. I even cut out the lining. His yacht is here too. I'm looking at it now through the kitchen window. He's been in the guesthouse. That's for sure. His clothes are in the bedroom closet. There's another suitcase on the closet floor. I cut out its lining too. The clothes in the closet are his, extra extra large. There's a pile of clothes on the bedroom floor."

"If Gonzalo's clothes are there, he's not running. What else?"

"He took the note I put on the refrigerator."

"Anyone been in the guesthouse since Gonzalo arrived?"

"I don't think so."

"What do you—*you* Doug— what do you know? Who's been there since Gonzalo arrived? Anybody?"

"I had a party. Planned it weeks ago. Wanted to keep Janet Griffin happy. She's the daughter of the banker you bought those buildings from. Remember, I used her realty?"

"Who else?" Jose demanded.

"Okay, besides Janet—Pepe was there, two couples from Bayside. They're friends of Janet. That's it."

"What the fuck were you thinking? You had business to transact with Gonzalo. Business, Doug." Jose glanced around. The people standing ringside were looking at him. Jose turned away again. He pressed the cell phone against his ear. "Bottom line, Doug. Bottom line."

"I don't have a clue about Gonzalo's whereabouts. He just vanished."

"That's it, then," Jose screamed. "It's out of my fucking

hands, Doug. I'm sorry. I have to send Luis Botero." He threw the cell phone against the trunk of the almond tree.

Jose walked in small circles with his head down before looking toward the nearest riding ring. Lucita's hands cupped her face as she sobbed, lying on her pony's mane.

# Chapter 22

### Washington, D.C.
### Friday 2400 ET

Michael Stone began his twelve-hour shift in the leads center by scrolling through new leads associated with his OEF tag that blinked persistently. He opened the first, a new Echelon intercept.

Doug Crosby had called Jose Valderrama. He looked at the telephone number Doug called. It had an asterisk next to it. Jose was using a cell phone. Michael enabled the real time Spanish-to-English translator. He listened to their conversation.

The second was an OEF Carnivore intercept, an e-mail sent from the same Acapulco library as the previous Carnivore intercept but from a different computer in the library. The e-mail was to someone named Royce Palmer in San Diego. Michael enabled the Spanish-English translator again.

No word from the east. Find out what's going
on firsthand.

Michael put OEF tags on the cell telephone number and Royce Palmer's San Diego telephone number. He forwarded both intercepts to Greg McNulty and Alan Dickie at the Miami field office. SIOC's Multi-Agency Operations and Intelligence didn't object this time.

Rapid Start responded. Royce Palmer's San Diego domestic telephone number required approval by an attorney general followed by a judiciary approval. The Acapulco cell phone number required the approval of the international Echelon oversight committee. He forwarded both approval requests to Vinny Campbell, marking each URGENT.

Michael brought up all the items his OEF tag had gathered. He sorted them by location—Key Largo, Acapulco, San Diego, and Bayside, Florida. He resorted them by name—Gonzalo, Doug Crosby, Jose Valderrama, Royce Palmer, Pepe, Luis Botero, and Janet Griffin.

Michael programmed Rapid Start to send him copies automatically of all intelligence containing any of the names or any of the domestic and international telephone numbers. His intelligence icon began blinking. It was an Interpol alert directed to FBI headquarters, Washington, D.C.

Luis Botero on Avianca Flight 22.
Arrival: Miami International Airport,
nine-eighteen a.m. ET this date.

Michael immediately forwarded the Interpol alert to Vinny Campbell, Greg McNulty, MFO, and the CIA Acapulco office.

# Chapter 23

### Reston, Virginia
### Saturday 0600 ET

Jack Taylor and Simon Tully exited the revolving doors of Taylor Associates' Reston, Virginia annex. On the other end of the long, tree-lined walk a gray limousine waited on the cobblestone drive. Its driver stood by its opened door.

Simon had trouble keeping up with Jack—a well-proportioned ramrod straight six-foot three who exercised most every day. When Simon fell behind because of his limp and was forced to run a few steps to keep up, he was glad Jack didn't notice how badly he limped. The two men settled into the rear seat.

"Integrating won't be easy," said Simon as he ran his fingers through his white pompadour.

"Think multipliers," said Jack as he stretched his legs full length.

Simon looked up at Jack. "Jack, we've been expanding at a twenty-three percent rate the past few years. This year we've exceeded $1.7 billion in revenue. We're in a recession." Jack rested his head on gray leather. Simon plunged ahead. "We've just hired that consulting firm to tell us what it will cost to go public. They need time." Simon glanced at Jack. His eyes were closed.

Thirty minutes later the limousine pulled up in front of the Crystal City building with "Taylor Associates" engraved in the gray marble above the entrance.

Simon followed Jack as they exited the elevator and headed for the conference room. "There are six firms," said Simon. "Four are outside the Baltimore-Washington corridor. Two of the four produce avionics, one communication and electronic countermeasure systems, and one satellite ground terminals."

Simon followed Jack as he threaded his way between those sitting at the conference room table and those sitting behind them along the wall. The two men sat in the chairs at the head of the large conference table. At the far end was a podium. Simon leaned toward Jack. "These four are eager to be closer to their government sponsors."

Jack took a small notepad from his jacket pocket, held it in his right hand, flipped a few pages before finding the one he wanted, and then scribbled $1.7 billion. "Let's get started," Jack announced to the room. There was a momentary pause. The room quieted. Jack leaned back in his chair. "Okay, let's hear first from the firms with the least federal dependency."

Simon flushed. He leaned toward Jack. "Jack, only Bauer Industries has no federal contracts. Carolyn is the least prepared. Our best teams are here. They're prepared to brief the four largest firms. Bauer is scheduled for eleven thirty." Jack remained silent. Simon addressed the room. "Bauer Industries has no federal contracts. They'll be first." He looked at Emily, sitting along the sidewall. "Emily, would you please ask Carolyn to come in."

Jack leaned toward Simon. "How's our cash position?"

"Excellent. Three hundred million plus."

# Chapter 24

### Miami, Florida
### Saturday 0615 ET

Holt Brown sat alone in Alan Dickie's outer office. In his hand was an Interpol alert he had received minutes before. He rose and went to Sally's desk. The folder he had put there last night at nine-thirty marked "Alan Dickie—Morning Briefing" hadn't been touched. He clipped the Interpol alert to the outside of the folder.

As Holt sat, Sally rushed in. "Morning, Holt."

Sally and Holt had had a good relationship over the years, often teasing each other. Sally respected authority. Holt took it in stride. Sally fought a constant weight problem. Holt couldn't gain an ounce. Sally dressed professionally. Holt never did. They liked each other.

"Slow down," Holt said. "Alan's not here yet."

Sally breathed a sigh of relief. "Thanks." She picked up Holt's briefing folder from her desk. "I'll be right back." She took the folder into Alan's office and left it on his desk.

Alan arrived fifteen minutes later. The look of his closely cut three-piece pinstriped suit was overshadowed by the too-small shirt-collar digging into his neck. "Give me a minute, will you?"

Alan had bristled at the criticism of the FBI since Waco and the Oklahoma bombing. The institution he loved had become an easy target. Now 9/11 criticisms appeared daily in newspapers, newscasts and talk shows. They all stressed the lack of interagency coordination. Sunday supplements blazed with accusations of missed opportunities and the lack of free communications between the upper ranks of the FBI and those on the front lines. Alan was convinced that FBI culture had to change.

The one criticism that annoyed Alan most was the bureau's alleged inability to gather and process intelligence. The FBI was being pegged as a law enforcement agency that should be restricted to law enforcement. Alan and many others in the FBI disagreed. They felt that if the FBI were restricted to law enforcement, its role in the post-9/11 era would be severely restricted.

Alan reread the Interpol alert Holt had clipped to the outside of his morning briefing folder. He looked for an indication of why Luis Botero was entering the United States. He found none. Since Botero was flying on Avianca, there was an excellent chance he was coming from Colombia, a proven international hot spot. Interpol's involvement proved Botero had an international reputation. The hint of a smile crossed Alan's face. This man could have used forged documents to board the plane, yet he hadn't. There was no need for a disguise. No law enforcement agency had yet been able to get a picture of him. It was almost as if this man was taunting authorities to catch him. The grin on Alan's face turned to a smile. Was this really Botero or possibly a feint to distract authorities while the real Botero waltzed into the United States unhampered? Gathering intelligence on this man—whether Botero or not—before capturing him would enhance Alan's reputation and skyrocket his profile within the upper ranks of the FBI.

Sally's buzzer sounded. It signaled that Alan was ready. Holt went in and sat on the arm of the chair furthest from Alan's desk.

"I see you added the Interpol alert this morning."

Holt nodded.

"Interpol claims a Luis Botero is on Avianca Flight 22. Probably coming from Colombia. Claims he'll be landing in Miami at nine-eighteen this morning."

"*Claims?*" asked Holt.

"Who else has seen this?"

"It just arrived," said Holt.

"Botero is one of our ten-most-wanted. I just looked it up."

"Extremely dangerous," Holt added.

"Age?"

"Not yet twenty," said Holt. "A killer who enjoys killing."

"The alert doesn't say why he's coming."

"Right."

"DEA in on this?"

"No, it's our lead," said Holt, as he slid from the arm of the chair into its cushion. "I've sent a message to our office in Barranquilla and to Interpol. Maybe one of 'em has a picture of Botero. We don't."

"Recommendation?"

"Have Customs shunt the punk to the side on some pretext. We'll be waiting. It'll be a high profile collar."

"Alternatives?"

"Hadn't thought any necessary," Holt said.

"Why not find out why he's here?"

"*Street surveillance?*" Holt said, sitting up straight.

"Exactly," said Alan. "Gather intelligence. We may be sitting on something here. Something big."

"Risky," said Holt. "If we lose him—"

"We won't lose him. Other downsides?"

"There's no time to set up a surveillance effort," said Holt. "He's in the air. Our internal coordination is monstrous…needs high-level approvals."

"That's my job," said Alan. "What else?"

"Coordinating customs, airport security, the Miami-Dade PD, positioning our team…"

"One at a time," said Alan, wanting to demonstrate his methodical course of action. "Customs?"

"Customs will be the least of our problems," said Holt. "I can handle them, Airport Security too. This is right down their alley. They have everything on site. With authorization, I can parallel those efforts and put our request in with both chiefs right there at the airport. They owe us one from last June. But the Miami-Dade PD…"

Alan ran a finger inside his collar to ease the chafing on his neck. "What's their problem?"

"If there's a politico or celebrity onboard with Botero, in the customs area, anywhere in the airport, or even within an hour of his arrival time, it could mean trouble. Those critters travel with their own security teams and may even have a relief team waiting. Some use freelance bodyguards. If anything goes wrong, they'll protect their own and get in our way. That is, unless they're alerted first. That'll take time. And then there's the press."

"You can handle the Miami-Dade PD. Right? I mean if it becomes necessary."

"And the unexpected," said Holt, standing and taking a step toward Alan's desk. "If this psychopath bolts, clears our perimeter, we'll need Miami-Dade PD as back-up to bring him down without collaterals."

"Please, Holt. Answer the question. Can you coordinate the Miami-Dade PD?"

"Fast track isn't Miami-Dade PD's specialty."

"Why do we need them?"

"If it gets rough, they provide foot soldiers, cruisers, even swat teams. However, they come with politicos attached. Politicos demand details, fallback positions, and guarantees. They'll want to know who's in charge. Who gets the credit. Who steps up if it fails. Who leads at the press conference?"

"Holt, you've got more reasons to do nothing than anyone I've ever met. We need a "can do" attitude here. Get with Customs right away. Tell them to delay Botero without alerting him. Delay plane dockings, claim no terminal berths free, whatever it takes."

"I'll suggest that." Holt headed for the door, anxious to get started. He was out of time before he started. "Customs will bring in airport authority, ground crews, traffic controllers, the FAA. I'll get the staff on this right away."

"Holt, there's no time for staff involvement."

Holt spun around, facing Alan in disbelief.

"You and I will take charge. Have an FBI back-up team ready before Botero clears Customs. Initiate 24-hour FBI surveillance."

"That overloads me," said Holt. "What about the Miami-Dade PD?"

"This'll be an FBI operation."

# Chapter 25

## Arlington, Virginia
## Saturday 0815 ET

The murmurs in the Taylor Associates third floor conference room ceased as Carolyn Hughes entered. She walked to the podium and faced her audience. Her smile, framed in shoulder-length red hair atop her statuesque figure, focused her audience.

"My name is Carolyn Hughes. I'm here to brief you on Bauer Industries, our newest merger candidate." Carolyn walked to a bank of switches on the wall. She lowered the conference room lights and then returned to the podium. "I will be pleased to respond to all questions... after my presentation." Those close to the podium heard her take a breath.

"Bauer Industries is a privately-held company incorporated twenty years ago this month. Gil Bauer runs the company on a day-to-day basis. His father, Charles, is the founder, CEO, and chairman of the board. Both are engineers by training. The information I will be presenting was obtained yesterday during my visit to Bauer Industries. I met with both Charles and Gil Bauer. Additional data from a variety of peripheral sources may become available. At the end of our meeting Charles Bauer gave me a letter." She paused and addressed Jack. "Mr. Bauer requested that I deliver the letter to you, Mr. Taylor, after my presentation." Jack nodded.

Carolyn clicked the remote on the podium. The words "Management Efficiency" appeared on the projection screen behind her. "Bauer Industries' management efficiency during the trailing twelve months expressed in terms of return-on-equity and return-on-assets are 37.1% and 24.6%, respectively. Their return-on-investment for the same TTM is 18.3%."

"Acquisitions have been their growth engine. Two years ago they acquired a software firm larger than they were at the time. Last year they acquired an e-commerce firm. This year they acquired a budding Internet service provider, gaining access to over two million subscribers."

Fifteen minutes later Carolyn concluded. "Charles Bauer told me he is flattered by our interest in his company and, as I said in the beginning, has given me an envelope addressed to you, Mr.

Taylor."

"Thanks, Carolyn," said Jack. "Can you and Simon stop by my office about three this afternoon?"

Jack Taylor returned to his office and opened the envelope Charles Bauer had given Carolyn.

Mr. Jack S. Taylor, CEO and President
Taylor Associates
2377-85 Crystal Drive,
Crystal City, Virginia 22202

Dear Mr. Taylor:

Although the possibility of a merger of our firms may appear advantageous, it will not be possible, now or in the future.

Sincerely,

Charles J. Bauer

Below his signature was a handwritten note: "I enjoyed meeting Carolyn Hughes. Her presentation and manner represented you and your firm admirably."

# Chapter 26

## Miami International Airport, Florida
## Saturday 1110 ET

A small boy sat on top of the dividing wall, his grubby, untied sneakers threatening to fall off. Every time the gray doors on the other side of the wall snapped opened, he looked for his cousins and aunt. Not seeing them, he'd turn, calling to his mother, "No, Mama."

The boy's mother, a woman fighting going over 340 pounds, lowered herself onto the cushioned seat that circled the only cement column in the waiting area. She welcomed the cool feel of the cement through the back of her sundress. With a sigh of relief, she braced herself with her left arm, closed her eyes and cleared beads of sweat from her face with a handkerchief already soaked with perspiration. She shifted her attention to the boy's three sisters. Despite her repeated warnings, they were testing her patience by wandering further and further away. Yielding to exhaustion, she closed her eyes again, giving silent thanks for the coolness on her back and the vigilance of her son.

Newcomers to Miami airport's international arrival waiting area found the sight of the boy perched precariously on the wall amusing. For those waiting a few minutes longer, the drumbeats of repeated "No Mamas" added to the irritation they were already feeling as they waited for U. S. Customs to free their own friends and relatives.

Alan Dickie sat next to the boy's mother, his right heel twitching to an unheard beat. He doubted Botero would be on incoming Avianca Flight 22, as the Interpol alert claimed. Why would an FBI ten-most-wanted travel so openly? Turning away from the boy's mother he said in a low voice, "Holt, is the hand-off team here?"

"They're heading for the terminal now," the voice in his ear responded.

"What's with Customs?"

"They're not happy. Holding planes off their berths causes havoc with the traffic controllers."

"Yeah, okay," said Alan. He stood and began strolling the waiting area.

Holt said, "Customs had the pilots tell their passengers—"

"Never mind what excuses Customs used," said Alan. "That's their business. Tell 'em their description of Botero isn't helpful. Tell 'em it fits a thousand people out here. Tell 'em we need more time."

"Too late," Holt said. "They're about to release everybody. He'll be out those doors any minute... This is it. They're all released... They're walking toward the doors as I speak."

"Shit," Alan said. "Holt, you in position?"

"I'll be coming through the release doors with the passengers."

Botero lingered near the front of the anxious crowd as it sensed it was about to be released. Those in front inched closer and closer to the gray release doors. Those behind tried to do the same. Luggage carts became barriers blocking those behind from forging ahead. In a moment Botero would be in the United States. If he could make it to the novelty shop before being recognized...

Botero emerged alongside a harried woman carrying a tattered suitcase bound with white cord and masking tape. Two little girls holding hands followed meekly behind, one clinging to the woman's flowing skirt. At the sight of his aunt and cousins, the boy atop the wall began screaming, "They're here, Mama. They're here."

The crowd cheered and began clapping, happy that the boy had finally spotted his cousins. The outburst startled the boy. As he turned to see what caused the sudden outburst and applause, he lost his balance and fell off the wall. A collective "Ohhhh!" rose from the crowd as he disappeared over the wall.

The boy's mother lumbered up and ran toward the other side of the L-shaped wall to retrieve her son. Shouts from those now looking over the wall tried to assure her that the boy was okay. In her panic she couldn't hear them. She screamed repeatedly as she bolted through the crowd, "My baby, my baby." From various corners of the waiting area her three little girls, never having seen their mother in such frenzy, raced after her.

A lone customs guard tried to stop the frantic mother from entering the restricted corridor area. He had no choice. He stepped aside not wanting to be bowled over. Several would-be rescuers and the woman's three daughters followed close behind.

The boy's aunt had seen her nephew fall. She dropped her bag and ran toward him. Her two girls froze at the sight of their mother running to their crying cousin sprawled on the floor. Their aunt rounded the corner, leading would-be rescuers. The fallen boy began screaming. His cousins and sisters screamed louder.

Their mother, turning and seeing her own children in a panic, reversed course and headed toward them. She collided with a young man who had scaled the wall to help, landing on top of him.

"We have a diversion in progress," Alan shouted. "I say again, we have a diversionary effort. Stay alert. Stay alert. Suspect is now our responsibility, Holt."

Holt spotted the only passenger not caught up in the chaos. He was on the escalator. Holt raced through the crowd in pursuit. "Suspect is on the upper level."

"Where the fuck is the backup team?" Alan yelled as he headed for the escalator.

"They're turning into the terminal drive," Holt said into his shoulder microphone.

"Shit," Alan said as he brushed past a woman bent over tying her daughter's shoelace. "Holt, where are you?"

"About twenty yards behind him. It's mobbed here. No, I've lost him. I'm heading for the ticket counters."

Alan raced up the down escalator. An irate man wouldn't let him pass. "Where's the backup, Holt?"

"Behind a Hertz courtesy bus."

Botero entered the novelty shop, went to a magazine rack in the rear, and extracted the bottom copy of *El Tiempo*, a Bogotá newspaper. If Pepe had done what he was told, Botero could make it out of the airport even if he had been spotted. He held the newspaper at its fold and shook it. A key fell to the floor. He checked the number on the key and went to the locker bay attached to the wall outside the shop. He opened a nearby locker, removed a brightly colored child's lunch pail and opened it. He took out a set of keys and put them in his pocket before setting the timer inside the lunch box for sixty seconds.

Fifty-six seconds. Holding onto the top of the open locker door, he turned to study the overhead direction signs. The baggage claim signs directed passengers to turn the corner located a hundred feet to his left.

Forty-one seconds. He searched the crowd. Without turning, he closed the locker, put the lunch pail under his arm, and strolled toward the corner on his left.

Twenty-six seconds. "I got him," Holt said. "Go straight ahead as you come off the escalator. Subject is fifty yards in front of you. I'm at the end of the Air France ticket counter, ahead on your right. In pursuit." Holt squeezed his way through the crowd, his eyes riveted on Luis.

Twenty-four seconds. "The backup?" Alan demanded.

Twenty-one seconds. "They're moving again," Holt said. "Will be at the entrance any minute."

Nineteen seconds. "Damn it," Alan said as he left the escalator and entered the upper level.

Seventeen seconds. "I see him," Holt roared. "He hasn't spotted me yet."

Sixteen seconds. Botero approached the corner where the baggage claim sign indicated he should turn left. As he did, he hesitated and glanced back. Holt's and Botero's eyes met.

"We've been made," Holt said. "He's turning the corner at T.G.I. Friday's. He's out of sight control. Repeat, subject out of sight control. He'll be coming out of the terminal, guys. Young male, big, greased-back hair with two stubby ponytails, has a yellow object in his hand, no luggage."

Ten seconds. "Roger that, Holt. Which exit?"

Holt didn't feel his shoulder microphone fall off as he raced after Botero. "International concourse," he yelled. Holt turned the corner, searching for his prey.

Five seconds. Botero dropped the yellow lunch box into the trashcan by the exit doors. He turned. His eyes narrowed searching the crowd. Suddenly, they locked on Holt in mid-stride. With an impudent smile Botero swaggered to attention. His hand arched high over his head before mocking Holt with a salute.

Three seconds. "Report," Alan screamed.

One second. "God damn it. *Report!*"

# Chapter 27

## Washington, D.C.
## Saturday 1110 ET

Sarah Stone had called Michael. She would be out shopping when he got home. Michael decided to eat in the cafeteria before he went home for the day. Standing in line in the FBI headquarters' dining room, he promised himself he wouldn't eat too much. His love handles were pinching more than an inch and pulling in his gut didn't show as many ribs as it used to. He was determined to be lean and mean when forty arrived.

Twenty minutes later, stuffed with shrimp scampi and chocolate yogurt, he hustled back to the fifth floor. He opened a flashing icon flagged as urgent.

Report to Vinny Campbell immediately.

Michael stood at Vinny Campbell's open office door. He should have found time to respond one way or the other to this man's administrative directives.

Vinny Campbell, a tall, thin man, was dressed in a crisp dark suit with a small American flag on his left lapel. "Come in. Close the door."

Michael stood in the middle of Vinny's office. "What's up?"

"What do you know about the Miami Airport bombing this morning?"

Michael's eyes widened. "Miami airport bombing?"

"At eleven o eight this morning," said Vinny. "What do you know about it?"

"Eleven aught eight?"

"Right. *Eleven o eight. This morning.*"

Michael's eyes rolled under his lids momentarily. "That's about when I went to the dining room. I just got back. This is the first I've heard about a bombing."

"Damn it, Michael, tell me what you know."

"I just told you, I don't know anything about a Miami airport bombing."

"This is no time to play games," Vinny said.

"Tell me something about it," said Michael. "Anything, it

may trigger something in my memory."

"Lose the attitude."

There was a knock at the door. A man leaned in, signaling Vinny to step outside. Vinny left without a word, closing his office door behind him. A moment later Vinny reopened his office door. "Come with me," he said.

Michael followed Vinny. "Where're we going?"

"The executive briefing room." Vinny paused. "Heard about Echelon, Carnivore?" asked Vinny.

"Sure," said Michael.

"Finally, your memory's coming back."

"Your point?"

"You put CIA tags on leads. I directed you to put FBI's PENTTBOM tags on them. You refused. Not once, but twice."

"Negative. I used SIOC's Operation Enduring Freedom tags. *We're all in this together. Okay?*"

"I don't like being surprised," said Vinny.

"Surprised?" said Michael. "Everything's in my reports. Including an Interpol alert."

Vinny swung around. "An Interpol alert?"

Michael stood toe to toe with Vinny but hesitated before answering. "Luis Botero arrived at the Miami International Airport on Avianca Flight 22—ten-ten this morning. I sent the alert to MFO. And to you."

# Chapter 28

### Miami International Airport, Florida
### Saturday 1400 ET

Taro Okada's grandparents had immigrated to Los Angeles during the 1930s depression, three weeks after their marriage in Tokyo. His grandfather, an architect experienced in designing earthquake resistant buildings wasn't able to find a job in his chosen field after arriving in the United States. He worked as a day laborer. His grandmother washed and ironed uniforms for local restaurants and hotels. They were lucky. Most of their friends and neighbors were unemployed.

Taro's grandparents became U.S. citizens in 1941, nine months before Japan attacked Pearl Harbor. Their children, a boy and two girls, attended the Los Angeles public school system.

Taro's grandfather had attempted to volunteer for military duty. The military would not accept him. Worse, he and his family were placed in an internment camp soon after Pearl Harbor. Taro's father, the first-born, and his two sisters were home-schooled until the end of World War II when the family returned to Los Angeles and the children reentered the Los Angeles public school system. Taro's father and mother graduated from UCLA, married, and then moved to San Diego. Taro, the couple's only child, was born two years later.

Taro had earned letters in high school playing center on the basketball team and linebacker on the football team. He had attended San Diego State but dropped out during his first semester. He was restless, couldn't decide what he wanted to do the rest of his life. He accepted a job on the other side of the country. He became a salesman in a Miami appliance store.

Three months later, while standing in line for a movie, Taro met the love of his life, the daughter of a Cuban exile. His carefree attitude about his future changed. He registered at the University of Miami and began pre-law courses seven months later, in September. The couple scheduled a May wedding for the following year, the first Saturday after Taro's spring semester ended. Their honeymoon would have to wait until after his graduation. Taro's summer session of classes would start the Monday after their Saturday wedding.

Three weeks before the wedding, Taro's bride-to-be went with her mother for the final fitting of her wedding dress. As they left the fitting, a bullet fired during a robbery two blocks away ricocheted off the storefront, striking his fiancée in the temple. She died on the pavement in front of the bridal store.

Nine months later the robber was convicted of robbery and acquitted of manslaughter. It could not be proven that the robber had fired the bullet that had killed his fiancée, even though no other gun had been fired. The ricocheted bullet was too damaged. Eighteen months after entering the prison system, the convicted robber was ordered released by court order as part of a program to relieve crowding in Miami's jails.

Taro joined the Miami-Dade Police Department while continuing his studies at night. Over the years he rose in the ranks, becoming chief of Miami-Dade detectives. He was one of the first law enforcement officers to arrive at the Miami International Airport after the bombing.

Taro leaned heavily on the Air France ticket counter. Around the corner, smoldering debris was everywhere. The airport entrance arch, no longer supported, sagged dangerously. Rescue workers in heavy and cumbersome garb dragged hoses, axes, oxygen bottles, and defibrillators through the entrance arch while comrades made makeshift braces to keep it from collapsing.

Victims were everywhere, crying, moaning, and writhing in pain. Many were alone, others in small family clusters. A few of the luckier passengers who were out of harm's way when the explosion occurred tried to comfort the less fortunate. They began to yield as the aid workers started the triage of the injured.

Saddest of all the victims was a family, or what was left of a family. They were on the floor just inside the concourse entrance, soaked in blood. The mother sobbed uncontrollably over her twin daughters lying in grotesque positions in front of her. The two little girls had taken the brunt of the blast. The father sat on the floor, his son cradled in his arms. He was shielding his son's eyes from the sight of his mother and two dead sisters.

Taro wanted the image of this former family sprawled on the concourse imprinted deep. He forced himself to take a deep breath. The smoke and smell began doing its job, etching the image deeper and deeper within his brain. He vowed to collar this wanton killer, this murderer.

Taro had been given the word. A passenger arriving on an international flight had caused the mayhem. Taro headed for Customs…

Taro made his way through the crowds of arriving passengers, flashed his badge to a customs officer scanning a passport, and headed for the chief customs officer.

Taro stood in front of Blake Pugh's desk. "Not now Taro, the alligators are stampeding."

"And how are you, Blake?"

"In deep shit, if you must know. Now what do you want?"

"Information on the bomb explosion," Taro said.

"Oh God, another alligator."

"You held some planes on the tarmac…"

"Close the door." The chubby Customs chief headed for the coffee pot. "What'd you want to know?"

"Everything," said Taro.

"Figures." The coffeepot timer had shut the coffeepot off hours ago. "This shit tastes awful." He turned to Taro. "Off the record, right?" Taro nodded. "Look, it was a favor, that's all. It just got out of hand."

"A favor?" said Taro.

"Sit down." They settled into old chairs that protested. "Holt came in this morning."

"Holt Brown—FBI?" said Taro.

"Yeah. Never seen him so harassed. Said Customs was his last coordination point. Said he knew we'd help."

"So you did," said Taro.

"We did." He started to take a sip of coffee, looked into the cup and decided not to. "Holt has a new boss and needed a favor."

"You said that before," Taro said.

"What?" said Blake.

"The favor." Taro's dark eyes watched him. "You already said Holt needed a favor. You agreed."

"Give me a break will ya." He forced himself to drink some coffee. "Holt showed me an Interpol alert." Blake handed the alert to Taro. "It says a Luis Botero will be arriving on Avianca Flight 22. It came from Barranquilla."

"He wanted you to arrest him," Taro said. "Right?"

"Wrong. His boss wants him put under surveillance. Wants to get some kind of intelligence before he arrests him."

"Go on."

"Holt wants us to stall Botero. Had a surveillance team on its way. I tell him no way, the morning's busy. He says Botero's a ten-most-wanted." Blake drained the bottom of the cup and coughed. "Holt's worked with us for years, hand in glove. We owe him big time—drug busts, smuggling. So I delay."

"Sounds okay."

"Traffic control begins bitching," said Blake. "I knew they would. Backups begin building on the tarmac. We bring Avianca 22 in. Unload them. Tell them there's a medical issue." Blake looked sheepish. "Off the record now." Taro nodded. "We lied. Oh yeah, Holt's wearing a shoulder mike and earpiece, talking to his new boss: someone called Alan Dickie."

"What'd Dickie want?"

"A description of Botero. So I have a Customs agent mingle. She ID's Botero. No problem."

"And tells Holt."

"She hears Holt relay her description to Dickie. Dickie wants better. Back she goes, this time for the works. Traffic Control has a fit. I have to release. No more room on the runway. This is Miami for Christ sake."

"What'd your agent get?"

"She's good. A couple of pictures, a print of his right palm, four left fingers including the thumb and index, and a cup he threw in the trash—DNA." Blake handed Taro copies of the pictures and prints. "I thought they'd be back for this by now."

Taro looked at the pictures. Botero was huge and young. Guys like him don't grow old, Taro mused. "Keep the cup within your evidence system."

"No shit," said Blake.

Taro returned to the concourse level. A planeload of passengers was being shepherded behind yellow tape to an exit normally used by concourse vendors. As the last passenger exited the service door, a policeman released the door from a stop. The sound of the heavy door slamming shut reverberated throughout the concourse just as another group of passengers began appearing at the far end of the strung out yellow tape.

# Chapter 29

### Bayside, Florida
### Saturday 1430 ET

Pepe slowed as he approached the stop sign. He glanced into his side yard. He turned off the car air conditioner and lowered the windows. The aroma of freshly-cut grass filled his nostrils. He drove into the garage. The sound of the garage door closing behind him didn't mask the sounds coming from the living room television. *Son-of-a-bitch. Those fucking gardeners have been in the house again. That's the last straw for those bastards.* Inside he tossed his keys on the kitchen counter, picked up the telephone, and punched in the lawn service number that he read from a magnetic clipboard on the side of the refrigerator.

"Hermano, porque llega tan tarde," Botero said.

Pepe spun around. Botero, towering over him, stood directly behind him. Pepe dropped the phone. It bounced off the keys on the counter, landing on the floor. "I'm not late," Pepe said, feigning composure.

Botero stepped closer to Pepe. 'Me estaba esperando a mi, no?"

"I wasn't expecting you to be in my house." Pepe picked up the telephone. "Speak English."

Botero cocked his head and looked down at Pepe. "How tall you man?"

"You've made the newscasts," Pepe said.

Botero stepped back. "You five-one, two?"

Pepe walked around Botero and headed into the living room. Behind him he heard his keys being picked up from the counter. "Did you have to use the bomb? It was for an emergency."

Botero played catch with Pepe's keys. "An emergency man. Right."

"Emergency? What emergency?"

"You no see guy on my ass. Bomb work great, man."

Pepe turned off the television and faced Botero. "Two little girls for Christ sake."

"I use your car, man. And house."

Pepe's eyes widened. "What? What am I supposed to do?"

Botero sauntered to the television and turned it back on.

'Where Gonzalo?"

Pepe went to the wet bar, poured a Scotch and sat in a chair on the opposite side of the room. "No idea."

"Jose no happy," said Botero. "Where Gonzalo, man?"

Pepe shrugged. "On the mainland. That's all I know."

"Doug no happy. Say Bauer deal stink. Say you promise."

Pepe was proud of the Bauer deal. "Doug can invest a lot of money. A lot."

"How pipsqueak like you get with Doug and Jose? Some fucking gambler. Right, man?"

Pepe downed the remaining Scotch. "Scott Graves. He was married to Janet Griffin. Her father owns the bank." Pepe headed back to the wet bar. "Scott's the worst gambler ever."

"You got Tequila?"

Pepe nodded and put a glass on the bar for Botero. "He bet on tips I gave him. It was so *fucking* perfect." A prideful grin crossed Pepe's face. "He owed me a bundle. *A hundred thirty grand.*" Pepe poured Botero's Tequila. "When the time came, I had muscle threaten to kill him. He went to daddy-the-banker. I had the money the next day." Pepe sat on a barstool. "The next week the bank's hit with a surprise audit. How fucking lucky can one guy get? The banker needs his money back. Just for a few days he says. I say *no way.* I tell 'em about this rich guy in Key Largo."

"Whoa, man," said Botero. "You no know about Bauer?"

"Bert Griffin, the banker, told Doug about Bauer," said Pepe. "Bert Griffin needed cash *real bad.*"

"You asshole, man."

Pepe glared at Botero. "What the fuck are you talking about?"

"Use fucking head. No gambler, no hundred thirty grand. No hundred thirty grand, no banker come Doug. Gonzalo no come."

Pepe decided Botero was dumb. "You're not making sense."

"You asshole, man."

Pepe glanced over his shoulder into his study. His desk had been pulled away from the wall, its chair lying on its side. "My computer's gone!" Pepe raced into the study.

"Relax man. We take your fucking disks."

"We? Who's 'we'?"

Botero crowded Pepe. Pepe backed into his desk. "Why you no happy? You have house. I here to help, man."

"Nobody told me we're looking for a disk."

"You got more disks?"

"This is about disks?"

"Do you, little asshole?"

Pepe walked past Luis and went back to the bar. "In my office."

"We there, man."

"What?" said Pepe. "You've been to my office?" Pepe poured his drink and retreated to the chair he had been sitting in.

"Talk man," said Botero.

"Doug has this party. Right off the bat Doug's pissed."

"Off the bat?"

"Right away, okay." Pepe waved his glass in the direction of the bar. "Help yourself." Botero headed for the bar. "Doug says Jose wants me to find Gonzalo. And his car. That's it. That's all I know. A six-four fat guy is on the mainland. He has Doug's Mercedes."

"No nice call Gonzalo fat." Pepe poured his Tequila. "What else, asshole?"

"I searched Doug's guesthouse."

"Guesthouse?" said Botero.

"A small cottage. It's down by the dock. I found a pile of wet clothes on the floor, some in the closet, and a suitcase with more clothes. Nothing else." Pepe's leg felt wet. He sipped his Scotch to keep more from spilling.

"That's it, man?" asked Botero.

"Shit no. I went to every joint between Doug's and the mainland."

"No Gonzalo?"

"Right, no Gonzalo," said Pepe. "I'll tell you this. Gonzalo's one religious fuck."

"Why you say that, asshole?"

"I found his scapular," said Pepe. "On top of his wet clothes."

"What scapular, man?"

"A scapular—religious people wear 'em, round their necks. Like a holy medal on a chain. Only a scapular is two pieces of cloth with religious pictures on them." Pepe took a healthy swig.

"One picture hangs on your chest, the other on your back. But this one's different. There's a pocket behind the pictures. To put religious medals in, I guess."

"The car, man?" Pepe drained his Tequila and poured another.

"Nothing," said Pepe. "The cops closed Route 1 because of a hurricane. Fucking shame. If they'd done it earlier Gonzalo'd been stuck on the Keys."

"A red Mercedes vanish?" said Botero. "No way."

Pepe nodded, trying to convince Botero. "Doug about shit a brick."

"Shit a brick?" said Botero.

"Doug wasn't happy, okay."

"Gonzalo hiding?" Botero asked. "To meet someone?"

"Doubt it," said Pepe.

"Shithead. Doug have party after Gonzalo arrive. Right, man?"

"So?"

"Someone at party hide him."

Pepe finished his Scotch. "What the fuck's going on here? Doug's looking for Gonzalo and a car. You're after computer disks."

"It Gonzalo disk. It opens door to Jose."

"Holy shit." Scotch splashed Pepe's pants again.

"Who at fucking party?" said Botero. "Every fucking name, asshole."

Carolyn looked at her watch as she pulled onto I-95N, heading for Bayside. Five after three. Not too bad. Even after a couple of hours cooped up on the plane, they could get to Bayside, check in and be in the bar about five. Perfect. Plenty of time for Mr. Taylor to get a little local color. Then it's dinner at Janet's. Carolyn rested her left elbow on the car's opened window and glanced over at Jack Taylor. He looked relaxed, taking in the scenery. Carolyn dropped her left hand out the window and started tapping on the door panel.

Carolyn and Jack walked into the Carp's Landing bar. Carolyn felt comfortable that she knew the surroundings as well as she did and was looking forward to introducing Jack to Charles and Gil Bauer.

The only other patrons were three men huddled deep in conversation at the far end of the bar. Natalie stretched and slid stems of glasses into the overhead rack. She walked to Carolyn and Jack. "Hi guys."

"You been a good girl since I saw your last?" Carolyn asked.

"Yeah, but wish I hadn't." Natalie wiped the bar pointlessly. "What'll it be?"

"The usual," said Carolyn, wondering if Natalie would remember she drank vodka tonics with a twist of lime.

"Coors light for me," Jack said.

"Coming up." Natalie went off.

"Carolyn," a voice called. "Over here." Gil Bauer stood, excused himself from the other two at the far end of the bar and headed toward her.

Carolyn flushed. *Oh God, Jack is going to wonder why I didn't recognize him when we came in? Stay alert, girl. Stay alert.*

"You just get in?" Gil asked as he sat next to Carolyn.

"Gil Bauer, this is Jack Taylor, our CEO. Mr. Taylor, Mr. Bauer."

The two men leaned in front of Carolyn, shaking hands. "You guys just come through the airport?"

Jack nodded, "The last time I saw that many policemen in one place was in the Big Apple on Fifth Avenue during a St. Patrick's Day parade."

"Just saw it on the TV there," said Gil pointing to the TV suspended from the ceiling at the end of the bar. "Really a bad scene. A couple dozen planes were just sitting on the runways."

Jack said, "Carolyn and I were sitting on one of those planes far from the terminal for two hours. When they finally let us off there were visual barriers everywhere. We have no idea what happened."

Carolyn said, "We were paraded single file behind a long stretch of this-is-a-crime-scene tape and herded onto a delivery ramp out back."

Natalie placed the drinks on small napkins. "One vodka tonic with a lime twist and a Coors Light."

# Chapter 30

## Washington, D.C.
## Saturday 1445 ET

Michael followed Vinny Campbell into the executive briefing room. Three arched rows of spacious seating spanned the full breadth of the amphitheatre. Behind the three arched rows was a wide aisle. Behind the wide aisle were five straight rows of seats tightly bunched in the center of the amphitheatre. They gave the appearance of being a fifty-person jury box. High on the wall in front of the amphitheatre were three large video screens.

The only person sitting in the room was Greg McNulty. He turned toward Michael and Vinny from his front-row seat. He gave Michael a half-hearted nod. I wonder if he changed that rumpled shirt since I saw him in the cafeteria, Michael mused before looking up at the video screens. Two screens displayed Michael's two spreadsheets.

Vinny glanced toward Michael as he made his way to the front row. "You know Greg McNulty." Michael and Vinny sat next to Greg. "All FBI field offices and more than a dozen federal police, military and intelligence organizations around the country have the ability to monitor and participate in whatever goes on in this room. Dozens of additional law enforcement sites can also."

Vinny turned to Michael. "Until I find out what's going on, I've shut down all external access to this room. Start at the beginning. Give us an explanation of what you've done."

Michael stood and strolled to the rear wide aisle in front of the jury box. Standing there, he began. "On the left screen is the chronological listing of a cluster of intercepts I've been following. On your center screen are the same intercepts listed by the name of the caller and then the person called." He moved along the wide aisle to the center of the room. "This all started with the Echelon intercept you see at the top on the left screen." Michael grasped the back of the plush green leather chair in front of him, pausing for questions.

"I'm listening," Vinny said.

"Everything follows from this Echelon intercept. I put an OEF tag on it to be sure I'd receive related intercepts."

"You used an OEF tag to track and access Echelon intercepts?" Vinny said.

"Echelon intercepts related to this particular intercept," Michael said.

"Go on," said Vinny.

Michael sat before continuing. "The OEF tag led to everything you see on the two screens. I'll start with the left screen, the chronological listing of intercepts."

Michael and Greg followed Vinny into his office. Vinny sat hard in the chair behind his desk. "Close the door." He began rocking back and forth as he stared at Michael. "Did you establish the need-to-know that allowed access to our Special Compartmented Information network?"

"Sir?"

Vinny scowled. "Echelon intercepts are transmitted via the SCI network and only the SCI network. It's our top secret network. Do you know if you even have an SCI or a TS-SBI clearance with us?"

"They were transferred from Langley," Michael replied with confidence.

"The efforts of Greg's Justice department task force are compartmented. They require SCI or TS-SBI clearance levels *and a need-to-know.*"

Michael's Langley training program in preparation for his assignment to the FBI's SIOC had included a presentation by the CIA's Office of Technical Services (OTS), the technical arm of the Clandestine Service. OTS had spent three hours going over previous OTS training he and other trainees had received, including reminding them not to be bamboozled or succumb to the vagueness of need-to-know, but rather to make every effort to remain fully informed at all times.

Michael glanced toward Greg. "Okay."

"*Okay?*" said Vinny. "That's all you have to say? Okay."

"The CIA operates under different laws and regulations than the FBI," Michael said.

"I know that," barked Vinny.

"With all due respect sir, I'm not the enemy," said Michael.

"We play by the rules here," said Vinny.

"The enemy doesn't carry signs saying 'here we are.'

They're clever bastards: resourceful, talented, and primed with hate, anger, and greed. Those bastards are exquisitely subtle— right in your face."

"Don't lecture me," said Vinny. "You didn't establish a need-to-know and therefore you couldn't have known Greg's task force was investigating money-laundering schemes. Without knowing, you couldn't establish any connection between the SIOC mission and the Justice Task Force. Without that connection there is no basis for approving a need-to-know and with it access to the SCI network."

Michael's eyes narrowed. "The intercepts on the screens occurred over a very short period of time. Time was of the essence."

"Being in a hurry doesn't buy you *a need-to-know*. You had no idea things were going to unfold with the speed they did. I'll ask again. How did you establish a need-to-know?"

Michael took his time sitting. "With all due respect sir, when you need to know, you find out."

"Cute. One last time, how did you establish a need-to-know on a compartmented task force?"

Michael glanced toward Greg. Greg stared at Vinny. Michael said, "I went to Justice and met Greg. He grants authorization for access to the task force."

"So Greg granted you the need-to-know," said Vinny.

*"I didn't say that,"* Michael corrected.

"Stop dancing around," said Vinny.

Michael peered at Vinny. Could he seriously be questioning my motives? "Follow the terror, you find terrorists, *sir*. Follow the money and you don't know where it will lead or what you'll find. From what I now understand, the FBI, Justice, Customs, the SEC and other agencies have been trying to uncover this particular money-laundering scheme for years. It's been on everybody's special back burner. I put it on a front burner, to apply international heat, *sir*."

"You made a command decision," Vinny said. "You never connected Justice's task force mission statement to the SIOC mission statement."

"The CIA works under different laws and regulations than the FBI," Michael repeated.

Vinny flushed, glaring at Michael. "That's a dangerous

divide, mister."

Michael stayed on message. "Cut off enemy money sources and they die."

"Let's sum up," Vinny grated. "You met with Greg and purposely gave him the impression you had the proper credentials, which you didn't. He granted you the need-to-know to compartmented information. With that need-to-know, you accessed the SCI network."

Michael got out of his chair and stood rigidly straight. "Greg approved a request that went through the *FBI*'s Multi-Agency Operations and Intelligence Office, *sir.*"

Vinny blanched and then shook his head in ridicule. "Obtaining access to a compartmented program and thus access to the SCI network without first obtaining specific and written approvals coupled to a need-to-know is a serious violation of security and you know it."

"*Sir*, are we here trying to assign blame or fight terror?" said Michael.

Vinny said, "I'm opening a formal inquiry to get to the bottom of all this."

"Your prerogative," Michael said.

"I'm not done," said Vinny. "The first phase of that inquiry will be your violation of SIOC administrative directives. Specifically my *two* requests that you use PENTTBOM tags."

"You're kidding," said Michael.

"A memo to that effect is in your personnel folder," said Vinny. "Prepare yourself for the second phase, a call from the FBI's inspector general." Vinny rocked slowly in his chair, looking intently for signs of wounds he knew he had inflicted. He didn't find them. He rolled his chair into his desk. "Now, what insights have you gained on the individuals listed in your spreadsheets?"

Michael took his time. "Even though Crosby, Valderrama, Palmer, Pepe, and Gonzalo reside in different parts of the world, it's almost certain they have been working closely for a long time. Crosby is careless. Valderrama is the opposite, has a temper. Valderrama's money-laundering scheme, whatever it is, may be in danger of being taken over by a rival. At the least, he's trying to protect it. Palmer is an advisor of some sort to Valderrama and maybe to Crosby. No idea what kind of advisor. It's no coincidence that Botero's arrival and the airport explosion occurred within minutes. Botero probably planted the bomb. Maybe it was Crosby, to cover Botero's arrival. Pepe is a wannabe or utility asset of some sort. Zip on Gonzalo except that everyone is looking for him... and Crosby's car. They're all involved up to their necks, no question."

Vince said, "What's Gonzalo's last name?"

"Don't know," said Michael.

Vinny grinned slightly as he threw Michael's words back in his face. "We have a need to know here, mister. *Find out!*"

Michael had thought he'd be escorted out of the building by now and riding the Metro home. He looked confused. "You want me to stay on the job?"

Vinny looked down at his desk. "Before your spreadsheets appeared, we had no idea why a bomb exploded at Miami International or what group might take credit."

"So you want me to stay in the leads center?" asked Michael.

Vinny looked up. "You've provided a cast of characters that seems to fit the crime. You're the only one I have with any insight into these scumbags. How they work together, what they're after. Nobody's going to jump ship until everyone responsible for this bombing is brought to justice."

"There's a problem," Michael said.

"What's the problem?"

"Congress decreed Echelon couldn't be used domestically."

"That's right. It's an international treaty. We'll live with it."

"On the other hand, the president and Congress have just enacted the Patriot Act."

"One hand gives while the other takes away," Vinny said.

"I've already logged a home and cell telephone conversation from Jose Valderrama. It's possible he'll be using other telephones. The Patriot Act authorizes roving wiretaps. We are going to need roving authority on all our wiretaps from here on."

"That's my job," said Vinny. "SIOC has the administrative procedures to handle it."

Now it was Michael's turn. "Can the procedures keep up? Can I count on getting approvals? Fast?"

Vinny looked at Michael and then nodded solemnly.

"Are you sure?" pressed Michael. "Those same administrative procedures delayed intercepts going from this

SIOC to the FBI's Miami Field Office for *twenty-four hours."*

Michael strolled back to the leads center. Before coming to SIOC he had seen Vinny on nationwide television a few times, standing at the side of the attorney general of the United States.

The press knew Vinny Campbell too. Michael had seen many stories describing the FBI's SIOC. They enhanced the image of the FBI at a time when enhancement was badly needed. The pressure was only going to get worse, intensifying every time Vinny turned the screw.

Michael knew no one in the city—certainly no one at SIOC other than those sitting near him. As part of his three weeks of training at Langley prior to being assigned to FBI headquarters, he had seen videos of Vinny describing the functions of the FBI's SIOC. Vinny's entire career had been at the FBI. He had been promoted recently into their highest ranks as a key advisor to the attorney general of the United States. How could he possibly counter an FBI deputy director, the very person responsible for the operation of the SIOC at FBI headquarters—the nexus of the nation's war on terror?

Michael called Langley from his console. He told them to expect a call from the inspector general of Justice.

Michael had never worked a case like the Miami airport bombing—or any case—while being confined to a chair. He wasn't in the field where he could talk to witnesses and suspects to get a feel for the truth and the lies of whatever was evolving. There wasn't a team of forensic scientists in the wings standing ready with laboratories of sophisticated analytical equipment to go over whatever evidence he might uncover.

His only view of the outside world came through the computer screen in front of him. There was nothing he could touch, no one to talk to, no body language or nuances to ponder. He was constrained to manipulating zeros and ones. The deputy director of the FBI, the head of the FBI's SIOC, had it in for him. He was alone. Vulnerable.

Michael fell back on the only thing he could think of, something his father had told him while he was in the third or fourth grade. Son, hard work will always be recognized. Rewards will follow.

*Dad, are you sure?*

Coming back from his meeting with Greg McNulty in the cafeteria at Justice, Michael had connected two dots, the Justice task force investigation of money laundering and the SIOC priority on identifying terrorist money-laundering schemes. He needed to know more about money laundering. He had taken a continuing education course a year or two ago that had spent less than an hour on money laundering. That night he searched his files at home and found his notes. He started to read.

> Conventional money laundering benefits from the rule-of-five. Money is wired from any country to a world financial center like England, then to France, and then onto at least three nations that do not have the financial infrastructure or are reluctant to disclose financial transactions. To trace such money, each sovereign country must give its approval in turn for each specific transaction to be divulged. Such a money trail is impossible to follow. Money simply disappears.
>
> Trade fraud is the oldest form of money laundering and a massive international problem. Worldwide trade barriers have been lowered over the years, resulting in trade fraud intensifying. Financial institutions around the world are being pressured to be more accountable but changes are slow to be implemented.
>
> Trade fraud overvalues imported merchandise. For example, a ten-dollar bottle of wine can be falsely valued at a hundred dollars. When the invoice is paid, a hundred illegal dollars goes out of a country. Ten dollars of assets are received—the bottle of wine.
>
> Trade fraud works with exports as well. Illegal cash buys a thirty thousand dollar car. The car is exported with an invoice value of five thousand dollars. When the car arrives, the five thousand dollar invoice is paid. A thirty thousand dollar asset, the car, is received. Twenty five

thousand dollars have been laundered. Double billing trades double the amount of funds laundered.

A trade can be fabricated when nothing is exchanged, yet money is laundered.

Trade fraud is so prevalent with Colombia it has been dubbed the Peso Exchange. Colombia estimates five billion dollars a year in ill-gotten U.S. currency is turned into Colombian pesos through the purchase and illegal import of American products, often through neighboring third countries.

American exporters consistently ship cigarettes, alcohol, appliances, electronics and auto parts from American manufacturers to Colombia. American manufacturers receive the orders in the form of wire transfers, checks or cash from random third parties with no connection to the transaction. The merchandise is sold illegally throughout Colombia and neighboring countries. Colombia views such illegal transactions as much our problem as theirs.

Customs is heading a task force called Operation Green Quest. It's investigating counterfeiting, fraudulent import and export schemes, drug trafficking, cash smuggling, and credit card fraud.

The United States froze Al Qaeda accounts in 1998. Al Qaeda had been obtaining tens of millions of dollars by working with the Revolutionary United Front in Koidu, Sierra Leone located on the west coast of Africa.

RUF rebels work in the rich alluvial diamond fields. Al Qaeda operatives buy the diamonds at below-market prices. Aided by the governments of Liberia to its south and Burkina Faso, the land-locked nation to its east, Al Qaeda operatives transport the diamonds from Sierra Leone across the Liberian border to the capital city Monrovia and a safe house protected by Liberia.

The diamonds are exchanged for briefcases of cash brought by diamond dealers who fly several times a month from Belgium to Monrovia.

A White House task force composed of the CIA, FBI and Treasury is examining a global network of paperless money exchanges called 'hawala.' Hawalas are legitimate money exchanges. They are used in countries such as Somalia, Yemen, and Afghanistan where banks and financial institutions are scarce. Hawala exchanges may be funneling tens of millions of dollars to finance terrorist activities.

Hawala dealers follow immigrants worldwide, exchanging money without leaving paper or electronic trails. Several hawala dealers are in the Washington, D.C. Metropolitan area and other major cities in the U.S. and around the world.

A hawala dealer is at both ends of the money exchange and may operate exchanges as a sideline to a tobacco or barber shop. Each dealer charges five to fifteen percent of the value of the exchange.

A customer gives the hawala dealer $100 cash to send his family. The dealer calls his counterpart dealer in a foreign country and, using a password, tells him to give $100 to the customer's family. Both dealers record the transaction. No money is exchanged. They assume $100 will come the other way sometime in the future. Gemstones or other goods are sent to rebalance the books.

In the United States hawalas are required to register with the Treasury Department and report suspicious money transactions.

Money orders have long been used to launder money abroad. Charitable organizations are sources of laundered funds.

Michael reached for the phone.

# Chapter 31

## Miami, Florida
## Saturday 1500 ET

Taro Okada drove behind the federal building and found a parking spot near the dumpster in the back corner of the lot. He seesawed the ends of his tie until they were even before getting out of his car. Leaning on the side of the car, he held his head back so as not to sear his eyebrow as the flaring match surrounded the end of the cigar butt protruding from his lips. He sent a series of small gray clouds drifting over the smelly dumpster before starting toward the rear entrance. With the cigar firmly anchored between his teeth, he dug his badge out of his jacket. He clipped it on the drooping pocket of his wash-and-wear shirt.

Taro tossed the cigar before entering the building. He welcomed the building's conditioned air as he threaded his way through the corridors to the front lobby. "Okada to see Dickie," Taro told the man sitting behind the reception desk.

The receptionist slid the guest book in front of Taro, scanned his computer, and picked up the telephone. A minute later he looked up. "Room 227. Stairs on the left, elevators on the right." He handed Taro an FBI visitor's badge. "Display it at all times," the receptionist told him.

"Yeah," replied Taro. He lumbered up the stairs, found room 227, and entered the outer office of Alan Dickie. "Taro Okada," he told Sally.

"Good afternoon, Mr. Okada," said Sally. "Mr. Dickie is on his way. I expect him back any moment. Please have a seat. Is there anything I can get you?"

"That's okay," said Taro. "He's expecting me. Two o'clock, right?"

"Oh yes. You're on his calendar. He called. Said he might be a few minutes late."

Alan Dickie arrived a half hour late. "This is Mr. Okada," said Sally as Alan crossed the outer office.

Alan acknowledged Taro. "Mr. Okada." He turned to Sally, "Any messages?"

"No sir, no messages since you went to lunch."

"I'll be right with you, Mr. Okada," said Alan. "Please give me just a moment more." Alan went into his office, reached back and swung the door closed.

Before the door reached its latch, it flew back open and bounced off the wall. Alan turned. Taro stood in the doorway. Taro mocked Alan's tone. "I don't have 'just a moment more.'"

Alan stepped backward. "Mr. Okada."

"That's right. Taro Okada, chief of Miami-Dade detectives. We had a two o'clock appointment. Remember?"

"You're here for?"

"I'm here to talk about the bombing at the Miami airport. You have heard about the Miami airport bombing haven't you? Two preschoolers slaughtered."

"The FBI is aware, Mr. Okada. Yes." Alan moved behind his desk.

Taro stood with his toes under the front of his desk. "What have you got to tell the Miami-Dade PD about the bombing, Mr. Dickie?"

"We're investigating, Mr. Okada."

"You're investigating? You're *investigating*. Isn't that nice."

"What do you want, Mr. Okada?"

"For starters, tell me about Botero."

"Botero?"

Taro stood erect. He took a slow deep breath. Suddenly he reached across the desk, grabbed Alan by the lapels, and lifted him out of his chair. "Listen, you son-of-a-bitch, two little sisters are dead, their brother is barely hanging on, twenty-four others are in Miami hospitals, thousands of passengers were delayed, millions of dollars have been lost."

Taro dropped Alan into his chair, stretched his full length, and spit his words into Alan's face. "Miami-Dade County is my county. Miami-Dade county people are my people. Every wart on every one of them. No one, and I mean *no one*, hurts any of them, if I can help it."

Taro turned his back on Alan. He walked to the middle of his office. In a slow and deliberate voice, still not facing Alan, he growled, "Interpol told you Botero's flight number and time of arrival. Customs closed the docking terminals, trying to help you. Nearly thirty planes belonging to seven different airlines and five different countries paid your price."

Taro turned, his black eyes raking Alan. "Customs violated the law at your request. Customs gave you a description of Botero before they released him. Customs told you exactly when Botero was being released. You and at least one other FBI Agent were there when Botero, an FBI ten-most-wanted mind you, walked through those gray release doors. Botero killed two little girls and blows up an airline terminal on his way to freedom. Freedom to roam the streets of my Miami-Dade County."

Taro walked slowly back to Alan's desk. "Now you tell me every fucking thing you know, or so help me, I'll make it my career to see that you are the shortest-reigning head of the MFO in this nation's history."

# Chapter 32

## Bayside, Florida
## Saturday 1930 ET

Carolyn stood in the kitchen doorway. She was listening to Gil Bauer, Bert Griffin, and Jack Taylor, who were sitting at Janet's dining room table. They were arguing about a controversial call giving the Redskins a 13 to 10 win over Dallas.

Janet walked up behind Carolyn. "Let's go outside." She led Carolyn across the dining room, through the living room, and out the sliding doors into the backyard. Gil, Bert and Jack didn't notice. The two women headed toward the pool.

"Male bonding seems to revolve around sports," said Carolyn.

Janet walked head-down through the surrealistic glow cast by the underwater pool lights, leading Carolyn to the far end of the pool, the deep end. They settled into overstuffed chaise lounges. "I thought we could use a break before dessert."

"Your father looks great," said Carolyn.

"Now he does." Janet put her drink on the table between them and embraced her knees.

Carolyn lowered her backrest, stretched full-length, and put her head on interlocked palms. "This is nice."

"It's a long story," said Janet.

"What's a long story?"

Janet wiggled deeper into her cushion as if to anchor herself. "Remember, just before I divorced Scott, when I visited you in Arlington?"

"Of course." Carolyn rolled her head on her palms to look at Janet.

"Scott was a lot of fun. We had dozens of friends. We went everywhere. Cruises, San Francisco, New York, Las Vegas, Key West... you name it, we did it." Janet retrieved her glass. "It was a ball. Well, just before the divorce Scott hammered me with a zinger. My father had given him $130,000. *Cash!*" Janet put her glass to her lips but lowered it without drinking. "Can you imagine? $130,000. *In cash.*" Janet looked at Carolyn. "I knew our credit cards were maxed out. But so what? Isn't everyone in credit card debt? I always thought so. But, oh no, I find out Scott has been gambling our money away. He's an inveterate gambler, Carolyn. I didn't know."

"Janet, I'm so sorry."

"I couldn't tell you. I was so ashamed. Bert knew Scott was a gambler. *My own father* knew and he didn't tell me."

"Did you talk to your father about it?"

"Scott knew how badly he had hurt me when he told me about the $130,000." Janet measured each word. "Scott told Bert that his bookie would have him killed if he didn't pay his gambling debt. An example would have to be made with that kind of money."

Janet hugged her knees, this time tighter and then lowered her forehead onto them. "I was devastated, worried sick for Scott's life, and crying my eyes out about my father. Bert and I talked. That was when I started one of my infamous weight-gaining sprees. I looked like a blimp when I saw you then."

"Janet, you're too hard on yourself."

"That's not all." Janet lifted her head. "Bert's bank was about to go belly up."

"The $130,000 wasn't bank money, was it?" asked Carolyn.

"Bert swears not. *Thank God!* I don't think I could have survived if my shit-for-brains husband caused Bert's life's work to go down the toilet. No, Bert says it was a streak of bad loans that caused the problems at the bank. My poor father, his bank is in serious trouble, he loses $130,000 in cash, and his only child turns into an emotional wreck."

Carolyn sat up and faced Janet. "Oh Janet, how terrible."

"You remember the guy I took up with after Scott?"

"You broke up with him. I remember."

Janet put her head back on her knees, her drink still clenched tightly in her hand. "Would you believe it? Another gambler! I know I didn't tell you that. Bert and I are hanging on the ropes. and I link up with another loser. Turns out he's into craps, 21, poker. You name it. He'd bet on two leaves falling from a tree. If it weren't for Scott, I wouldn't have noticed so soon. I was dumbfounded, up sixty pounds and packing it away at breakneck speed." Through nervous laughter, Janet stammered, "I could hardly walk. My thighs were challenging each other to see which would be rubbed raw first. How many of those guys are out there anyway?"

Carolyn smiled. "Been there, done that, girl."

Janet sniffled and then wiped her cheeks dry with the back of her hands. "You know that loser tries the same thing. Tells me he owes a lot of money. Can I lend it to him? No problem this time. 'Blow it out your ass,' I tell him. Finally, I'm into self-preservation. Who am I? What's life all about? That sort of thing. Only now I'm a twenty-seven-year-old blimp."

Janet took several shallow breaths, "Anyway, the first thing I do is become Ms. Janet Griffin again. I think I lost ten pounds just doing that."

"You look absolutely great," said Carolyn.

The automatic timer turned on the pool filter system. The sudden sound of the whirring motor startled them. They stood and began drifting back toward the house.

"Bert told me to get off my fat ass. That's exactly what he said: 'Get off your fat ass and dust off your realtor's license.'"

"That's not what I remember," said Carolyn. "You told me Bert imitated Audrey Hepburn in *My Fair Lady* as she stood pressed against the race-track rail pleading with her mount, 'Move yer bloomin' arse.'"

"Yeah, I guess he did."

"Within months you're back in the money. I was so jealous, sitting back in Washington in my small cubbyhole, surrounded by ancient furniture, metal file cabinets, and paper covering every horizontal square inch. Including most of the floor, I might add. You. You buy this beautiful house."

Janet smiled weakly. "Remember..." She shook her index finger at Carolyn. "Jealousy's a sin. But yeah, Bayside Realty took off."

"Wasn't Pepe supposed to be here tonight?" Carolyn asked.

"I'm not sorry he's not here. He tried to jump my bones last night. Can you believe that?"

"Pepe? I didn't know you two were a thing."

"God no," said Janet. "He's a sad case, one pain in the ass to just about everyone. He offered to drive Nicole and me to Key Largo. I felt sorry for him. I thought, why not? That was a mistake. But since we're on the subject, I've been dying to ask. Are you interested in Jack Taylor?"

"He's my boss," said Carolyn. "Actually, he's my boss's boss."

"I see the way you've been looking at him."

"Oh for God's sake, Janet. It's business. Strictly business. I hardly know the man. Knock it off. No, I don't have the hots for Jack Taylor. If this is your way of bringing up Greg..."

"Just checking." Janet grinned broadly. "Screw Greg."

Carolyn nodded.

"I'm happy to say I'm still losing weight," Janet said.

"Pepe noticed last night," Carolyn needled.

Janet jumped at Carolyn, pretending to push her in the pool. Carolyn recoiled, laughing.

# Chapter 33

### Miami, Florida
### Sunday 0800 ET

Sally, sitting behind her desk, looked up at Holt. "You should have been here."

"God, I wish I had been," Holt said, not trying to hide his pleasure.

"I almost called security. But Mr. Okada is a Miami-Dade detective, right?"

"He just kicked the door open?"

"It almost hit Mr. Dickie."

The corridor door opened. Taro came in, nodded to Sally, and then turned to Holt. "Let's go."

The two men entered Alan's office.

"Where's Dickie?" Taro asked.

"With your bosses," said Holt. "They're powwowing with the Miami mayor, a few councilmen, two state representatives, and three or four citizen organizations, trying to explain exactly what's being done to find the airport bomber and ensure the future safety of Miami-Dade county citizens and tourists."

"Better them than us," Taro said.

"You got that right."

Taro sat in one of the cracked-leather chairs. Holt sat on the couch opposite him.

"What ya got?" Taro asked.

Holt began. "Luis Botero. He's the one that set off the bomb in the airport. He's an enforcer for Jose Valderrama. Jose lives in Acapulco. Botero lives in Colombia. Jose heads a syndicate that's laundering money. We're not sure where he's getting the money. We know it's a huge operation. Back to Botero. We're not sure why he came to Miami."

Taro evened the ends of his tie. "Hard info?"

"There's a guy in Washington, Michael Stone, who's started sending us good info. He's using Echelon."

"Echelon? What's that?" said Taro.

"It's a massive complex of eavesdropping systems. They suck up virtually all voice, data, and video transmissions worldwide."

"Where are these systems?"

"Everywhere, here and abroad. On farms, hillsides, mountaintops, satellites, planes, ships, and submarines. One of Echelon's largest antenna farms is in North Yorkshire, England."

Taro looked skeptical. "Who manages the information these systems 'suck up' as you say?"

"The National Security Agency, at Fort Meade, Maryland."

"Let's get back to earth," Taro said. "What's Echelon doing for us?"

"Good question. Monitoring traffic in Acapulco and Bogotá."

Taro tinkered with his visitor's badge. "Why Bogotá?"

"There's heavy communication traffic between Bogotá and Jose's Acapulco compound during the last few days. Most is encrypted."

Taro watched enviously as Holt put his left ankle on his right knee without thinking about it.

"Jose's operation seems to have become vulnerable some way," said Holt. "We don't know why or how. All we know is that he's laundering hoards of cash."

"Using brute force, how long to decode?" Taro began fingering the two cigars protruding from his shirt pocket.

"Years," said Holt. "Miracles might happen. The basement of Fort Meade is testing new code-busting techniques. Weird stuff. Molecular electronics or something. In reality, it may be easier to cure all types of cancer than to decode encryption these days."

Using hand signals, Holt encouraged Taro to ask more questions. Taro shrugged him off. "We're using Carnivore too, another eavesdropping tool. Carnivore equipment sits at Internet service provider gateways intercepting targeted e-mail traffic. Carnivore intercepts can present encryption problems too. We're hopeful though."

*"Why?" asked Taro.*

"Why what?"

"Why hopeful? You said encryption takes years to decode."

"Depends how you skin the encryption cat. Key loggers in Crosby and Valderrama's computers might just do the trick."

"Keep it simple," said Taro.

"The code name for key loggers is Magic Lantern. Magic Lantern software installs keystroke loggers in targeted computers."

Taro's eyes narrowed. "Go slow."

"Keystroke logger software monitors encryption programs. It records the keystrokes used to open the encryption program in order to gain access to the encryption key. With this encryption key, you can decrypt whatever has been encrypted."

"Okay, how do we get your hands on keystroke loggers?"

"They're not commercially available. Not yet anywise. Magic Lantern is like a virus. The computer owner never knows key logger software is in the computer or when it transmits the keystrokes back."

Taro took one of the cigars from his shirt pocket. "That's legal? Putting things on people's computers?"

"There are strict criteria to be met before a request can even be considered. The Patriot Act among others requires prior authorization from a state attorney general or from the U.S. Attorney General and then judiciary authorization."

Taro shook his head in wonderment. "Sounds like magic to me. What about the content of the conversations you're intercepting with Echelon, Magic Lantern and—what was the other one?"

"Carnivore." Holt sat back, uncrossing his legs. "What we get is limited. Echelon can't be used in the U.S. Federal laws and regulations restrict the domestic use of the Patriot Act, Magic Lantern and Carnivore. Privacy rights are serious counterweights."

Taro raised the cigar to his ear and rolled it between his fingers. The crinkling sound of cellophane seemed to focus him. "Okay, we've used your tool box to pry open messages. What'd you learn?"

"A few names—Botero, Gonzalo, Pepe, Jose Valderrama, Royce Palmer, and a new one, Janet Griffin. We're trying to ID Pepe locally."

"There are thousands with the name Pepe in Florida."

"Sure," said Holt. "But thousands is a finite number. Computers handle finite numbers."

"Anything else?"

"Doug Crosby is Jose Valderrama's son. The two are looking for Gonzalo and Doug's car. We don't know why. That's about it from this side."

Taro put the cigar back in his shirt pocket and sat erect. "We've got a few pictures of Botero. Taken by Customs." Taro handed an envelope to Holt. "Also partial prints, again courtesy of Customs."

"I'll fax the prints to our print ID center," Holt said.

"The car rental companies at the airport can account for their vehicles. No reports of violence or stolen vehicles anywhere near the airport within two hours either side of the bombing. Botero may have taken a cab, had a car planted, or someone waiting. We're still checking the cab trips."

"Oh yeah," Holt interjected. "We're checking the sources of the explosives."

# Chapter 34

## Bayside, Florida
## Sunday 2030 ET

Carolyn Hughes put a scoop of vanilla ice cream on the final square of fudge and returned the ice cream container to the refrigerator. Janet poured her father's cappuccino.

"I don't know how Bert handles the caffeine so late in the day," Carolyn commented idly.

"Addiction, pure and simple," Janet said.

"Let's go in and sit down," said Carolyn. "I can't wait another minute for this dessert."

Nicole smiled as Janet moved Freddie to the side and put a bowl of fudge a la mode in front of her.

Janet reminded Nicole this was grown-up time. "Recuerda, este es tiempo para los adultos."

"So you're into system engineering?" Gil asked Jack as Janet sat. "Working on the next generation of the Internet, wireless, optical middleware… that sort of thing?"

"It's an exciting time," said Jack.

Gil smiled, happy to find someone familiar with his craft. "We're working on communicating faster with seamless middleware and embedded diagnostics. But my father should be in on this conversation."

"Absolutely," said Jack.

Nicole dropped her spoon.

Gil replied, "He's playing a charity golf tournament tomorrow."

Nicole took another spoon from her mother and began chasing the ball of ice cream around the bowl with it.

Gil asked, "Then why don't you and Carolyn join Janet, Nicole and me tomorrow on an Everglades tour. You can meet my father the next day, when he's back from the golf tournament."

"Great idea," Jack said.

"Wish I could go," said Bert. "Tomorrow's a busy day for me."

The ball of ice cream flew out of Nicole's bowl and landed on Freddie. While cleaning up, Janet said, "I meant to tell you guys. Pepe told me Crosby is interested in Bauer. He wants to provide them with venture capital."

Jack looked to Gil. "Is that right?"

"Doug and my dad have talked. That's all I can say."

In the car on their way back to Carp's Landing, Jack turned to Carolyn, "What do you think about this Doug Crosby?"

"Not sure. But look, I'm going to skip the Everglades trip tomorrow to see what I can find out about him. Okay?"

"I'll stay with Gil," said Jack.

"I'll have to tell Crosby we're interested in Bauer," Carolyn said, looking for approval.

"Might as well get right to the point. Have you met him?"

"No. I was supposed to go to the Key Largo party Janet mentioned but I cancelled when I got Bauer's Q2 Report."

"Any idea yet who gave you the report?"

"I don't know," Carolyn said. "I'd guess Gil Bauer."

# Chapter 35

### Vienna, VA
### Sunday 2235 ET

Linda Ann and Kathleen were upstairs sound asleep for the night. Michael and Sarah were cooking breakfast together. Sarah was in charge of the omelets; Michael the coffee and English muffins. Watching Sarah and having breakfast this way reminded him of their first apartment after returning from their honeymoon. They shared the cooking often then, before children. Those mornings were great. This morning meal late at night was just as great.

Michael entered the near-empty Metro car and took a vacant window seat. Several stops later a tall man wearing tattered jeans and a white muscle shirt sagging from bony shoulders came into the car. The man looked the passenger car over before sitting next to Michael. A woman headed for the two empty side-riding seats in front of them. The tall man stretched his legs and reclined until his head rested on the seatback he and Michael shared. His legs blocked the woman's access to the side-riding seats. She looked at his tattered jeans punctuated by bare feet in filthy beach sandals. The man looked up at her and smiled. The woman turned and headed down the aisle. The man rolled his head toward Michael. "How's it going, man?"

Michael snuck a look at the man. He didn't want to strike up a conversation. The man's smell was overpowering.

The man mumbled, "I wouldn't talk to me either," rolled his head forward and closed his eyes.

Michael looked out the window. The train was beginning to match the speed of the cars on Route 66. Michael didn't see the man sitting next to him roll his head toward him again. In a barely audible voice the man said, "You're family."

Every sense in Michael's body jumped to attention. It took all the discipline he could muster to keep looking out the window at the cars on Route 66.

"One of your In-Q-Tel teams sent you that Echelon intercept," the voice said.

The Metro slowed going into the Virginia Square station.

The man opened his eyes, made a show of getting up, and moseyed to the doors.

Michael didn't recognize him standing there at the doors. The doors opened. The sagging muscle shirt and tattered jeans exited the car. Michael watched him clomp his way along the concrete platform. He forced himself not to smile. He knew this man. He was family.

Michael was assigned a new terminal located on the side of the leads center, closer to the investigators' room. It was one of four stations that shared a common table.

The FBI analyst Michael relieved said, "Director Ward has mustered an army down there in Miami. That's what the press says anyway. Couldn't tell it sitting here. What do you think about Vinny's edict to concentrate on intelligence gathering?"

Michael grinned.

# Chapter 36

## Bayside, Florida
## Monday 0600 ET

Carolyn Hughes woke early and dressed in her running clothes. It was way too early to call Greg. She left her room and went into the Carp's Landing bar. A young man was beginning to unfold large tablecloths. They would cover the bar to convert it into a breakfast-buffet table. She asked him for a glass of orange juice.

"No problem," the man said. He dropped the tablecloths on the bar and disappeared into the kitchen. He soon reappeared with a tumbler of orange juice.

Carolyn took the glass and meandered around the area as she drank. When she finished she went out onto Bell Boulevard and looked both ways. She decided to jog east toward the ocean.

At seven, Carolyn stepped from her shower, wrapped a towel around her hair, and a second one around herself. Sitting on the side of the bed, she dialed Greg's number. She knew he was an early bird. His secretary didn't arrive until seven-thirty. Once in a while they had used these minutes to play. Just before the third ring she heard, "This is Greg."

She copied his monotone. "This is Carolyn."

"Where are you?" said Greg. "It's good to hear your voice."

She loathed the insincerity she recognized in his voice. "In Florida. Need a favor."

"What are you doing in Florida?"

*Forget it dick.* "Information on Crosby Limited?" Carolyn was pleased with the detachment she was feeling. "All you have. That's C, R, O, S, B, Y."

"What're you up to?" Greg asked.

"Crosby Limited. In Florida."

"Will you be in town anytime soon?"

"Crosby Limited. Who's in charge? Sources of capital? That sort of thing."

"I'd love to see you again, Carolyn."

"Will you bring the children?" Carolyn cursed herself for venting.

"That's not fair and you know it."

"Crosby. Yes or no?"

"We can't research a firm and provide information to just anyone," Greg said smugly.

"It's a simple question, Greg. Yes or no."

She was about to hang up when Greg said, "Your timing may be good. I have a few SEC guys coming in on the hour. I'll see what they can do. How can I reach you?" Carolyn reminded Greg of her cell number, hung up and then dialed Janet.

Janet rolled onto her back and stretched to reach the telephone on the end table. "Hello."

"Sorry it's so early."

"Carolyn?" said Janet.

"Is it okay to talk?"

"What'd ya mean?"

"Is someone with you?" Carolyn asked.

"I wish."

"I want to meet Doug Crosby. What do you think if I just call him, say I'm your friend, and invite myself to his home?"

"Just like that?" said Janet.

"Yup."

"Oh, go ahead," said Janet.

"Got his address and telephone number?"

"Oh God Carolyn, you're going to make me get up. Aren't you? Hold on." Carolyn could hear Janet groan as she rose. A minute later Janet gave Carolyn the telephone number, address, and directions on how to locate his home in Key Largo.

"Thanks, gotta go." Carolyn recorded the number Janet had given her onto her cell phone. She stood and headed back to the bathroom. The towel wrapped around her fell to the floor.

Carolyn headed west to pick up Florida's Turnpike, marveling that the traffic wasn't anything like Northern Virginia's. A half hour later she picked up her cell phone and speed-dialed Doug. The phone on the other end rang twice.

"Hello."

"Mr. Crosby, my name is Carolyn Hughes."

"Yes?"

"I'd like to stop by and talk to you for a few minutes." Carolyn paused. "Is that possible?"

"Do I know you?"

"We have a mutual friend—Janet Griffin."

"So?"

"You're the man to see about venture capital. Right?"

"I only do large, mature deals."

"I'm talking about Bauer Industries."

"Where are you?"

"Driving south on Florida's Turnpike, approaching Florida City."

"You know how to get here?" Doug asked.

"Janet told me, Mr. Crosby." Carolyn accelerated to get by an eighteen-wheeler so she could hear better. "I can be there in a half hour." Doug didn't reply. "If that's okay." The line remained quiet. "Janet and I are close friends."

"How close?"

"We went to college together. I had dinner with Janet and Bert last night. Gil Bauer was there, too."

"Who else was at this dinner?" asked Doug.

"Janet's daughter Nicole, Jack Taylor. Anyway, your name came up. I'm interested in talking to you."

"Who's Jack Taylor?"

"May we discuss that when we meet?" said Carolyn.

"This morning?"

"Around ten?"

# Chapter 37

### Miami, Florida
### Monday 0820 ET

The mayor's point man called Taro twice a day, early in the morning and late in the evening. Taro was expecting his morning call at any moment. Waiting, he focused his attention on a fax from Holt. The Coast Guard had flown over coastal waters to evaluate the effects of Hurricane Fabian. There was minor damage between Savannah and Boca Raton, with one craft adrift in the ocean. The owner of the craft had claimed it; nothing there. There was considerable damage north. The inland areas of the Carolinas were hit hard. No crafts south of Boca or on either side of the Keys were reported missing. There was some beach erosion. The Keys got off light this time. Taro sat back wondering why Holt had sent him this report. The next line told him.

A red car had been found in the surf off Key Largo.

# Chapter 38

### Key Largo, Florida
### Monday 0830 ET

Doug Crosby put the telephone down and walked past Botero and Pepe to the bay window. He looked past the lanai pool, lawn and guesthouse to Gonzalo's yacht docked just beyond. "Pepe, do you know Jack Taylor?"

"Never heard of him."

"Well he, Gil Bauer, Janet, and Carolyn Hughes had dinner at Janet's house last night," said Doug. "So where were you?"

"I was supposed to be there, but I didn't have my car."

"What does that mean?" asked Doug

Pepe shot a glance at Botero. "Botero took it," said Pepe. "Said he needed it until he'd found the disk."

"That's bullshit!" roared Botero. "You no call a cab, man?"

Doug ignored the exchange. "Carolyn Hughes will be knocking at my door in a few minutes. Says she wants to talk about a venture capital deal with Bauer." Pepe and Botero said nothing. Doug spoke to Botero. "When she arrives, you go into the bedroom. Leave the door ajar. You'll be able to listen from there."

Botero walked to the bedroom door, looking in. "No way out, man," said Botero. "The kitchen door to the garage."

"The kitchen then." Doug turned to Pepe. "You stay with me."

Carolyn sat in the armchair in Doug's living room. Doug sat opposite her on the couch, his legs stretched and crossed at the ankles. Pepe sat in a chair near the sliding doors.

Doug asked, "Well, Ms. Hughes, what's this about a venture capital deal?"

"I work for Taylor Associates in Arlington, Virginia. It's an engineering firm."

"And this Jack Taylor you mentioned?"

"He's the owner. I work for the CFO."

Doug's head bobbed subtly. "Chief Financial Officer. So you're visiting Florida?"

"My second trip this week. We saw an article in *Forbes*—"

Pepe jumped in. "We saw it too."

Doug turned toward Pepe, the intensity of his irritation canceling the need for a verbal reprimand.

Carolyn continued, "I came the first time to meet Mr. Charles Bauer."

Doug sat up. "You meet him?"

Carolyn nodded. "Yes. He's playing a charity golf tournament today. I hope to meet with him again tomorrow."

"Why? For what purpose?" Doug asked.

"Taylor Associates is considering a merger with Bauer Industries," Carolyn said. "As I understand it, you're considering providing venture capital as mezzanine financing to assist Bauer. Is that right?"

Doug said, "I told you we aren't early-stage investors. We don't deal in crapshoots or educated guessing games."

"Bauer's no crap shoot," Carolyn said.

Pepe glowered. "I met you at Janet's. You didn't mention you were coming here. Why did you?"

"I'm trying to evaluate alternatives," Carolyn said.

"Like what?" Pepe demanded.

"Pepe, let me handle this."

"It's a fair question," said Carolyn. "One alternative is Mr. Crosby provides venture capital and Taylor Associates goes home. Another, Taylor Associates invests and Mr. Crosby finds other venues for his capital. A third, there is no IPO or merger and we both go home. A fourth is Bauer and Taylor Associates merge. A fifth… Oh, I think you get the idea."

Doug had had enough. "What triggered this visit, Ms. Hughes?"

"Venture capital funds are used when the money needed cannot be borrowed from banks. Hearing that Bauer was considering venture capital raised a red flag. I'm under the impression they're going great guns."

"I'll tell you why," said Pepe. "Bert Griffin is a friend of mine. I suggested he meet Doug here, he's another friend of mine."

Carolyn studied Pepe. "Why would Bert Griffin, a bank owner, want to do that?"

"I told you, he's a friend."

"Interesting," said Carolyn. She turned to Doug. "Can you tell me the amount of money you're considering investing?"

"Absolutely not," said Doug. He sat bolt upright. "You know better than to ask that. Can you speak for Mr. Taylor?"

"I'm authorized to discuss, within reason, our interests in Bauer Industries and convey all responses. That's about all we can hope for today."

"Exactly how long have you worked for Taylor Associates, Ms. Hughes?"

"Two days."

"Two days: Where's Mr. Taylor?"

Carolyn looked at her watch. "About now he's leaving Bayside for lunch at the Marco Island Marriott."

The doorbell rang insistently. Pepe sprung to his feet. "I'll get it."

Doug said, "Ms. Hughes, how'd you learn about Crosby Limited?"

"May I have a glass of water?" said Carolyn.

Botero retreated to the garage, leaving the door slightly ajar. He continued listening.

Pepe opened the front door. He gasped.

"Pepe," said Taro. "Fancy meeting you here."

Pepe stepped out onto the porch, closing the door behind him. "You're here to see Doug Crosby, right?"

"So tell me," Taro said to his snitch. "What's going on between you and Doug Crosby?"

"No big deal," said Pepe, his forehead beginning to sweat. "We do deals now and then. Nothing much. Small stuff."

"Well let's see what Doug has to say." Taro reached past Pepe, opened the door and went in. Pepe followed.

"Doug this is Detective... " Pepe stuttered, confused. He turned to Taro. "I can't think of your name."

"Okada," Taro told Doug. "Taro Okada, Miami-Dade PD. You're Doug Crosby?"

Doug remained seated. "What can I do for you?"

"And the lady is...?" asked Taro.

"Carolyn Hughes." She started to get up. "Shall I leave while you talk with Mr. Crosby? I can wait outside if you want."

"Not for my sake," said Taro. "In fact, I'd like you to stay." Taro turned to Doug. "I've news for you, Mr. Crosby. We've found your car. A red Mercedes convertible, right?"

Pepe's eyes shone. "Where'd you find it?"

"The Coast Guard found it a few blocks from here."

"What?"

"Anything strange about finding it so close, Pepe?"

"I guess not."

"At low tide it's just barely under the water," said Taro. "Probably traveling too fast and into the drink it went. The winds may have driven the car further from the roadway than might be expected. Eventually, its wheels hit the bottom." Taro looked at Doug. "Is that about when you missed the Mercedes? During Hurricane Fabian?"

"Anybody hurt?" asked Doug.

Taro walked to the sliding doors and looked out. "You mean was anybody in the car?"

"Of course," said Doug.

"The driver's door was open. If the driver got to shore he's one lucky son-of-a-bitch, that's for sure. Why didn't you report the car missing?"

"A buddy of mine borrowed it." Doug got up and walked to the wet bar, desperately trying to think of a name to give Taro. "Jose Guzman" Doug blurted out. "Anybody for a drink?"

"Have you heard from this Jose Guzman?" asked Taro.

"No, but that's not unusual. These are the Keys, you know. People come and go around here all the time. Strange things are always happening." Doug put ice in his glass and poured himself a Scotch. He waved his glass at Taro and Pepe. "Anybody?"

"Your car is submerged with no one in it. You didn't report it missing. The driver might have drowned. If he didn't, he doesn't tell you about the accident, let alone tell you where your car is. That's not unusual?"

Feigning disinterest poorly, Doug turned away and wiped the counter behind the bar. "Not really." He tossed back his drink, poured another, and headed back to his chair.

"There are no active missing persons reported on the Keys," said Taro.

"Where can I pick up my car?" Doug asked.

"It's impounded," said Taro. "Active investigation."

Botero eased the door from the kitchen to the garage closed. He made his way to the BMW on the side of the house. Carolyn and Taro's cars blocked his way. He drove on the grass around them, headed north on Route 1, and dialed his cell. When the receiver at the other end was picked up, Botero said, *"Meet me at the heliport. I'll need three men in fifteen minutes."* He hung up without waiting for confirmation that he had been understood.

"For Christ sake, it's my car," said Doug.

"And you didn't report it missing," said Taro. "Maybe, we can help you find out who stole it."

"I didn't say it was stolen."

"Beautiful place you have here," said Taro, his voice dismissing Doug's protests. "Those your boats?"

Doug headed back behind the bar. "They're mine."

Botero redialed, this time an international number.

Jose Valderrama grunted, "Yeah."

*"Gonzalo's alive."* Botero hung up.

Taro turned to Carolyn. "It's Carolyn. Right?"

"Carolyn Hughes."

"You work for…?"

"Taylor Associates."

"Never heard of them," said Taro.

"We're based in Virginia."

"Why are you in Key Largo?"

"We're looking at a company named Bauer Industries."

"We?" Taro asked.

"My boss, Jack Taylor and I," said Carolyn. "I was just telling Mr. Crosby before you arrived that Mr. Taylor and Mr. Bauer are on their way to Marco Island. They're having lunch at the Marriott."

"What d'ya mean you're looking at Bauer Industries?" asked Taro.

"We're considering a merger," Carolyn said. "Nothing definitive."

"Where are you staying while in Florida, Ms. Hughes?"

"At the Carp's Landing Hotel in Bayside."

"And what brings you to Crosby's home?" asked Taro.

"It's a long story," said Carolyn. "May we continue this discussion, say in Bayside?"

"I can't right now," said Taro as he started walking toward

the front door. "Maybe later."

Carolyn faced Doug. "Thank you for seeing me on such short notice. I'll be leaving with detective Okada.

Taro handed Carolyn his card. Turning to Doug he said, "You'll be staying in town for a while. Right?"

Taro adjusted the ends of his tie before tucking them under the straps of his safety belt. He looked out his side window and saw the BMW's tire tracks on the still-saturated lawn. They hadn't been there when he had arrived. He wrinkled his brow and drove out of the driveway, making his way to Route 1. Was it Gonzalo or Botero? Gonzalo wouldn't make much sense. Whoever left those tire tracks had been eavesdropping, heard everything, and high-tailed it out of there. Taro turned north on Route 1 and called his office. He asked them to call the Coast Guard and have them inspect the two boats at Crosby's dock. He held on, wanting confirmation that they would. If Gonzalo took the convertible, it would explain why Crosby didn't report the car missing. He'd ask the Monroe County PD lab to go over the car with a fine-toothed comb. He listened as his office confirmed that the Coast Guard understood exactly where the sailboat and yacht were moored.

Taro pondered; if it was Botero in the house, he could have just stayed hidden. Instead, he bolted. Taro dialed the Collier County PD and asked them to meet him at the Marco Island Marriott. He turned west on Alligator Alley and then glanced at his watch. One o'clock. He hit the siren.

Carolyn drove off the Keys onto the mainland. She was concerned that a Miami-Dade County detective had visited Doug Crosby's home. The detective's tone had been barely polite. There was no question that he had more on his mind than just recovering a missing car. Doug Crosby had parried every one of Taro's questions. Her cell phone rang. "Hello."

"Carolyn, Greg. Got some news for you."

"Shoot."

"There aren't any public records on Crosby Limited," said Greg.

"Who handled the incorporation?"

"A San Diego lawyer.  Royce Palmer."

"What else?"

"Carolyn, why are you asking about Crosby Limited?"

"Not now, Greg."

"The SEC wants to talk to you."

Carolyn hit the end button on her cell.

# Chapter 39

### Acapulco, Mexico
### Monday 0824 CT

Jose shook his head and returned the telephone to its cradle. Unbelievable, *now Botero is calling me at home. These telephone calls are going to have to stop.*

Jose called for his car. He had to visit the Acapulco general library.

# Chapter 40

### Washington, D.C.
### Monday 1100 ET

It was eleven o'clock in the morning on a bright sunny day in Lafayette Square, across the street from the White House. Within the hour Michael would be out from under Vinny's thumb, heading home. He settled on his favorite bench to watch the show. Long ago it had become a part of America's heritage. Although he'd seen it many times and the plot rarely changed, he always enjoyed watching the different players.

He unwrapped the sandwich that he hadn't had time to finish earlier. He'd take only a bite or two. He didn't want to spoil his appetite. Sarah had gotten a babysitter and he'd promised her she wouldn't have to cook. They would go to the Amphora restaurant on Vienna's Main Street. Sarah would have lunch while he ate dinner. Then the big decision, which of Amphora's fabulous desserts would they choose?

He looked toward the southeast corner of Lafayette Square. The protesters had finished mustering their faithful. Their leader had presented their permit to the U.S. Park policeman. It authorized the protesters to exercise their constitutional right to demonstrate at this hour and place. In just a few minutes they would be cleared to carry their signs across Pennsylvania Avenue and march in front of the high, wrought-iron fence guarding the north portico of the White House. The shouting and waving of signs and banners would last less than ten minutes, enough time for the press to can enough footage for the evening news. The protestors would then return to Lafayette Square, turn in their signs, and disperse.

Michael decided not to wait. He trashed the unfinished sandwich and headed back to the SIOC. Maybe he could get away just a few minutes early.

Michael hustled to his terminal. A little cleanup and he would be out of there. Several intelligence icons were blinking. The first was a cell call to Doug from Carolyn. The cell towers revealed Carolyn was traveling south on the Florida turnpike. Michael listened. Carolyn Hughes was on her way to Doug's Key

Largo home. An asterisk alerted him—Carolyn's cell number required authorization if it was to be monitored.

The second icon was an Echelon intercept. It captured a cell call to Jose Valderrama, the same telephone number the previous Echelon intercept had captured. The two-word one-way message had already been translated from Spanish.

Gonzalo's alive.

Another asterisk appeared— this new originating cell number required authorization in order to be monitored.

Michael put his OEF tag on both cell phone numbers and sent a request to Vinny for immediate authorization to have them monitored.

The OEF tag caused Rapid Start to respond with the information it could provide without authorization. The first cell phone number was registered to Carolyn Hughes. Michael already knew this. He had heard Carolyn introduce herself when she called Doug. The second cell belonged to an Ernesto Soto, a Florida City resident. An FBI report followed:

Ernesto Soto is an illegal alien.
He works as a crop-dusting helicopter pilot.

The third icon Michael clicked was a Carnivore intercept. Carnivore had captured an e-mail from the Acapulco general library to someone named Royce Palmer in San Diego. Michael read the translated text:

Botero closing in.

This e-mail had originated from a different computer at the library than the previous e-mails from the same library.

The fourth icon was a call that originated from northwest Washington, D.C. No caller number was available. Michael listened to the conversation. He recognized both voices. Greg McNulty had called Carolyn Hughes. There was something in Greg's voice that Michael couldn't pin down. There were new leads too—a corporation named Crosby Limited and the name Royce Palmer, the same name uncovered in the third intercept.

Michael called Greg on his red phone.

"Carolyn worked for me for a few years," Greg explained. "She up and quit a few days ago. I was surprised to get a call from her in Florida, more surprised that she asked about Crosby Limited."

"Why?" Michael asked.

"What the hell she's doing in Florida, I don't know. Asking about Crosby Limited shocked me. We've just started investigating that firm. It's new. We have zip on it."

"Anything else?" Michael asked.

"Yeah, another shocker. She asked who incorporated Crosby Limited. When I looked it up, it turned out to be Royce Palmer, a San Diego lawyer. He's been in our crosshairs for a while. Nothing yet, but it sure is funny she hit two of our nerves just a few days after leaving Justice."

Michael wanted to know as much as he could about anyone now in his OEF database. "Tell me about Carolyn."

"She's good, a superior analyst."

"But what?" Michael asked, catching hesitancy in Greg's reply.

"Well, I don't mean to be judgmental," said Greg. "She's naïve. You know what I mean?"

It wasn't a question but Michael responded. "Tell me."

"Like I'd never bring her in on SIOC business."

"Why's that?"

"Let her be a roving innocent," Greg said. "I'll extract any info that might be pertinent. No problem."

Michael let it go. True, there was more to this than Greg was telling, but this wasn't the time to press. It was time to organize, pull out all the stops, apply resources.

Michael searched his databases. He added every FBI District Office and their emergency command centers to his coordination list of telephone numbers. Next he called Alan Dickie. Alan was not in his office. Sally gave him Alan's direct line and his cell number.

Sally added just before hanging up, "Oh, you'll want Holt Brown's number too. He's Alan's chief of staff and responsible for the coordination with the Miami-Dade County PD."

Michael called Holt. Holt suggested he add the office and cell phone of Taro Okada.

Michael searched his databases again. Thirty minutes later he had added all of Florida's state, county and municipal emergency command centers to his coordination list. Then he wrote a summary report explaining SIOC's role in the investigation of the Miami International Airport bombing, and highlighted the frenzy of activity that had erupted in southern Florida since the bombing. He sent it to all those now on his coordination list.

His intelligence icon began blinking.

Request for attorney general authorization for
Carolyn Hughes and Ernesto Soto wiretaps
remains under administrative review. Prepare a
brief that the attorney general can present to a
judge to justify such action.
Vinny Campbell
Deputy Director SIOC

A second intelligence icon began blinking.

U.S. attorney for the eastern district of Virginia
authorizes monitoring Carolyn Hughes and
Ernesto Soto's cell telephones.

Michael looked at the two messages. Which one applied? Vinny hadn't forwarded his request. He was asking Michael for further justification. The second message approved his request.

Michael reviewed both messages carefully. The second was transmitted five minutes after the first. He scrolled down to the name of the approving authority on the second message. It was the U.S. attorney for the eastern district of Virginia, located in Alexandria, Virginia. He had authorized the request within minutes of Michael's original request, but the authorization hadn't been forwarded to him until now.

Michael mulled the two documents.

The tall man wearing tattered jeans and a white muscle shirt sagging from bony shoulders must have used excerpts from his summary report to support the monitoring request and sent it to the eastern district court. He must have then held it in deference to the FBI's SIOC. Seeing Vinny Campbell's response, he forwarded the approval of U.S. attorney for the eastern district of Virginia.

Michael made a mental note. Bony-shoulders would be welcomed at his house anytime.

Michael entered the authorization to monitor the two new cell phones. Rapid Start automatically back-checked for calls made since the time on the authorization request. Soto's cell phone had made a call to the Homestead General Aviation Airport, ten miles west of the Homestead Regional Airport. The caller had ordered his crop-dusting helicopter readied.

Just before entering the executive briefing room for the 4 p.m. briefing, Michael remembered he hadn't called Sarah. He broke out into a sweat. Things had just started to turn around at home. Shit. He had missed their Amphora restaurant date too. No time now; he would call Sarah for sure after Vinny Campbell's briefing of law enforcement officers, investigators and prosecutors from around the world. He entered the executive briefing room.

Vinny Campbell told him without warning to take center stage during the briefing. When Michael finished presenting his findings, Vinny directed him to present updates at both the 7 a.m. and the 4 p.m. briefings until further notice.

Michael's world had changed.

# Chapter 41

## Marco Island, Florida
## Monday 1100 ET

Janet sat on the overstuffed couch a few feet away from the Marriott concierge's desk. Nicole slept soundly by her side. Gil scanned the rack of tourist brochures near the registration desk on the far side of the lobby. Jack finished talking with the concierge. He headed toward Janet. Gil noticed. They met at the couch.

"We're all set," Jack said. "The concierge says it's just a few miles south. Shouldn't take long to get there."

"Great," said Janet. "As long as I've lived in Florida, I've never been to the Everglades."

"Here, let me carry Nicole," said Jack. Nicole was oblivious to the transfer. As they walked out the Marriott's entrance, the concierge ran up behind them. "Sir, sir. You left this on the couch." She handed Nicole's koala bear to Jack.

"Oh, thank you," said Janet. "It would've been a disaster if we lost Freddie." Janet took Freddie from Jack and stuffed him into her tote bag.

Fifteen minutes later Jack turned right into a dirt parking lot. He pointed to the creek on the other side of the road. "That must be the inlet the concierge told me about," he said. "If we want to see alligators, that's the place. I'll get the tickets and see when the next boat leaves."

"Sounds like a plan," said Gil.

Janet bent over and whispered, "Estamos en la tierra de los cocodrilos."

Nicole, still sleepy, strained her seat belt trying to sit up. She asked in Spanish, *"Will the alligators eat Freddie, Mommy?"*

Janet reached into her tote bag and handed the koala to Nicole, while saying in Spanish. *"Not as long as you hold onto him."*

Jack returned to the car and spoke through the window. "It'll be about forty or fifty minutes until the next boat." Opening the door he said, "So let's go alligator hunting."

On the other side of the road, Janet pointed to the creek with the alligators. "Nicole, ahí es donde están los cocodrilos." The creek was at the bottom of a steep gully. A few parents with children lined the embankment peering into the creek far below.

An elderly lady in sandals and shorts standing next to Janet pointed. "Over there honey. On the far shore… in the grass by that rock."

"Alligators?" Janet asked.

"Two babies," the woman said.

Janet stood and waved for Gil and Jack to join them. Not wanting a crowd of children to descend on them she whispered to Nicole in Spanish, *"Look. By the rock, honey. Two baby alligators. One's floating in the water. Only his snout is on the bank. See? By that rock. It's a baby alligator. Isn't he cute?"*

In her eagerness to see better, Nicole dropped Freddie. The stuffed animal teetered on the edge before starting down the embankment to the creek. *"Freddie! Freddie!"* Nicole yelled and started after Freddie.

With one sweeping motion, Jack bent over and snapped Nicole and Freddie from the embankment's edge. "Gotcha," he said. He swung them both around in the air to keep Nicole from becoming frightened. "Nothing like being at the right place at the right time," he told Janet as he put Nicole down and handed Freddie to her.

Janet and Gil followed Nicole into one of the long rows on the top deck of the tour boat. They wanted Nicole on the end so she could see over the side of the boat. Jack sat in the row behind them. As the boat moved away from the dock, the captain announced over the PA system that there would be a demonstration of how to wear the life preservers that were stored in boxes located on each deck. When a deckhand finished the demonstration, the captain came back on the PA. "If for some reason you do find yourself in the water don't panic. My recommendation would be that you just stand up. The Everglades are only two feet deep."

Within minutes they were among the islands of mangrove trees. "It's the nesting season, so we don't want to frighten the birds if we can help it," said the captain. "If you look ahead on the left you'll see an osprey nest. It's in the top branches of the highest tree about a hundred yards ahead. I'm going to be quiet now. We'll get as close as we can without disturbing the nest."

Taro turned left off Alligator Alley onto Route 92, heading toward Marco Island. His hands-free cell phone rang. "Yo."

"Taro?" said Holt Brown.

"Right, Holt."

"More intercepts."

"I'm listening."

"One was Carolyn Hughes's cell. She made an appointment with Doug Crosby for this morning."

Taro smiled. "I met her there."

"Another intercept was to her cell, from a Greg McNulty in D.C. They talked about Crosby Limited. No real info passed. The SEC wants to see Carolyn for some reason."

"What else?"

"Two intercepts from a guy named Ernesto Soto. He called from Key Largo. The gist… he ordered a helicopter from Homestead. FBI says Ernesto Soto is an illegal alien. Flies a crop-dusting chopper."

"It wasn't Soto, Holt. It was Botero. I'm a few minutes behind him."

"You sure?"

"Pretty sure," said Taro. "Things are popping. You may want to get over here."

"I'm not done," said Holt. "Carnivore picked up an e-mail from Jose to a Royce Palmer in San Diego. This Palmer guy is on his way east. I'm checking Miami's San Diego arrivals."

"Hold on, Holt," said Taro. "I'm just pulling up in front of the Marco Island Marriott. Two Collier PD cruisers are out front."

A man walked up to Taro's car window. "Detective Taro?" he asked. Taro nodded. "I'm Detective George. Sorry we couldn't get here sooner. We missed the folks you told us about. The concierge remembered them. Said they left a little before we got here. Taking an Everglades tour. We can lead you there if you want."

"I want." Taro turned back to his cell. "Listen Holt… Jack Taylor, he's the CEO of Taylor Associates, and Gil Bauer are going on an Everglades tour with Janet Griffin and her daughter. I think it's a certainty Botero is running them down. Don't know why yet."

"Is that the Everglades tour boat just south of the Marriott?" Holt asked.

Detective George nodded.

"Yes," Taro told Holt.

"I took the family there a couple of months ago," said Holt. I'll hop a chopper, meet you there in about thirty... forty minutes."

As the tour boat approached another osprey's nest, the captain said, "Unfortunately, on your left, you'll see one of the Everglades' biggest problems... speedboats that don't throttle down. Sadly, their propellers slice into the backs of the manatees grazing on the marsh grasses below."

The speedboat slowed, its bow settling in the water. The four men aboard stared at the tourists on the open deck. Two used binoculars. As the boat got closer one of the men with binoculars pointed toward the upper open deck. The speedboat roared to life and sped away.

"Haven't seen anything like that before," said the captain. "Most of the time they just speed on, hoping not to be reported. Look ahead on the sandy area on the right. Far ahead. That's a great blue heron standing like a statue. He's fishing. If he doesn't move, the fish think his legs are just reeds."

After quietly cruising past the blue heron the captain said, "Here comes that speedboat again. This time he's on the wrong side of the channel."

The speedboat headed directly for the tour boat, cut its engines, and glided toward it. A man stood up and threw a line onto the tour boat. A tour boat deckhand instinctively grabbed the line and pulled the speedboat alongside.

Two men on the speedboat pulled semiautomatic weapons from under a tarp. In three quick steps they were aboard, screaming that no one move. "Ninguno se mueve. Ninguno se mueve." Tourists began screaming. Nicole melted into her mother's side. Jack and Gil braced themselves.

One of the gunmen stayed where he had boarded. The other came down the center aisle. He stopped at the row behind Janet, Nicole and Gil. With one foot in the aisle he waved menacingly with his automatic at Jack. "Usted, venga con nosotros. Muévase! Pero ya!"

Jack looked to Janet. "What does he want?"

Janet wrapped both arms around Nicole and yelled at the gunman, "El no entiende español." In a calmer voice she told Jack, "They want you to go with them."

The gunman at the front of the boat fired a burst from his AK-47 into to the air. The sky darkened with birds flying in panic.

"Muévete!" the gunman in Jack's aisle shouted again. "Pero ya!" The gunman stepped into the row, grabbed Jack's arm, and began yanking him out of the row.

Jack resisted. The gunman jammed the butt of his gun into Jack's stomach. Jack fell dazed onto the long bench seat. The gunmen dragged him out of the aisle and sent him sprawling onto the deck. Jack staggered to his feet. The gunman shoved and pushed Jack until he stood on the tour boat's deck by the speedboat. The gunman gave Jack a shove. He fell onto the deck of the speedboat. Jack got to his hands and knees, a gunman standing guard over him. Suddenly Jack rose. With a vicious uppercut he sent the gunman over the stern. A second gunman rammed his gun into Jack's chest. Jack fell unconscious.

"Vámonos! Vámonos! Saquen a esos malditos de aquí! Ahora! Ahora!"

The speedboat roared to life, sending Jack Taylor rolling against its stern. Within seconds the speedboat disappeared behind a mangrove island.

No one on the tour boat spoke or moved. Suddenly a woman standing at the rail where the speedboat had been started shrieking. A pool of blood swirled in the churning silt below her. Suddenly, the gunman who had gone over the side of the speedboat burst to the surface. The speedboat propeller had severed his foot.

# Chapter 42

### Key Largo, Florida
### Monday 1120 ET

Doug sat by the pool watching the Coast Guard 44-footer head for his dock. As the craft entered the only open slip, Seaman Guy Franklin jumped off and secured the bowline. Coxswain Raul Salinas cut the engines and waved to Doug.

"Wouldn't you like to have a spread like this?" Guy asked Raul as he finished mooring the small boat.

"Sure would," said Raul. "Any markings on that yacht?"

"DESCIFRAR, across the stern," said Guy.

Doug didn't get up as the two men approached. "Good morning, I'm Raul Salinas. This here's Guy Franklin. How's it going today?"

"Watched you come in," said Doug. "What do you want?"

"Checking the coast for hurricane damage," said Raul.

"Any on Blackwater Sound?"

"Nothing serious. That CIFRAR, one beautiful yacht."

"What can I do for you?"

"Nothing really."

The two coastguardsmen looked at each other and then headed back across the lawn. Raul freed the bowline and then jumped onto the small boat. "That guy doesn't own that yacht."

"Yeah, I noticed that too," said Seaman Guy. "If he owned it, he'd have known it's name was DESCIFRAR and not what you told him, CIFRAR."

# Chapter 43

### Everglades, Florida
### Monday 1225 ET

Two dockhands stood amid the tourists waiting for the Everglades tour boat to return. Suddenly, a woman employee came rushing out of the souvenir shop and hurried toward them. When she was within earshot of the waiting tourists on the dock she began shouting. "We're sorry, really sorry, but all tours have been cancelled for the day. Please return to the ticket counter for a full refund. We're very, very sorry. Please go now. There will be a full refund." The crowd didn't move. Ticket holders wanted a fuller explanation. The woman kept repeating herself until the crowd began to drift to the souvenir shop for their refunds.

Several minutes later the woman stood on the dock alone, watching two police cruisers and a white Ford sedan pull almost onto the dock. "How did you get here so soon?" she asked. Taro stepped out of the car. "Oh, it's terrible. Like I told you, the captain radioed that gunmen had boarded our boat. They kidnapped a passenger." The tension had tired the woman. She sat in a chair near the boarding ramp. "When will the ambulance be here?"

"Ambulance, ma'am?" said Taro.

"Yes, of course. I told you, the captain said one of the kidnappers lost a foot. I don't know how. It's just awful."

Detective George stepped up. "Ma'am, I'm from the Collier PD. An ambulance will be here soon." Looking at Taro, Detective George said, "I heard the report on our way here."

"Where's the tour boat, ma'am?" Taro asked.

"The Captain said they had to get the gunman out of the water. Then it was something awful, stopping the bleeding and all. They'll be here any minute." She looked past Taro. "There they are. See? The white boat."

Detective George said, "Taro, what's going on here?"

"We're running down Botero," said Taro. "He's our chief suspect in the Miami airport bombing."

The tour boat docked. The injured man was treated and put in the ambulance while the Collier County police corralled the tourists in a corner of the parking lot.

"I have pictures of Botero," Taro told Detective George. "We'd appreciate it if you'd put out an APB. This guy's extremely dangerous."

"No problem," Detective George said. "I'll have the tourists look at it too. See if he was among the kidnappers." The detective glanced at the photo and passed it on to a blue shirt standing at his side. "See if anyone can identify this punk."

Taro said, "There are a few tourists I'd like to speak to: Gil Bauer, Janet Griffin, and Jack Taylor."

Detective George hailed the officer to whom he had just given the photo. "See if you can identify Gil Bauer, Janet Griffin, and Jack Taylor."

A helicopter began hovering in preparation for landing. "That'll be Holt Brown, FBI," Taro told Detective George.

The officer Detective George dispatched returned with Gil, Janet, and Nicole. Nicole's face was buried in her mother's shoulder, protecting her from the noise, wind and dust caused by the whirling blades.

"This is Gil Bauer and Janet Griffin," the officer shouted. "They say the guy in the picture was the leader of the kidnappers."

"Mr. Bauer, I'm Detective Taro Okada, Miami-Dade PD. This here's Detective George, Collier PD. Coming out of the helicopter over there is FBI Agent Holt Brown. Now, who was kidnapped?"

"Jack Taylor," said Gil. "He resisted and took a beating for it. He could be seriously injured."

Holt Brown ran toward Taro. "What do we have, Taro?"

Taro said, "Botero used a speedboat to snatch Jack Taylor off the tour boat. We've got positive ID. A couple dozen witnesses."

"When did it happen?" asked Holt.

Gil said, "About twenty-five minutes ago."

"Come on," said Holt. "We'll use my chopper. See if we can track 'em. They can't be far." Holt and Taro boarded the FBI helicopter.

"Gus, this is Taro, Miami-Dade PD," Holt told the chopper pilot. Gus nodded. "Follow the shoreline south. We're looking for a speedboat, three maybe four passengers. One's a hostage." Looking toward Taro he said, "North is too urban. They'll have to come ashore soon."

Jack lurched getting off the speedboat, falling face down into knee-deep water. The swamp water felt cool and helped flush his grogginess. Wanting to avoid another blow, he forced himself to his feet. He stumbled to shore, dropping onto the narrow strip of sand. "What do you want?" he gasped.

Botero yanked him to his feet and pushed him toward the helicopter waiting in a clearing.

"Where's the other man?" the pilot yelled over the noise of the rotating copter blades.

"He's staying behind," Botero yelled. "Let's go."

Holt peered over the shoulder of the pilot. "That could be them. Dead ahead," he said into the noise-muffling mouthpiece connected to his helmet. "Three men, two have automatics," said Holt as he peered through binoculars. "We can't match that firepower. Not much we can do but follow. The Coast Guard should be in the air in a few minutes."

"Coming from?" asked Taro.

"From Homestead."

"Can't wait," Holt said to Gus. "Circle. Let them know we're here."

"What good will that do?" Gus asked.

"Confusion. Delay," said Holt. "I don't know. Let's find out. Try it."

"Confusion. Delay. We can do that," said Gus. He headed out to sea, gaining altitude as he did.

"Where're you going?" asked Holt.

"Their open door is on the left side, facing north. We'll approach high, from the southwest. With any luck, they won't hear us over their own engines. Maybe they won't see us. We'll be on top of them before they know it."

A half-mile out at sea Gus warned, "Hang on." He banked sharply and headed for Botero's helicopter.

As they approached Botero's helicopter, Holt said, "They're still on the ground. The door's still open."

Gus slowed and then hovered high above the helicopter on the ground. He wanted to avoid the low-density air caused by the rotating blades of Botero's helicopter. Holt opened the door and leaned out, peering through binoculars. "Take a look," Holt said, handing the binoculars to Taro.

Taro changed places with Holt. Taro focused the binoculars and then smiled. "Hard to believe. The crop-dusting rig is still attached." As he handed the binoculars back to Holt, he said, "No sign they know we're here."

Gus turned the volume control of the loudspeakers on the outside of his helicopter to full volume, while fixing his gaze on the flex of the crop-dusting rigs.

Suddenly Gus barked into his microphone, "This is the FBI. Do not take off. Exit your craft with your hands over your head." Not waiting for a response, Gus dove and headed south traveling low and fast over the Everglades while repeating his command, "This is the FBI. Do not take off. Exit your craft with your hands over your head."

Botero jumped from the helicopter, his finger poised on the trigger of his Uzi. He spotted the FBI on the opposite side of his helicopter but couldn't get a clear shot without firing through his own craft's whirling blades. He ran to the other side of his helicopter. A dark cloud of scattering birds rose, obliterating his view. He fired angrily in the general direction of the FBI chopper, screaming "son-of-a-bitch." A few birds fell to earth. He ran back to the helicopter and jumped in, leaving the door open. "Go. Go." he shouted.

"Can't," shouted Soto. "Too many birds!"

"Hang on!" Gus yelled. He banked hard to the right, gaining altitude, and circled back. When he arrived at a spot east of Botero's helicopter, he hovered. "We'll wait here for him to take off again. He'll go straight up to avoid the birds. Not much more we can do but track him till the cavalry arrives."

"Does the cavalry know where we are?" Taro shouted to Gus.

"I've been sending our GPS coordinates. They'll be heading right for us."

"So what are we going to do this time?" Holt asked Gus.

"Stay a half mile or so behind him. That way the Coast Guard pilot will know exactly where we both are."

"They're taking off," said Holt. "The door's still open."

Botero shouted to Soto. "Get me to that mother-fucking chopper, man."

"Are you crazy?" said Ernesto. "No way."

Botero pointed his Uzi at Ernesto's head. "Do it man!"

"All right," yelled Soto. "All right."

Botero threaded the safety belt through the belt on his pants in the back, and sat in the open doorway, his feet dangling. "Go straight at those fuckers, man."

"Here he comes," said Gus.

"He knows we won't fire with the hostage aboard," said Taro.

"We can run," said Gus.

"Go straight at him," said Taro.

"What?" Gus asked.

"He's got to turn to fire from the open door. Stay at the same altitude. We'll be closing fast. Real fast. Go!"

Gus headed toward Botero's helicopter.

"He'll have to turn south to get his shot," said Taro. "When he starts to turn, you gain altitude fast. Real fast. And turn north."

Botero leaned out of the helicopter door, straining to see the FBI helicopter ahead of him. "The fuckers are coming at us."

"Yeah," said Ernesto.

"They want to play chicken. We'll play chicken. Keep straight at 'em. I'll tell you when to turn. We'll blow those mother fuckers out of the sky." Botero stood on the helicopter's landing skid, squinting, the wind pinning his hair to his scalp.

"We're closing too fast," Ernesto said.

"Keep going straight," shouted Botero.

"We've got to turn. We'll crash."

Botero leaned further out and grinned. "Turn. Those mother fuckers are mine."

The FBI chopper rose almost straight up as it turned north. Taro and Holt felt their weight press them hard into their seats. Their safety belts cut into their bellies.

Botero sighted his Uzi, its muzzle following the rising helicopter. A blur appeared as Botero was about to fire.

"Don't shoot. Don't shoot," Ernesto screamed. "You'll hit our blades."

"Mother fuckers." Botero climbed back into the cabin. "Follow those cocksuckers. I'll kill you if you lose them."

"FBI, can you hear me?" Gus heard in his headset.

"Roger that," Gus replied.

"This is the Coast Guard. We're on our way. I say again, we're on our way."

"Glad to hear from you, buddy."

"What are you doing over there? Your position is changing mighty fast. What's up?"

"We're in a dog fight with a crazy," said Gus. "He has a hostage aboard. Repeat. Crazy has a hostage aboard."

"Roger that. Helicopter dogfight. Crazy has hostage."

"How soon will you be here?"

"Ten, twelve minutes."

"Can't you get here faster?"

"Head east on Alligator Alley. We'll follow it west."

"Roger, turning due east," said Gus. "Will follow Alligator Alley."

"Where's the crazy?"

"Don't know."

"Keep coming east. We'll close on you."

"Roger that."

Three rapid high-pitched pings echoed through the cabin. "What was that?" said Taro.

"Don't know," said Gus.

"There it is again," said Holt.

"Holy shit! We're being fired on," said Gus. "Where is he?"

Holt and Taro strained to locate Botero's chopper but saw nothing. "He's not in front of us," Gus said.

"He must be behind us," said Taro. "He's firing through that open door, so he's gotta be heading south."

"Right." Gus turned north and began descending toward the Everglades canopy. "Maybe we can use the birds again."

"Don't," shouted Taro. "He knows that maneuver."

It was too late. Gus was deep into his dive.

Botero leered. He was already turning to keep the open door facing his prey. He welcomed the larger target provided by the descending FBI helicopter. Botero squeezed the trigger spraying bullets back and forth across the circle of the whirling blades.

"Your position is changing mighty fast," said the Coast Guard pilot. "What's going on?"

"We're hit," said Gus. "Repeat. We're hit. Going down."

"Roger, you're going down," said the Coast Guard pilot. "Can you maintain control?"

"Repeat. Can you maintain control?"

# Chapter 44

### Everglades, Florida
### Monday 1300 ET

Jack Taylor had sat blindfolded in the helicopter, his hands bound behind his back. Botero yanked him off the seat and tossed him onto the floor. Pain shot up his backbone as it hit the sharp edge of the opened sliding door. He felt the rush of hot air as the chopper took off and had to brace his feet against the base of the seat Botero had just tossed him off to keep from falling out.

The gunfire had almost deafened him. When it stopped, he heard cheers and then Botero and the pilot yelling back and forth. He couldn't understand that Botero was telling Ernesto to fly below the treetops and close to the Everglades shoreline as they rounded the southern tip of Florida. That they would approach Key Largo from the west.

Or that Ernesto was telling Botero he knew how to fly low–real low. He was a crop duster pilot.

With the chopper in steady flight and his body not pressed against anything, Jack realized his arms and hands had lost feeling. He rolled more onto his back, freeing them from the sharp edges that had cut off the blood flow. When his limbs regained feeling he began rubbing his bonds against the sharp edge that had been causing the loss of blood flow. He used a steady pace, one second per stroke.

He pressed hard with the start of each count. One... two... three... 458, 459, 460, 461.

Ernesto suddenly realized he had lined up with the wrong Key Largo inlet. Crosby's place was a mile further north. He began a steep bank to change course.

Jack felt himself about to tumble. There was nothing between him and the open door. He jammed his feet harder and harder against the bulkhead as the bank steepened. Jack screamed, urging his legs to win their fight with gravity. As suddenly as the bank began it ended. Jack's head slammed into the bulkhead, knocking him out.

Doug heard the helicopter approaching. He went out onto his lawn. The chopper landed hard, the skids and crop-dusting rigging flexed dangerously close to their breaking points. The impact awakened Jack. Ernesto shut the engine off. Botero jumped out, his Uzi still strapped to his arm. He reached back in and yanked Jack out. Jack went sprawling onto the lawn. Botero jerked him to his feet and shoved him toward the guesthouse. Inside he sent Jack, still blindfolded, sprawling again, this time on a bedroom floor. Doug watched as Botero grabbed Jack by an arm, dragged him to the foot of the bed and tied him there. Without a word, Botero left the guesthouse. Doug followed.

The ends of the chopper's blades almost touched the ground. Ernesto was looking up at the tail rudder. "What's wrong with the chopper?" Doug asked Botero.

Botero stomped the crop-dusting rigging. "It piece of shit, man."

Botero made his way across the lawn to the main house, his steps measured, his face blank. Doug followed him through the patio doors. Botero went straight for the wet bar, poured, and downed a shot of Tequila. He poured a second, studying it for a moment before downing it too.

"You can't leave that guy here," said Doug.

Botero wanted the chopper airborne. He went to the patio doors. Ernesto stood by an opened toolbox, staring up at the tail rotor.

"Who is that guy?" said Doug.

Botero turned back to Doug. "Jack Taylor, man." He had no idea why Doug didn't know. It was so obvious. But he couldn't deride him. He was Jose's son. "He the key, man. Wanta buy Bauer."

Doug's eyes bulged. "Jack Taylor? Are you crazy? Why the hell did you grab him?"

Botero walked back to the bar. "Man, you blind? He come to see Bauer."

"He's not the only one."

Botero slammed his empty jigger onto the bar and spun around. "What you mean, man?"

"Charles Bauer told me he's had a ton of inquiries."

Botero picked up the tequila bottle by the neck and waved it at Doug. "You tell Jose only one."

"As far as I know."

Botero's legs hurt more than his arms ached. Firing the Uzi

while not holding on had strained his leg muscles. They threatened to quit on him. "He sent that bitch. She talk to Bauer, bring Taylor, man." He waved the tequila bottle at the chair Carolyn had sat in, Tequila splashing from the bottle. "She sit in fucking chair."

"So you decide to snatch Jack Taylor. In broad daylight!"

Botero shook his head, wondering why Doug couldn't understand. He'd had enough. "Where Gonzalo, man?"

"Christ, I don't know. I never saw him. We don't even know if Gonzalo's alive."

"He alive, man. Car door open."

"That doesn't prove shit," said Doug.

Botero tried to pour Tequila into a glass on the bar. His hand shook, splashing Tequila over the bar. He brushed the glass to the floor and drank from the bottle. "Taylor and the bitch... They the ones, man. She lucky she no on boat." More Tequila drenched his stomach. "She got disk, man."

"How would she know about the disk, for Christ sake?"

Botero didn't want to explain. Too damned obvious. "I check everyone at your fucking party, man," he said disgustedly.

"You what?"

"Their computers filled with shit." Botero's hands wouldn't stop quivering. He cradled his best friend with both hands and drank. "Pepe, he scared shitless. Too dumb, man. It someone not at party, man. What other thing happen?"

Doug echoed what Botero asked. "What other thing happen?"

Dumb, dumb, dumb. "The bitch shows up, man."

"Oh, for Christ's sake, how could she know anything?"

Again Botero pointed to the chair Carolyn had sat in. "What she say when she sit right there, man?" Doug didn't answer. "You no remember? She know you invest in Bauer. She ask who your investors. Remember? She goading you, man. She know about Jose."

"Bullshit."

Botero walked back to the patio doors but forgot why. "Maybe Gonzalo hid disk here and the bitch come get it."

"Are you saying Taylor, Carolyn and Gonzalo are all in cahoots?"

Botero lost track of where the conversation had gone. He

retreated to what he wanted, the helicopter airborne. "We wait. They get that hunk of shit up, then we go man." He went to the patio doors. Again he forgot why. He went to the couch.

Three swigs later he was asleep, the Tequila bottle draining between the cushions.

# Chapter 45

### Bayside, Florida
### Monday 1945 ET

Carolyn Hughes sipped her vodka-tonic as she watched Natalie heading back to the bar after having taken her dinner order. The sun had set and the light from the string of multicolored lanterns was dancing on the surface of the stream that threaded its way among Carp's Landing's patio tables. Taro... now that's a nice name, she thought. Seems to fit... strong, masculine, decisive.

In a few minutes Natalie returned to Carolyn's table. "There's a telephone call. It's from Janet. You can take it in the bar." They walked to the bar together.

Carolyn picked up the phone. "Janet?"

"I'm so glad I got hold of you."

"What's up?"

"A police cruiser is escorting us."

Carolyn couldn't believe her ears. "You're being escorted by the police?"

"Please listen, Carolyn. Gil is following behind in his car. We're just about home. Can you come over? Please, Carolyn. It's important."

"Is Jack with you?"

*"Please, Carolyn."*

# Chapter 46

### Bayside, Florida
### Monday 2110 ET

Janet Griffin tucked Nicole in. "Te quiero, princesa." Nicole tumbled onto her side in the big bed and burrowed her head in the pillow. "Y Freddie?"

Janet stroked her daughter's hair, saying in Spanish. *"Would I let Freddie sleep in my bed if I didn't love him too?"* Janet kissed Nicole and then Freddie. *"Of course I love Freddie."* She pulled the sheet up to cover Nicole's back. *"I'll be downstairs. The bathroom and hall lights are on and I'm leaving this door open. Okay sweetheart?"* Nicole burrowed deeper into the pillow.

The doorbell rang as Janet entered the living room. Gil volunteered. "Let me get it."

It was Taro. In the living room he asked, "You guys okay?" Janet and Gil nodded. "Two men are posted outside. 24/7."

"What about Jack?" Janet asked. Taro sat on the edge of the chair by the screen door. "We found the speedboat a couple of miles south of the dock, on the shore near a clearing in the swamp. They had a helicopter waiting." He pursed his lips. "I'm sorry. They got away. Our chopper went down."

Janet gasped. "Is Jack dead?"

"There's no reason to think so. It'll be a while until we can pinpoint where the helicopter landed. Air Traffic Control hasn't been able to pick up their chopper's track. They're still trying, using enhancement techniques."

Carolyn Hughes turned off Bell Boulevard, heading for Janet's, her mind racing. Why would a police car be following Janet home? Did Nicole fall off the boat? Oh God no. Please no. A police escort. No way they broke the law—oh maybe speeding. An accident. That's it. Someone was hurt. Hurt badly. Not Janet, she sounded okay. She always buckles Nicole in. It's Gil. He's the one who's hurt.

Carolyn turned onto Janet's street. Her heart skipped a beat when the flashing lights from police cars nearly blinded her. Blue uniforms mingled between Janet's front door and the nearest police car. She threaded her way as close as she could to Janet's house, double-parked next to a cruiser, and raced up Janet's driveway.

The policeman at Janet's door questioned her and then announced her entry. "We're in the living room," Taro called from the living room.

Carolyn made a beeline for Janet. "You okay?"

Janet's eyes teared. Her voice choked. "Jack's been kidnapped."

*"What!"*

"It was horrible," said Janet.

Carolyn stepped back. "Jack Taylor's been kidnapped!" She looked to Taro. "Jack Taylor's been *kidnapped?"*

"Don't know why," said Taro. "We thought you might have an idea."

"Me? My God, what's going on here?"

"Nobody knows," Gil said.

Carolyn turned to Janet. "Talk to me. What happened?"

"This speedboat just appeared," said Janet. "Out of nowhere. It was awful."

"There's got to be a reason," said Carolyn. "Maybe they got the wrong person?"

"They went directly for Jack," said Janet. "He resisted. They hit him with a gun butt."

Carolyn's hands flew to her face. "He's been *injured!"*

"Jack knocked one of them into the swamp," said Janet. "Oh Carolyn, I'm so sorry."

"Is Jack *alive?"* Carolyn asked.

"I think so."

*"You think so! You think so!"* Carolyn closed her eyes in utter disbelief. "I've got to call my boss." She turned to Taro. "Who's in charge?"

"Have your boss call Alan Dickie at the FBI," said Taro. "I'll give you his number." Taro wrote Alan's number on the back of his card. "Give him my name too."

Carolyn went into the kitchen, moving her head slowly from side to side.

"I'm leaving," Gil told Taro. "I have to tell my father."

Taro wrote Alan's number on the back of another of his cards. "You and maybe your father should contact the FBI too."

"Will do," said Gil. He left.

Carolyn returned from the kitchen and handed Taro the phone. "It's Simon Tully." Taro took the telephone and went to the kitchen. A few minutes later, Taro returned. "Carolyn, these folks have been through hell. They need rest."

"I can't just *leave*."

"I have men outside," said Taro. "Can we go someplace? I need your help."

Not knowing what else she should be doing, she replied despondently, *"I can't just leave!"*

Janet took both of Carolyn's hands. "We'll be okay. Nicole needs me to help her sleep. It's okay."

Carolyn didn't want to leave, but didn't want to upset Janet. Her eyes probed Janet. "You sure?"

"Why don't I follow you back to Carp's Landing?" said Taro. "We'll talk in the restaurant."

Carolyn nodded reluctantly. Janet hugged her best friend and walked her to the door. They hugged again. Outside Carolyn headed to Carp's Landing. Taro started to follow, then stopped. He went back into the house. "I meant to ask. Anyone know a Royce Palmer?"

"I do," said Janet. "He lives in San Diego. How can he have anything to do with this?"

Taro said, "Who is he? What does he do?"

"Royce Palmer is a friend. A lawyer," Janet said.

"Has he ever been east?"

"Not that I know of."

"He's never been to Florida then?"

"He'd call me if he did," said Janet. "I'm sure he would."

"Sometimes things come to you when you least expect it," said Taro. "Give me a call if anything does."

Taro handed Janet his card and left.

# Chapter 47

### Washington, D.C.
### Monday 2130 ET

Vinny Campbell sat in the front row of the executive briefing room. He didn't see the woman in jeans, a blue blouse, and sneakers, walking crouched-over across the front of the room toward him. She was trying not to disturb the ongoing briefing. She needn't have bothered. Every man in the auditorium followed her jeans. She reached Vinny and whispered, "You have an urgent call from Alan Dickie at MFO." Vinny signaled Michael. They both headed for Vinny's office.

Vinny closed his office door and activated the speakerphone. "Alan, Vinny Campbell. Michael Stone's here too."

"Stone, you son of a bitch," said Alan. "You turned my office into the news capital of the world."

Vinny glared at Michael. "What'd you do, Stone?"

"I'll tell you what he did," snapped Alan. "He's brought every goddamned law enforcement agency in southern Florida in on our investigation. It's chaos here. The phone's ringing off the hook. The press is hounding me. The mayor and a U.S. senator want to know exactly what the FBI is doing. They're both pissed about the press knowing more than they do."

Vinny knew this wasn't the time to bring Stone down. "What's causing the chaos, Alan?"

"A lot has happened in the last hour, Mr. Campbell. There's been a kidnapping. A man was taken at gunpoint from a boatload of tourists in the Everglades. They used a speedboat to snatch him. Automatic weapons were fired." Alan's tone turned to pride. "We were right on this one, chief. Holt Brown, my chief of staff, was on his way to the scene in our helicopter before the kidnapping took place, sir."

"Before the kidnapping?"

"Yes sir, before the kidnapping. We have great cooperation with the locals. A detective—Taro something."

"Taro Okada," Michael chimed in.

Alan ignored Michael. "Holt picked up Taro at the tourist boat dock and went in hot pursuit. They found the speedboat beached in the swamp a few minutes later. There was a crop-dusting helicopter waiting in a clearing nearby." Alan paused. He wanted to give Vinny an opportunity to congratulate him for having up-to-the-minute intelligence that allowed his office to be at the scene of a crime almost before it happened.

Vinny wondered why he had to tell Alan to continue. "Go on."

"Holt fought a valiant delaying action but their helicopter was able to get airborne. There was an air battle." Alan hesitated again not knowing how to phrase his next comment.

"Go on, for Christ sake," Vinny demanded.

Vinny's anger startled Alan. He answered without thinking. "Our helicopter was shot down." Embarrassed, he added quickly, "No one hurt, thank God."

"A crop-duster helicopter shot down an FBI helicopter? Is that what you're telling me?" Vinny was up pacing. "Who the fuck was kidnapped?"

"Witnesses say it's a Jack Taylor, from Virginia. ATC hasn't located their helicopter track yet. They're hopeful, though."

"They may have gone to Doug Crosby's place," said Michael.

"Good guess, Stone," Alan said snidely before returning to his agenda. "Timing, location, and the violent behavior of these kidnappers tell me they're the ones responsible for the airport bombing." Alan couldn't slow down. "If it's the Keys as Michael suggests, Route 1—that's the Overseas Highway—is their only avenue of escape. I say we hit 'em. Hit 'em hard at Crosby's house."

Vinny's adrenalin surged. "A SWAT team?"

"These guys are kidnappers. They have a hostage. They shot down an FBI helicopter. I'm sure they're the ones that bombed the Miami airport. I say we go with FBI hostage rescue. Two HRT teams."

Hostage Rescue Teams were the FBI's crème de la crème. They do the impossible. When everyone else says it's impossible, they'll come at you balls out. If you hold someone hostage and the FBI sends a hostage rescue team to extract that person, you had better surrender that person or chances are you'll die before you know it.

Vinny sought confirmation he should even think about using hostage rescue. "You sure?"

"I'm sure," said Alan. "Two teams. It's a small site, just two buildings. It's on the water. Blackwater Sound."

"Go on," said Vinny.

"We have hundreds of satellite photos of the Keys. I've got them processing images taken from north-south and south-north passes. Should have 3-D images of Crosby's neighborhood soon. We'll use 'em for planning the assault."

From Vinny's experience, the planning of an assault was always the bottleneck, choked with procedures, reviews and approvals.

"Coordination and planning take time," he said. "At best we can have a team airborne from Andrews sometime within the next four hours."

Alan said, "Add another hour or so to Homestead, plus another hour to stage in Key Largo... Not good enough. They could be gone by then."

"That's the best we can do," said Vinny resignedly.

Alan jumped on his reply. "Quantico tells me they have two teams in the air, on the same transport. They're returning from gigs in Afghanistan and Turkey. They can be at Homestead in ninety minutes. If you concur, of course, sir."

"They'll be tired and jet-lagged."

"They're professionals."

"Are you guaranteeing me that the hostage will be there?"

"At Doug Crosby's Key Largo home?" added Michael.

"Guaranteed," Alan snapped, not wanting Michael to squash the possibility of a HRT team going into action. "It's where the Coast Guard found Gonzalo's yacht. It's got to be the place. I'd bet on it."

"Doesn't sound like a guarantee to me," Michael said.

The room went silent as Vinny pondered his options. He had been privy to three previous FBI hostage rescue efforts. The assaults were brutal, done after days of planning, coordination, and practice. There were endless approval cycles beginning at HRT headquarters in Quantico, Virginia and ending in Washington, D.C.—after being bounced between an endless number of agencies with the power to deny and only one with go-ahead authority.

The teams practiced using full-scale mock-ups of the hostage locations and everything in and around them. Every eventuality was scripted. Battle-dressed teams of assaulters did the hand-to-hand, going in and surgically removing the hostage while snipers provided cover. The assault teams exhausted themselves going through all possible scenarios. Success depended on split-second timing, surprise, speed, and overwhelming force. Nothing was left to chance. Everyone knew his or her assignment. They knew they could depend on each other for their lives.

The hostages would be extracted alive. No guarantees for others.

To be responsible for initiating the use of hostage rescue was something that Vinny had dreamed of doing. He had to be careful. "Walk me through the planning cycles."

Alan was poised to respond. If he didn't screw up, he would have approval within minutes. His name would bounce off the walls of FBI headquarters. Everyone would know Alan Dickie. His fast track rise in the FBI ranks would gain momentum.

"Prelim staging at Buzzard's Point is out. Quantico and the teams will do it en route using 3D satellite images. They're experienced and have worked together many times. Our Tactical Operations Center stays in control. They'll do the countdown. I'll have an FBI agent and the local U.S. attorney on a hotline in case we need an extra warrant or two along the way. Don't know. May have to enter neighboring property."

"What about local law enforcement?" said Michael.

"That'd be Monroe County PD," said Alan, not the least bit annoyed. He had thought about this query too. Besides it was Vinny who would give him the go-ahead, not this interfering CIA agent. "We don't need them to clear the area of unfriendlies. No time to bring 'em in on it. As I've said, there's only one road in and out of the Keys. This'll be an FBI operation."

Vinny wasn't convinced. "Procedures require coordinating with locals, Alan."

"Okay, I'll take it on."

"What about compromise authority?" Vinny asked. "Don't you think they'll have guards, lookouts? The teams may have to kill to get near the extraction site."

"Sir, it's a residential community—commuters, retirees, and tourists. That sort of thing. I'm thinking two vans—they shouldn't be noticed anywhere on the Keys—will be the team's final concealment point, right on the curb bordering the site. The snipers will fan out from the vans first. They will establish perimeter control, protecting the backs of the assaulters. Piece of cake. No way we'll need to shoot our way to the hostage extraction point."

"And the strike plan?"

"These teams are experienced. One has worked as a team for three years, the other five. Quantico is working with them as we speak—using the 3D satellite images as I said. Quantico will write the ops plan and rules of engagement. TOC stays in control as usual. They do the countdown."

Vinny paced back and forth. He looked to Michael.

Michael frowned. "Out of my depth."

Vinny didn't like Michael signaling less than wholehearted endorsement. "What's your problem?" Vinny barked.

"The water egress," said Michael.

Alan heard Michael. "Snipers will provide three-sixty cover for the assaulters. That includes the shoreline."

Vinny couldn't put his finger on exactly what was bothering him. There was something in Alan's voice, more than just being cocky. The bastard's daring me to say no. But it wouldn't be his ass on the line if all this blew up. He doesn't have authority to authorize HRT assaults. Vinny made his decision.

"We'll wait until ATC guarantees the hostage is at Crosby's place." Vinny's hand hovered over the speakerphone about to disconnect. On the other hand, if this son-of-a-bitch who shot down an FBI helicopter over U.S. soil escaped?

"Alan, you still there?"

Alan sucked up. "I'm here, chief."

Vinny swallowed hard. "You're authorized to use the HRT teams."

Alan Dickie had his first HRT authorization.

# Chapter 48

### Bayside, Florida
### Monday 2100 ET

Taro Okada was about to get out of his car in the Carp's Landing garage when his cell phone rang. He flipped it open. "Taro."

It was Alan. "The Coast Guard says the yacht at Crosby's place doesn't belong to him."

"Figures. I'd guess it belongs to this guy Gonzalo." Taro opened his car door and leaned back in to remove the ignition key and silence the chimes. "Thanks." Taro started toward the garage stairway leading to the Carp's Landing lobby.

"Wait," said Alan. Taro pressed the cell to his ear. "ATC says they're still checking, trying to find the track of the kidnapper's chopper."

"Got it. Hey Alan, Janet Griffin is home with her daughter tucked in for the night. It's off 43rd Avenue in Bayside. I gave them your name. Gil Bauer was with them when Taylor was snatched. Gil said he'd contact your office in the morning after he talks to his father. Oh, by the way, I think we may have a lead on that guy Royce Palmer you mentioned."

"Whatcha got?" said Alan.

The stairwell door slammed shut behind Taro. "Janet Griffin knows him."

"What?"

Taro raised his voice. "Janet Griffin. She says he's a friend of hers who lives in San Diego."

"She's in on this. I'm sure she is," said Alan.

Taro didn't bother to reply.

Alan didn't mention the hostage rescue team.

Carolyn Hughes sat at a corner table in the Carp's Landing bar. Clusters of twenty and thirty-somethings strained to hear each other over music booming from two large black-shrouded speakers on either side of three musicians. A female vocalist was singing into a microphone pressed to her lips.

Taro entered. From the far corner, Carolyn stood, waving for him to join her.

"I was lucky to find this booth," Carolyn shouted when Taro arrived at the corner table. "It's a little noisy in here. Isn't it?"

Taro smiled.

"Why don't we go out on the patio?" Carolyn hollered. "It's got to be quieter."

The string of Chinese lanterns hung across the patio had been dimmed since the dinner hour.

"So you work for Jack Taylor," said Taro as he sat with Carolyn.

"That's why I was at Doug Crosby's this morning."

"Uh huh," Taro said, signaling for more.

"Taylor Associates is a system-engineering firm doing quite well even in this recession. We're investigating merger options. Mr. Taylor spots a *Forbes* article hinting that Bauer is on the verge of becoming a major player in the Internet. He's interested. Sends me to see what I can find out."

"Why you?"

"I worked as an investigative analyst for Justice. Antitrust. I've mined cases using sophisticated software."

"Okay."

"I called Charles Bauer, got an appointment, and hopped on a plane."

"You called him cold?" said Taro.

Carolyn studied Taro's facial features before replying. "The direct approach works more often than not." Carolyn grinned. Taro didn't recognize her double entendre. "When I arrived in Bayside, I met Janet in the bar inside there. We were college roommates. Low and behold, Gil Bauer, Charles' son, comes in right after me. Janet introduces us. Nice guy. Janet had to leave. I stayed. Gil and I talked for over an hour. I told him what we do. He opened up some."

"Keep going."

"The next day I met Charles Bauer. Charles is the CEO."

"He's interested?"

"No. He's a laconic Southern gentleman and scooted out for a golf date." Taro was listening intently as a detective, alert to every inflection in her voice. She decided to open up more than she had planned. "The receptionist gave me Bauer's Q2."

"Q2?"

"Second Quarterly Report. It turns out Bauer's doing even

better than the *Forbes* article suggested."

"Let me get this straight," said Taro. "Charles Bauer just gave you his Q2 at your first meeting with him? I thought you said he scooted out to play golf."

"I'm not sure who left it for me. Charles Bauer and I never developed what you would call a relationship." Carolyn talked to Taro's eyes. "Look, you're the first person from Bayside that even knows we have the Bauer Q2. I wasn't supposed to tell anyone."

"Go on."

"Back in Virginia I briefed Mr. Taylor. His interest shoots straight off the charts. I bring him to Bayside. We have dinner at Janet's. The next day everybody goes on the Everglades tour. Except me. I go to Crosby's. The rest you know." Carolyn leaned back smiling, feeling safe and tranquil.

"Why Crosby's and not the Everglades?"

"During dinner, we learned Bauer Industries is considering going public, issuing an IPO."

"An initial public offering."

"Exactly," said Carolyn. "The equity market will pay Bauer big bucks for an interest in the firm. If you're lucky enough to buy Bauer at the initial IPO price, any pop in the price when it begins trading is yours. There's less frenzy when the markets are down like now, of course. There's rarely a dearth of money willing to take a flyer. Bauer's one of the very few diamonds left in the dot-com rough."

"Talk to me about IPO's."

Carolyn decided she'd have to satisfy his thirst for detail before she'd have any possibility of switching agendas. "Here it is in a nutshell. Venture capital firms gather money from a variety of investors. They listen to business plans from companies wanting those funds. If the investors like what they hear, they invest. It costs millions to develop and beta test concepts... things like that."

"What's the incentive for the investors?"

"A percentage of the company," said Carolyn. "Oh... say eight or ten percent. They become owners at a price that's below the IPO price too."

"Sounds like a good deal."

Taro's tone told Carolyn he was beginning to finish gathering information. *His eyes are so clear.* "It's a crap-shoot too. Companies go belly-up, products bomb. Outsiders, investors who bought after the IPO, get hurt first. The brokerage firms get their money regardless."

"You never told me why you went to Crosby's."

*Is he ever going to let up?* "Janet told us Crosby is interested in investing in Bauer." She cut it short. "I was getting uncomfortable when we met at Crosby's."

"Why's that?"

"I just was," said Carolyn. She sat up straight, pressing her shoulder blades into the back of her chair. She was feeling warm, bed-warm. "There's something about Crosby, hard to put your finger on it." She stretched her arms above her head. Her back arched. "I'm tired."

"Sorry," said Taro. "Let's go."

"No need to be sorry."

# Chapter 49

### Bayside, Florida
### Monday 2115 ET

Gil Bauer drove up his father's long driveway and parked on the side of the house. He walked around the back. Chimes announced he had opened the door. "Dad, where are you?"

"In the den," said Charles.

Gil went through the kitchen into the den. His father was sitting in a chair, reading. "How you doing, Dad?"

Charles looked up. "What are you doing here?"

Gil stood awkwardly in front of his father. "There's news. I don't know how to start."

Charles smiled. "It can't be that bad."

Gil decided to blurt it out. "Jack Taylor's been kidnapped."

"What?" The hardcover book Charles was reading cracked closed. "Kidnapped?"

"Jack Taylor, the CEO of Taylor Associates. He's been kidnapped."

Charles stood. "I know who he is. I'm meeting him in the morning. What the hell happened?"

"You were at the golf tournament."

"Get on with it."

"Mr. Taylor, Janet, her daughter Nicole and I went on an Everglades tour." Gil looked around the room nervously. "A speedboat came alongside. Armed men boarded. They grabbed Jack Taylor and took off with him."

"You weren't hurt, were you son?"

"No," Exhaustion caught up with Gil. He sat heavily. "They hit Jack a few times. The speedboat sped away with Jack rolling unconscious on its deck."

"How badly was he hurt?"

"Don't know." Gil looked down. He hadn't gotten to the bad part. "I've been with the Miami-Dade PD. They're looking for the men. So's the FBI."

"Why the hell did they kidnap Jack?"

The question came sooner than Gil expected. He took a purposeful breath to help him say it. "I caused it."

"I doubt that." Charles looked closely at his son. "You look awful."

"I feel awful."

"I'm not surprised. You've been through a lot. Now relax for a minute."

"I wish I could relax," said Gil. "I can't." He pursed his lips. "Remember that article in *Forbes*?" Charles nodded. "I wrote it for *Forbes*."

Charles smiled. "I know, son. I still have a few connections, you know." Gil smiled weakly. His father continued. "I don't think you should have done it. It put a lot of pressure on me, turning everyone away like I did."

"I know, Dad. I'm sorry." Gil couldn't let his father leave without telling him. "That's not all, Dad."

"Oh?"

"Remember Carolyn Hughes?" said Gil. "From Taylor Associates. She spoke with you."

"Of course I remember. She's one competent lady. I told her boss so."

"Listen, Dad. I met her. At Carp's Landing Bar. The night she came to town. Before you met her."

"I know that too," said Charles.

"This is the hard part, Dad."

Charles moved to the chair next to Gil and sat on the front edge of its cushion. "Go on."

"Janet left, but Carolyn stayed. We talked. We talked a lot."

"So you talked..."

"By the time we were done, I had heard more about Taylor Associates than you did."

"Tempting, huh?" Charles sat back in his chair. "But, you know I want us to keep this business in the family." Gil's father had engaged the old argument between them.

"We can't, Dad. It won't work." Gil realized he had shunted the conversation off track.

"We've had this discussion before. Let's not get into it again now."

"By the time we ramp up to get the expertise we need, the opportunities will be gone." Gil surprised himself. This time it was he who engaged. He couldn't stop. "It'll take too long. Merger or acquisitions are the only way to go. We're going to have to buy capability. There's no time to develop it internally."

"This has always been a family business," Charles replied.

"That's the problem, Dad. We need new technology. *Now.* We need it more than we need Crosby's money, that's for sure."

Charles rose from his chair and started to leave. "We're not going to discuss Crosby's financing again."

Gil couldn't let his father go. He blurted out, "Dad, I gave Carolyn our Q2 report. The same Q2 report you gave Crosby. Everything."

Charles turned, glaring at his son. "You *what?*"

"I came back to the office after talking with Carolyn, made a copy, and then put it in a sealed envelope for her. The temp handed it to Carolyn after you went down in the elevator. I'm sorry, Dad. Maybe I shouldn't have, but I did."

"So that's what brought Jack Taylor down here."

"And that's why it's my fault he was kidnapped," said Gil.

# Week Two

# Chapter 50

**Bayside, Florida**
**October 30, 2001**
**Tuesday 0230 ET**

The sound of the water in the shower seeped under the bathroom door and enveloped Carolyn, warm under the sheets. She curled tighter, his pillow wedged between her thighs and breasts. She inhaled slowly, savoring his scent. The water stopped. She heard the shower door snap open. She rolled onto her back. Her body tingled as her fingertips, barely escaping the top of the sheet, grasped the headboard. Her toes stretched, seeking the footboard well beyond their reach.

The bathroom light flooded the room. She froze, listening. Nothing. She released the headboard and cleared the sheets from her head and shoulders. He was facing away, bending over. His boxer shorts dangled from his right hand. He lifted one foot, then the other as he put them on. He bent over again to pick up his shirt from where he'd dropped it a few hours before. With one arm in the shirt, he turned.

"Good morning," Carolyn whispered.

"It's time," said Taro, his free arm hunting for the second sleeve.

Carolyn sat on the edge of the bed, searching for her nightie somewhere under the sheets. "What time is it?"

Taro finished buttoning his shirt and turned away, looking for his tie. "Two thirty."

"You're kidding." Carolyn stood. She held the silk nightie at arms length over her head, waiting for Taro to turn back toward her. When he did, she stretched onto her toes, took a slow deep breath and then released the silk. "Give me a second. I'll be right with you." She gathered her red hair behind her ears and tippy-toed barefoot into the bathroom.

"Have to go," said Taro.

She leaned against the bathroom doorframe. "I won't be long."

Taro continued dressing, not looking at Carolyn. "I'll call when I have something new."

"Come on, I got my boss into this mess. I'm not just going

to sit around and wait." She closed the bathroom door behind her.

Carolyn stepped out of the shower and wrapped a towel around herself. Glowing, she opened the bathroom door and went back into the room. Her face flexed to a pout. Taro had left without saying a word. Almost as quickly, the remembrance of the events of the previous day refocused her.

Making contact with Royce Palmer was a must. She sat on the edge of the bed and dialed information. Her right heel quivered as she waited. She reached out and picked up the pen and small pad from the end table as she waited for the recorded options to play out. An operator came on the line.

"Residence listings," Carolyn said. "Palmer. San Diego. In the business section, listings beginning with Palmer." The operator didn't reply. Carolyn silenced her quivering heel.

The operator came back. "Two individuals, a David and a Royce and a business listing, Palmer Investments."

*Bingo.* "Royce Palmer and then Palmer Investments please."

A computer voice provided the numbers. She wrote them down and then dialed Palmer Investments. She turned, looking at the clock radio on the other end table. She decided to let the Palmer Investments number ring anyway. A recording answered. "Mr. Palmer will be out of the office for the rest of the week. In an emergency, dial 858 …"

Carolyn dialed the 858 emergency number. The phone rang three times. "Royce Palmer." She was startled. At this hour she hadn't expected to hear a man's voice.

"Mr. Palmer, my name is Carolyn Hughes."

"Yes."

"Mr. Palmer, you don't know me but we have a mutual friend. Actually, two friends."

"Okay, I give up. Who are they?" Royce responded.

"Janet and Nicole Griffin."

"I know a Janet Griffin," said Royce.

"Nicole is Janet's four-year-old daughter."

"What can I do for you Ms.—?"

"Carolyn Hughes, Mr. Palmer. My name is Carolyn Hughes."

"I see, Ms. Hughes. Now, what can I do for you?"

"I'm sorry to bother you so late."

"I'm in a cab, arriving back at my hotel in Miami. Now, what can I do for you?"

"I would like to meet with you, as soon as possible."

"About?"

"Crosby Limited," said Carolyn.

Royce remained silent.

Carolyn spoke slowly, "Is it possible we could meet? Say in the morning? At the Carp's Landing Hotel? It's in Bayside, about twenty minutes north of Miami." Royce still didn't respond.

"Say eight o'clock in the lobby?"

# Chapter 51

## Miami, Florida
## Tuesday 0300 ET

Taro knew just how far to lean back in his low-backed wooden chair without toppling over. Without a word he hung up the phone. It was the mayor's point man, *again*. This time he wanted to be triply sure Taro knew how important it was to nail the Miami airport bomber. Like anybody needed to tell him. He sat forward in his chair thinking about the eavesdropping tools Holt had told him about—Echelon, Carnivore and what was its name... Magic Lantern, that's it. And, oh yeah, the Patriot Act.

Taro didn't like to hear a lot of technical gobbledygook, but he did want to understand. He took out the sheets Holt had faxed to him and began reading.

Echelon is controlled by the U.S. National Security Agency under treaty with the United States, Great Britain, Australia, New Zealand, and Canada. It's a global network of ground, sea, air and satellite eavesdropping systems. Every day it scoops up faxes, e-mail traffic, telephone calls, and data in just about every language in the world, whether it's encrypted or not. There are hundreds of millions of intercepts every day.

During the last decade there has been an explosion of traffic volume, languages, dialects and codes. NSA, with its limited resources, can barely keep up with the very highest priority requests of the international oversight body that directs and monitors the intercepts.

Targeted intercepts are typically foreign leaders, criminals, terrorists, and drug dealers. There are huge technological barriers to be overcome before Echelon comes anywhere close to being a real time, all-hearing, all-seeing system.

A Mind-Boggling Problem

Every day hundreds of millions of video, imagery, text, and voice intercepts are collected by the CIA.

Every day a million new pages appear on the Internet. They are in hundreds of languages, dialects and accents.

Individual analysts must understand this mass of raw data so they can answer specific questions. For example, what is a country's doctrine concerning electronic warfare, surveillance, undercover agents or sabotage while taking into account competing military, academic, governmental and private industry interests?

"Data mining" is a term used to explain how analysts extract knowledge from gigabytes of raw data. Sophisticated software programs are used to comb raw data. They prepare it for analysts to mine. Examples:

Software transcribes audio and web pages in Chinese, Russian, Japanese, and other languages into English.

Software links an individual's phone calls, bank deposits and airline travel.

Multilingual search engines use "natural-language" (e.g. what is Castro's favorite meal?) instead of rigid "key word" searches.

Combining computer translations with web-based searches improves the accuracy and timeliness of data mining.

A software package called Fluent performs searches of web sites in Chinese, Russian, Japanese and seven other languages. It translates them almost instantaneously into English.

The Defense Advanced Research Projects Agency has developed a computer program called Oasis that uses speech recognition to turn audio feeds into searchable text. It is currently learning various English accents. The CIA is pushing for Chinese, Arabic and Korean.

Half-hour intercepted broadcasts are being processed and readied for mining in 10 minutes.

A CIA "surge tool kit" allows teams of analysts to search and assess huge quantities of "open source" information in order to provide analytic reports for the president and his chief advisors during times of crisis.

Carnivore

Carnivore is an FBI system approved by Congress. After receiving judiciary approval and informing the Internet sevice provider, Carnivore equipment is placed at the gateway of the Internet service provider. It targets e-mail traffic.

Taro turned to the Miami-Dade PD report he had requested.

> Active surname files:
> Gonzalo: Twenty-eight
> Gomez: One hundred three
>
> Previous seven day:
> House break-ins: Six
> Locations: Four-Miami, two-Bayside

Taro wondered, where's the light at the end of this tunnel?

# Chapter 52

### Key Largo, Florida
### Tuesday 0315 ET

Botero was jolted awake by the roar of the helicopter engine on the lawn. He staggered from the couch, making his way to the patio doors. The chopper blades were whirling faster and faster as they responded to the full-throttle command of the engine. Botero made it out to the side of the helicopter and yelled to the man standing in its door. *"Low, man. Fly low. No radar track you. Okay man?"* The man nodded and disappeared into the chopper. Doug joined Botero as the chopper began a slow rise. They watched as it headed out across Blackwater Sound.

"Why'd you let it go?" asked Doug. "We should be on board."

"It coffin, man." Botero took a device from his pocket. "See the chopper, man?"

The helicopter crossed Blackwater Sound, heading north. It was barely visible when Botero pressed a button on the device in his hand. A black cloud appeared where the helicopter had been. The sound of the blast arrived moments later. Botero smiled.

Doug turned, crouching in horror. Then he retched.

Jack Taylor was stiff all over when the chopper blades began their slow rhythmic beat. He worked his wrists trying to break the final threads he hadn't been able to slice through while on the helicopter. Without a sharp edge he knew it would be useless. He twisted his wrists, working the threads over his hands toward his fingers. Finally his hands worked free.

He ripped the tape from his mouth and eyes and then freed his legs. He went to the window. Two men stood alone on the lawn. He ran to the kitchen and searched the drawers frantically for a weapon. He slid a steak knife between his belt and pants just as the sound of the explosion filled the guesthouse. He raced back to the window.

The two men were heading for the guesthouse. Jack dashed to the bedroom, dialed 911, and slid the handset under the pillow without waiting for an answer. He sprinted through a bedroom onto the deck. He vaulted over the rail and lay prone, pressed against the hot tub side of the deck. He heard the guesthouse front door open.

Botero shouted, "The fucker's gone. Check the fucking boats."

Jack stopped breathing as Botero checked the hot tub above him and then watched as Botero and Doug ran toward the boats. Botero boarded the yacht. Doug boarded his sailboat.

With both men below deck, Jack raced across the lawn, past the main house, up the driveway and began jogging along the street, his heart threatening to burst free of his chest. Headlights appeared in front of him. He flagged down the car and stood gasping by the driver's window.

"What's going on?" said the driver.

Jack wheezed, "Kidnapped." He pointed toward Crosby's driveway. "That house..."

"Hop in," said the driver.

Jack staggered to the other side of the car and got in. The car started down the road. Suddenly Pepe leaned on the horn and swerved into Doug's driveway. "What are you doing?" Jack shouted. He reached for the knife and drove it deep into Pepe's forearm. Pepe screamed. Jack stabbed his arm again. In anguish Pepe jammed his foot on the accelerator. The car careened across the lawn, crashing through the garage doors. It wedged itself catty-corner in the garage. Pepe fell on the horn in pain.

Botero and Doug ran toward the blaring horn. They didn't see Jack racing down the driveway. Botero pulled Pepe off the horn. Doug flipped on the garage light.

Jack's heart leaped a dozen beats faster. He would be a sitting duck in the glare of the garage lights. He threw the knife further up the driveway, ran to the shrubbery and dove onto the woodchips. He backed against the privacy fence and braced his head in the corner formed by the fence and a stone knee-high wall lining the street.

Jack heard Pepe. "I'm telling you this guy said you kidnapped him. Then the fucker stabbed me. Twice."

"You closed the massage parlor, didn't you?" said Doug.

"What the fuck are you talking about?" said Pepe.

Doug knew the massage parlor never closed. "You were fucking those cunts, weren't you?"

Botero and Doug started down the driveway. Botero turned,

yelling at Pepe. "Turn out that light, man."

Before Jack's pupils could adjust to the new ambient light, he heard Doug. "I found his knife."

Several minutes later, he saw the silhouettes of Doug and Botero coming back from the roadway. They walked up the driveway, through the garage, and into the house without saying a word.


Two Chevy vans pulled off Overseas Highway in Key Largo at Taylor Creek Village. They drove a short distance along Taylor Drive and turned around before they pulled off to the side of the road.

Four snipers carrying two rubber boats exited the van. Water presented a unique threat.

Eighteen men crouched silently in the vans. They would be asked to risk their lives soon. None were pleased with this sudden assignment. There hadn't been any practice drills. The site details remained sketchy. Exactly how high was the stone wall that lined the curb? Was barbed wire strung along its top? Was it crowned with pointed rocks? Was the helicopter on the grounds? Had it been confirmed that it had ever been there? Were any of the walls of the house made of stone? How many rooms were there? In the main house? In the guesthouse? How were the rooms laid out? How many people were in the house with the hostage? What room was the hostage in? What armament did the targets have? The unknowns were serious distractions. When risking your life, distractions killed.

This wasn't the first assault for any of them. They were all veterans and had worked together. On this gig they were counting heavily on each man's skills, and the knowledge they had of the other's moves in almost any situation, to carry them through. As they waited, they began steadying their breathing in an attempt to remain calm. Every man had his own technique.

Each van had two additional snipers. They would be the first out and would take positions on the street side of the stone wall, two on each side of the driveway. They would use the stone wall to steady their rifles, that is, if the top of the wall was the right height and clear of barbed wire and sharp-edged stones.

Fourteen long minutes later the Tactical Operations Center gave the order to proceed. The two vans pulled back onto the

Highway, drove south, and headed for Crosby's home on the other side of the highway.

Jack Taylor willed himself not to panic. He had to think clearly. He peered out from his bed of woodchips. The guesthouse and dock had both proved dead-ends. The roadway was pitch black and hadn't proved to be a much better option. He began to wonder why he was thinking of moving at all. He looked toward voices reaching him. Botero, Pepe and Doug were crossing the lawn toward the guesthouse. He watched them go onto the dock and board the sailboat.

A few minutes later the sound of the sailboat's motor gave him heart. He stood, brushed off the wood chips still clinging to his skin, and watched the sailboat moored in the slip. After an eternity it left the slip and headed out of the inlet.

As Jack started for the front door to call for help, something made him look toward the road. He raced back to his hiding place where a new set of woodchips dug into his flesh. He raised his head above the stone wall. A black Chevy van glided to a stop just before the driveway, a few feet from his hiding place. A second black Chevy van glided past the first. It stopped on the far side of the driveway. The two vans sat silently on the side of the dark, asphalt-covered road.

The Beta assault team leader in the van on the far side of the driveway listened as the Alpha assault team leader asked Tactical Operations Control, "Permission to go Yellow."

"Hold one," came the reply. Everyone checked his or her gear a final time. They knew it wouldn't be long now before they would be out the van's door. "Permission to move to yellow granted," TOC replied.

The starting gun had been fired.

In unison two black rubber rafts landed on the sound side of the inlet. Four snipers scrambled like bugs across the top of the jetty. Eight seconds later they were all but invisible, their bodies wedged firmly against granite, their rifle stocks wedged against the bone of their cheeks. When they finished adjusting their infrared scopes and gun sites for distance, wind, and humidity, they began the rituals of calming their pulse rates. The trigger pull must only respond to a mental command.

Jack didn't hear the van's roadside cargo doors slip open or see snipers from each van take up their assigned positions against the stone wall.

Exactly one minute later Alpha team in full battle-dress raced knees-bent up the driveway, fanned out across the lawn, and surrounded the house. One of the seven assaulters sprawled prone just a few feet in front of Jack. He aimed his shotgun through the garage to the kitchen entrance of the house, a .45-caliber pistol strapped to his right leg. Jack couldn't see the second forty-five holstered on the chest of the man's Kevlar vest.

The seven Beta team assaulters swarmed over the stone wall on the far side of the driveway. They ran in the same crouched posture toward the guesthouse and dock. A direct hit by a .50-caliber round would shatter the ceramic trauma plate on their chests, putting any one of them down. Most other rounds would slow their advance. Four of the Beta team assaulters surrounded the guesthouse. One squatted on the dock by the yacht's bow post around which Gonzalo had thrown a triple clove hitch. The other squatted by the sternpost. The seventh assaulter positioned himself with a clear view of the guesthouse, the length of the dock, and the lawn between the guesthouse and the main house, now surrounded by Alpha Team. Alpha and Beta had established their fields of fire.

Every cell in Jack's body was cocked to respond to whatever message it might receive. From his front row seat he watched law enforcement setting up their lines of attack, marveling at their discipline, body armor, and teamwork. Jack knew they would easily gain access to the interiors of the two buildings and the yacht as they obviously planned to do. These were no-nonsense professionals, prepared to kill and to die if necessary.

If Jack came out of hiding, anyone of these battle-ready specialists might consider him the first of the enemy emerging from cover. Every option Jack could think of failed when compared to staying put and letting them do whatever they had come to do. He put his adrenaline on standby.

The man lying prone in front of Jack lowered his night vision goggles and began moving his head slowly to his right. Jack fought panic. When this man started turning his head back to the left it would be only seconds before his green-vision world would glow from his body heat. Jack pressed his back hard against the fence and squiggled closer to the stone wall until a sharp edge of stone began digging into the top of his head. He put his chin on his chest to get less than an inch closer and drew his knees hard to his chest until they locked in a fetal position. There was no better position.

The assaulter's head held at its far right position. Could he have spotted someone? Something? The NV goggles started back to his left. Jack made a decision. If he were spotted, he would sit up tight to the corner of the wall and fence and thrust his hands as high in the air as they would go without raising his butt a fraction of an inch off the woodchips. The goggles passed center and started toward Jack. Were they moving slower? Was the glow from his body heat beginning to appear? The assaulter's head stopped just as it had when he looked hard right. Jack stared at the side of the man's head. He watched for the slightest motion that might tell him that the man had spotted him.

The goggles started moving right.

The fourteen assaulters held their positions. Arm and hand signals did the communications. "Clear. No ninety-eight point sixes." The words startled Jack. They hadn't come from the man lying in front of him. They were said as someone might say on a Sunday afternoon, "Want to go to a movie?" Jack searched for the source. Instead of a man, Jack found the barrel of a rifle directly above his head. The man holding the rifle was a foot away, on the opposite site of the stone wall.

Jack knew then that staying put had been the best decision of his life.

Every assaulter heard, "TOC to Alpha and Beta. Permission granted to go green."

One assaulter from each team rose and crouched their way to the two buildings. They set breach charges against the front doors before retreating backwards as they guided the detonator cords to control boxes.

A short way up the dark road, an ambulance driver turned on his siren and flashing lights. The policeman in the Monroe County PD cruiser leading the ambulance did the same.

The snipers were trained to protect the assaulters from all threats unless restrained by TOC. With the sound of the sirens one sniper on each side of the driveway swung around on the balls of his feet. They followed the sound of the police cruiser with the muzzles of their drawn forty-fives. The cruiser's front wheels began to turn into Doug's driveway just as the breach charges blew the front doors. The roar from the explosion smothered the reports coming from the muzzles of four snipers and the sound of four tires exploding.

The HRT plan was working, so far.

The Monroe County cruiser with its tires blown skidded to a stop on the graveled driveway, its siren demanding the right of way.

Before the front doors of the house and guesthouse hit the ground, assaulters were inside tossing flash bang grenades to blind anyone inside and rupture their eardrums. The assaulter lying in front of Jack got up, raced through the garage and used his shotgun to demolish the kitchen door. With fingers on the triggers of forty-fives, shotguns, and MP-5 machine guns, the Alpha and Beta teams began their systematic room-by-room search for Jack Taylor.

The ambulance turned into Crosby's drive. Again, four sniper bullets took out the ambulance tires, two from behind the stone wall took out the rear tires, and two from the jetty took out the front tires. The ambulance went into its skid and rammed the back of the cruiser. The ambulance driver and EMT were too stunned to move. The cruiser and ambulance sirens continued dueling for the right of way.

The cop jumped out, crouched by the fender of his cruiser, waving his gun in every direction, sure he would find something to aim it at. *"Backup. Backup,"* he screamed into his shoulder-mounted microphone.

# Chapter 53

### Biscayne Bay, Florida
### Tuesday 0400 ET

The Coast Guard coxswain Raul Salinas pushed the throttles of the Chrysler engines forward. The bow of the 44-foot small boat lifted up over the low swells as it sped south on the Intracoastal Waterway toward Biscayne Bay.

"What do you think it was,?" Guy Collins shouted over the roaring engines and swirling winds engulfing them.

Raul's eyes remained focused past the bow, watching for anything that might cause him to alter course. "Don't know. Hope someone stayed around long enough to show us where the explosion was."

Guy unfolded a chart and pressed it onto the small clear area in front of him.

"After Barnes Sound, what?" Raul asked as the small boat passed under Card Sound Road Bridge.

Guy studied the chart. "Route 1 Bridge, past Sexton Cove. Then Blackwater Sound."

"That's Key Largo. Where the Miami-Dade PD had us check out that yacht. What was that name printed on the stern? DESCIFRAR?"

"Right. Think there's a connection?"

"I'd bet on it," said Raul. "How long before we get there?"

"The GPS says…"

"Get us there before the chopper." Raul Salinas went full throttle. The deck of the small boat rose another eight degrees as it flew across Barnes Sound.

Raul throttled the engines back. The deck began leveling as it entered Blackwater Sound. "See anything?" He began an inward spiraling search pattern.

"Not much, too dark," said Guy. Raul turned on the searchlight. Guy reached for the grappling hook. "Port side. Twenty meters." The bow sliced the calm water. "Slow, slow… I've got it."

"What is it?"

Guy said, "Looks like a… It's a seat cushion. Doesn't look like it's from a boat."

Raul explored with the searchlight. "What's that over there?"

Guy squinted as Raul idled the boat closer. "A little closer."

"Okay?" said Raul.

"It's a… oh lord." Guy slumped on the gunwale. The grappling hook fell onto the deck.

Raul cut the engines, went to Guy, and looked over the side. Black hair fanned on the surface of the water. It was the torso of a man. Both legs were missing below the knees. It had only one arm. Guy heaved.

Raul looked over the debris field. "Whatever happened here was no accident."

# Chapter 54

## Biscayne Bay, Florida
## Tuesday 0415 ET

Doug had been at the helm since fleeing in his sailboat from Blackwater Sound, yet he couldn't remember leaving his dock. Over and over he watched the two men on his lawn repairing their helicopter, heard the chopper sputter and then roar to life, listened to Botero instruct the pilot to fly low below the radar, and moments later — the blinding fireball, its plume rising straight up, a brief monument to the existence of the helicopter crew.

"This tub don't go no faster?" Botero snarled.

Doug looked around. They were passing under Card Sound Road Bridge.

"Man, you no deaf."

"It's a sailboat for God sake," Doug spat back.

Pepe emerged from below deck, his right arm in a makeshift sling.

"Little asshole," said Botero.

Pepe staggered to a deck chair. "Where are we?"

Doug pointed in the direction of the clouds ahead glowing in the light from Miami. "Miami."

Botero grasped the rail, staring into the dark water. Without warning, he whipped around, growling at Pepe, "Where fucking disk?"

"I don't know," Pepe said. "Doug can vouch for me. Right, Doug?"

Doug looked to Botero. "Maybe Gonzalo, dead or alive, still has it. Maybe he didn't bring it. Who knows?"

"Feelers out man," said Botero. "Gonzalo easy spot."

Pepe grinned. "Why?"

"He tall and fat, asshole."

Pepe laughed. "There are thousands of tall, fat bastards in the states."

Botero drew his gun and put it in Pepe's face. "Why I no waste you, asshole?"

Pepe crouched, his face frozen in fear. "Didn't I get the bombs for you?"

Botero pressed the nozzle of the gun against Pepe's nose. "You shark, man. He snickered. "Shark eat garbage, asshole." Doug joined in. "He's not an asshole. Assholes have a purpose."

"Where disk..." Botero demanded.

Pepe's eyes bulged, the muscles in his shoulders balled. "Wait."

"Why I wait?"

"You want the disk, right?" Botero moved his gun away from Pepe's face. "Gonzalo left it in the guesthouse. Just like you said."

"What you talk about?" said Botero.

"Someone must have found it. Right?"

"We're listening," Doug said.

"Who was in the guesthouse after Gonzalo arrived?"

"You dumb shit," said Botero, pressing the gun to his Pepe's forehead. "I check that."

"Maybe no," said Pepe. "Maybe someone just took it?"

"Yeah, like who?" said Doug.

"What about Janet?" said Pepe. Botero drew back. Sensing an opening, Pepe challenged. "Anyone check her out?"

Botero swung around to Doug. "Who this Janet?"

Doug's face dropped. He hadn't mentioned Janet. He blurted, "Pepe brought her."

Botero put the muzzle of his gun to Pepe's wounded arm. "You little son-of-a-mother-fucking asshole." Botero took several rapid breaths. He pressed the nozzle deeper and deeper into Pepe's wounded arm with each word. "Tell... me... everybody... at... party." Pepe doubled over, fell to the deck, unable to speak. *"Everybody!"* Botero forced Pepe's wounded arm out of its makeshift sling.

Pepe rolled over, drawing his knees to his chest, wheezing, fighting heaving. "No one else."

"There better not be," said Doug. He kicked Pepe in the back.

Pepe's mind flooded with visions of Janet that night on the couch after he took her home from Doug's party, her look of disgust, her screaming rejections. He spewed vengeance. "We've got to check the bitch out."

"Where she, man?"

"I can find her," said Pepe. "I know I can."

# Chapter 55

## FBI headquarters, Washington, D.C.
## Tuesday 0420 ET

CIA Agent Michael Stone hadn't been able to concentrate during his Metro ride to work. He never opened the paperback he had planned to start. He cleared the Federal Triangle Metro station and exited onto 12th Street. *Who cares? The way things are going I won't be around much longer anyway.* He began a slow jog. Two blocks later he crossed Pennsylvania Avenue and headed for FBI headquarters. For some reason, the Capitol lights usually seemed a little brighter from this side of Pennsylvania Avenue. Tonight they didn't. He lost his desire to jog.

Sarah had taken the children to Ohio. She had said he shouldn't mind if the children spent a week or two or three with their grandparents. He certainly wasn't spending quality time with them. They were always asleep when he was home. Besides, it certainly wouldn't be her that he'd miss. He had demonstrated that time and time again. Well it was the truth, wasn't it?

At his break Michael had left the headquarters building for a change of scenery and a breath of fresh air. Outside, he stood on the corner in front of FBI headquarters with no desire to go back in. Vinny had told him he must provide a detailed explanation of exactly how he had obtained access to the Echelon intercept. The inspector general would use it as evidential material in his investigation to see if Michael had violated security laws. Yeah, it was going to be a great day— or rather, a great night. No question about that.

Downtown Washington was a ghost town. No one wanted to be standing alone on a street corner much after 7 p.m. At midnight you felt like the last person on earth. Michael tried to shake the blues. Maybe the silence was just a sign that the city was sleeping well. After all, the F-14s were still flying, protecting the nation's capitol. He looked up. The empty sky didn't help one bit.

Michael sat at his terminal in the leads center. The Capitol-building icon he had created so enthusiastically a few days before was blinking. There was an intercept he hadn't read. He smiled. Using Echelon, Carnivore, Magic Lantern and Rapid Start as an integrated eavesdropping team had proven to be like fishing with four poles in a school of starving fish. He opened the blinking capitol-building icon. This time his eavesdropping team had snared three new intercepts.

The first was a Carnivore intercept. It was another e-mail from the Acapulco Library to Royce Palmer. Michael read the translation.

> No word from east.
> Find out what's going on first hand.

The second was the domestic tap that had been approved on Royce Palmer's office phone. Someone had called from Florida, a place called Carp's Landing. The comment column displayed a single word: Recording. Michael dialed the number. He listened to the same message Carolyn Hughes had listened to a few hours earlier. He wrote down the 858-exchange number the recorded message gave to all callers. He entered it in Rapid Start. He was casting fresh bait into the ether.

Later, a third intercept. Bony shoulders was still on the job. It was Royce Palmer's cell phone call back to Carp's Landing. Michael listened. Carolyn Hughes answered. She would be meeting Royce at eight in the morning. Fishing was best in early mornings.

Michael studied his spreadsheets—the names, times, and places of the intercepts. Then he reread every message. He was gleaning a better feel for this cast of characters. He could almost see them in Acapulco, San Diego, Key Largo and riding along Florida's highways. Each had a distinctive voice and style of speaking or writing e-mails.

There was no doubt in Michael's mind. They would end up at the same place at the same time. The question was, where? when? Wherever, it would be a volatile mixture that would require the least little spark to ignite. Michael had no idea what was causing the feeding frenzy, where his zeros and ones were taking him.

Michael couldn't ignore it any longer. The administrative

icon would never stop blinking if he didn't open it. He opened it. It was what he thought, a message from Vinny Campbell. Vinny wanted to know when he would receive Michael's explanation of how he had accessed the Echelon intercept.

Michael typed his reply: "New intercepts. Terrorists first."

Michael began summarizing the new intercepts. He had to be sure the summary told the story as seen from SIOC—no embellishments, just clear statements of fact. The summary of the latest intercepts would build on his previous summaries. Focus on the Miami airport bombing. Maybe someone else could figure out what was going on better than he could.

Vinny Campbell would receive his copies when everyone else did.

# Chapter 56

### Miami, Florida
### Tuesday 0350 ET

Taro Okada walked into his office and turned on the lights. He didn't realize he was adjusting the ends of his tie as he settled into his low-backed swivel chair. The phone rang. "Taro."

"Taro-san, Alan. There's news."

Taro was tired. "Go."

"The Coast Guard found the helicopter. More precisely they found what's left of its crew. Gruesome. The chopper went down in Blackwater Sound."

Taro took off his tie and folded it ceremoniously. "Don't tell me. Blackwater Sound is near Crosby's."

Alan said, "It exploded. Body parts everywhere."

Taro put his folded tie in its reserved space in the desk drawer. "Say it, Alan. A bomb."

"Yeah, a bomb. Our hostage rescue team raided Crosby's place."

Taro closed the drawer slowly, putting his only tie away for the night. "Oh?"

"Good news first," said Alan. "Jack Taylor's safe. He heard the explosion, dialed 911, and left without hanging up. When the 911 operator didn't hear anyone on the line, she assumed the worst. She dispatched an ambulance. Ambulances are accompanied by police cruisers in that county."

"Monroe County," said Taro. "Go on."

"They arrived as HRT teams detonated charges to gain access to Crosby's house and guesthouse."

"Talk about bad timing."

"A lot of explaining and paperwork," said Alan. "Bottom line. No one home. Jack was hiding in the shrubbery. Like I said, he's fine."

"Good," mumbled Taro.

"We're going over the house, the guesthouse, the yacht, and grounds with a fine tooth comb. We should get prints and DNA evidence. We'll have to corroborate what Jack saw."

"What'd he see?"

"Botero and two others left in a sailboat."

"You'll have trouble finding it," said Taro.

"Tell me about it.   By the time we closed the circus at Crosby's place, talked to Jack, and sent a chopper aloft... we couldn't find it."

"Who was with Botero?" said Taro.

"Jack didn't know.  If I had to guess, one was Crosby.  We don't know who the other guy might be."

Taro said, "I'd guess my snitch, Pepe.  Look Alan, I'll contact C.G. search and rescue.  See if I can get the guys that went into Crosby's inlet earlier in on this.  They'd have the best chance of finding the sailboat.  They saw it.  They know Crosby."

# Chapter 57

### Biscayne Bay, Florida
### Tuesday 0440 ET

Small boat Coxswain Raul Salinas stood behind the podium. Navigational maps of the Keys and Biscayne Bay were projected on the two screens behind him. Raul's shipmate Seaman Guy Collins sat in the first row with a Miami-Dade precinct captain and three plain-clothes policemen—two male, one female. Scattered in the remaining rows were two other 44-footer C.G. crews and six coastguardsmen armed with rifles. Holt sat with the C.G. helicopter crew. All the coasties wore sidearms.

"Gentlemen, we're looking for a sloop, a single mast sailboat," said Raul. "No real distinguishing features. Three men are known to have been aboard when it left Key Largo's Blackwater Sound. Both the Miami-Dade county police and the FBI have classified these men as heavily armed and extremely dangerous. One of them is responsible for the Miami airport bombing of a few days ago." Gasps rumbled in the room. "His name is Luis Botero." Raul pressed a button on the remote. Two pictures of Botero replaced the navigational maps. Raul's face tightened. "Two Miami-Dade children died in that bombing."

"Botero is known to have kidnapped a civilian from an Everglades tour boat just south of Marco Island. He escaped with his victim in a speedboat and then to a waiting crop-duster helicopter. He stood on its skids and downed an unarmed pursuing FBI helicopter." Again, gasps filled the room.

"Our C.G. helicopter crew is sitting in the last row there." Everyone turned to look at them. "They were first on the scene. Rescued the crew of the downed FBI copter. Unharmed, I may add. Holt Brown there—Raul encouraged Holt to stand— was in that downed helicopter. He wants Botero bad. Really bad. He will fly with our crew."

Holt nodded to his onlookers.

Raul walked in front of the podium and continued. "After Botero exited his helicopter in Key Largo, the chopper took off and exploded over Blackwater Sound. Botero used a bomb to slaughter his own crew."

Raul pressed his remote. The navigational maps reappeared. He pointed to a spot on Blackwater Sound. "The helicopter went down here. Raul and I were first on the scene. It was gruesome. The remains recovered are of two individuals."

The C.G. station captain took the podium. "Communications will remain open at all times between all units. I'll be the C.G. focal point and coordinate with the Miami-Dade PD. Holt Brown, flying with our helicopter crew, will be the FBI focal point."

The C.G. captain followed with the radio frequencies to be used, concluding with, "Gentlemen, this will be in the press. You know what that means. They want *gotcha headlines*. We're all being put under a microscope. They'll be watching every move we make, headlining every flaw, real or imagined. So if you spot anything, I repeat *anything*, report it immediately. Do not take any action on your own unless you are in immediate danger. God's speed to you all."

Raul and Guy were the first to exit the building. They headed toward their 44-footer moored at the pier.

Sunrise was an hour away.

# Chapter 58

### Bayside, Florida
### Tuesday 0605 ET

Carolyn Hughes walked out of the Carp's Landing Hotel. She found a public telephone outside a drugstore and called Janet. "Everybody okay?"

"We're still shook up, but we're fine," said Janet. "I guess."

Time was critical. Carolyn got right to the point. "Your home telephone may be being tapped. That's why I called your cell."

"What are you talking about? Where are you, Carolyn?"

"On Bell Boulevard."

"You think someone's tapping my telephone?"

"Could be. Listen Janet, get out of there."

"Why?"

"Taro says we're dealing with a lunatic, that's why."

"Taro has two men watching us twenty-four hours a day," said Janet. "We'll be fine." Janet heard something and looked out her bedroom window. "Would you believe it? Nicole just jumped into the pool after her beach ball. It's just after six in the morning, for God sake."

"Jesus, Janet, get her inside," said Carolyn. "It's not safe. We're dealing with a lunatic."

"What *exactly* are you saying?" asked Janet.

*"Get out. Now."* She put the telephone closer to her mouth, turned toward the wall, and said in hushed tones, "Call the airlines. Go to my apartment."

"You're serious, aren't you?"

"I'm *dead* serious. *Now go.*"

"Come on, Carolyn, why would they be after us? We have nothing they want."

"Mr. Taylor didn't have anything they wanted, either. As soon as they realize that he doesn't have whatever the hell they're looking for, they'll start looking elsewhere."

"You're scaring me."

"Good— *now go!* " said Carolyn.

"How can we?" said Janet. "The police are guarding us."

"Right." Carolyn stared down Bell Boulevard. On the next block was a supermarket. She turned back to the wall. "Call a cab. Tell 'em to meet you behind the supermarket on Bell Boulevard, at the rear loading dock. Tell 'em you're coming off shift."

"Huh?" Janet said.

"The police will follow you. When you're in the supermarket go to the ladies' room. It's usually in the back where they're moving stock, cleaning fish, that sort of thing. Don't dawdle. Keep going, out onto the loading dock. Get to the airport. Don't even tell your father until you're in my apartment. No, call your father from a pay phone in the Crystal City underground."

"Taro won't like this."

"Just go, Janet. *Please!*" Carolyn hung up. She went into the drugstore for a roll of quarters. Returning to the pay phone, she called Simon Tully.

Emily answered. "Mr. Tully's office."

"Emily, this is Carolyn."

"Are you okay?" said Emily. "Is there any word on Mr. Taylor?"

Carolyn couldn't think of any way to sugarcoat it. She didn't want to. "I'm afraid not, Emily. We're doing everything we can to get him back safe and sound."

"We haven't seen anything in the press yet."

"The FBI and police don't want—"

"Oh, thank God, the FBI is in on this. Why would anybody kidnap Mr. Taylor?"

"We just don't know at this point. Look, I have a favor to ask."

"Anything," said Emily.

"Call HR. Have them send you my personnel folder, okay?"

"Sure, but why?"

"I don't want anybody to know where I live. Okay, Emily?"

"I'll lock it in Mr. Tully's safe," said Emily. "But can't they just call information?"

"I have an unlisted number."

"Oh good. Where can I reach you?"

"I'll be on the go. My cell battery died. Leave messages at the Carp's Landing Hotel if it's a dire emergency. Gotta go."

Carolyn looked at her watch. Royce Palmer was due in the Carp's Landing lobby within the hour.

# Chapter 59

### Biscayne Bay, Florida
### Tuesday 0630 ET

Pepe felt nauseous as he watched Doug and Botero go below. The makeshift sling on his arm hung loose around his neck, undone by rolling on the deck as he tried to protect himself from Doug and Botero. He grasped the rail with his left hand and followed them into the cabin. He lowered himself onto a cushioned seat. Doug handed him his cell phone. Pepe dialed. Janet answered.

Pepe smiled up at Botero and Doug. "Janet, this is Pepe."

"Can't talk now," said Janet. "Gotta go."

Pepe looked up at Botero with a feigned I'll-know-soon smile. "Where?"

Janet clamped her head over the masterpiece. Pepe pressed the telephone hard against his ear. He heard Janet chastise Nicole in Spanish, "*Move! The plane won't wait. Aunt Carolyn lives in Virginia, not around the corner.*"

Janet uncovered the mouthpiece, saying while hanging up, "Goodbye."

Pepe said after Janet hung up, "Okay, Janet … I understand. Goodbye."

"So?" said Doug.

Pepe gloated. "Janet's on her way to the airport."

"The airport?" said Doug.

"She and Nicole are catching a plane. It's leaving for Virginia."

Botero said, "Who Nicole, man?"

"Nicole's her daughter," Doug said.

Botero pulled Pepe to his feet, shoving him toward the ladder. "This all start with your fuckin' mark, didn't it, man?" Pepe crawled up to the deck. Botero followed and then yanked him to his feet.

Pepe pulled loose from Botero, staggered to the stern, and jumped into the water.

"You son-of-a-bitch," said Botero. He waited for Pepe to surface. Looking him in the eye he smiled. "Man, you go with fuckin' sharks." Botero aimed carefully. He shot Pepe in the shoulder. Pepe screamed in agony and disappeared below the water. Botero waited. Pepe resurfaced, floundering in his blood. Botero smiled. He fired again. Pepe's other shoulder exploded.

Botero turned to Doug, "Go shore, man. Fast."

# Chapter 60

### Bayside, Florida
### Tuesday 0650 ET

The unmarked police cruiser followed several car lengths behind Janet as she turned into the supermarket parking lot. The officer chose an empty back row where he could see both Janet's car and the entrance to the supermarket. "They're getting out of the car," said the driver unnecessarily. He turned the engine off. "We'll be here awhile."

"I'll pick up a couple of coffees," said the driver's partner.

"I'll go with you," said the driver. The two plain-clothes policemen entered the grocery store. They watched Janet and Nicole go to the back by the meat and dairy counters. Janet spoke to a butcher who had been loading the meat case. The butcher listened and then pointed to the area separating the meat and dairy counters. Janet took Nicole's hand. The two women disappeared behind white swinging doors with small windows.

"Where're they going?" said the driver's partner.

"Keep an eye on their car. I'll check."

The driver's partner retreated toward the entrance. He looked out the floor-to-ceiling front windows pasted with large advertisements of the week's specials. Janet's car was clearly in view.

The driver returned. "The little girl had to go to the bathroom."

# Chapter 61

## Biscayne Bay, Florida
## Tuesday 0700 ET

Guy Collins pressed the eyecups to his eye sockets, his elbows pressing against his body to steady the binoculars. "This is our last marina."

Raul turned to the two riflemen standing behind him. "See anything?"

The taller of the two said, "Nothing unusual. Any more on that body?"

"Yeah," said Raul. "Found it floating about two kilometers from here, south of Fisher Island, off the Virginia Key. Male, in his forties. Took two bullets, one in each shoulder. They're hoisting the body up to our helicopter as we speak. Could be a connection. Nothing definite."

Guy scanned the sailboats anchored off Miami Beach Marina. "Over there," he said. "Those two are awfully close."

Raul pressed the port throttle a slight bit forward, heading for the two craft. "They're moored together, that's all."

"Yeah, but I don't see bumpers," said Guy. "I can't get a clear view of the second boat." Raul adjusted his course as they glided smoothly through the calm water.

"That's them," Guy said. "Same sailboat we saw at Key Largo." Both riflemen stood. They twisted their rifle straps tight around their biceps.

Raul turned his small boat west, away from the Miami Beach Marina. He picked up his microphone and said in clear firm tones, "We've found them, captain. They're one hundred meters south southeast of us. They're lashed to another boat off the marina." He looked at his GPS receiver and relayed his coordinates.

"Roger that," the C.G. captain said. "Activity onboard?"

"Negative," Raul replied.

"Boats 2 and 3, rendezvous with 1. Full throttle, Raul's the lead on this."

Raul listened as the captain told the C.G. chopper now over the hospital of Raul's success. He heard Holt say he'd brief Alan Dickie on his way to the marina.

# Chapter 62

### Miami, Florida
### Tuesday 0730 ET

Taro flipped onto his back and searched for the ringing telephone. His elbow hit the corner of the night table. "Jesus," he bellowed as he sat up on the edge of the bed, his eyes closed against the pain. He reached for the phone, knocking it off the end table. It landed on his foot. "Damn it," he screeched. He picked up the receiver. "What?"

"You're in a bad mood," said Alan.

"Yeah."

"Our taps hit," said Alan. "We intercepted a call to Royce Palmer's office."

Taro refused to open his eyes. "So?"

"Got his answering machine."

"You woke me up to tell me that?"

"The call originated from Carp's Landing," said Alan. "In Bayside."

Taro opened his eyes. They hurt. He blinked rapidly. "You're shitting me. What time?"

"2:56 a.m." said Alan.

Taro's brain was grinding. That was about when he had left Carolyn. "What time is it?"

"Seven thirty," said Alan.

Taro shook his head. The math wasn't easy but he remembered he had gone to bed about four hours ago. "That's a few hours ago. More."

Alan said, "It takes time to process data and get the word out. The hotel uses a console. We don't know where in the hotel the call originated. I've sent someone to check the registry, look around. Thought you should know."

"Yeah, okay. Thanks, Alan." Taro hung up and started toward the bathroom. The phone rang again. "What now?" he muttered as he picked up the phone. "Taro Okada."

"We've lost them," said the stakeout driver. "In a supermarket."

"You're telling me a lady with a kid shook your stakeout?"

"Sorry, boss."

Taro lowered the phone to his side and then brought it back to his ear. "Okay, any idea where they are now?"

"None. Doesn't look like they were abducted."

Taro couldn't think of anything else to say. "It's going to be one of those days."

"That's not all, boss."

"What?" said Taro.

"We made the front page."

# Chapter 63

## Carp's Landing, Bayside, Florida
## Tuesday 0800 ET

Carolyn sat in the Carp's Landing hotel lobby waiting for Royce Palmer. She wanted to size him up, if only for a moment, before they met. She watched a couple at the registration desk checking out. A second couple stood behind them, waiting, their bags at their feet. He should have been here by now, she thought. She picked up a copy of *USA Today* from the table in front of her. The front page had a picture of a helicopter, its tail rotor entangled in the branches of a mangrove tree. The caption read:

> FBI Chopper Shot Out of the Sky: Virginia Executive Seized

"Carolyn Hughes?" Carolyn's head snapped up. Her breath stopped. The man standing on the far side of the glass-topped table was striking—tall, piercing dark eyes set with Hollywood-handsome features, a thousand-dollar suit draping from broad shoulders. "I'm Royce Palmer." Carolyn extended her hand. Could Janet possibly be right about this man? He looks so normal. Nothing like what she said about him. "You wanted to speak to me?"

"Perhaps we could go into the restaurant. They're serving breakfast."

"I've eaten, thank you," said Royce. "You wanted to talk to me about a financial matter?"

The desk clerk leaned around the couple checking out. "Carolyn." The clerk was busy and insistent. *"Carolyn."* Carolyn acknowledged with a hand gesture. "There's a call for you," said the desk clerk. "You can take it on the house phone." The clerk signaled to her left. "Over there."

Carolyn excused herself. Royce looked aggravated as she went to the house phone. "Hello."

"Good news," said Taro. "Jack Taylor's safe. He's frazzled but otherwise in good shape."

"Oh, thank God," said Carolyn. "Put him on."

"I'm in my cruiser. He's with the FBI. They're debriefing him as we speak."

Carolyn turned tightly to the wall. She put the phone on her lips. "Do they know who kidnapped him?"

"A killer named Luis Botero. He's from Colombia. He's the one who set off the bomb in the Miami airport a few days ago."

"I can't believe this. Why Mr. Taylor?"

"Don't know. But one thing's for sure, it's something important to Botero's boss."

"Who's that?" asked Carolyn.

"A guy named Jose Valderrama. But your boss doesn't have anything Botero wants."

Carolyn recognized Taro's attempt to stay level. She wanted to get as much information from him as she could. "Apparently, Botero doesn't agree with you, Taro. What's he looking for?"

"Maybe a computer. Or at least information on a computer. Look Carolyn, there's something else I have to tell you. The Coast Guard found a body floating in the ocean off south Miami Beach. It may be Pepe Gomez."

"Janet's Pepe?"

"Yeah, the same guy you and I met at Crosby's place yesterday. The C.G. says the tide may have floated his body out of Biscayne Bay, into the Atlantic. There's more."

Carolyn went numb. Pepe, a man she'd met at Janet's and then again at Crosby's home, was dead, floating in the Atlantic. "Go ahead," she told Taro despairingly.

"The helicopter that the kidnappers used landed on Doug Crosby's lawn."

*"What?"*

"Remember how you said you were getting anxious when I arrived at Crosby's?" said Taro. "Well, your instincts were right on."

"Oh, my God," Carolyn gasped. "That's when I…" Carolyn held her hand over her mouth in shock.

"When what?"

"When I told Crosby about Mr. Taylor. He didn't even know his name before I mentioned it. I'm almost sure of that."

"Another puzzle piece," said Taro. "Back to the helicopter. Botero and Mr. Taylor got off at Crosby's place. Later, the helicopter exploded right after it took off over Blackwater

Sound."

"What happened?" asked Carolyn.

"Another bomb is what happened," said Taro. "Bombs are Botero's M.O. Anyway, Mr. Taylor is one clever guy. He escaped not once, but twice. It's a long story. Right now everything seems to be centering on Crosby."

Carolyn gasped.

"What?" Taro asked.

"The party at Crosby's home—a couple of days ago. I was supposed to go. I begged off and flew home."

"What party?"

"Janet, Pepe and two Spanish families. Friends of Janet. They all went to a party at Crosby's Key Largo home."

"And then Janet went on the tour boat with Jack Taylor and Gil Bauer. Another puzzle piece."

"I was supposed to go with them," said Carolyn. "I begged off as I said and went to Crosby's place instead. That's when you and I met."

"Look, this is important, Carolyn. Janet purposely shook our security. Do you know where they are?"

Carolyn pursed her lips and said in the most reassuring tone she could muster, "They're safe."

"What does that mean?"

"They'll be fine. Where are you?"

"If you know where they are and don't tell me, you're obstructing justice."

"They're safe. Don't worry."

"Carolyn, they're Miami-Dade County citizens. I'm responsible for their safety. Now, damn it, where are they?"

Carolyn surrendered. "They're going to my apartment—in Virginia."

"Jesus." said Taro. "They're on their way to *Virginia*?"

"They'll be safer there. Away from this lunatic."

"Son-of-a-bitch," said Taro. "Listen, wherever they are, they're unprotected. This man is a killer, Carolyn. He kills on whim."

"You're the only one I've told."

"Where exactly is your apartment?"

Carolyn leaned against the wall, squeezing her eyes shut. She realized she might have put Janet and Nicole in danger. She gave Taro her Crystal City apartment address.

"One more thing," said Taro. "This is extremely important Carolyn. Did you call Royce Palmer?"

Carolyn gasped. "Yes. I did." She sneaked a look toward the reception area. Royce was sitting behind the glass-topped table, reading the paper.

"Carolyn, that man is as dangerous as Botero. They both work for that guy Jose Valderrama."

Carolyn turned back toward the wall. "Taro, he's here, in the lobby. We're about to talk."

"Carolyn, get out of there. *Now!*" Taro hung up and then turned on his cruiser's siren and flashing lights.

Carolyn kept the telephone to her ear even though Taro had hung up. She needed time to think. In a loud voice she said,"When did it happen? Oh, how horrible. I'll be right there."

Carolyn returned to the lobby. "Royce, I'm so sorry. I have to go. A good friend has just had a terrible accident."

Royce looked up at her sullenly, not sure what to make of this sudden change of events.

"I'll call you as soon as I can. I'm sorry." Carolyn turned and rushed into the hotel.

# Chapter 64

### Key Largo, Florida
### Tuesday 0830 ET

Three days after entering the boarded up home Gonzalo woke, feeling weak and dazed. Coral had inflicted razor sharp cuts on much of his body and many of the cuts remained inflamed. For the past few days he could do little more than shower, scavenge from a paltry selection of canned foods on pantry shelves, and sleep in his tattered clothes.

This morning he had to leave. During the night he had heard sirens and explosions. That meant police activity in the area, the last thing he needed.

Gonzalo exited through the same window he had used to get into the house. He replaced the sheet of plywood before making his way along the rocky coastline. Ten minutes later he looked ahead. He couldn't believe his eyes. It was Doug's dock and his beloved yacht, *Descifrar*. He fell to his knees.

*"A miracle. Another miracle."*

He ducked under the crime scene tape and entered Doug's guesthouse, heading directly for his pile of clothes on the side of the bed. The pocket in the scapular was empty. He looked everywhere he had been and then at the date on his watch. In another seventeen days it wouldn't matter who found the disk. The time lock embedded on the disk would shred the data on the disk.

He changed, taking clothes from the closet and then carried his tattered clothes aboard *Descifrar*. He would follow the Key Largo shoreline south, praying for one more miracle—a gasoline loading dock.

# Chapter 65

## Bayside, Florida
## Tuesday 0900 ET

Charles Bauer sat in his car outside the Bayside Savings Bank, waiting for Bert Griffin. He lowered the car window to enjoy the cool morning air.

Bert walked up along the side of the car and leaned in the window. "What are you doing sitting out here this early in the morning?" Charles jumped. Bert laughed. "You didn't expect me to be walking to work, did you?"

The two long time friends walked across the street and went into the bank. Bert tossed a bag of Dunkin Donuts on a counter next to the coffeepot in his office. "They're my morning indulgence—forbidden delicacies with my coffee and paper."

Charles didn't want to banter. "Things are changing."

"You're serious, aren't you?" Bert said.

"I want to talk about Crosby," said Charles. "Remember what I promised?"

Bert nodded. "He'd offer cash."

"At a rate higher than venture capitalists," said Charles.

The coffee began to drip into the coffeepot. "What's on your mind?" said Bert.

"Last night, Gil told me he gave Carolyn Hughes our Q2 report."

Bert knocked a doughnut on the long faucet arm. Powdered sugar showered the sink. "So Crosby and Taylor Associates both have it."

"That's not the point," said Charles. "Carolyn flew back to Virginia, gave the report to her boss, Jack Taylor, and the next day, she brought Jack Taylor to Bayside." Charles looked at Bert with a no-nonsense expression. "Tell me about Crosby."

Bert walked to the window and stared across the Intracoastal Waterway. "Janet's ex, Scott Graves, had a gambling problem. A $130,000 problem. A loan shark threatened to kill him."

"Scott told you this?" said Charles.

"No. Pepe," said Bert. "I told him I couldn't come up with that kind of cash. He said he knew this guy who could."

"Crosby?" said Charles.

"Yes." Bert looked back toward the coffee counter. "Coffee's ready." They merged at the coffee pot. "Crosby loaned me the $130,000, bought two large properties with dead mortgages I was holding, and used Janet for the closings."

"Sounds good."

"It was," said Bert. "You know I'm on the board at Bayside Venture Capitalists."

Charles touched his mug to his lips. The coffee was too hot. "Right, BVC."

"When you told me you were thinking of using BVC for your initial public offering of stock, I told Crosby. The rest is history."

Charles said, "Crosby called, told me he's your friend."

Bert headed for the twin chairs bracketing a corner table. "He was my friend. His money saved Scott's life and my bank. To top it off, his commissions gave Janet her self-confidence back. After all that happened between her and Scott, she needed the boost."

Charles settled into the wing-backed chair. "Life is full of surprises. Gil seeds the *Forbes* article, Jack Taylor reads it in Virginia and sends Carolyn, Janet's best friend, to Bayside." Charles bit into his doughnut, put the mug on the table, and then wiped his mouth clean of powdered sugar. "Carolyn calls me, tells me Janet is her best friend. I say, come on in. We'll talk." Charles sipped from his mug. "I was surprised when Gil told me he gave Carolyn our Q2 report."

"Because that report brought Jack to Bayside?"

"Brought Jack to Bayside to be kidnapped, that's what it did. Bert, what exactly do we know about this Doug Crosby?"

"You think Crosby—"

"Damn right, I do," said Charles. "Somehow, that son-of-a-bitch, with all his fucking money, is why Jack Taylor was kidnapped."

# Chapter 66

## Arlington, Virginia
## Tuesday 0915 ET

Janet didn't want to move but needed to change position. If she did it slowly enough, Nicole wouldn't wake up. She pulled her leg up, rolled onto her other side and put her head on her palm. The sound of Nicole's rhythmic breathing was a relief. Now if only her eyes would close and stop roaming aimlessly around Carolyn's bedroom.

So much had happened in such a short time. Telling Nicole that they were going to fly to Aunt Carolyn's home to surprise her had worked okay. Nicole had asked a million questions about their trip and Aunt Carolyn's apartment. Janet answered Nicole's questions, giving her daughter a sense of wonderment and excitement.

Janet promised Nicole that she would see the wonderful sights of the nation's capital. She described everything she could remember from visits while Carolyn attended George Washington University and worked at Justice. Seeing Nicole's eager expressions as she described the adventures ahead had been a godsend for Janet too. It took her mind off the gruesome events of the recent past.

Nicole's breathing had become a part of the room, like the rug or closet door. Janet was being encased in silence but her mind refused to relax.

Everything had started so suddenly, Carolyn showing up in Carp's Landing, introducing Carolyn to Gil, the next day crossing Alligator Alley and lunching at the Marriott, and then the Everglades.

The first sight of the speedboat racing through the swamp had nothing to do with them. They were spectators. Suddenly, it was like someone put life on fast forward. It couldn't possibly be happening to them. Yet here she was, lying with Nicole in Carolyn's bed, her mind insisting she relive every blurred minute in slow motion: Jack struggling as the gunman yanked him out of the aisle, thousands of birds fleeing the roar of automatic gunfire, Jack knocking that man into the swamp and then being rendered unconscious, the boat disappearing around an island with only white foam as ephemeral proof it had ever been there. And, oh God, that poor man without his foot.

Janet let Nicole kick off her covers and slide out of bed. Janet closed her eyes and didn't hear Nicole walk around the bed, but knew she was standing inches away, studying every wrinkle on her mother's face.

Janet wasn't quite ready to face whatever the day might bring. She steadied her breathing and immobilized every muscle. Several breaths later there wasn't a doubt. Nicole still hadn't moved from in front of her face. Janet let out a snort. That usually convinced her. Through the blurred slates of her eyelashes she watched Nicole leave the bedroom.

Nicole wandered into the living room. A pigeon was preening on the balcony rail. Nicole ran to the sliding doors. The pigeon flew away. She tugged at the balcony door. It slid open easily. She stood at each end of the balcony holding onto the rail, fascinated at how high she was, how far she could see.

Tiring from standing on her toes to see over the rail, Nicole sat at the balcony's edge, wiggled her legs under the railing and dangled her feet over the side. She held her koala on the outside of the rail. She wanted Freddie to see better than she could.

Nicole studied the cars below going back and forth and then the white buildings of different sizes and shapes on the other side of the Potomac. Before long she became intrigued by the airplanes that kept appearing on her left and disappearing a short time later behind the same covey of trees on her right. She held Freddie facing each plane as it appeared and until it disappeared.

Janet's eyes popped open. There wasn't a sound coming from the living room. Nicole hadn't turned on the television to watch her favorite cartoons as she always did when Janet insisted on sleeping in. Janet turned onto her back and listened with both ears. Nothing. Nicole didn't want to turn on the television in a strange house? No way. Nicole didn't know the channel for her favorite cartoons? More probable, she couldn't find the remote. The remote was always getting lost. But Nicole knew the channel up and down button on the TV.

Janet bolted out of bed, found her way into the living room, and then the kitchenette. Nicole was nowhere to be seen. Janet raced back into the living room. The front door was chained. She looked around. Her heart stopped. How could she have missed it? The sliding door to the balcony was open. She ran to the balcony. *"Nicole!"*

Nicole smiled as her mother crouched by her side and grasped her arm trying desperately not to convey a sense of panic.

Nicole kicked her feet to show her mother there was nothing under them, and then pointed to an airplane about to disappear behind the covey of trees. "Avión!"

*"Yes, airplane,"* said Janet in Spanish between kisses to Nicole's arm. *"Let me have Freddie."* She helped Nicole get her legs out from under the rail. *"Are you as hungry as I am? Let's eat, get dressed, and then go shopping."*

Janet held Nicole's hand as they went into the living room. *"We can't live the rest of our lives in these old clothes, you know."* Janet closed and locked the balcony door.

*"You and I are going to shop in stores that are underground. Won't that be fun? Then you know what?"* Nicole shook her head. *"We're coming back here to put on our brand new clothes—oh, you'll look so pretty. Then we'll take a train under that river you saw from the balcony. And then honey, we'll walk among those white tents we saw from our window in the airplane. Remember, the white tents? Just before we landed? I wonder what's under them. Don't you?"*

Carolyn tried to adjust the pillow against the plane's window. There was no way it would ever allow her to be comfortable against the bulkhead. It was too damned small. She'd been looking out the plane's window a long time and seen enough of the Virginia countryside. Her back and neck ached in protest. She loosened and then tightened her seat belt as she straightened herself in the seat. "How long are you going to stay testy?" she asked Taro.

Taro frowned. "What?"

"Just kidding. But you haven't said a word for the past hour."

"Sorry, I was thinking."

"I think you're still pissed because Janet and Nicole shook your stake out."

"Those guys blew it. Be honest now. Did you tell Janet how to lose my guys?" Carolyn gave Taro a knowing smile. "Did you know I got a call from a Florida senator?"

"No I didn't, oh quiet one," Carolyn teased.

"The senator was inquiring on behalf of a Mary Jacobe."

"Who's Mary Jacobe?"

"She just happens to be the late Ambassador Jacobe's wife, the former Mrs. Bert Griffin."

"Janet's mother?"

"Yep, and her constant calls don't help."

"I've never met Janet's mother but I'm not the least bit surprised she's having a senator call you. I would if I were her. After all, her daughter and granddaughter were sitting next to Mr. Taylor when terrorists snatched him. And an Uzi was fired a few feet away from her daughter and granddaughter. Another Uzi was inches from Janet's face when Mr. Taylor was yanked out of the aisle behind her."

"You're right," Taro said.

"What do you think it was like seeing Mr. Taylor rolling on the deck of a speedboat as it raced away? And when was the last time you saw a foot amputated by a propeller blade? What mother wouldn't be concerned?"

"All right already." Taro's eyes rolled as he smiled his surrender.

"What about nailing whoever *sent* Botero?"

"That's kind of what the FBI wants to do. Not me. I'd have arrested Botero as soon as he set foot on American soil. Two little girls would be alive if someone had just arrested the bastard." Taro loosened his seatbelt and turned toward Carolyn. "Let's talk about you."

"Okay."

"Why'd you go to Crosby's—cold turkey?"

"Crosby claims to be a venture capitalist. He's interested in Bauer Associates. Venture capitalists target big capital gains—within months or a year or two at most. A venture capitalist can be a single wealthy individual, several wealthy individuals that band together, or a firm that bundles funds from a variety of sources. Mostly they're wealthy individuals."

"Got it," said Taro.

"Banks turn down emerging firms that are desperate for cash to bring their ideas to market. Too risky for them. Venture capitalists are eager to take those risks. High risks and returns go together."

"What're ya gettin' at?"

"Bauer isn't an emerging firm, so why is Bauer talking with Crosby, a venture capitalist? If Bauer were so in need of money... well, it wouldn't be the firm described in *Forbes*." Carolyn's head and shoulders slumped. She took a breath to recover. "Pepe—oh God. He's dead. Pepe introduced Bert Griffin to Doug Crosby. Why is, or rather was, Pepe so connected?"

"The shapes and colors of your puzzle pieces aren't meshing with mine."

Carolyn decided not to acknowledge his double entendre. "Before arriving at Crosby's, I called Justice to see what they knew about Crosby Limited."

"And?"

"They'd call back later. I went to Key Largo—cold turkey."

"Just like that, you go into the lion's den."

"How'd I know it was a lion's den? I told you I was feeling uneasy when you arrived." Carolyn rolled her head toward Taro. "Justice called back when I left Crosby's. They're looking at Crosby Limited. The SEC wants to talk to me about why I'm asking about Crosby Limited. Kind of like what you're doing now." Carolyn smiled. Taro didn't. "Justice will be my first stop when we land. Then the SEC."

"First, let's let the Arlington PD know we're in town," said Taro.

"Why do you think Botero is after Janet? She doesn't have anything he could possibly want."

"Botero thinks she does. Janet's dealing in large chunks of cash, those commercial buildings in Miami. What happens to all that cash?"

"Bayside Savings Bank handles the transactions."

"That's Janet's father," said Taro.

Carolyn closed her eyes. The pilot banked for the final time over the Potomac River as he lined up with the runway.

Taro peered past Carolyn out the window. Rows of white tents lined the Mall between the Capitol and the Washington Monument. "What's going on down there?"

Carolyn didn't open her eyes. "It's the annual Smithsonian Folklife Festival. This year they're highlighting New York City and Bermuda."

Emily looked toward the ceiling, stretched her arms straight up and then twisted her wrist so she could see her watch. It was 11:25 a.m. Startled, she got up and tapped lightly on the conference room door before opening it. She caught Simon's eye. "Sorry to bother you." Simon was sitting with four members of team two, the team analyzing the merger candidate specializing in satellite ground terminals. Simon looked up and nodded to Emily. "Royce Palmer is due in a few minutes."

Simon told those at the table, "I'm sorry, that'll have to be it for now. I think we're on target."

Emily walked to Simon's side as the two women and two men gathered their belongings and began leaving his office. "Do you need anything for your meeting with Mr. Palmer?"

"This will be his meeting, Emily. I'm just going to listen."

# Chapter 67

## Key West, Florida
## Tuesday 1100 ET

Gonzalo docked *Descifrar* at the Hilton Marina in Key West. He paid cash for a two-month stay. He ate at the grill but was still feeling groggy. He decided to walk it off along Duval Street. Key West had changed. The excitement was gone. The crowds were now a distraction. He crossed to Whitehead Street. He needed time, fewer interruptions to think clearly. He had lost control of Jose's financial empire. He had to decide what to do.

By the time he reached the southernmost point in the continental U.S., he had downed four bottles of water and his knees had stopped complaining. He crossed back to Duval and found a small deli shop. While eating a yellowfin tuna sandwich, he decided there was nothing he could do. The disk was lost and that was that. It must have fallen out of the scapular when that swell toppled him from the deck chair. Probably washed overboard during the hurricane, or when he jumped from *Descifrar* and landed hard on his chest against the side of the dock, or… It didn't matter where. It was lost. Period.

Anyone finding the disk would never realize what it really contained. Hadn't he disguised it so? Weren't there millions of PoKéRoM disks all over the world? Kids were inserting them into their computers to initiate PoKéRoM educational games with wide-eyed cartoon characters. So what if one was found? No one would be surprised if it didn't work. They would assume it had been discarded for just that reason. Besides, hadn't he planned for just such a loss? He looked at his watch. In sixteen days the time lock embedded in the disk—his final defense against exposure—would scramble the zeros and ones on the disk. The disk would become useless to everyone. He would get on with his life. Just disappear. He'd be free for the first time in his life.

Gonzalo strode back along Duval feeling like a new man, a free man—until he looked up. He was standing in front of Ripley's Believe It or Not. No one would believe he hadn't stolen a small fortune. It would be folly to think that such a collection of superegos that were so accustomed to having their every whim satisfied would just let him vanish and lose control of all that cash. They would track him down, no matter what he did or how hard he tried to disappear.

Gonzalo wandered into the Hog's Breath Saloon, sat at the bar and ordered a beer. "Any brand," he told the bartender. His mother and grandmother would take the brunt of his decision to disappear. They would be harassed, their phones tapped, their every move watched—that was all a given. They would be terrified, griefstricken. The thought of their sorrow engulfed him. Their future agony weakened him. And there was nothing he could do to temper their distress or his. He could never see them again.

When he didn't call they would believe he had died. Gonzalo swept the bar clear with both arms, let out an anguished howl, and slammed his fists onto the bar. His shoulders heaved. Tears flowed onto the varnished wood. They would mourn and he would mourn. He knew in his heart that they would understand. They would want him to live if it meant they had to believe he was dead.

But how would he disappear? It wouldn't be easy. Powerful men convinced that he had absconded with their fortunes would track him down. In time they would realize that nothing had been lost. His policy of staying fully invested meant the bulk of the money belonged to the corporations that Royce Palmer had created. The one problem, a serious problem, was how to allocate the wealth among Jose's clients. That's what was on the tiny PoKéRoM disk, the names of Jose's clients and what he had done with their money. A few had hit it rich. A few had taken a bath. No one knew how the money should be divided, not even Gonzalo. Like a surgeon, he never got involved.

Gonzalo assigned any future allocation of the empire to Jose and Royce. They, not he, would have to deal with the clients. After all, he had never met any of them and had never wanted to—a true surgeon in his way.

By the fourth beer, Gonzalo decided a year should be enough time. Jose's clients would have redistributed their wealth among them—if they recovered it—hot tempers would have been soothed, and having lost his scent, the yelps of the hounds would be silenced.

Not contacting his mother and grandmother for a year might

prove to be his Achilles' heel. He'd have to be strong. *Forgive me Momma. Forgive me Grandma. The year will pass and we will be together again.*

Gonzalo found his way to the car rental store and rented a full-sized four-door sedan. He drove north the length of the Overseas Highway and didn't notice Key Largo when he passed through. He crossed to the mainland, found his way to the Miami address on the back of the rental agreement, and returned the car. He ate, walked a few blocks, and boarded the metromover. Twenty-five minutes later he withdrew nine thousand dollars from an account at Citibank. A transaction over ten thousand dollars would be reported automatically to U.S. authorities.

He took a cab to the Miami International Airport, where he paid cash for the next flight to Atlanta. He ate again in the Atlanta airport and paid cash for the next flight to Orlando. He had heard so much about the Magic Kingdom and thought his mother and grandmother would love to visit it when they joined him. Besides, Disney World would be a wonderful place to work. Employee turnover was high, an ideal cover for the upcoming year.

# Chapter 68

### Arlington, VA
### Tuesday 1200 ET

Alan Dickie had taken the reports on the downed FBI helicopter home and studied them until two in the morning. He woke up late. There wasn't enough time to stop by the office. He went directly to the airport. He'd call Sally from the airport and tell her he had to go to Washington. She would fax his clearances to FBI headquarters while he was in the air.

Alan sat silently as the American Airlines plane climbed to cruising altitude out of Miami. He pulled his bulging briefcase from under the seat and took out the thinnest file—Vinny Campbell. Sally had arranged his e-mails in chronological order. He studied the top one, a request from Vinny that he be at FBI headquarters this date at 10-hundred hours for consultations.

He studied the word *consultations.* An FBI helicopter being shot down was more than enough reason for a consultation. Alan waved off the flight attendant's offer of a beverage and went to the folder marked "Helicopter." He would be prepared to answer every question regarding the downed chopper, including the names and backgrounds of those aboard, mission purpose, flight path, photos of the helicopter entangled in the mangroves...

As the plane banked following the Potomac River on its approach to Reagan National, Alan finished studying the last of the detailed reports he had stuffed into his briefcase. He crammed them all back into the briefcase, snapped it closed, and buckled the two leather straps around the briefcase.

Alan looked around for the first time since opening his briefcase. There was a newspaper on the seat between him and the woman sitting on the aisle. The woman nodded. She had finished with the paper. Alan picked it up. The front page had a picture of an FBI helicopter with its tail rotor entangled in the branches of a mangrove tree. The caption under the picture read:

> FBI Chopper Shot Out Of The Sky: Virginia Executive Seized

Alan scanned the article and then grinned.  The no-comment edict he had imposed on the FBI's MFO was holding.  No tainted reports would reach Vinny Campbell or the attorney general of the United States before he presented the documented facts that he had in his attaché case concerning the downing of the helicopter.

Alan was engulfed by swarms of reporters and photographers when he emerged from the exit ramp of the plane to enter the airport boarding area.  Not wanting to hear their questions and blinded by lights, he barged through the mob and headed for the main lobby.  His briefcase was knocked from his hand.  He snapped it up and held it tight against his chest with crossed forearms.  A sea of microphones bobbed in front of his face.  Reporters barraged him with questions.

Alan relied on the overhead baggage claim signs to guide him.  His only thought: find the limousine Vinny Campbell had sent to pick him up.

Several times reporters in front of him stopped abruptly and held their ground.  Alan used his briefcase held in his folded arms to brush them aside.  Howls of assault, claims of damaged equipment, and threats of lawsuits rang out.  Alan didn't miss a step.  At the curb he ducked into the FBI limousine.  The driver pulled into traffic and headed across the river to FBI headquarters.

Alan had studied every aspect of the FBI chopper loss.  He had reviewed it all again during the flight to Reagan National.  Every detail would be his friend.

He vowed he'd make an impression at headquarters that wouldn't soon be forgotten.  He'd use his attaché case material as backup only if his memory failed.  It wouldn't.  He had memorized every detail on the tapes of the initial cell calls between Holt and Taro.

Holt's decision to commandeer an FBI helicopter and fly to the Everglades, the helicopter tapes—Taro's and Holt's in-flight conversations, the ensuing dogfight, the crash and the recovery—Holt's later statement in his office, the ATC and Coast Guard preliminary reports, and the hostage rescue team's report.  For insurance he had brought along the tape of Vinny Campbell authorizing the use of the FBI HRT.

During his ride to headquarters, Alan refreshed details in an attempt to maintain his edge. He started with the names of the three men in the downed helicopter, special agent Holt Brown, his chief of staff—he'd have a one-on-one with Holt about his casual appearance as soon as he returned to the MFO. Taro Okada, a Miami-Dade county detective. Was Taro chief of detectives? Yes, chief of the Miami-Dade county detectives. Who else would the director of the FBI's MFO deal with? The FBI helicopter pilot, what was his name? Alan's mind went blank. He began undoing the briefcase straps as the limo lurched into the FBI headquarters driveway, over the sunken barrier, and then plunged down the ramp into the underground garage.

The reception desk at FBI headquarters couldn't locate Alan's clearances— the receptionist insisted they hadn't arrived from the MFO. Alan called Sally. When he heard her voice he said, "Sally, my clearances haven't arrived."

"Where are you?" Sally asked.

Alan suddenly realized he hadn't called Sally from the airport to tell her he had gone directly from home to the airport. "I'm at FBI headquarters in D.C."

"What are you doing there? Everybody's looking for you."

Sally promised to fax his clearances immediately.

Alan was twenty minutes late. Vinny Campbell stood as he entered the large conference room adjacent to the executive briefing room. "I'm Vinny Campbell. We've been expecting you."

Alan had envisioned Vinny as a linebacker dressed in a business suit. After all, he was in charge of SIOC. Instead, a beanpole of a man with an American flag on his lapel stood in front of him. Alan dropped his briefcase on the floor next to an empty chair. "Sorry I'm late."

Vinny waited as Alan settled into to his seat before speaking. "A Florida state senator and a U.S. senator from the state of California have asked the director for daily reports on the Everglades kidnapping. Director Ward wants to know if you have any information on this, any information at all, Alan."

"Forrest Ward wants to know?" Alan said, startled. "No sir. This is the first I've heard about senators calling."

"Any information at all?"

*Ask me anything about our downed chopper, please.* "None."

"On my right is Greg McNulty," Vinny continued. "Greg heads a Justice task force. Next to him is Michael Stone. You know Michael."

Alan was still pissed at Michael. By alerting local law enforcement agencies he had effectively negated his stonewall edict. He kept focused on Vinny. "We've corresponded." Alan didn't want to stumble again. He picked up his briefcase and put it on the table in front of him.

"What was your plan of action when Greg assigned you the lead on the Interpol alert?"

"Sir, to put Luis Botero under surveillance."

"You put an international ten-most-wanted under surveillance?" Michael said. "The man that detonated a bomb in the Miami International Airport."

*Fuck you Michael.* "Botero came through Customs. They gave me no indication he was armed or carrying explosives."

"Where did he get the bomb?" Vinny asked.

"No idea, sir."

"Did you have back up?"

Alan smiled. At last, a question he could answer. "Absolutely, sir. Unfortunately, they went to the wrong airport entrance. They couldn't recover in time."

"Taro Okada and Carolyn Hughes landed at Reagan National this morning," Michael said. "Do you know why they're here?"

Alan gave the only answer he could. "No."

"Do you know Carolyn Hughes?" Vinny asked.

"Michael has sent me copies of her telephone intercepts. I have never met Ms. Hughes."

Michael said, "In one of those intercepts Carolyn asked Greg for information on a company named Crosby Limited."

"Privileged information," Greg emphasized. "Do you know anything about Crosby Limited?"

"No."

Greg said, "Earlier last week Carolyn worked for me."

Michael added, "And Greg told me he is not prepared to vouch for the loyalty of Carolyn."

"That's right," Greg confirmed. "Carolyn worked for me for a couple of years. She quit a few days ago. The next thing I know I receive a call from her in Florida. She's asking me about Crosby Limited." Greg looked smugly at Vinny and Michael before continuing. "She wouldn't tell me *why* she wanted to know. That concerns me." Again he looked righteously at Vinny and Michael. "She never *appeared* to know what was going on outside of her little world."

"Do you know a Janet Griffin?" Vinny asked Alan.

Alan said despairingly, "No sir, I do not."

"Michael tells me Janet's a friend of Carolyn Hughes," said Vinny. "It's Janet's mother who has been asking the state department and a U.S. senator for daily updates from the director's office." Vinny hesitated, wanting to give Alan time to assimilate what he was hearing. "Her second husband was a U.S. ambassador. Terrorist in Yugoslavia kidnapped the ambassador. Janet's mother paid a million-dollar ransom to get him back. The terrorists decapitated the ambassador."

Again Vinny hesitated before continuing. "Now her only daughter and granddaughter become involved in this Everglades kidnapping. Yesterday, her daughter and granddaughter eluded protective custody. There's a chance Botero may be trying to kidnap them both."

Alan sat dazed. Everything had turned to shit.

Royce waited in the lobby of Taylor Associates near the reception desk. He took the small envelope out of the breast pocket of his jacket and looked at the tickets inside, two seats at a Saturday performance at the John F. Kennedy Center for the Performing Arts.

He didn't see Emily approaching. "Mr. Palmer?" she asked.

Royce put the tickets back in his pocket. He followed Emily across the lobby to the elevators. On the third floor she led him into Simon Tully's office, opened the conference room, and introduced Royce to Simon, who was still sitting at the conference table.

Simon rose, beckoning Royce to sit in the same chair that Carolyn had used when his staff interviewed her three days previously. "You say you've met Carolyn Hughes, Mr. Palmer." Simon began as the two men sat facing each other.

Royce took his time settling into his chair. "Yesterday morning. In the lobby of her hotel in Florida. The Carp's Landing

Hotel, I believe. She called me." Royce studied Simon. Simon sat stoically. "She suggested we meet. Before breakfast."

Simon's head drew back. "Oh?"

Royce smiled. "I head a venture capital firm—Palmer Investments. Carolyn said you're considering a merger. Correct?"

"Carolyn has our full support, Mr. Palmer."

"Please, it's Royce." He leaned forward a little. "You wouldn't be considering a merger with Bauer Industries?" Simon didn't reply. "You asked what you could do for me. Well actually… nothing at the moment." Royce sat back. "I'm in town on business. Thought I'd take the opportunity to introduce Palmer Investments to Taylor Associates. Within the hour I'll be locked into back-to-back meetings, probably late into the night."

"These are busy times," Simon agreed.

"I'd like you to consider Palmer Investments if you ever feel the need for venture capital." Royce slid his business card across the table.

Simon left the card on the table. "I see."

Royce pushed his chair back from the conference table and stood. "Oh, one more thing. Would you mind telling Carolyn I have the Orioles' tickets for tonight's Camden Yards game?" He took the ticket envelope from his jacket pocket, holding it so Simon wouldn't see the Kennedy Center logo on the envelope. They're playing the Blue Jays." Simon followed him to the conference room door. "She's a huge Orioles fan, as you probably know."

"Carolyn may not stop by until tomorrow," Simon said.

"She's one busy lady," Royce agreed. "What do you suggest I do with these tickets? I'd hate to see her miss the game."

"We can get the tickets to the receptionist at her apartment nearby."

"Great." Royce started to hand the envelope to Simon and then withdrew it. "I can drop them off. No problem. Your call."

"It's a few blocks," Simon warned.

"Well then," Royce said. "It's settled. I'll drop them off."

"She lives in Crystal Park 3. It's on the same side of the street as this building, west along Crystal Drive." Royce grinned. "If she calls before she goes home, Emily will tell her where you left them."

"Perfect," said Royce. "Now I really have to go."

Alan Dickie got off the elevator in the bowels of the FBI headquarters garage and checked out a bureau car, or burcar as they are called. He made his way across the 14th Street Bridge into Virginia. Seventeen minutes later he had passed through security and stood in front of the Arlington Courthouse directory. He ran his finger down the directory glass, found the Arlington county PD, and then rode the elevator to the eighth floor to meet Taro and Carolyn.

Taro introduced Alan to Don Hutchings, his Arlington county counterpart and to Carolyn. "I was just telling Don that Janet and her daughter are unwittingly bait."

"God, Taro, how can you say that?" said Carolyn. "There's no way Janet and Nicole are bait."

"I'm afraid he's right," said Don. "Without other leads…"

"Damn it, Taro, I wish you had told me this on the plane. I would have gone directly home." Carolyn took out her cell and dialed Janet.

"We're on our way," said Taro.

Don added, "Arlington county officers are probably there by now."

Don addressed Taro. "One more thing before you go. We're in Virginia. Just a couple of miles away are D.C. and Maryland. Our Arlington command center has alerted both the D.C. and Maryland command centers and faxed them Botero's photos." Taro nodded. "In the District, the secret service could be anywhere covering dignitaries, their wives, whatever. The principal federal authority you'll encounter if you go on the Mall will be the U.S. Park Police. Since this guy's tossing bombs around, we've alerted our bomb squad as well as the DCPD and the Maryland bomb squads."

"Kidnapping is federal," said Alan. "The FBI has jurisdiction here. Two FBI agents have already been to Carolyn's apartment."

"When the hell were you going to tell us that?" Taro bellowed.

"You didn't tell me you were flying to Virginia," Alan snapped back.

"Like hell I didn't," said Taro. "Check your voice mail for

Christ sake. What did your FBI agents find out?"

Alan scoffed. "The lobby receptionist told them a woman with a child came off the elevator, asked for directions to the Crystal City underground. They'd returned some time later. A short time after that they left for a second time. He believed they were going to the Mall."

Carolyn snapped her cell closed. "Damn, Janet's cell is off. I left a message."

Taro started to leave. "Where you going?"

Taro said, "The Mall."

"You don't have jurisdiction."

Taro didn't look back. "As far as I know, only Carolyn and I can ID Janet Griffin and only Carolyn can ID Royce Palmer." Taro, Carolyn and Don headed for the elevator.

"Wait," said Alan.

Taro yelled over his shoulder, "What?"

"The lobby guard said they weren't the first to ask about them."

The three froze. Taro glowered, "Don't make us ask."

"A man in his forties, business suit, tall, medium weight."

"That's not Botero," said Taro. "It could be…"

"Royce Palmer," said Carolyn. "Let's go."

"Shit. They're making fools of us," grumbled Taro as they all got on the elevator.

Don asked, "Who's making fools of us?"

"Botero and now this Royce Palmer. They're always a step ahead. Botero bombs the Miami Airport and escapes, even though the FBI is waiting for him. He beats us to the Everglades and kidnaps Jack Taylor. He downs an FBI helicopter. With me aboard! He downs a second helicopter off Key Largo, killing his own men. He escapes the FBI's hostage rescue team in Key Largo and then probably killed Pepe Gomez on Biscayne Bay. He even beat us here to Virginia. Even Royce Palmer, from *San Diego* beat us here."

# Chapter 69

### Washington, D.C.
### Tuesday 1200 ET

B otero sat on the bench outside the Mall entrance to the Smithsonian Castle. He stretched both legs and crossed his ankles as he watched Janet lift Nicole high so she could mount the silver horse on the outer ring of carousel horses. He smiled as Nicole waved a stuffed animal above her head while Janet worked the long leather strap attached to the brass pole around her tiny waist. When Janet finished, she mounted the black and white horse next to Nicole.

Botero leaned back, put his face to the sun and closed his eyes. His t-shirt was emblazoned with a picture of the Capitol building. Bold letters below said Washington, D.C. He covered the image with two plastic shopping bags filled with street vendor wares and waited for the carousel music to begin.

Taro, Carolyn and Don stood on the Mall at the corner of 14th Street and Jefferson SW. Taro asked Don, "What do you suggest?"

Don said, "We'll spread out along 14th Street here and walk the three aisles between the tents and head toward the Capitol building. We'll check in with each other as we pass the north-south aisles. Let's meet in front of the reflecting pool on 3rd Street. It should take, oh, fifteen minutes."

Carolyn said, "This place is wall-to-wall museums. They could be in any one of them."

"Our best chance is if they're outside on the Mall," said Don. "The park police are distributing Botero's photos. Who knows, maybe we'll get lucky. Where'd Alan go?"

Taro said, "Don't know."

At lunchtime a tall thin man in a freshly-pressed suit left FBI headquarters. He made his way through the crowds attending the Smithsonian's folklife festival on the Mall to the Air and Space Museum. He found a public telephone.

"This is all background, off the record," the man said to a *Washington Post* reporter.

The reporter said, "From an unnamed high government official speaking on the condition of anonymity. No problem."

"You've got his name, where he works, what he does at SIOC?"

The reporter said, "Michael Stone. Being investigated for violating administrative procedures and possible security breaches. Got it."

"Good," the man replied.

"We'll slip it in as filler somewhere," said the reporter. He hesitated. "That's the way you want it. No bold headlines. Right?"

"Right."

"Next week okay?"

*"Tomorrow,"* the man said. "It's important."

"Okay," said the reporter. "Identifying an alleged security risk… that's news."

The man pressed, "Okay then?"

"It'll only be a couple of lines buried somewhere in another piece."

"That's what I want."

"You know when it appears, the news wires will pick it up."

"And that's what you want."

Janet looked at Nicole astride her silver mount. Speaking Spanish she said, *"I love carousels. Isn't this fun, honey?"* The carousel began to move. Nicole grabbed the pole with both hands. Freddie fell to the floor of the carousel. *"Hold on, honey, Freddie will be fine. Here we go."*

Janet grinned as multi-colored lights began flashing and carousel music resounded. Nicole's pony began dipping as Carolyn's steed rose. Nicole clung to the pole, staring at Freddie riding the floor of the carousel. As their mounts leveled, Janet put her hand across Nicole's back. *"Freddie's just fine, honey."* Nicole looked down at her mother as her silver mount rose and smiled.

Janet and Nicole emerged from the porta-potties on the Mall a few minutes after Carolyn walked by. Mother and daughter walked hand-in-hand along the wood-chip aisle. Janet was startled when someone tapped her on the shoulder. She grasped

Nicole's hand more firmly as she turned around.

"What are you doing here?" Janet asked.

Royce hugged Janet gently. "Business. This is almost like our first meeting in the San Diego airport. I can't believe it. What are *you* doing here?"

"Staying with a friend for a few days."

Royce looked at Nicole. "Who's this little lady?" He squatted to talk with Nicole.

"This is my daughter Nicole," said Janet. Speaking Spanish she said, *"Nicole, honey, this is Mr. Palmer."*

Royce smiled. *"Hola Nicole."* Nicole grasped her mother's hand. Royce stood erect, towering over Janet. "It's just about five. Why don't you two have dinner with me? I'm at the Willard Hotel. The chef in the Willard Room rivals any in town."

Janet hesitated. She hadn't actually told Royce she had no interest in continuing their relationship and had been concerned he might become abusive whenever she did. This would be as good an opportunity as any to tell him, in a restaurant with people all around.

"All right," Janet said coolly.


Carolyn, Taro and Don stood in front of the Capitol reflecting pool with three U.S. park policemen and two undercover D.C. cops who had joined them.

Alan pulled his burcar to the 3rd Street curb next to them and turned on its blue flashing light. As soon as he joined the group, he pulled Carolyn aside. "Your meeting with Justice has been shifted to the FBI headquarters building. They're waiting."

Carolyn looked baffled. Why would he bring up such a thing at this time? "Forget it. They can wait. We have to find Janet and Nicole first."

# Chapter 70

## Washington, D.C.
## Tuesday 1710 ET

R oyce held the cab door open for Janet and Nicole and guided them across the sidewalk, through the revolving door, and into the Willard's 1850 beaux-arts lobby. Two-story-high marble columns separated an elaborately carved ceiling from a mosaic floor. Upholstered Victorian furniture rested on plush Oriental area rugs and ringed a giant bowl of colorful flowers. A warm glow emanated from huge bowl-shaped chandeliers suspended on brass chains from the ceiling, showering the spectacular expanse with light.

They crossed the lobby, walked up a few stairs, and entered the Willard Room, a two-story, oak-paneled, turn-of-the-20th-century dining room.

The maitre d' smiled. "Good afternoon, Mr. Palmer."

"Ramon," said Royce. "My usual table."

"I'm afraid it's not available. I've reserved a special table for you."

"I'm sure that'll be fine," said Royce. "What's going on?"

"A private dinner party, Mr. Palmer." Ramon picked up the menus and led the three past a grand piano and through the empty dining room to a table isolated by an oak-paneled divider accented with crystal lamp sentinels sporting frosted-glass shades. After the three sat, Ramon put menus in front of Royce and Janet.

Nicole said, "Tengo que irme."

Janet whispered in Spanish, *"But you just went honey. When we got off the carousel."*

"Tengo que irme," Nicole insisted.

"Please excuse us," said Janet. "We'll be right back." Janet and Nicole threaded their way among the empty gold-colored upholstered chairs surrounding elegantly set tables.

# Chapter 71

## FBI Headquarters, Washington, D.C.
## Tuesday 1717 ET

Carolyn had protested vehemently about coming to FBI headquarters. Alan had emphasized that assisting the FBI with fresh intelligence might be the best way to get Janet and Nicole out of harm's way. Meanwhile, the officers on the Mall would continue the search.

Carolyn was shocked to find Greg-the-Bastard in the conference room Alan had escorted her to. She sat in the chair Alan held out for her. Alan sat directly opposite her. Greg-the-Bastard sat to Alan's left. Carolyn didn't know any of the others at the table.

Alan began. "Royce Palmer and Doug Crosby, both of whom you've met, work for one Jose Valderrama. Jose heads an international money-laundering scheme. We believe it may be supporting terrorism."

Alan looked at Greg, then back at Carolyn. "After the Miami airport bomb explosion, you contacted Greg McNulty here."

Carolyn's eyes narrowed, forcing herself to focus on Alan.

"Then you went to Mr. Crosby's home. Within hours, Mr. Taylor was kidnapped and Pepe Gomez was found floating in the Atlantic." Alan sat back.

Carolyn looked down and shook her head slowly before replying. "My name is Carolyn Hughes. I work for Taylor Associates. Taylor Associates is headquartered across the river in Arlington, Virginia." She reached into her purse, took out her business cards, and fanned them to those sitting at the conference table, to everyone except Greg-the-Bastard. "Why was I brought here and who am I talking to?" Carolyn sat back, her arms crossed.

Alan said, "Carolyn, we're only trying to…"

Carolyn interrupted. "Obviously, this is an interagency group of some sort, Justice and FBI at least."

The man sitting to Alan's right slid his business card facedown to Carolyn. "Let me be the first to introduce myself. I'm Forrest Ward, director of the FBI. You are sitting in the Strategic Information Operations Center, or SIOC as we call it.

It's the heart of the investigation of the September 11 terror attacks. On my right is Vinny Campbell, my deputy. He's in charge of SIOC."

Carolyn snapped Forrest's card over but didn't look at it.

Forrest said, "You were brought here, Ms. Hughes, to see if you could help us in our investigation of the Miami airport bombing. Mr. Michael Stone, sitting to Vinny's right, is in charge of our Miami airport investigation." Forrest sat back. "I'll let Vinny Campbell give you a little background on SIOC."

Vinny leaned forward, putting his arms on the table. "Our intelligence-gathering efforts here at SIOC are coordinated with every FBI field office, as well as a wide array of other law enforcement and intelligence agencies both here and abroad. We are all in this together. We share everything openly and freely."

*Yeah, right. You're forgetting I worked at Justice.*

Business cards began sliding across the table toward Carolyn. She gathered them as a poker player might gather a pile of chips after a winning hand and put them aside. She wanted to give those at the table time to tell her why they had brought her here.

Vinny continued. "Greg McNulty, whom you know, heads an interagency task force investigating money-laundering." Carolyn tensed. "Greg doesn't know if or how his task force might be involved in the Miami bombing."

"Not surprised," Carolyn muttered, immediately cursing herself.

"As the director said, Michael Stone here on my right is in charge of the Miami airport bombing investigation. He's CIA and has some interesting ideas on what might be going on."

Carolyn looked at Michael. He was sitting four seats away from Greg-the-Bastard. She relaxed her peripheral vision.

Michael began."When you asked Greg about Crosby Limited, Greg seemed evasive with his reply."

"You're eavesdropping on my calls?" Carolyn fired back.

"Doug Crosby's phone had the tap," Michael explained calmly. "When you called him from your car while driving past Florida City, we picked up your call. That's when I learned your cell number. We obtained approval for your cell to be subsequently monitored as part of the Miami airport investigation. When you placed your next call, we picked it up.

I recognized Greg's voice. I had talked to him the day before."

Greg said, "You're eavesdropping on *my* calls?"

"No. As I said, we eavesdropped on Carolyn's cell call to you."

Carolyn explained without looking at Greg. "The Patriot Act authorizes the use of roving wiretaps on multiple telephones with the approval of an attorney general and follow-up authorization by the judiciary."

Michael nodded his agreement. "Greg's comments to you were again evasive. I did a little checking on Crosby Limited."

"And?" said Carolyn, happy to find someone who seemed to understand.

"Thousands of paper millionaires blossomed during the 90s. We have to assume the world's most notorious criminals haven't been blind to this."

Carolyn encouraged. "Go on."

"Crosby Limited is incorporated in San Diego by the same lawyer that incorporated dozens of other companies there in the last few years. A lawyer named Royce Palmer."

*This guy understands.* "Janet's friend."

"Right. All of those companies, bar none, are or have been acting as venture capital firms. If these companies are investing in emerging companies during their pre-IPO phases, as most venture capitalists do, then they're getting as much as ten percent ownership in the companies they invest in."

"Plus equity growth if the company succeeds," Carolyn added.

Michael nodded. "Right. If these same venture capitalists are investing dirty money, then we're seeing a new and sinister money-laundering scheme that's attacking the basic fabric of our nation's corporate structures."

"Is this what's happening?" asked Carolyn.

"It may be worse," said Michael. "If any of the corporations they're investing in obtain contracts with critical government agencies like the FBI, the CIA, the Department of Defense, the White House… well you get the picture."

Forrest said, "This is potentially a serious breach of national security."

"We're in a recession," Carolyn said. "They must be concerned about the other side of the coin—the loss of their money."

"They have a much larger concern. Being exposed," said Forrest.

"They sent Botero to keep them from being exposed. Is that what this is all about?" Carolyn asked.

Michael agreed. "You got it. Our focus is twofold. Arrest Botero. Expose the money-laundering scheme."

Carolyn leaned forward. "Drug dealers?"

Michael said, "So far, no hint of drug money."

"Al Qaeda, Hezbollah, Hamas?" Carolyn suggested.

"Don't know. We've been slow catching on. You know how it is. You worked at Justice."

A quiver went down Carolyn's spine. *I like this guy's style.*

Forrest said, "SIOC wasn't aware of Greg's task force until Michael identified it a couple of days ago. Justice was focusing on enforcing SEC regulations. As Michael explained, our concerns are much broader. Is it a terrorist organization like al Qaeda, Hezbollah or Hamas? Or even a consortium of terrorist organizations? Are there links to the 9/11 attacks in New York and Virginia, and the plane crash in a Pennsylvania field? We simply don't know."

Michael said, "There may be hundreds of millions of dollars invested through the venture capital companies that Royce Palmer has incorporated. Doug Crosby on the East Coast may be doing the same thing."

Forrest stared at Carolyn. "Successfully prosecuting a case this size would send a powerful message."

# Chapter 72

## Washington, D.C.
## Tuesday 1725 ET

Janet and Nicole sashayed back across the Willard Room hand-in-hand, Nicole twirling Freddie, and Janet in deep thought.

"Welcome back ladies," said Royce, rising slightly in his chair. When the two ladies sat, Royce said, "You know Janet, I was thinking. We're in the same business, sort of."

"Not," said Janet.

"You broker real estate," said Royce. "I broker capital."

"That's one big difference."

"Oh, it's not that big a difference," Royce said.

Janet began. "I'm kind of glad we met today."

"Me too," said Royce.

"No, Royce, not that way." Janet wasn't sure exactly how to begin. However she told him, it wouldn't be easy. She had to do it. This was the ideal time.

"I want to talk to you, Royce."

# Chapter 73

## FBI Headquarters, Washington, D.C.
## Tuesday 1730 ET

Taro stood back while his security escort opened the door to the large SIOC conference room. He entered, found Carolyn, and sat next to her. Facing the others, he said, "Taro Okada, Miami-Dade PD."

Vinny introduced himself and others around the table.

Carolyn leaned toward Taro and said, "Michael Stone was just telling us what might be going on with Crosby Limited."

Michael continued, "From Echelon intercepts, we believe Gonzalo may be key."

Taro leaned over to Carolyn. "This should be interesting."

"Gonzalo's brilliant," said Michael. "And a video game freak. Our Bogotá office reports he's won several international video game competitions. His other passion: yachting. He belongs to the Barranquilla Yacht Club. It's on the Caribbean coast of Colombia. As far as we know, this is the first time he's ventured this far from port. In fact, we didn't know he had left Colombia for almost two weeks. It took another week or so for Customs to locate his yacht. We lost him when he left the Hilton Marina in Key West—Hurricane Fabian." Michael took a pager from his belt. "Sorry, I have to leave." He slid his notes to Vinny.

Vinny continued. "Two coastguardsmen reported they've seen Gonzalo's yacht in Crosby's cove. Said the Miami-Dade PD sent them there. Was that you, Taro?" Taro nodded. "A Coast Guard chopper found Pepe Gomez floating in the Atlantic, just outside Biscayne Bay. It was Jose Valderrama who sent Botero to find Gonzalo. Gonzalo may be the key to Valderrama's empire."

Carolyn gathered the business cards in front of her and snapped one face up. She turned to the woman sitting on her left. "Justice."

"Susie Thomas, DOJ task force prosecutor—"

Carolyn snapped another card onto the table. "Denise Hogan?"

Denise said, "Investigative assistant to Greg McNulty."

Carolyn studied her replacement. "We'll have lunch." She

snapped another card over. "J. E. Breingan, DEA."

J. E. leaned back in his chair and stretched. The bad blood between the FBI and DEA seemed to have existed since the start of time. "We do exactly what everybody thinks we do."

Vinny said, "We're all in this together, J.E."

"In plain words, Ms. Hughes, ever since you asked Greg to divulge confidential governmental information, your subsequent cell phone call to Doug Crosby, and your appearance at Crosby's home minutes later... well, an awful lot of things have been happening."

Vinny repeated, "Everybody in this room is on the same team."

J. E. said, "Some recommended we brief you on all this. Greg wasn't among them."

Carolyn looked levelly at J. E. without saying a word.

J. E. said, "Greg adamantly refused to vouch for your loyalty, Ms. Hughes."

Carolyn's spotlight materialized: Greg with outstretched arms accepting her plaque from the attorney general. His wife by his side looking up in awe. His daughter's eyes radiating adoration. His son, cradling his younger brother wrapped in a blue blanket, proud as a peacock of his father.

Carolyn leaped to her feet, her chair crashing to the floor. Her eyes burned through Greg-the-Bastard. "You bastard. You fucking bastard."

"Please, Ms. Hughes," said Vinny.

Taro stood next to Carolyn. "This is all bullshit," he barked at J. E. "I was with Carolyn in Crosby's home. So drop any suspicions your pea-sized brain might have."

"Please Taro," Vinny pleaded.

Taro glanced toward Carolyn. She was fuming. He turned, firing at Vinny. "Two Miami-Dade residents are on your goddamned Mall. They're in mortal danger. What's anybody in this fucking room doing to protect them?"

"Calm down," Vinny pleaded.

Taro roared louder. "Royce Palmer is on your Mall."

"You know this for a fact?" Forrest Ward said.

"Alan Dickie knows it for a fact too," said Taro. Vinny glared at Alan as Taro continued. "Royce was in Carolyn's lobby an hour ago. The receptionist told FBI investigators that Janet and her daughter had gone to the Mall. Royce is stalking them, for God sake." Taro scanned the table. "Carolyn and I were on the Mall looking for them when Alan shunted us here." He looked around the table again. "Listen, you pinheads, your first job is law enforcement, not intelligence-gathering."

Vinny said, "That's not warranted."

"In spades it's warranted."

Carolyn headed for the door.

Michael clicked on his blinking Capitol building icon. His spreadsheet appeared displaying a 703 area code telephone. The comments column contained one word: recording. "This is Carolyn. If you'll leave a message, I'll call you back."

Michael listened, "Hi Carolyn. Janet. Can you believe it? We met Royce Palmer on the Mall. Nicole and I are at the Willard Hotel having dinner with him. We'll be back in an hour or two. Loved shopping in the Crystal City underground. See you soon."

# Chapter 74

### Washington, D.C.
### Tuesday 1740 ET

A Willard Room waiter began rearranging the table setting although it wasn't necessary. With his back turned to Janet, he mouthed to Royce, "Just nod."

Royce dismissed the waiter with an annoyed glance. Turning to Janet he said, "You wanted to tell me something?"

They were the only ones sitting in the Willard Room. Janet had planned to ease into telling him she was breaking up with him, perhaps near the end of dinner when they were both feeling more comfortable and there were other diners. "This room is gorgeous. Do you eat here often?"

"Whenever I'm in town."

"I didn't know your business brought you east," Janet said. "You never mentioned it."

"Like I said, whenever I'm in town."

"So how often does your business take you to Washington?" Janet asked.

Royce became annoyed at Janet's evasiveness. "Let's not talk business. You wanted to tell me something?"

"Maybe later. Give Nicole and me a few minutes to enjoy these surroundings. They're all new to us."

"Okay then. I want to talk to you about Doug's Key Largo party."

"What about it?"

"I don't know how to say this, but… did you take anything from Doug's house?"

Janet laughed. "Like what, an ash tray?"

If Royce couldn't get Janet to tell him if she took the disk, he would have no choice but to turn her over to Botero, waiting in the kitchen. A nod would do it. "I'm just asking. Did you? You can tell me."

Janet's irritation at the suggestion she was a petty thief morphed into a rush of words. "I don't think we should see each other anymore, Royce." *There, I did it.*

Royce sat dazed, not believing what he heard. "What are you talking about—you don't think we should see each other anymore?"

Janet squeezed her lips together. She'd tell him like it is. "You're always hurting me."

"I'm always hurting you?" Royce asked sarcastically. "How in heaven's name have I been hurting you?"

"For one, when we last parted in the San Diego airport."

"What are you talking about, girl?"

"When I could hardly breathe. Remember?"

"No."

"You enjoy embarrassing me."

"I do not," Royce said mockingly.

*He has no idea what I'm talking about. He isn't even interested.* "It's later than I thought." Janet began to stand. "We really must go."

Royce's anger gushed, his vision blurred. *"Sit down!"* He looked down, trying to control himself and then looked back at Janet. "I'm sorry. I didn't mean that. Come on, you don't want to spoil a good time. The night is young. The food, excellent."

"We must go."

Speaking in Spanish, Royce turned to Nicole. *"You're not tired sweetheart? Are you? You want to stay, have anything you want to eat, don't you?"*

"Royce, that's not fair," said Janet.

Royce snickered. "It doesn't hurt to spoil." His expression changed again. "You're trying to make me mad, aren't you?" He turned to Nicole, smiling. In Spanish he said, *"Wouldn't your koala bear like to stay too?"*

"Please, Royce."

Royce seized Janet's wrist. *"Stay!"*

"You're hurting me, Royce."

"I want you to stay."

"We can't. I told Carolyn we're coming home."

Doubt swept Royce. "No you didn't." He looked for confirmation. "When?"

"On the telephone," Janet said. "Outside the powder room."

Royce could hardly see. *"Don't lie!"*

"I'm not," said Janet. "Now, let go of me."

Royce slumped in his chair. "I wish you hadn't done that." He looked across the dining area. He nodded to the waiter on the other side of the Willard Room.

# Chapter 75

### FBI Headquarters, Washington, D.C.
### Tuesday 1745 ET

Michael Stone stared at his screen in near disbelief. The call to Carolyn Hughes's apartment had come from Janet Griffin. She was dining in the Willard Hotel with Royce Palmer. Michael rose from his console, raced out of the leads center and down the long SIOC hallway to the conference room. He burst through the door. The door almost hit Carolyn. He nodded a perfunctory apology and went directly to Vinny's side. "Royce Palmer is in a dining room at the Willard Hotel." He looked at his notes. "14th and E. Janet Griffin and her daughter are with him."

"The Willard Hotel?" Vinny exclaimed. "Are you sure?"

"I'm sure."

All eyes riveted on Vinny as he dialed and then shouted into his cell, "The First Lady's having dinner at the Willard. Get her out of there. Now!"

# Chapter 76

### Washington, D.C.
### Tuesday 1748 ET

Janet Griffin was overwhelmed with anger and fear. Her wrist throbbed. She and Nicole had to get away. She rose from the table and told Nicole they were leaving.

Royce jumped up, his chair tumbling over.

Two men in business suits suddenly appeared on the sides of the oak-paneled divider. One faced the table. He said in a polite yet firm voice, "Please sir, it will only be a minute." He turned. Both men braced, facing the dining room, feet apart, hands clasped behind their backs.

"What's going on?" said Royce.

The first man turned his head toward Royce. "Please, sir."

A third man appeared. He took a position with the first two. All exits from the table were blocked. On the far side of the dining room a loose cluster of patrons appeared, passed the grand piano, and headed for the maitre d' station. When the last of them disappeared, the third man to appear at the alcove walked to the center of the dining room, stood, and looked around before walking toward the maitre d' station. As he disappeared from view, the second man who had appeared at the alcove repeated the same routine. The third man relaxed. "Thank you, sir. You are free to leave."

Royce, Janet and Nicole watched him start for the exit.

Janet took Nicole's hand and looked up. Her mouth fell open. Both hands cupped her mouth, her body hunched in fear. "Oh my God," she screamed.

The last man to leave the alcove hadn't quite left the dining room. He whirled around. His suit jacket flew open, his hand on the gun in his belt holster. He looked toward Janet. He never heard the muted report from Botero's silencer on the other side of the dining room.

# Chapter 77

## Washington, D.C.
## Tuesday 1758 ET

Carolyn Hughes sat in the last row of seats in a limousine being escorted by motorcycle policemen through the streets of Washington. Taro Okada sat beside her. In the seat facing them was the director of the FBI, Forrest Ward.

The limousine, its blue and red lights flashing through the front grill, followed the motorcycles as they threaded their way through the maze of D.C. police barriers guarding the entrance of the Willard Hotel. Forrest emerged first. Carolyn and Taro followed. The FBI director's entourage engulfed them. The three fell a step behind two German shepherds held on short leashes by secret service agents.

Janet, Nicole clinging to her side, spotted Carolyn across the lobby. "Carolyn! We're over here." Forrest nodded to a stocky secret service agent standing just inside the lobby. Carolyn rushed across the lobby and embraced Janet. The stocky secret service agent blocked Taro.

Janet sobbed as they hugged. "It was terrible," she said. "Terrible." Nicole burrowed her head deeper into her mother. "We're okay. We're not hurt or anything. They won't even let us tell…"

The secret service agent standing with Janet interrupted, "Please, we'd like to take individual statements first."

Forrest scanned the crowd of men and women in the lobby. Bold letters on the back of their jackets told who employed each—secret service, FBI, ATF, the DCPD. Forrest spotted his secret service counterpart, John Callahan. He hurried to his side.

In hushed tones John told Forrest, "We lost an agent tonight."

"I'm sorry, John," said Forrest. "Deeply sorry. I passed the word as soon as I knew."

"We appreciate that. The president and first lady are safe. They were just getting into their limousines…"

"The president was here too?" said Forrest.

"He came to surprise the first lady," said John. "Today's the anniversary of the day they met. Thank God your alert came in time." Forrest touched John's arm. "They were getting into their limousines, ready to go back to the White House when we first noticed our man missing. It took less than a minute to locate him. It was too late. The bullet entered the side of his skull."

"The shooter?" asked Forrest.

"A pro," said John. "He used two diversionary tactics: a fire in the kitchen and a third floor false elevator alarm. I doubt he's still in the building though. But if he is, we'll nail the bastard."

"We have to talk," said Forrest.

John massaged the side of his temple with the palm of his hand. "I'm listening."

"Across the lobby there," said Forrest. "Behind me. The woman with the child." John looked over Forrest's shoulder. Janet was sitting with Nicole on her lap. "That's Janet Griffin. You've got Royce Palmer, right?"

"We separated him from Janet as you suggested," said John. "He's in a room on the tenth floor. You said the shooter might be someone named Botero?"

"Let's go somewhere private," said Forrest.

John said, "I've commandeered the Oval Suite. We can talk there."

Carolyn and Taro were left in the lobby near the entrance, out of the way of a seemingly endless number of law enforcement officers with urgent assignments keeping them in constant motion. Janet and Nicole sat on the far side of the lobby.

Carolyn noticed a blue-jacketed officer searching the crowd from the top steps of a staircase. Their eyes met. With a slight wave, the officer acknowledged Carolyn and headed toward her. Carolyn told Taro, "It seems not everybody has forgotten us."

The officer arrived at their side. "Would you both please follow me?" Without waiting for a reply, he turned and headed back across the lobby. Carolyn and Taro followed the officer up the staircase. The officer knocked lightly before opening the door. He held it open for Carolyn and Taro.

Carolyn and Taro entered the Oval Suite. On the floor was a wall-to-wall rug with a pattern of overlapping golden wedges that narrowed as they approached the small round table in the middle of the room. Four red upholstered chairs sat around the table. The back of a gold-colored love seat followed the oval wall. Matching chairs were scattered along the circumference of the room. Two open archways led to rooms beyond.

Forrest Ward and John Callahan rose from center table chairs as Carolyn and Taro entered. The officer retreated into the corridor and closed the door silently behind him.

"Sorry to keep you waiting," Forrest said. "It's been hectic, as you might imagine. This is John Callahan, chief of the secret service." John gestured for Carolyn and Taro to sit in chairs at the center table. Carolyn did. Taro waved him off, preferring to stand.

"Janet Griffin will be joining us in a moment, then we'll go over…" There was a light tap on the door. Janet entered, Nicole sound asleep on her shoulder.

Carolyn went over and put her arms around Janet and Nicole. "You guys okay?" Both women wiped away tears.

"You can put the child in the bedroom," said Forrest, pointing to an archway. "When she's settled we'll talk."

Carolyn and Janet returned from the bedroom and collapsed on the love seat.

John Callahan said, "We haven't finished interrogating Royce Palmer. We have him in a room eight floors above."

"What about the shooter?" said Taro.

Vinny said, "Janet told us the man that killed the secret service agent is the same man who kidnapped Mr. Taylor from the Everglades."

"Botero," confirmed Taro.

"Let's go back a little in time," said John. He looked at Janet. "The president and first lady were dining in the room next to you. That's why you were shunted off to the table the maitre d' gave you." Addressing his remarks to everybody, he continued. "We received a call from Vinny that the presidential party was in danger. We immediately asked the president and first lady to leave the Willard Hotel. The three men blocking your table, Janet, were secret service agents protecting the presidential party."

Carolyn said, "Janet was prevented from leaving so the president could? Is that what you are saying?"

"Exactly. The president and first lady arrived separately, so there were two details of secret service agents in the restaurant."

Taro said, "You knew something might happen."

"As I said, Vinny alerted us," said John.

"Alerted you to?" pressed Taro.

"The fact that Royce Palmer was stalking Janet Griffin in a Willard dining room."

"Taro, this isn't an interrogation," said Vinny.

Taro's frustration rose with each word. "And you hustled the presidential party out of the hotel while blocking the exit of the very people you were told were being stalked."

"Our duty is to…"

Taro said, "You're told there's a killer in the hotel and you didn't alert his target. Did you alert anyone in the hotel?"

"We have a job to do and we did it," said John.

"Couldn't someone in the two details have called for backup?" said Taro. "Alerted the DCPD? Or the hotel security staff?" Taro turned and walked to the other side of the room. "Is Botero holed up at the Willard?"

"We believe he was out of the hotel about the time we found our agent on the dining room floor."

Taro said, "Why the hell didn't you just put the Willard on lockdown when Forrest alerted you?"

John said, "Our duty is to protect the president and first lady."

Taro said, "So now Botero's still after Janet and we'll have to wait until he calls or strikes again.."

Vinny said, "Botero's after Gonzalo, who has an encryption key. We're after the encryption key."

Taro said, "Doesn't anyone believe in law enforcement any more? Arrest Botero *first*. Two little girls in Miami are dead because you guys didn't arrest Botero in the first place. If you had, he'd be in jail right now."

"Please, Taro," said John. "We have to move forward."

Taro shook his head. "Botero's slipped through our fingers twice now. Five are dead in Florida and now one in D.C." Taro headed to the door. "Unbelievable." Taro turned to Carolyn, "I'll stay in touch."

"Taro, don't get in our way here," said Vinny. "I'm letting you in on this as a courtesy." Taro never looked back.

Janet said, "Thank God Nicole's asleep."

"I'll have an agent drive you home," said Forrest.

After Carolyn, Janet and Nicole were seated in the black sedan, the FBI agent slid into the seat next to the driver. He turned to Janet and Carolyn. "Is there anything you'll need?"

"I'm okay," said Carolyn.

"Maybe a few new PoKéRoM game disks," Janet said. "Nicole loves them. If we can get her involved in a new game when she wakes up…"

The agent flipped open his cell phone and said while dialing, "I'll have an agent pick up a game or two and meet us at your apartment."

"They're in breakfast food boxes," Janet told the agent.

# Chapter 78

## Arlington, Virginia
## Wednesday 0800 ET

Carolyn put her hairbrush on the bathroom counter, tightened the belt on her robe and strolled into her living room, her hands folded across her waist. Taro was reading *The Washington Post*. The coffee cup in his hand was about to spill. They grunted mutual acknowledgements. In the kitchen the toaster released the English muffin halves. The secret service agent found one too hot. The agent juggled the half. It landed on the floor.

Carolyn heard a car passing on the parkway below and meandered to the sliding doors. Janet was standing at the balcony rail, sobbing quietly. Carolyn went onto the balcony and put her arms around her best friend. "You're not alone, you know. We're in this together. It's all a terrible shock."

Janet spoke in slow, distressing tones. "What have I done wrong?"

"You've done nothing wrong," said Carolyn. "Nothing."

"Then why is that terrible man after me? I must have done something."

"You've done nothing. Now stop this."

"Taro tried to protect me in my home and now the secret service is protecting me in your home. What's going on?"

"Whatever it is, it has nothing to do with you. Believe me, Janet." Carolyn sat Janet down in a wrought iron chair and sat in the one next to her. They looked toward the Washington Monument without seeing it or hearing the hum of the traffic below. "Look, it's complicated," said Carolyn. "It's all my fault. If I hadn't come to Bayside, none of this would have happened. It'll all be over soon."

"Even Royce. He told me it's my fault the secret service man was killed. Said if I hadn't screamed, the man would be alive."

"No. No. Royce is pushing the blame onto someone else. You were the closest."

"That man was after me," said Janet. "I could see it in his eyes. After he shot the secret service agent, he came for me. Royce grabbed me. He wouldn't let me move. My arms still hurt where he held them."

"Janet…"

"I don't know why that man stopped coming after me. He just did. He turned and ran back into the kitchen."

"Janet, Royce is…"

"My arm is black and blue," said Janet.

"Royce may be involved with that man, Janet. Do you hear me? Royce may be involved with the killer."

"I don't know if I believe it."

"Royce may be laundering money," Carolyn said. "Dirty money."

"He lives in San Diego."

"They think he's laundering money from around the world."

The telephone rang. Carolyn rushed inside and went into her bedroom. She stood next to the telephone on the nightstand waiting for the secret service agent to signal it was okay to pick up.

"Hello."

Botero said, "Is Janet there?"

"How'd you get this number?" Nicole began to awaken.

"Tell whoever listen no bother, man," said Botero. "I hang up thirty seconds."

"What do you want?"

The secret service agent signaled Carolyn to keep him on the line.

"Ten seconds gone man. Where Janet?"

"What do you want?" Carolyn insisted.

"Janet know," said Botero.

"You're the one who killed that man in the hotel, aren't you?" said Carolyn.

"Twenty seconds gone."

"Janet doesn't have anything you want."

Nicole heard her mother's name. She stood up in bed. *"Mommy, Mommy."*

"Janet baby, right? She die."

"Tell me what you want. If I can get it, I will." Botero hung up. Carolyn put the phone in its cradle, picked up Nicole, and went into the living room.

"Good," said the agent. "He's hooked."

Carolyn settled Nicole beside her on the couch.

"Who's hooked?" said Janet.

"That was Botero," said Carolyn. "He says you have what he wants."

"What?" said Janet. "I don't have anything that man could possibly want."

"We believe you," said Taro.

"Come on, come on," said the agent. "There isn't much time."

"It doesn't matter how much time there is," said Janet. "I have *nothing!*"

The agent said, "Even if you don't have what he wants, he thinks you do. He'll get in touch again. For now, that's all we've got. Let's hope he doesn't call back soon."

"We need more than time," said Carolyn.

"Botero wants something to do with computers," said the agent.

"We've been over this a dozen times," said Janet. "We know nothing about that kind of stuff."

"You were at Crosby's party, right?" said the agent.

"I told you that."

"Did you talk about computers while you were there? Did anybody?"

"Not that I heard," said Janet. "It wasn't that kind of a party. Small talk. That's all."

"Please, Janet," said Carolyn. "Think. Did you see anyone using a computer or... anyone talk about computers or CDs before, during, or after that Key Largo party?"

Nicole squirmed free of Janet's arms and scurried off into the bedroom.

"You told me you're not even sure this maniac is looking for a stolen computer or disk," said Janet.

"I know," the agent nodded. "But we better have something in mind before he calls back. Even if it's a bluff."

"No bluffs," said Taro. "You don't bluff crazies. They'll call you every time."

"I'm open to suggestions," said the agent.

Nicole returned from the bedroom with Freddie clutched in her hand. She looked at Carolyn and reached into Freddie's pouch.

"What do you suggest, detective Okada?"

"Easy. Collar Botero. Forget about computers and codes."

"We're dealing with national issues here," said the agent. "The president and first lady. Congressional committees. National and international press. Our country's prestige."

"You keep putting living breathing citizens in harm's way because of your so-called national issues," said Taro.

Nicole pulled out a brightly colored PoKéRoM disk and gave it to Carolyn.

Janet smiled as she watched Carolyn study the PoKéRoM disk.

What did Janet tell me back in Bayside? Carolyn mused. This thing is a CD? She turned the PoKéRoM disk over. The underside reminded her how surprised she was when she had first opened the CD tray to play a PoKéRoM game with Nicole. The CD tray actually accepted two different sized CDs, the normal CD diameter everyone uses and this much smaller diameter. She remembered thinking, what the heck, if you didn't need to file away an entire dictionary, why use a large disk if this small one is all you need.

Suddenly it hit her. Hadn't she just asked Janet if anyone at the Key Largo party had said anything about computers or CDs? Hadn't Nicole been at the Key Largo party? Hadn't Nicole just handed me a CD?

"You have no idea what we're all in for, detective Okada," said the agent. "This isn't Miami-Dade."

"Right. It's Disney World."

Carolyn looked at Janet. "Tell Nicole I'll play with her."

"Now?" asked Janet, surprised.

"Right now," confirmed Carolyn.

*"La tia Carolyn dice que jugara contigo,"* Janet told Nicole.

A broad grin spread across Nicole's face as she took Carolyn's hand and marched off to the bedroom.

Janet followed Carolyn and Nicole. "What are you two doing?"

Carolyn held up the PoKéRoM disk. "Your precious daughter may have what Botero wants."

Taro joined them in the bedroom. "What are you thinking?"

Carolyn rose, taking Nicole's hand. *"Señorita ven conmigo."* They headed for the computer.

"What is that thing?" the agent asked.

Carolyn said with more than a hint of pride, "As a good

friend said to me not too long ago, you haven't been around kids recently, have you?"

"So what is it?" insisted the agent.

"A PoKéRoM educational game disk," said Carolyn "Get it?"

"No," said Taro.

"It has a child's game on it," said the agent. "Right?"

"Exactly," said Carolyn.

Nicole sat on the bed. Carolyn sat at her computer. "PoKéRoM is a Pokémon computer game. There are Pokémon cards like baseball cards, dolls, and a zillion collectables. One of the biggest movies is Pokémon."

Carolyn held the PokéRom disk so the agent could get a good look at it. "This is a CD that's been cut to the size of a business card—except its ends are rounded to match the smaller curve in the CD tray. PoKéRoM disks are really CD-ROMs—CDs with read-only memory. Each PoKéRoM disk contains an educational game. Get it?"

"I'm listening," said the agent.

Taro added, "I'm hoping she'll explain soon."

Carolyn put the disk on the CD tray and closed the tray. Nothing appeared on the screen. She ejected the PoKéRoM disk and tried again. Again the CD motor came up to speed and nothing appeared on the screen.

Carolyn ejected the disk. She put it in Freddie's pouch, winking at Nicole. Back in the living room Carolyn said, "Remember, someone said Gonzalo was an expert at computer games? That he won computer game contests?" Carolyn glanced around. No one said anything. "Well, am I right?"

"Michael Stone told us," said Taro. "While we were at FBI Headquarters."

"Okay then," Carolyn said. "… Nicole was at the Key Largo party. Somehow she found Gonzalo's disk and put it in Freddie's pouch." The room fell silent.

Janet picked Nicole up and hugged her warmly. In Spanish she told her daughter, *"I love you, darling. You're just wonderful."*

Nicole squirmed and pulled Freddie from between them. *"Y Freddie?"*

*"Yes, and Freddie too. We're going to take your disk and*

*solve a big mystery. Mommy is so proud of you."*

Taro chimed in, "So Nicole found the disk while she was at the party, and thinking it was a real PoKéRoM game disk, took it. You're suggesting Gonzalo stripped this disk of game information and put his codes, passphrase, data or whatever on it."

Carolyn stretched her arms out with her palms up. "Bingo."

"I'll have NSA check out the disk," said the agent. He headed toward the balcony doors as he flipped his cell phone open.

Nicole twirled Freddie over her head. Freddie went flying, landing on the floor by the bedroom door. Nicole ran after Freddie, picked him up and then went back into the bedroom. She took a new PoKéRoM disk from among those the agent had delivered the night before.

Carolyn and Janet sat quietly on the couch, late that afternoon. Nicole was in the bedroom at the computer. Carolyn leaned toward Janet. "I'm telling you we can do it."

"This isn't a game," Janet said pensively.

The intercom buzzer rang. Carolyn headed for the door and waited before pressing the button. They listened to the lobby receptionist together. "Royce Palmer is here, Ms. Hughes."

"Send him up," Carolyn said. She turned to Janet. "We did it in Manhattan. We'll do it here. Think of all the guys we scammed in college. Remember Bruce?"

"Royce isn't Bruce," said Janet. "Besides, I broke up with Royce in the Willard Hotel, just before the secret service agent was murdered. Royce wasn't a happy camper, I can tell you that."

"Oh Janet, just run into his arms when he comes in the door and he'll forget whatever you told him."

"I don't know."

"Remember, we're a team. We can do it." Their eyes locked. They grasped hands.

"Okay," said Janet. "I won't have a problem duping Royce. I really won't. Not after all you told me about him. If I get squeamish, I'll touch the bruises he put on my arms. They still hurt."

"Okay then," said Carolyn. "We'll just let him discover our quote, *little secret,* unquote all by himself. Convincing him not to tell the police will be a no-brainer. Getting him to go with us to meet Botero for the exchange will be harder, but between us we can plead and cry at the appropriate times if the going gets rough. We work as a team bamboozling Royce until he gives Botero the disk later tonight. Okay?"

"Why wouldn't Royce just take the disk and run?"

"He's running a multi-million dollar operation out there in San Diego. He doesn't want to break his cover. Besides, if he runs, his clients and the feds will all be after him."

"Say he runs and the FBI gets him, then what?"

"Then it's plan B. You and I will give Botero the disk."

"Either way it's scary," said Janet. "Royce goes with us and two bad guys are at the exchange. He doesn't go, it's just you, me and Botero at the exchange."

"Come on Janet, we've got the FBI, the secret service, the park police, and the DCPD backing us up."

"Why am I still uncomfortable?" said Janet with a weak smile. "Hey, where's your little hottie, Taro? I'd feel a lot better if he was in on this."

"I'm sure he will be," said Carolyn.

"What does that mean? Where is he?"

The doorbell rang twice in quick order. Carolyn rose and went to the door. Before opening it, she looked back at Janet. Janet replied with a confirming nod. Carolyn opened the door.

"Royce, where have you been?" said Carolyn, an anxious look on her face. "We've been worried sick about you. You haven't called or anything." Carolyn turned, heading back into the living room. "Janet's inside." Carolyn winked at Janet as she entered the living room walking in front of Royce.

Carolyn and Janet were on stage.

"So much has happened," said Royce. "That man shot in the hotel—*he died.*"

"They told us," said Janet. "I feel so awful. It's my fault. I shouldn't have screamed, like you said. And Royce..." Janet looked poignantly into Royce's eyes. "I shouldn't have made you mad. I'm sorry. I really am." She ran into his arms.

"That man's death isn't your fault," said Royce. "You've got to forget it." He turned toward Carolyn. "What'd the police do with you two?"

"Kept us waiting," said Carolyn. "Forever. Questioned us

separately, together, and then separately again. Same questions over and over. One dumb question after the other. It took hours before we could go. We can't leave town."

Janet said to Royce, "They let us go last night. What happened to you?"

"Same thing that happened to you," said Royce. "Questions, questions, questions. Except they asked me to stay overnight so they could check with San Diego this morning. They kept telling me you guys were okay."

"We're not. We're jumpy as hell," said Janet.

"We're so glad you're here," said Carolyn. "You'll know what to do. We got a call from the gunman. He's looking for something and we don't know what. He's demanding we hand it over."

"I hope you called the police," said Royce.

"No way," said Janet. "He said he'd kill Nicole, if either of us called the police. The way he looked at me at the hotel, what he did—I'm scared. …I believe him."

Royce sat on the arm of the couch. "What'd he want?"

"No idea," said Carolyn. "We were hoping you'd know."

"What exactly did he say?" asked Royce.

"He insisted Janet knew what he wanted," said Carolyn. "He threatened to kill Nicole if Janet didn't hand it over. Whatever it is."

"We've racked our brains." Janet's face broadcast despair. "I haven't the slightest idea what he wants."

"We figured it must be something important," said Carolyn. "A killer like him doesn't risk his own life for nothing."

"So help me God, I have no idea what he wants," said Janet. "Or why a scumbag like that would think I had anything he'd want. It just doesn't make sense. No sense at all, Royce." Royce stood as Janet ran into his arms again, crying this time.

"Tell me again, what exactly did he say?"

Carolyn said, "I don't remember exactly what he said, Royce. He scared me, too."

"Okay, we have something he wants," said Royce, stroking Janet's hair. "Now, let's figure out what it is. By the way, where's Nicole?"

"She's in the bedroom playing on the computer," Janet sniffled. "She finally stopped crying."

"Until I bought her some new PoKéRoM disks, that little lady was a real pain in the butt, said Carolyn."

"Come on, Carolyn," said Janet, turning to Carolyn defiantly. "She's a four-year-old who saw a man killed."

"For Christ sake, I didn't mean anything. It's okay she's a pain in the ass."

"It was that damned disk." said Janet.

"What disk?" Royce asked.

Carolyn said, "I couldn't get her disk to work in the computer. I went from the help section to the trouble shooting section, back to the help section. I couldn't find out why it wouldn't work."

Janet said, "It kept us busy, at least."

"Us?" snapped Carolyn. "You didn't do a damn thing. You just lay on the bed watching me push the mouse around."

"What are you getting so huffy about?" said Janet. "It isn't a big deal."

"Oh no?" said Carolyn. "You don't think anything's a big deal. Royce is missing. A man's shot dead. The police questioning us over and over again. No big deal?"

"Okay, let's settle down," said Royce. He looked at each of them. "Nicole's on the computer now. How'd you fix it?"

"There's not a damned thing wrong with the computer," said Carolyn. "It's that PoKéRoM disk Nicole carries around in the pouch of that stupid koala bear."

"Oh, for Christ sake," said Janet rolling both her face and eyes to the ceiling.

"So what did you do with it?" said Royce.

"With what?" said Janet.

"The disk that wouldn't work," said Royce.

"Take a guess," said Carolyn.

"He's just asking," said Janet. "Don't get huffy."

"Look, I just started a new job. Everything's going great. I bring my new boss to Bayside. He's kidnapped. My world explodes. Literally, explodes."

"Cool it Carolyn," said Janet.

"Cool it? Where do you get off—"

"Royce just asked what you did with the disk."

"I trashed it, Royce. That's what I did."

"You trashed it?" said Royce.

Carolyn began crying. "Which word didn't you understand?"

"Oh, come on," said Janet, dripping sarcasm. "The baby's not going to start crying, is she?"

Carolyn shook her head, her red hair flying back and forth across her shoulders. "Everything's getting to me, Royce. I put the disk in the kitchen garbage. So sue me." Carolyn headed for her bedroom, sniffling. "I'm a mess. I need some tissues."

"Jesus, Carolyn, what's wrong with you?" Janet said. She followed Carolyn into the bedroom and closed the door behind them.

Carolyn and Janet had exited the stage.

# Chapter 79

### Vietnam Memorial, Washington, D.C.
### Thursday 0200 ET

Carolyn forced herself not to look for the law enforcement officers she knew were watching. She did the only thing she knew would work. She looked down.

Janet said, "It's crazy to be standing here at the entrance to the Vietnam Memorial at two in the morning." She squared her shoulders to Carolyn. "And you expect this killer that the entire U.S. government is after will just walk up to us, take a kid's computer disk, and go away?" In a slow cadence she said, "I...don't...think...so."

"You're not going to quit on us?" said Carolyn. "You're okay, right?"

Janet crossed her arms and squeezed her bruises hard as she shuffled around with her chin on her chest. "How would I know if I'm okay?" She stopped in front of Royce and began laughing. "I can't help it," she told him. "You look stupid standing there holding that stuffed koala bear." Janet looked past the bronze statue of the three fighting men, to the Wall. She spoke to Carolyn without looking at her. "Royce doesn't think this is going to work, either."

"It's going to work, Janet," said Carolyn. She turned to Royce. "You've got the disk. Right?"

Royce tossed Freddie from hand to hand. "To be precise, this koala bear's got the disk. Let's hope it satisfies this Botero and we all get out of here alive." Royce looked at Freddie. "Why am I the one holding this dumb animal?"

"Because men believe men," said Carolyn. "This guy Botero would never believe Janet or me. Besides, you're the one who figured this out. So you tell him how you did it, how Nicole took it home with her from Crosby's Key Largo place. He'll believe you, get his disk, and let us all go."

"We should have told the FBI, the D.C. police, or someone," lamented Janet. "I'm telling you this is crazy. We're alone, defenseless against this maniac."

"One thing's for sure," Royce said. "We have what he wants."

Janet squeezed her bruises again. "Why the hell didn't he just tell us to leave it somewhere? He could then pick it up anytime he wanted."

"Sure, with police waiting in the shadows," said Royce. "That doesn't make sense. He's using us as insurance."

Janet swung around, confronting Royce. "Oh that's great. Just great. First I'm bait, now I'm insurance."

"Take it easy, Janet," said Carolyn. "Botero knows what he wants. He wants to make sure he's getting the right disk."

"And if it isn't marked like he thinks it's supposed to be marked?" said Janet. "How are you going to handle that, Royce?"

"What do you expect from me?" said Royce. "Heroics?"

"Just be here. Act like a man," Carolyn pleaded.

Janet looked up the grade toward the Vietnam Memorial souvenir shacks. "Is that guy here all the time?"

"Someone is here 24/7" said Carolyn. "Those shacks are manned by vets dedicated to their fallen comrades."

The veteran sitting in a wheelchair next to the shack turned his wheelchair and looked toward them. "Shit," said Royce. "He'll just get in our way."

"Stay cool," said Carolyn. "If these guys see anyone looking like they need help finding a loved one on the Wall, they want to help. We've been standing here a while. I'm guessing he thinks we need help. Don't worry, he'll leave us alone when we tell him we're okay."

The man in the wheelchair grasped both wheels and with a quick motion began rolling toward them. When he was about halfway down the incline, Royce said, "He's lost both legs."

The man rolled his wheelchair in front of Carolyn. "Janet?"

"I thought it might be you," said Carolyn.

Botero spoke in a low voice. "You the bitch on phone."

Forrest Campbell peered through night goggles from the roof of the Federal Reserve on the far side of Constitution Avenue. "Anybody. Can we confirm Botero in the wheelchair?"

The sniper on the roof of the National Academy of Sciences next door peered through the scope on his rifle. "Can't be sure. This guy's legless below his knees. Land mine, probably."

A sniper lying prone on the knoll separating the Lincoln Memorial Reflecting Pool from the Wall said, "I can't see his face the way he's wearing that cap. His jacket and cap have a hell of a lot of buttons on 'em."

Forrest said, "Stay alert. If this isn't Botero, he'll turn up soon." He focused his goggles on the roof of the Lincoln Memorial. "Taro, you up there?"

"He just left," a voice responded. "He's not happy. Says he's seen all this before. Doesn't like it."

"Can you see the wheelchair?" Forrest asked.

"Both my guys up here have it in their crosshairs."

"Remember, ground-level shooters, fire only in self-defense, Forrest said. We don't want bullets hitting a passing car or flying into the streets of D.C."

Botero said to Carolyn, "You got wire. Pull it off, bitch."
Carolyn froze, her eyes riveted on Botero.
"Pull it off, bitch! Slow."
Carolyn didn't move. "Are you for…?"
"Do it, bitch. Slow."
Carolyn sneezed and pulled the microphone from under the lapel of her blouse.
"You bitch!"
Janet looked at Carolyn in disbelief. "You had a microphone on?"
"Taro made me wear it," said Carolyn.
Botero said, "Who this Taro, man?"
"A Miami-Dade detective," said Royce. "He's pissed you killed two little girls in the Miami airport."
Botero sneered as he inspected the mic. "Tough." The microphone was embossed with the initials M-D PD. Botero murmured, "Miami-Dade."
Carolyn said, "Royce, give him the koala bear. I want out of here."
Royce threw the bear on the blanket covering Botero's legs.

Botero looked at the stuffed animal. "What this, man?" He tossed Freddie to Carolyn. "Keep it bitch." He turned the wheelchair toward the souvenir shacks. "We done, man."

The knoll sniper said, "The man gave the guy in the wheelchair something but he flipped it back to one of the ladies."

The sniper next to Forrest said, "Confirm that."
Forrest said, "Stay cool everybody."

Botero rolled toward the path leading back up to the veteran's shack. Carolyn called after him. "We gave you what you asked for."
Botero stopped and turned his wheelchair sideways to the grade. "Where the disk, man?"
"In the koala bear's pouch," said Royce.
"Why don't you just get up and walk?" said Carolyn.
"You no want me out of this chair, bitch."
"We'll bring the disk to you," said Carolyn. Botero waited. Royce pushed him up the rest of the grade. Botero rolled to the souvenir shack and stopped at the door on its far side.

Forrest couldn't see the shack's door from the Federal Reserve roof. "Talk to me. What's going on?"

The sniper on the roof of the National Academy of Sciences said, "Out of sight."

The voice from the Lincoln Memorial said, "We've got two sets of crosshairs on 'em."

The sniper on the knoll said, "In my crosshairs."

Royce said, "The disk is in the koala's pouch. Janet's daughter found it at Crosby's party. She just took it. No one knew she had it."
Botero flipped his cap off. A broad grin spread across his face. "You shit me."

The sniper on the knoll said, "Confirmed. Botero in the

wheelchair."

"Stay cool, everybody," said Forrest.

"I found it a couple of hours ago," said Royce. "In Carolyn's apartment. The disk was in the koala bear's pouch."

Carolyn tossed Freddie to Botero.

Botero found the pouch, took out the shiny metal, and looked at Royce. "This it, man?"

"That's it," said Royce. "Gonzalo put the codes on it. With the Internet, he can control everything from anywhere in the world. He's a genius."

Botero studied the disk, turning it over and over.

"Satisfied?" said Carolyn.

"You ask for it, bitch." Botero stared at Carolyn before wheeling through the entrance and into the darkened shack. The owner of the wheelchair was under the cot, bound and gagged. Botero's chair rolled through his blood on the shack floor.

The knoll spotter whispered, "Can't see inside the shack."

Royce followed Botero into the shack. "Give me the disk. Your job is done." Botero handed the disk to Royce. "Now let's get out of here."

Royce left the shack. Botero rolled backward through the entrance after him. Botero started toward the path leading back to the bronze statue.

The man under the cot kicked it over. Carolyn and Janet heard it hit the ground. They looked into the shack.

The sniper on the knoll said, "The guy in the wheelchair is rolling. I'm losing him. Out of sight."

"Perfect," said Forrest. "We want him isolated."

The legless veteran struggled furiously against the tape binding him. Carolyn knelt by the side of the cot and ripped the tape from his mouth.

"Get out!" he screamed. "There's a bomb!"

Janet screamed, "Royce!" Carolyn lifted the cot but there wasn't room to get it out without folding it up.

"Royce!" Janet shouted. "Where are you?"

The Lincoln Memorial voice said, "Wheelchair's really moving. He's headed for the 'Nam flagpole."

The sniper next to Forrest said, "Wheelchair's below grade. Out of sight. Repeat. Out of sight."

"Out of sight," said the sniper on the National Academy of Sciences.

The spotter on the Lincoln Memorial said, "The man that was with those two women is running toward the side of the Lincoln Memorial. He's out of sight. What the...? Who's...? It's Taro. He's running across the roadway toward the shack...."
The Lincoln Memorial sniper followed the wheelchair in the crosshairs of his scope as it headed for the Vietnam flagpole. "Wheelchair out of sight."

Royce sprinted alongside the marble staircase until he reached the rear corner of the Lincoln Memorial. Panting, he half squatted, pressing his back against the cool white marble.

Carolyn ran toward Taro as he crossed the circular drive. "There's a man in the shack. And a bomb."
Taro ran past her. "Run!" he shouted, pointing toward the knoll leading to the reflecting pool. "Over there. Go! Now!" Taro disappeared into the darkness of the shack.

The knoll spotter stood and shouted to Janet and Carolyn. "Here. Over here."

Botero let the wheelchair freewheel toward the bronze memorial statue.

Taro carried the bound veteran out of the shack. The sniper guiding Carolyn and Janet saw Taro struggling with the weight of the legless veteran. He ran to Taro, snatched the vet from Taro's arms, and flung him over his shoulder. Together they raced toward the knoll and tumbled down toward the reflecting pool.

At the tallest panel on the Vietnam Memorial Wall, Botero jumped out of the wheelchair. He crouched near its base, waiting for the timed explosion. The walk lights cast a giant silhouette of Botero and his Uzi onto the Wall.

"I'm okay," said the Vietnam veteran.
Out of breath, Taro signaled the sniper that he was okay too.

Royce protected his face with his arms and hands and forced his way through the low branches of trees. Emerging on the other side, he stopped to get his bearings. The car lights crossing the Memorial Bridge provided the perfect guide. He raced down the sloping lawn. The explosion threw him to the ground, his momentum sending him tumbling into the closed roadway circling the Lincoln Memorial.

Botero ran further along the walk and scaled the first panel he could. He ran across the grass toward Constitution Avenue and fell, crossing the curb of the cobblestone maintenance road. He hobbled across Constitution Avenue and up the street between the National Academy of Sciences and the Federal Reserve buildings.

Taro ran under the billowing white cloud that had replaced the fireball and then ran along Henry Bacon Drive. His lungs said enough when he reached the grass above the corner of the Wall. With his hands on his knees and his heart and lungs maxed out, he looked across Constitution Avenue for signs of Botero.

"Here. Over here," Royce heard, as he ran along the low stone wall confining the Potomac. A man stood on the wall holding the mooring line of a boat in his hand. "What a fucking blast."
Royce hopped on the boat. "Let's go," he panted, as he collapsed on the deck.
The man jumped onboard and took the wheel. The boat headed toward the Theodore Roosevelt Bridge.

Taro saw Botero. He was limping badly. As Taro caught his breath he watched Botero limp up the street between the National

Academy of Sciences and the Federal Reserve, turn right at the corner, and disappear behind the Federal Reserve building. Taro raced toward the street on the other side of the Federal Reserve. A car hit him as he crossed Constitution Avenue. He rolled across its hood and kept on running.

Forrest looked down from the roof of the Federal Reserve at the car screeching to a halt. A man rolled across the hood of the car. "That son-of-a-bitch is going to get killed...." Forrest used his binoculars. "Goddamn. ... It's Taro." He watched Taro run across the front of the Federal Reserve building and up the street to his left. "He's going behind us." He tapped the back of the sharpshooter. "Come on," said Forrest. They raced across the roof of the Federal Reserve to the back of the building.

Botero could hardly walk. He crouched low on the C Street sidewalk. Almost sitting, he massaged his broken ankle.

Forrest scanned the street below with his goggles. "I don't see a goddamned thing. TOC, come in."
"This is TOC."
"Fugitive on C between 20th and 21st NW. Armed. Automatic weapon. Extremely dangerous. Request assistance."
"Roger. Fugitive on C between 20th and 21st NW. Armed. Automatic weapon. Extremely dangerous. Assistance requested."
"TOC to Little Birds. Fugitive on C Street between 20th and 21st NW. Armed. Automatic weapon. Extremely dangerous. Alpha to C and 20th. Beta to C and 21st. Cleared to green."

Royce heard the helicopters before he saw them. "Stay here," he shouted to the man at the helm. The man didn't respond. Royce shouted in Spanish. *"Damned it, stay under the bridge until the helicopters pass, you idiot."*

Taro reached the far corner at the back of the Federal Reserve. He sat on the curb, his back to Botero, his lungs heaving.

Botero groaned as he put weight on his broken ankle getting up. He staggered forward, his head down, his left hand clutching his ankle, his right the Uzi.

"I see him now," Forrest said. "Holy shit, Taro has him boxed in."

The Washington Harbour was crowded with moored pleasure boats. Their occupants had heard the blast from the Lincoln Memorial and were standing on their decks watching its plume drift over the Potomac toward them. No one noticed Royce's boat being lashed to the last boat on the pier. Royce stepped onto the pier, walked through Washington Harbour, up Wisconsin Avenue, and then into Georgetown.

Botero hobbled a few more steps and looked up. He spotted Taro sitting on the curb. Botero yelled, "You, man." Taro ignored him. "Get your fuck'n ass outta here, man." Taro staggered slowly to his feet, his head lolling on his shoulders.

Botero raised the Uzi. "Who the hell are you?" The rumbling roar of the Little Birds engulfed the two men.

Taro's knees flexed, his shoulders hunched, his eyes dared Botero to act. He shouted over the roar. "It's over, Botero."

Botero squinted at Taro. "Fuck you, man...." He raised his Uzi.

Suddenly MD530 helicopters appeared at each end of C Street. Their spotlights turned night into day. Two snipers stood on the skids of each of the Little Birds. Alpha's loudspeaker demanded, "Put down your weapon."

Botero pointed his Uzi at the Little Bird over Taro. His finger squeezed the trigger. Botero heard only the first two of the twenty rounds he fired before his head exploded. Eight of his rounds crashed through white tents on the Mall. Nine cut a path in the Mall grass on their way toward the Smithsonian Castle. Two sprayed gravel in front of the carousel.

Botero's body hit the ground as his last bullet hit the rump of the silver horse Nicole had ridden the day before.

# Chapter 80

### Vienna, Virginia
### Friday 1500 ET

Michael rolled the lawn mower into the garage and left with the weed whacker. Twenty minutes later the lawn and garden were trimmed. He grabbed his t-shirt from the hook in the garage, flung it over his shoulder, walked to the back of the house and sat on the broad low deck.

Sarah came out of the house with two large glasses of ice water. She handed Michael one and sat in the chair next to him. They drank in unison. "Your shoulders are beet red. Want me to put something on them?"

"Maybe later," Michael said absent-mindedly.

"You're still brooding aren't you?"

"Blame me?"

"A little," said Sarah.

"How long do you think I should just sit on my ass, Sarah?"

"It's only been a day. You're just on administrative leave. Government machinery is slow."

"I'm supposed to just sit here while it grinds?"

"We're going to the beach with the kids tomorrow," said Sarah. "That will be fun."

"If I lose my security clearances... End of story."

"Who planted that crazy story?" asked Sarah.

"Vinny Campbell. I know it. He knows I know it."

"I thought you said he denied it before announcing his retirement," said Sarah.

"He's hiding behind a reporter's shield." Michael got up and started to go into the house. "It's a win-win for them both."

"Where're you going?" asked Sarah.

"I can't just sit here," said Michael. "I'll be back in an hour or so. Don't worry."

# Chapter 81

### Arlington, Virginia
### Friday 1510 ET

Carolyn sat on her narrow balcony with Janet and Taro. They were watching another plane bank over the Potomac as it completed its approach into Reagan National. The drone of rush-hour traffic rising up from the GW Parkway provided proof that the world hadn't missed a beat. A rasping buzzer broke the silence.

Carolyn squeezed past Taro and Janet. On her way to the intercom she peeked into the bedroom. Nicole was moving Tonka vehicles across her computer screen.

"Forrest Ward's here to see you," said the receptionist. "Claims he's the director of the FBI."

Carolyn grinned. "Send him up." Returning to the sliding doors, she leaned out saying, "You won't believe this. Forrest is on his way up."

"What now?" said Taro.

"Stop complaining. Come on in." Taro and Janet dragged themselves into the living room. The doorbell rang.

"What's up?" said Taro as Forrest entered the living room.

Carolyn waved Forrest to a chair. "Something to drink?"

Forrest said, "Can't stay. Due on the Hill."

Carolyn sat on the couch with Janet and Taro. "Everything okay?"

"No," said Forrest. "NSA tells me the PoKéRoM disk we gave them is just that—a PoKéRoM disk."

Carolyn said, "The disk didn't have codes on it? The Michael Stone theory is wrong?"

Forrest said, "I'm not saying Michael is wrong—only that there's no proof. On the other hand, Greg McNulty has done a great job. His task force is right in the thick of things. We're proud of the work he's doing."

Carolyn froze. *"What?"*

Forrest looked to Carolyn. "I know you two don't get along. But we have to look at the facts. Greg has been working the task force for years, putting in yeoman's work. We're running down every lead he has. He's going to break this wide open. Soon."

Carolyn glared at Forrest, unable to speak. She turned and walked out onto the balcony.

Forrest said, "There's one more thing. Royce Palmer escaped. We'll get him. Just a matter of time."

Taro said, "You had him in custody and released him, hoping to gather intelligence. That's exactly what you guys did with Botero in the Miami airport, at the Willard, and then again at the Wall."

Forrest said, "You planted that microphone on Carolyn, didn't you?"

Taro said, "Botero needed to find one."

Forrest said, "Her sneeze was your idea too." Taro nodded. "What about never bluffing? You told one of my men never bluff a crazy."

"I didn't bluff."

"When you sat on the curb? You were bluffing, taking a chance Botero wouldn't use his Uzi."

Taro said, "No way. When that car screeched to a halt on Constitution Avenue and I went over its hood, I knew you'd see me from your rooftop perch. Given a little time, you'd cover me. So I bought time. I sat on the curb."

Forrest grinned and shook his head in admiration. "Gotta go." Nicole came from the bedroom and stood by Janet. Seeing Nicole, Forrest said, "Oh, before I forget." He pulled Freddie from his attaché case and handed the koala to Nicole. Nicole looked at Forrest as if he had stolen Freddie.

Janet walked Forrest to the door. Taro joined Carolyn on the balcony. After Forrest left, Janet joined them. Taro and Carolyn were standing at the patio rail. Carolyn had her arms folded across her stomach, her head down. She muttered, "This place is a zoo."

The rasping buzzer interrupted again. Carolyn welcomed the interruption. No need to expose others to her despair. She went inside to answer the buzzer. The receptionist said, "There's a man here. Says you know him. Michael Stone."

"Send him up," said Carolyn. Nicole came out of the bedroom to see who was coming.

A few minutes later Michael stood in the living room. He wore a grubby t-shirt, grass-stained sneakers, and needed a shave. "Look, I'm sorry to bother you, but…"

Carolyn said, "Absolutely no bother. Sit. Want a cool one?"

"No thanks. I can't stay. My wife and kids are waiting at home."

Taro said, "What can we do for you?"

"Do you have any other PoKéRoM disks?" asked Michael.

Nicole clutched Freddie and ran into the bedroom.

"We have a few," said Carolyn. "The FBI bought them for Nicole."

"Can I see them?" said Michael. "Please?"

"They're in the bedroom," said Carolyn. "Give me a minute." Carolyn returned with several PoKéRoM disks. All were still sealed in plastic wrapping.

"Any others?" said Michael.

"Three or four," said Janet. "We brought them from Florida." Janet went back into the bedroom and retrieved three.

"Can I have these? I'll return them."

"You think the code will be on one of these?" said Janet.

"I don't know, but I'd like to find out. Any others? You said three or four."

"That's all I could find," said Janet.

"Just a minute," said Carolyn. She turned and summoned Nicole. *"Nicole, ven aca por favor."*

"You speak Spanish now?" asked Janet.

"Two years in high school," said Carolyn.

Nicole came into the living room. She pressed Freddie tight to her body and squinted her eyes, daring anyone to try to take Freddie.

Carolyn turned to Janet. "Please ask Nicole if there's a disk in Freddie's pouch."

There wasn't.

# Chapter 82

## Acapulco, Mexico
## Saturday 0800 CT

Royce looked back before rounding the grove of trees. Confident that he could find his way back to his car, he started up the final grade. With every step he flicked sweat from his brow into the tall meadow grass engulfing his Bruno Maglis. He stopped to catch his breath and looked ahead. Jose was standing on a grassy knoll just beyond the smaller riding ring.

When Royce arrived at Jose's side, the young girls in the smaller ring were lining up their ponies like a company of cavalry ready to charge. The woman standing in the ring in front of them studied her clipboard. Beside her was a girl a few years older than those astride ponies. She held a collection of different colored ribbons at the ready.

"They told me I'd find you here," said Royce. Jose ignored him. Royce looked into the ring. Nothing was happening. He tried again. "How many more events?"

"Quiet," said Jose. "Can't you see the judge is about to make her decision?"

The riders sat motionless in their saddles. Somehow the ponies understood that they shouldn't misbehave. The riders all looked alike—black riding helmets anchored with chinstraps, black or blue riding jackets over pressed white shirts sporting bow ties, and flared jodhpurs that disappeared into shiny black calf-high boots resting on stirrups.

"See?" said Jose. "The heel of her boot in her stirrup? It's lower than the toe. A sign of a trained equestrienne."

Royce couldn't think of a proper response.

The clipboard lady looked up. "The blue ribbon for the best-in-show goes to…" A gust of wind sent dust swirling and the pages on her clipboard flapping. The lady smiled apologetically and meticulously laid each page flat again before displaying the results.

Jose groaned. "Why doesn't that bitch announce the fucking winner?"

The lady smiled at the crowd once more and positioned her clipboard. "The winner is…" She lowered her head to read from the clipboard. "Ladybug, owned and ridden by Lucita Alonzo."

The crowd cheered. Jose's eyes watered when his granddaughter waved gleefully to him. The judge nodded to the teenaged girl. She peeled the blue ribbon from those on her arm, ran to Ladybug, and secured the ribbon to the side of Ladybug's bridle. Delighted, Lucita lowered herself onto Ladybug's mane and wrapped her arms around her pony's neck.

Lucita was first to exit the ring. As she came through the gate Jose took her hand and reached for Ladybug's bridle. His fingernail caught Ladybug's nostril. The pony reared, her front hooves flashing in front of Jose's face. He jumped back but didn't let go of Lucita's hand. Lucita landed on top of Jose. Together they tumbled on the oiled red clay.

Royce and Jose sat at the glass-topped table. A maid entered and served Bloody Marys. "To a great day," said Royce. "Congratulations."

"Don't congratulate me," said Jose. He tilted his wrought iron chair onto its back legs. "It's Lucita who deserves the credit. Blue Ribbon! Best in Show!"

"Absolutely," said Royce, knowing exactly what Jose wanted to hear.

"She sat so straight in the saddle." Jose sat straight. "In every event she rode tall." He drank and then raised the soles of his feet off the tiles. "She kept her heels down, see?"

Royce smiled.

Jose turned pensive. "What ya got for me?"

Royce handed the PoKéRoM disk to Jose. "This is it."

"This is it?

"Yep. We have it. All's safe."

"You didn't make a copy?"

"No. I hate computers. You know that."

Jose held the disk up admiring it. "Luis?"

"The papers said he was killed. Shot in the head."

"Good. He died quickly. Gonzalo?"

"His yacht is at the Hilton Marina in Key West. Can't confirm whether he's alive or not."

Jose studied the green leaves on the celery stalk. "My son?"

Royce pursed his lips. "Luis left him at the Biscayne Bay Marina. No way he'd go back to Key Largo. Luis told me he was heading for the Caribbean… George Town I think he said."

Jose shook his head slowly from side-to-side. "Fucking shame. I liked that Key Largo place." He bit into his celery. "And?"

"Botero said he'd be where you took him for his first time."

A broad smile crossed Jose's face. "I'm telling you Royce, that woman had talent." Jose looked out over his gardens and inhaled deeply. "You're right. It's a great day all around." Royce followed Jose through the French doors into the study.

Jose said, "When'd you get laid last?"

"What?" said Royce.

"A holiday. What d'ya say? A week in Cartagena. Recharge the old batteries." Jose strode to the wet bar. "We had one close call. You know that?"

"Very close," said Royce.

"One thing, though."

"What's that?"

"I think Gonzalo's dead too."

"You may be right."

Jose offered Royce a cigar. "I'll be in charge of the codes from now on. You'll be my key in the States."

Royce accepted the cigar. "I'm honored."

"I'm telling you Royce, when things go well it makes you feel great all over. We'll leave tonight." Jose strode to the Elizabethan chair in front of the Mahogany picture frame he had chipped when he threw the Waterford crystal glass at it. "It's been a long time since I've had a good woman." He plopped down into the chair.

# Chapter 83

### Cartagena, Colombia
### Sunday 1700 ET

The small casino was rarely crowded. It had three blackjack tables, two crap pits, a fair number of slots, and a few other opportunities to tease money from those seeking sudden riches. Its location, a short walk from the Cartagena Hilton, was ideal for Jose and Royce. They stood at one of the crap tables.

"Seven," called the croupier. "The lady's a winner!"

Jose and Royce watched the winner clap her hands silently. She left her feet and bent over the edge of the table to retrieve the dice the croupier had purposely left just out of her reach. Her cleavage revealed all but the nipples of firm breasts.

Jose looked at his watch. "One last bet, the whole damned pile. Double or nothing." Jose pushed his chips forward.

The woman smiled at Jose. She rolled the dice in a cupped hand high above her head. She offered Jose an opportunity to blow on the dice. He shook her off. With a shriek she sent them bouncing the length of the table. "Seven. Seven," she pleaded. The dice bounced off the anechoic side of the table. The first one settled—a one; the second spun on its corner and then displayed another one.

"Snake eyes." The croupier's rake swept the table. Jose's chips were piled so high they spilled over the rake. The croupier gathered them quickly. They belonged to the house now.

Jose said, "What the hell. I own twenty percent of this place." As he left the casino, he kicked the door. "We've got a little time before the banquet."

The last thing Royce wanted to do was sit at a banquet table and listen to speeches given by people he didn't know. "What's with this banquet?" said Royce.

"The guys booked it as an executive committee meeting of some Cartagena business group," said Jose. "Actually, it's a private party."

"If you want to eat at a banquet, I guess it's okay with me," said Royce. "To tell the truth, I was looking for a little action tonight."

Jose said, "We're going to have a lot of action, my friend."

"At a banquet?" said Royce. "Right."

"At this banquet. Right!" said Jose. "The guys are bringing the best broads in Cartagena. Young bitches. Teenagers."

"Bullshit," said Royce.

Jose grinned from ear to ear. "There'll be a raffle."

"Sure, a raffle," said Royce.

"With a great first prize."

"Which is…?"

Jose was hardly able to contain himself. "Twins." Jose moved closer to Royce, whispering, "Twin virgins."

# Chapter 84

## Cartagena, Colombia
## Sunday 1900 ET

Royce thought about calling Jose before he left his top floor suite for the banquet. He decided not to bother. He'd meet Jose on the Hilton's mezzanine as they had agreed. He left his room and walked the newly-carpeted hall toward the elevators. Turning the corner he saw a woman standing in front of the elevator bank. She was talking on her cell phone. There was something about this woman Royce couldn't place. Then he did. The woman was a prostitute.

Prostitutes visiting upper class hotels dress elegantly and stride through lobbies with a sense of purpose. They create just enough doubt in the minds of the hotel staff that they are rarely stopped. If the members of the staff are wrong once, and the woman turns out to be the daughter or wife of a hotel guest, they might lose their jobs. There aren't many jobs in Cartagena.

Prostitutes dress to deceive wives more than hotel staff. Wives are far more dangerous to the livelihood of the hotel staff than prostitutes. If one wife finds out prostitutes frequent a hotel, the word spreads and is followed by an immediate fall-off of business-class registrations. Reclaiming a lost reputation is time-consuming and costly.

Once on the floors, prostitutes let their guard down. With this woman, the giveaway for Royce was the fit of her dress. Men know married women or daughters with parents in residence never wear a dress molded to curves like this woman's dress.

This woman was being careless. The nonchalant way she stood—her hip out to the side, the toes of her shoes pointing in different directions, her cocked head—were dead giveaways.

As Royce neared, he heard the caustic tone of her voice. "No way. I will never do that with you or anybody else." *This is one blunt-speaking whore.*

The woman noticed Royce approaching. She assumed a ladylike posture and lowered her voice. As he got to the elevator doors she lowered her cell phone, pressed a key on its pad, and put the cell back to her ear.

Royce faced the elevators. The down button had already

been pushed. He listened, anxious to hear her conversation.

"No, Javier. You asked me if you could do that to me last night," the woman said in a low calm voice. "I said no then. I'm saying no tonight." A moment later, "I just don't do that." Another pause followed by an emphatic, "Some do. *I don't.*"

Royce stepped forward. He pressed the still-glowing down button. The woman remained silent. Royce faced her. "Is there anything I can do to help?"

"Unfortunately, no." The woman put the cell in the small purse hanging on a gold chain from her shoulder.

Royce wondered if the caller had cancelled. A soft bell announced the elevator's arrival. Royce stepped forward, facing the elevator doors. When the doors opened he was startled to see an empty elevator shaft.

The woman shoved him from behind.

Royce's fall was so unexpected he didn't scream.

Jose called Royce's room but didn't get an answer. *Royce is predictable, always early. Good.* Jose tied his shoes and put on his dinner jacket. Moments later he left his room. The raffle dominated his thoughts. It would go as planned. The Cartagena chamber of commerce would have its biggest night ever. When the winning raffle ticket for the twins was drawn, it would be Jose's ticket. He had outbid three others the night before. It had cost him a small fortune. What the hell, having twin virgins in bed with him, having them watch each other being deflowered. That didn't come around every day.

When he turned the second corner in the corridor, he saw a woman bending over. She was adjusting a strap on her shoe. He stopped, taking in the view. Her skirt rode high, exposing a sliver of red rayon. As the woman stood, Jose cleared his throat.

"Oh God," she said, turning around. "I didn't know you were there."

"The elevators are slow, aren't they?" said Jose.

"I've been here forever."

Jose liked the way the woman studied him. "Going to the banquet?"

"I wasn't planning to."

*If it wasn't for the twins watching each other while I...* He looked the woman over. "Where're you off to?"

A faint smile appeared. "Maybe the casino. You're going to the banquet, I gather."

"I'm supposed to," said Jose. "To tell you the truth, it may be a little formal for my style."

The woman's eyebrows rose. "Oh?"

*Shit. Why does she have to show the same night as the twins?* "I have to go, meeting a friend."

"What's her name?"

*She wants me. No question. Maybe... No, I can't give up the twins. The three of us in bed. It'll be their first time. I have to look into their eyes when I...* "Not a she, a he."

"Too bad," the woman said. She opened her cell phone and pressed a key. "Sure you have to go?"

*Stop lady. You're killing me.* "I'm sure."

The bell signaled the elevator's pending arrival. The woman said, "Damn, I left my compact in the room." She stepped back searching her purse. "Where is that key?"

*The twins first, then this broad?* "Maybe I'll see you later. What d'ya say?" The woman shook her head no and turned her back on him. Jose turned to the elevator as the doors opened.

The woman drove the heel of her spiked shoe into the small of Jose's back sending him flying into the empty elevator shaft. He screamed all the way down to the second basement. He landed askew on Royce.

# Chapter 85

### Grand Cayman
### Thursday 1230 ET

Doug Crosby couldn't stop smiling as he rode in the cab from the airport to his hotel. He put his head on the seatback. He was twelve and with his father the last time he stayed at the same hotel. Jose had told him his time had come. Doug remembered the woman his father had chosen for him. He thought of her often. He couldn't stop thinking about her now.

How she sat him on the side of the bed and then knelt in front of him, her red silk robe revealing the sides of her breasts.

How he was too scared to move for fear he'd do something wrong.

How the tips of her fingers wandered his face, her smile telling him he was the only man in the world she would ever love.

How she unbuttoned his shirt and slid it slowly off each shoulder.

How she cradled the sides of his head in her warm hands while she brushed his eyes, nose and then his cheeks with her lips.

How she ever so slowly laid those lips on his and then didn't move, their mere presence making him mad to taste them.

How, when he finally did try, she denied him.

How she smiled while easing him down onto the bed.

How she brushed her draping hair back and forth across his shoulders and chest.

How her red lips parted, cupped each of his nipples in turn, unleashing her hot tongue.

How she sat up smiling with the face of an angel as her red silk robe floated onto the bed beside them.

How she grinned playfully as her hands unzipped.

How her eyes branded his soul just before she squeezed.

How the warmth traveled from his chin to his chest and then down across his stomach.

How surprised he was when he opened his eyes and found that she and her red silk robe were no longer in the room.

By early afternoon, Doug had teamed up with a group of four women who were best friends. They were relaxed, carefree, and welcomed him into their presence. They were just what the doctor ordered. One, Maria Paula, became particularly warm and affectionate. She was someone he sensed wouldn't ask about his past. Someone who actually liked him.

Maria Paula and Doug left the three other ladies. They went to a quiet restaurant on a side street. It was there that Doug confided he wanted to buy a sailboat. Maria Paula's eyes smiled as if she already knew.

At the second boatyard Maria Paula took him to, Doug found the boat of his dreams, a brand new 56-foot raised cockpit sloop equipped with all the bells and whistles—an in-the-mast roller furling sail, electric winches, auto-pilot, radar with repeater, forward looking sonar, and SSB and VHF radios. It was the largest sailboat Doug felt he could handle alone. Together with insurance, marina and slip fees, transportation to the dock, outfitting, maintenance and yard agreements, and an extended warranty, the single mast sailboat cost $1.43 million. Doug excused himself and returned to his hotel. He took the cash from one of the two steel-lined suitcases he had deposited in the hotel vault.

Doug wanted to celebrate. He took Maria Paula to what she told him was the best restaurant in George Town. It was during their late dinner that Maria Paula told Doug about her boyfriend Javier, a girlfriend Rosalia and two other women she really didn't know but whom Rosalia told her were seasoned sailors.

Rosalia was the owner of a two-mast schooner, the only two-mast schooner in George Town at the moment. Javier was an experienced sailor. Rosalia paid him well to captain her schooner. The schooner had left port under power that afternoon, soon after Maria Paula and Doug had met. It would return after a couple of days of testing its two overhauled engines.

Maria Paula's descriptors of Rosalia included gorgeous, filthy rich and a blatant flirt, the latter being something Maria Paula wasn't happy about. Javier swore to Maria Paula it was only her money that interested him. Maria Paula didn't believe him but, with her fear of the sea, there was little she could do. She was hopelessly in love with Javier. Javier treated her well. Maria Paula didn't hide her hope that Doug and Rosalia might enjoy each other's company.

# Chapter 86

## The Caribbean
## Friday 1115 ET

Maria Paula stood on the George Town dock waving goodbye to Doug as he took his new sailboat out for its shakedown cruise.

Doug stood behind the helm smiling as he waved back to Maria Paula. If he watched his radar, he would easily locate the two-mast schooner and Rosalia Arteaga.

The steady 30-knot easterly breeze a few miles from shore produced six to eight-foot swells with widely scattered white caps, perfect weather for a vigorous shakedown. Doug squinted to see through the wind washing his face. It made him understand why dogs loved putting their faces out of the windows of moving cars. He was thrilled with his new purchase. His elation was about to get better.

Doug had tested every instrument and control three, some, four times. He had tacked hard under full sail to strain the mast, keel and rigging as violently as his skill and the Caribbean breeze allowed. That's what warranties were all about.

Now it was time to find Rosalia.

Doug's spread legs braced as the sails, riggings and keel responded again to a tack command. The bow turned. The sails began falling off when he first saw it—Rosalia's two-mast schooner. He cancelled his tack command, aligning his bow toward her schooner. The two-mast schooner appeared dead in the water, its sails stowed. A few minutes later he made out the wake. The schooner's engines were maintaining the bow's heading.

As the gap between the ships narrowed he saw three women frolicking on the foredeck. Suddenly one of the women leaped onto the schooner's railing. She turned, facing the deck. She was naked.

Doug maneuvered the wheel until his sails flapped lifelessly. The woman on the railing used both hands to keep her wind-blown hair off her face while bantering with the two women on the deck below her. Doug heard the two women begin a faint chant. "Go. Go."

The woman on the rail cupped her face in her hands, crouching in laughter, her hair flying in every direction. The two women pressed their chant. "Go. Go." The woman on the rail stood, spun around, and faced the sea. The chanting grew louder and louder. The woman on the rail spun around screaming, "Okay, already."

The chanting stopped. The woman on the rail pirouetted, faced the sea again, her hair now waving free behind her, over the deck. She looked skyward while taking deep breaths to saturate her body with oxygen. With the wind pinning her hair to the sides of head, she looked out across the water. She spotted Doug and waved with both hands high above her head.

Doug saluted her with a rigid hand to his eyebrow. *One night. Just one night.*

The woman pantomimed. She would dive and swim to his boat.

Doug used long sweeping motions of his arm to encourage her before looking down and flipping a switch. The sails began coiling into the mast. A second switch brought the boat's motor to life.

The woman nodded, their agreement sealed. She coiled, sprung high above the rail and dove into the sea. She entered the water between swells with hardly a splash. The two women stretched, leaning over the rail, waiting for her to surface. More than a minute passed before she did. She surfaced on the crest of a swell. She bobbed in the sea from swell to swell as she gulped air. Finally, she wiped the hair from her face, spotted her schooner, and waved to her two friends. She then turned, waved to Doug and began swimming toward him.

When Doug was satisfied his maneuvering and motor rpm would drift his boat broadside toward her, he locked the helm and then lowered a ladder over the side. He watched as she snagged the bottom rung. With each swell she grasped a higher rung until she put a foot on the ladder's bottom rung. She clung to the ladder with one hand and cleared her face of wet hair with the other before looking up. She smiled at Doug, took a few more breaths and began her short climb.

Doug took her hand, helped her over the railing, and offered a towel. "Welcome aboard."

She held the towel, bent over and put her hands on her knees. "Whew!" she gasped between breaths. Still breathing hard she stood and looked around. Again between breaths she said, "Never dive into a trough." She began wiping her face. Panting, she introduced herself. "I'm Rosalia." With the towel draped around her neck, she bent over and meticulously squeezed the water from her hair.

"Maria Paula told me you would be out here," said Doug. "Said to look you up."

The sight of her long neck, tapered back, and taut buttocks seared itself into Doug's brain. She stood. Their eyes met. "Doug Crosby," he said.

"I'm more out of shape than I thought," said Rosalia as she wrapped the towel around herself. She extended her hand in greeting. "What are you doing out here? Are you all alone?"

Doug didn't object when Rosalia held his hand longer than he knew she should. "Sailing. Needed time, to think."

Rosalia nodded, let go of his hand and smiled. "Know what you mean." She looked around the deck. "Maria Paula's a trip, isn't she?" She ran her fingers through her hair. "If you don't have to get back to shore right away, why don't you come on over? We're about to have lunch."

Doug adjusted the bumpers between the schooner and his sailboat before looking toward Rosalia. She tossed his towel onto his deck and scurried effortlessly across the railings to her schooner. He was pleased Rosalia didn't notice how much less agile he was. On the deck of the schooner she locked his bent arm to her side. Her breast was firmer and warmer than he imagined. Arm-in-arm they paraded to the stern of the schooner.

Rosalia broke away from Doug. "Everybody, this is Doug," she announced with the flare of her arms toward Doug. "A friend of Maria Paula." The two women who had chanted, "Go. Go," were lounging on air mattresses. "On your left is Graciela. On the right, Marina." Graciela saluted Doug with a half-empty glass. Marina rolled onto her side, squinted up, and nodded her greeting. Beside her was an empty glass. Both were naked.

A man stood at the wheel behind the women. "And that's Javier," said Rosalia gesturing to the man at the helm. Javier raised his hand in greeting. "Doug will be staying for lunch," she told all. Looking toward Doug she grinned. "At least for lunch."

Rosalia guided Doug to the cushioned bench seat on the far side of the stern. Before he sat, she said, "Make yourself a drink first." She pointed toward a table amidships. "The fixings are over there. Give me a minute." Rosalia scooted across the deck, down the ladder, and disappeared below deck.

Doug put ice in a plastic glass and poured Chivas over it. The two women and Doug exchanged guarded smiles. He returned to the bench seat, stretched his legs out, and took in the schooner from bow to stern.

Marina got up and walked over to Doug. She sat beside him, smiling provocatively.

Rosalia emerged from below decks. "Hey," she said, raising a tray she was carrying in their direction. Marina returned to her air mattress. Rosalia offered Doug a selection of tea sandwiches from the tray.

Doug took a swig of Chivas before selecting one. "Thanks."

Rosalia took the tray to a table between Javier and the two women and returned to Doug. Still naked, she sat on one leg facing him squarely.

"This is some schooner," said Doug. "Maria Paula didn't do it justice."

"What's a nice-looking guy like you doing out here all by himself? The pleasures of sailing should be shared. You don't have someone to share the ocean with?"

Doug sneaked a look at her left breast. "It's a long story."

"Javier says I'm a chameleon."

"A chameleon?"

Rosalia threw her shoulders back, her breasts taunting. "Chameleons hide right in front of you, don't they Doug?"

Doug grabbed the back of the bench and twisted until he faced Rosalia. "You're not hiding anything." A Cheshire grin crossed Rosalia's face. "You looked great standing there on the rail. You look great now."

"The girls were teasing me."

"I thought for sure you'd fall off. You're fantastically agile… turning, squatting. Moving around like you did up there as the schooner rolled and pitched. It was as if the rail was three feet wide."

"It's attitude." Rosalia looked across the deck at Graciela and

Marina. They were lying on Graciela's air mattress, cuddling and giggling. Rosalia walked over and spoke to them. They nodded in unison, got up, and disappeared below deck. Rosalia said something to Javier. He heard Javier reply in Spanish. *"You got it."*

When Rosalia returned, Doug asked, "What was that all about?"

"Graciela and Marina like each other. I don't mind. I really don't." Rosalia sat on her ankle, again facing Doug squarely. "Later if you like, we can go below and watch. They won't mind. Now, where were we?"

Doug shifted to face Javier, taking the opportunity to adjust his pants. It didn't help. "Attitude. You were saying it's all attitude."

"Oh yes." Rosalia stood. "Stand up." She extended her hands to Doug.

Doug took her hands, letting her pull him up. "Now look down at the deck. What do you see?"

"The deck."

"I mean look at the deck," said Rosalia. "What do you see?"

"I see the deck, what else?"

"Don't you see the boards in the deck?" Rosalia grinned. "Now kick those deck shoes off and put one foot on any three of the boards. You pick 'em."

Doug did as she said.

"No problem, right? Now take a step forward. Put your other foot on the same three boards." Doug complied. "Okay, would you have any problem walking the length of the deck while staying on these same three boards?"

"Of course not."

"Okay then, let's do it." Rosalia stood in front of Doug. She put her feet on the same three deck boards. "Let's head toward the bow." Rosalia went to the balls of her feet. "Follow me."

Doug followed her long tapered back and rounded buttocks as far as the three boards allowed.

"Okay, now it's your turn to lead." They turned around. He didn't see Rosalia signal Javier or notice Javier respond by raising his phone.

Back at the bench seat, Doug sat. Rosalia said, "Now that wasn't hard was it? The rail is just as wide as those three boards you just marched up and down the deck on. So why can't you walk on the rail?"

"It's not the same."

"Why not? The schooner's rolling and pitching exactly as the deck rolls and pitches. Not a little more. Not a little less."

She skipped down the deck, pivoted, and skipped back, her breasts bobbing ever so slightly. He didn't notice that she made no attempt to stay on the same three boards.

"See, it's all attitude. If you can do it on the deck you can do it on the rail."

"You can..."

"You can, too." Rosalia hopped up on the cushions. "Give me your hand."

Her crotch was just above his eyes. He abandoned pretense.

"Oh come on, don't be a scaredy-cat." Rosalia bent low, pleading with her eyes.

Doug took her hands and stepped onto the cushions. She awarded him a slow full-body hug while looking over his shoulder at Javier. Javier was talking on the phone.

Rosalia stepped back and hopped onto the rail. "The first thing is to just stand. Come on. I'll hold you."

Doug stiffened, refusing to straighten his arms.

She bent toward him enticing. "Come on. Just stand. Don't worry, I won't let you go."

Doug refused to budge.

She squatted. "If you'll just stand on the rail, we'll go below deck." Doug watched as her nipples hardened. "Remember, it's just attitude." She tugged on his hands while rising slowly from her squat.

Doug smiled nervously.

"Just step onto the rail. That's all. And you've done it."

Doug put one foot on the rail. Rosalia pulled. He put his second foot on the railing.

"Now just stand up."

He held her hands tightly and started to rise. She pulled him all the way up.

"You've done it!" she said and then nudged him overboard.

Doug hit the water face first. His eyes were wide open.

The schooners engines roared to life.

Rosalia watched tippy toed as Doug thrashed about in the churning water behind the schooner. When she could no longer see him, she used the bench cushion to trampoline from the rail to the deck.

She shouted through the Caribbean breeze to Javier. "The deposit confirmed?"

"She transferred the money the moment I told her you had him on the cushions," shouted Javier. "She wanted to know every detail, just like at the Hilton."

"I wonder why?" Rosalia combed her hair with her fingers.

"I asked," said Javier.

Rosalia strode to the two mattresses on the deck in front of Javier. "What'd she tell ya?"

"Said these three guys tried to kidnap her daughter and granddaughter."

Rosalia gasped. "Oh lord."

"And that they should have known better than to get between a mother and her children."

"I like that Fannie, whoever she is." Rosalia's hand hovered over the tea sandwiches. "Three million bucks. Three million tax-free American dollars in just five days." She snatched a tea sandwich from the tray and popped it into her mouth. "Go several more kilometers and then scuttle that damned boat of his."

At the top of the ladder leading below deck, Rosalia turned to Javier, "Call Maria Paula. Tell her she's earned her $50,000." Rosalia leaned forward, grasping both railings. She threw her feet out in front of her body and slid on the rails below deck.

# Chapter 87

### Bayside, Florida
### Monday 1200 ET

Natalie acknowledged the chef as she put the tray of food on the far end of the bar. She finished rinsing the cocktail mixer and dried her hands before picking up the tray and heading out to the patio.

Janet spotted Natalie as she crossed the carp stream on one of the arched bridges two tables away. "I think I see our lunch coming."

"Good. I'm starved," said Carolyn.

"This is the second time you've just shown up in Bayside," said Janet.

"I had to get away. The beltway commentators are hammering the FBI, the CIA, and the administration for not connecting the dots in the Miami airport bombing."

"Want to hear something funny?"

"A little levity would be nice," said Carolyn.

Janet twisted the pepper mill over her salad. "I enrolled Nicole in an English speaking pre-kindergarten. She loves it."

"So she'll be speaking English soon," said Carolyn. "How's Bert doing?"

Janet laughed. "He's taken up golf. Playing with Charles, twice a week now."

"That's great, two old friends…"

Janet broke off a piece of pumpernickel. "I'm going to open an office in Miami. Going after the commercial market." She offered the breadbasket. Carolyn declined. "I've listed the three Crosby buildings there. Should give me a start. Have you seen Taro since you arrived?"

"We spent the weekend together," said Carolyn.

"*You what!*"

"You heard me. We spent the weekend together."

"Talk to me," Janet pleaded.

Carolyn couldn't hold back. "Taro and Forrest Ward have bonded."

"The FBI Director and Taro have bonded?" Janet repeated skeptically. "I thought Taro didn't care for the way the FBI handled Botero."

"True. But they are both law enforcement officers. Taro says Forrest wants to shake up his troops. He called Taro and offered him a job—FBI special agent."

"Amazing," said Janet.

"He's a hunk, isn't he? Have you heard from Royce?"

Janet's brow furrowed. She picked up her purse and pulled out a folded newspaper clipping. She handed it to Carolyn.

Carolyn studied Janet's face before unfolding the clipping.

> *El Tiempo* reported two bodies were found at the bottom of an elevator shaft in the Cartagena Hilton Hotel. The bodies were identified as Jose Valderrama, a former resident of Bogotá who lives in Acapulco, and Royce Palmer, a U.S. citizen from San Diego, California. Authorities estimated the bodies had been at the bottom of the elevator shaft for 24 hours.
>
> Preliminary indications are that the elevator doors opened while the elevator was stuck on a higher floor. Investigators believe that Mr. Palmer fell into the empty shaft and that Mr. Valderrama tried to save him, only to fall to his death on top of him.
>
> Authorities theorize there may have been a malfunction in the elevator's control module as well as the control module's backup. One possible cause of such a rare dual malfunction may have been an interfering radio signal. Sources of such an interfering signal are under investigation.

Carolyn looked up. "How terrible. This must be so hard."

Janet nodded. "So sudden. Out of the blue."

Carolyn handed the clipping back to Janet. "Everybody's been wondering about Royce. Just disappearing into thin air that night."

"I dated him too long," said Janet. "He was using me. I had no idea."

"That's exactly what Greg-the-Bastard did to me."

"Do you think it was an accident?" said Janet. "I mean, both of them dying at the same time. In the same place like that?"

"One thing it proves, they worked together," said Carolyn. "If it wasn't an accident as the paper suggests…"

"You think it was made to look like an accident?" said Janet.

"It comes to mind, doesn't it? They moved in a violent world."

"God, Carolyn. How'd we get involved in such a mess anyway?"

"Taro asked me the same question last night."

"What did we do to get ourselves almost killed?" Janet repeated.

"Forrest told Taro the FBI still hasn't made progress on uncovering the money-laundering syndicate."

"You look happy," said Janet. "I thought the disk had secret codes or something on it and the codes would expose a worldwide money-laundering syndicate. That was Michael Stone's theory, right?"

Carolyn stabbed a tomato wedge. "I'm happy because Greg isn't getting another…" Carolyn smiled, leaned forward and enunciated each word. "Because Greg-the-Bastard isn't getting another plaque he doesn't deserve."

"Royce must have gotten away with the disk, don't you think?" said Janet.

"If Royce and Jose died together like *El Tiempo* says, maybe Royce tried to keep the disk for himself in order to rip off Jose or the syndicate."

"Or…" said Janet.

Carolyn finished her sentence. "Royce never had the right disk."

Janet leaned toward Carolyn. "Correction. Or… Royce-the-Bastard never had the right disk." Janet enjoyed the tingle of the words on her tongue. "Royce-the-Bastard."

Carolyn broke into laughter. "Don't you have to pick up Nicole?"

Janet rose from the table. "You'll be at the house, 'bout seven?"

"I'll be there," said Carolyn. "Looking forward to seeing Nicole. I'll settle up with Natalie."

Janet smiled. "That's fine with me. You're the one who's loaded now."

# Chapter 88

### Bayside, Florida
### Wednesday 1730 ET

Carolyn rang Janet's doorbell. A moment later she heard Nicole hit the inside of the door and fall.

Janet opened the door as she bent to help Nicole up. "You're going to hurt yourself someday, honey." Janet looked up at Carolyn. "Come on in. Dinner's almost ready."

"God, it smells good in here," said Carolyn. "You always were a good cook." Carolyn handed Nicole a gift-wrapped box.

"Thank you, Aunt Carolyn."

Carolyn's hands flew to her mouth, her eyes widen. "Did she— she did, didn't she? Oh, my God." Carolyn looked to Janet. She was grinning from ear to ear.

"I've been dying for you to hear her. Pretty good, huh?"

"So fast," said Carolyn.

Nicole tore the wrapping off and opened the box. The box and wrapping fell to the floor as Nicole hugged her new koala. Suddenly she screamed, "Wait. Wait." She ran down the stairs.

"What's that all about?" asked Carolyn.

"You'll see," said Janet.

Nicole came racing back, slid to a stop on the hardwood floor, and fell again. She reached up, handing Freddie to Carolyn.

"Ever since Forrest gave her Freddie back—remember, the FBI found it at the Vietnam wall after it fell off Botero's wheelchair—she hasn't let it out of her sight."

"Well thank you, Nicole. I'm glad to see you've taken such good care of him, her. Oh, whatever."

Nicole stood and pointed at Freddie's pouch. "I put PoKéRoM there."

Carolyn crouched, looked directly into Nicole's eyes. "I know. That's how you and I first met. Remember?"

"No, Aunt Carolyn. The disk is in there." Nicole took Freddie back. She extracted a disk from the pouch.

Carolyn said. "We'll play after supper. I'm starved."

Nicole looked to her mother.

"What, honey?" said Janet.

"It doesn't work," said Nicole.

"We'll get you another one," said Janet. "Don't worry."

Nicole threw Freddie down the hall and stomped after it.

"Wait here," said Janet.

Janet followed Nicole down the stairs into the rec room. She cornered Nicole by the toy box. "What's this all about?"

Nicole sulked.

Janet softened her voice. "Aunt Carolyn is a guest in our house. It's our job to see that she has a good time. You know that."

"You don't understand," Nicole pouted.

Janet knelt by her daughter. "Understand what, honey?"

Nicole fought for words. "Aunt Carolyn liked it."

"Liked what?"

Nicole mumbled with her head down. "At her house."

Janet took Nicole's hand and walked her to the couch. They sat side by side. Janet asked softly, "What about Aunt Carolyn's house?"

Nicole took the PoKéRoM disk from Freddie's pouch. "It doesn't work."

Janet stared at her daughter, a quizzical look painted across her face. Nicole smiled. Janet jumped up and ran to the staircase. "Carolyn. Come on down here."

When Carolyn entered the rec room, Janet showed Carolyn the PoKéRoM disk Nicole had just given her. "Could this be the disk we should have given Forrest?"

Carolyn read the title: 133 EeVee™. Attacks: Tackle, Sand Attack, Quick Attack, Tail Whip. "Don't know. Do you think they all have this picture of a weird looking big-eared-bulging-eyed-bunny-cat with a fluffy bib collar and a too-full tail?"

"No," said Janet. She looked at Nicole. "Where did you get this?"

Nicole cowered.

"It's okay, honey," said Carolyn. "There's nothing to worry about. Is this the one that wouldn't play when we went to Carolyn's home?"

Nicole nodded.

"Where did you get it?" said Carolyn.

A weak don't-get-mad-at-me smile appeared. "The dollhouse."

"She doesn't have a dollhouse," said Janet.

"She does somewhere," said Carolyn.  She looked at Nicole.  "Where is the dollhouse, honey?"

"By the water."

"A dollhouse by the water…" said Carolyn.

"I've got it," said Janet.  "At Crosby's party, someone mentioned his guesthouse looked like a dollhouse the way it was gleaming in the sunlight."

"I saw it," said Carolyn.  "It did look like a dollhouse.  Did Nicole go into the guesthouse?"

"I was sitting by the pool and saw her go in." Janet said.  "When she came out, she ran to me, almost like she was afraid. "

"But I thought we gave this disk to Forrest," said Carolyn.

"Apparently not," said Janet.  "Somehow, my wonderful daughter never gave up the disk she found in Crosby's guesthouse."

"Do you know what we have here?" said Carolyn.

"Wait," said Janet.  "Are we sure this is the disk everybody is looking for?"

"Not one hundred percent, but…

"Dare we call Forrest?" said Janet.

"Think about it.  We thought we gave Forrest this disk.  The NSA thought they had this disk.  Royce thought he had it.  Who really had this disk?  Our little Nicole."  They turned to Nicole chanting, "Nicole had EeVee.  Nicole had EeVee."

Carolyn finished what was left of her grilled salmon, broiled red potatoes and long green string beans.  Sated, she looked at Janet, smiling.  "That was simply delicious." Janet rose to clear the table for dessert.  "This is so exciting." "An FBI man coming to my house.  What did he say his name was?"

"Holt Brown.  Remember, Nicole deserves the credit."

"You too."

"Oh no," said Carolyn.  "You're her mother."

"We all deserve the credit," said Janet.

Nicole pointed to Freddie sitting high on the bookshelf.

"Freddie too," said Janet and Carolyn in unison.

# One Year Later

# Chapter 89

**September 3, 2002**
**Vienna, Virginia**
**Monday 2315 ET**

Michael was in high spirits, proud that he had kept his promises to Sarah. He had limited the workweek to a maximum of fifty-eight hours except during heightened alerts and cut his jogging in Nottoway Park to three times a week. In a few weeks he would report to Langley to start his new assignment—a dream assignment. One that might lead to a directorship. He leaned across the front seat and kissed Sarah before stretching over the bench seat to kiss his girls. He got out of the car and walked to Sarah's side. She blew him a lingering kiss before driving off. Michael followed the family car until it turned onto Nutley, heading for White Cedar Court in Tall Oaks.

A full moon showed Michael his shadow as he headed for the Vienna Metro station.

Michael strolled along 12th Street, crossed Pennsylvania and meandered east. On the corner of 10th and Pennsylvania, he stood listening as he did on the first day of his assignment to FBI headquarters a year ago. He didn't hear a sound. F-14s no longer patrolled the skies over Washington.

In the leads center, his Capitol building icon blinked insistently. Michael hadn't seen the icon blink for months. He double clicked the icon. It was a Carnivore intercept, an e-mail from Orlando, Florida to Bogotá, Colombia. Michael read the translated message.

> *Come to Disney World. It's a nice place for you*
> *and your mother to celebrate a birthday.*

The Orlando Internet terminal was a public terminal in Disney World. Michael didn't have access to the reverse directories for Bogotá. He sent a NIACT to the CIA chief in Bogotá. Two hours later his terminal displayed the reply to the question he had posed.

*The telephone number belongs to an Elsa Santes*
*Bogotá, Colombia.*

Michael sorted his spreadsheet by name. A match appeared.
Gonzalo Santes. The comments column read: Last known
whereabouts: Key West.

Michael sent a second NIACT to the CIA chief in Bogotá
requesting pictures of Elsa Santes, her mother, name unknown,
Gonzalo and their birth dates. An hour later Michael forwarded
the Carnivore intercept, the pictures, and the background
information he had received to Alan Dickie at the MFO.

Thirty minutes later Holt Brown's reply appeared on his
screen.

Alan Dickie is on indefinite special assignment.
This could be the icing on our cake.
Thanks Michael.

Michael smiled. Zeros and Ones. Zeros and Ones.

# Chapter 90

### September 11, 2002
### Arlington, Virginia
### Tuesday 0900 ET

Carolyn busied herself in the kitchen waiting for Janet to finish the *Washington Post* article she had told her to look at. She couldn't wait. She stuck her head around the corner. "What d'ya think? An okay picture, huh?"

"Thank God I stuck to my diet," said Janet.

"It's going to be a week-long series," said Carolyn.

"What's this reference about Mafia bosses being nabbed in upstate New York?"

Carolyn went into the living room. "In 1957 the New York state police got a tip from a Sicilian Mafia boss. The U.S. Mafia bosses from around the country were gathering for a powwow in Apalachin, New York." Carolyn turned the page to show her the picture of the lodge. "The cops staked the place out. While the U.S. Mafia bosses were having dinner, the state troopers broke in. They arrested them all."

"I still don't get the connection," said Janet.

"They're saying the CIA turned the same trick with a current day worldwide gathering of crooks. Move over." Carolyn plopped down next to Janet. "Only this gathering was a virtual gathering—a twenty-first century cyber-gathering of crooks."

Carolyn took the paper from Janet. She turned ahead a few pages. "See, here's the rogue gallery of the twenty-first century bosses." She pointed to a sidebar listing the cyber crooks. "Almost all are from the Middle East, Central Asia, or the Balkans."

"But I thought we were dealing with drug dealers," said Janet.

"Me too," said Carolyn. "If not druggies, then terrorists like al Qaeda, the Taliban, Hezbollah, or Hamas. But no. It was these crooks."

"Where'd these guys get all this money?" said Janet.

"They're corrupt government officials, black marketeers in third world countries or freed communist states, oil sheiks, arms merchants feeding rebel causes, deposed heads of state…"

"And they were all laundering money?"

"Looks that way. Tons of it. Jose Valderrama had a knack for finding ' em. He'd convince them to seed some of their riches with him. He'd give them a sixty-day trial period with a money back guarantee. He played the greed card."

"Nothing to do with drug dealers?" said Janet.

"Not so far."

"Nothing to do with terrorists—al Qaeda, the Taliban or anything like that?"

"Not so far," Carolyn repeated. "Governments worldwide are now following these money trails."

"Mostly just crooks?"

"That's right," said Carolyn. "Your everyday, garden-variety crook." Carolyn turned the pages again. "See, this box. It names the tools the CIA brought to bear against these crooks—Echelon, Carnivore, Magic Lantern, Rapid Start, the Patriot Act—and tells how each works."

"Weird names," said Janet.

"They're code names," said Carolyn. "Anyway, these cyber tools aren't biased. They're equal opportunity twenty-first century tools."

"Tools?" said Janet.

"Michael says they're nothing more than zeros and ones."

"How do they work?" said Janet.

"I don't know," said Carolyn. She started flipping the pages again, finally giving up. "Somewhere it says this all worked because the CIA clustered these tools, working them as a team."

"How'd we get in the middle of this?" said Janet.

"It all started at New York University when we were assigned the same dormitory unit in Goddard Hall, overlooking Washington Square Park back in Manhattan."

Janet laughed. "Come on. You know what I mean."

Carolyn opened the paper again and found the flow of intercepted calls. "Here you are: 'Doug Crosby calls Janet Griffin.' Here I am, 'Carolyn Hughes calls Doug Crosby.'"

Janet pointed toward Royce's name. "And Royce worked for Jose Valderrama?"

"Right. Explains why they were found at the bottom of the same elevator shaft."

"So they were just crooks laundering money from other

crooks," said Janet.

"With a new twist," said Carolyn. "Unlike the U.S. Mafia bosses that knew each other, these crooks didn't know each other. They had no idea that anyone else had discovered their 'wealth enhancer' as Jose called his money-laundering system. Each crook fed Jose streams of money. Each then got what amounted to a quarterly 401(k) statement of his investments." Nicole came running from the bedroom. "And it was Nicole's PoKéRoM disk that had the keys to Jose Valderrama's vault."

Nicole hit the couch but didn't fall. "Look, Mommy." She pressed a brightly-colored drawing into Janet's lap.

"Oh, that's beautiful," said Carolyn. "Can I put it on the refrigerator?"

Nicole handed it to Carolyn and ran back into the bedroom.

Carolyn headed for the kitchen. "She hasn't used my computer this trip."

Janet joined her. "She's into Barbie dolls. Big time."

Carolyn hung the drawing. "Look okay?"

"Tell me about Royce," said Janet.

"Royce set up the corporations that posed as venture capital firms. These venture capital firms had a sixty-day half-life. The SEC would get suspicious and before they knew it they were bogged down tracing convoluted ownership trails. With their limited budget and staff, the SEC never accomplished much. They say a CIA agent improved the efficiency of worldwide law enforcement by displaying the initiative to integrate these eavesdropping tools."

"Investing in tech companies wasn't the best idea in the world," said Janet. "They must have lost a fortune when the market tanked."

"For a few years they were multi-billionaires." Carolyn went back to the couch and newspaper. "Look at this chart of their total worth. If Nicole had found that disk just a couple of years earlier..."

Janet said, "I like those code names—Echelon, Carnivore, Magic Lantern, Rapid Start and the Patriot Act. And Stone used them?"

Carolyn smiled. "CIA agent Michael Stone sits deep in the bowels of FBI headquarters orchestrating eavesdropping systems like a maestro. I'm telling you Janet, this guy saved our lives a couple of times."

"How come I don't see his name here?"

"He's CIA," said Carolyn.

Janet rolled her eyes. "Yeah, right. The CIA in FBI headquarters."

"These are changing times."

"Okay, if he's such a hero, why isn't the president honoring him today?"

"The CIA avoids taking credit. But don't worry, you'll be meeting Michael again today." Carolyn sprung off the couch. "Come on. We don't want to be late for the president."

# Chapter 91

### Orlando, Florida
### Tuesday 0930 ET

Holt Brown waited well to the side of the Disney World ticket booths. He and his chief-of-staff drank from oversized plastic cups as they milled with the crowd. Holt asked, "You don't speak any Spanish?"

"Sí, no, gracias, bueno, buenos días, and errrr... adiós," his chief-of-staff replied. "One or two more. Maybe."

Holt smiled. "Your accent is horrible." He glanced toward the ramp. The ferry was docking. "Here they come."

Gonzalo's grandmother used a four-legged cane. His mother helped his grandmother walk off the ramp of the Disney World ferry. The ticket booths ahead were mobbed. His mother and grandmother decided to wait.

His mother gazed back across the man-made lake. "Gonzalo loved the water." His grandmother nodded her agreement.

Gonzalo's mother stood at the ticket booth while his grandmother waited by the turnstiles. She slid her money through the opening. "Two please." She looked up. Her knees weakened. She grabbed the small opening of the ticket booth for support. "Gonzalo! Gonzalo! Oh I knew it would be you."

Gonzalo slid the money back through the opening.

His mother put her hand over his. "Happy birthday, my son."

# Chapter 92

### Arlington, Virginia
### Tuesday 1020 ET

Carolyn got into the back seat of the cab first. She slid behind the driver. Nicole followed and then Janet. "Lafayette Square, 16th and H," Carolyn told the driver.

Janet said, "Remember, I want to see the north portico of the White House before we go to the Rose Garden."

Carolyn insisted on buckling Nicole. "You will. Don't worry."

Janet said, "Now, tell me why Michael Stone isn't going in with us."

Carolyn was enjoying keeping Janet in the dark. "You'll have to wait."

The cab rolled to a stop in front of St. John's Church. Carolyn, Janet and Nicole piled out. "This way," said Carolyn as she led them across H Street into Lafayette Square.

"Oh, there it is," said Janet. "Look baby, the White House." Nicole whirled Freddie over her head.

"There's your north portico," said Carolyn. "Not in a million years did I ever think we'd get an award handed to us by the president of the United States. *In a Rose Garden ceremony.*"

Janet beamed. "I can show you the invitation if you like."

"Will you put that thing away?" Carolyn teased.

"Fannie said to watch for her," said Janet. "She'll be on the left end of the first row."

They crossed Pennsylvania Avenue and stared at the north portico through the same wrought-iron fence that picketers march in front of during their lunch hours.

"We'll be meeting Michal Stone and his family after the Rose Garden ceremony," Carolyn said, pointing to the ground floor windows on the left corner of the White House. "Over there in the East Room."

"What?" shrieked Janet.

"We'll be standing on the inside of those windows with the president and the first lady within the hour. It's a private ceremony for Michael Stone. Can you believe it?"

"Oh my God. We're going into the East Room of the White House with the president and first lady?"

"Your mother's coming too," said Carolyn.

"It's hard to believe, three generations of Griffins—Fannie, Nicole and me— in the East Room of the White House with the president of the United States and the first lady."

"That's not all," said Carolyn. "After the East Room ceremony, the first lady will take us for a tour of their private quarters on the third floor."

Janet was speechless.

They walked toward 15th Street and turned onto the East Executive Avenue pedestrian walkway between the White House and the U.S. Treasury.

"Will you look at the length of that line?" Janet said.

"There's Taro," said Carolyn.

Taro waved to them. "Come on, get in here. We're next. I thought you'd never get here."

# Epilogue

Greg McNulty's task force was disbanded.

The president's national security advisors began monitoring State Department negotiations with foreign governments for their expanded cooperation and investigation of money-laundering operations.

Congress reopened hearings on joint intelligence operations.

The SEC subpoenaed the records of several brokerage houses and venture capital firms. Public hearings were held.

Gonzalo was sentenced to fifteen years in a Florida federal penitentiary. *Descifrar* was confiscated.

Michael Stone arranged for Gonzalo's release nine months into his prison term. Given a new identity, he is now a consultant to In-Q-Tel. He lives in Arlington, Virginia. *Descifrar* is moored in Annapolis, Maryland.

Michael Stone's Vienna, Virginia home on White Cedar Court in the Tall Oaks development was sold thirty days before the White House Ceremony in the Rose Garden.

The whereabouts of CIA agent Michael Stone and his family are unknown.

## *—END—*